Dorothy Eden's
SPEAK TO ME OF LOVE....

"THIS IS PROBABLY DOROTHY EDEN'S BEST
NOVEL. . . . THE DRAMATIC TWISTS AND
TURNS PLAYED OUT AGAINST THE CHANG-
ING SOCIAL AND POLITICAL SCENE OF ENG-
LAND AND EUROPE, MAKE COMPULSIVELY
ENTERTAINING READING ALL THE WAY."
—*Publishers Weekly*

"Another Eden triumph."

—*Miami Herald*

"THIS IS DOROTHY EDEN'S MOST AMBI-
TIOUS, MOST SUCCESSFUL NOVEL. . . . IT
IS BIG, DRAMATIC, FULL OF CONFLICT AND
IMMENSELY READABLE, WITH A GRAND
AND UNFORGETTABLE HEROINE—AS BRIL-
LIANTLY RUTHLESS IN BUSINESS AS SHE IS
HEADLONG AND IMPULSIVE IN LOVE."
—*New York News of Books*

"The story is one that makes you not want to put
down the book until you come to the very last page."
—*Columbus Enquirer*

Dorothy Eden

Speak to Me
of Love

FAWCETT CREST • NEW YORK

SPEAK TO ME OF LOVE

THIS BOOK CONTAINS THE COMPLETE TEXT OF
THE ORIGINAL HARDCOVER EDITION.

Published by Fawcett Crest Books, CBS Educational and
Professional Publishing, a division of CBS Inc., by arrangement with Coward McCann & Geoghegan, Inc.

ISBN: 0-449-23981-0

Selection of the Doubleday Book Club, January 1973

Grateful acknowledgment is hereby made to the authors and
publishers for permission to quote from the following copy-
righted work:
The title and chorus of "Speak to Me of Love" by Bruce Sie-
vier and Jean Lenoir *"Parlez-moi d'amour,/Redites-moi des
choses tendres./Votre beau discours,/Mon coeur n'est pas las
de l'entendre. . . ./Pour vu que toujours vous répétiez ces mots
suprêmes,/Je vous aime. . . ."*
Copyright © 1930 by Editions Smyth
Copyright © 1931 by Ascherberg, Hopwood & Crew, Ltd.
Copyrights Renewed Southern Music Publishing Co., Inc.
Used by permission.

Printed in the United States of America

18   17   16   15   14   13   12   11   10

To my smallest friends,
PAUL, RACHEL, AND SIMON

Parlez-moi d'amour,
Redites-moi des choses tendres.
Votre beau discours,
Mon coeur n'est pas las de l'entendre. . . .
Pour vu que toujours vous répétiez ces mots suprêmes,
Je vous aime. . . .

Chapter 1

So here she was, in the autumn of 1881, Beatrice Florence Bonnington, aged twenty-four years, being dressed for her wedding.

The three women revolving around her, Mamma, Miss Brown from Ladies' Fashions in Papa's shop, and Hawkins, her maid, each wanted to be responsible for making her a beautiful bride.

The material on which they had to work was not highly promising. Beatrice had no illusions about her looks. She was of short stature and cozily plump. Because she held her head high to make herself taller she gave an impression of arrogance of which she had none at all. She had gray eyes and the rosy complexion of a country girl although she had always lived in the city. Her fair hair was plentiful, but difficult to manage, her smile warm, but she had too serious a nature to smile a great deal.

Now, dressed in the overelaborate expensive wedding dress which Miss Brown had chosen for her, she looked stiff and composed, giving no outward sign of her turbulent thoughts, her mixture of uneasiness and elation, happiness, apprehension and downright disbelief. For little Beatrice Bonnington, who, with her self-confessed desire to be a shopkeeper like her father, and with no looks to speak of, had surely been destined to be an old maid, was marrying the catch of the season.

No one, of course, was deceived about romance, not even the bride herself. She had worked toward this day as single-mindedly and coolly as Papa would have approached an important business transaction.

She had always known about business methods, for, from a tender age, she had been commanded by Papa to visit

7

his grand new shop in the Bayswater Road, scarcely a stone's throw from Marble Arch and the hurly-burly of Oxford Street. Bonnington's Emporium.

Dressed in a fur-trimmed bonnet, and with a matching fur muff, her head just level with the polished mahogany counters, she remembered following Mamma down the narrow aisles, smugly aware of the respectful bobs from the black-garbed shop assistants. The splendid head floor-walker himself led them to their destination, the impressive gilt cage of the cash desk where Papa was to be found surveying his empire.

These excursions had been all the more heady because they gave Beatrice a sense of importance that was lacking in every other part of her life. At home she was expected to trot obediently after her mother's rustling skirts, or to submit meekly to her governess's orders. She was considered to be a plain and rather dull child, and nobody ever bothered to discover what her feelings were.

But in Papa's shop, which had grown so impressively from the little haberdashery he had inherited from his father, she was Miss Beatrice, a personage, the crown princess—since to Papa's everlasting disappointment there was no crown prince.

Apart from the personal satisfaction this adulation gave her, Beatrice was wholly delighted by the shop itself. It was an Aladdin's cave mesmerizing her. The cascades of lace and French ribbons, the enormous ostrich feather fans, the flower-trimmed bonnets like a lush, permanently blooming garden, the cut-glass scent bottles, the rows of elegant, shiny buttoned boots, the ruffled petticoats and shifts, and the cool gauzy materials of the Indian room, not to mention the rich satins, brocades, and velvets—this was heaven to a child with a lively imagination and a hankering for beauty.

On her promenade with Mamma the pause to speak to Papa was necessarily brief, for he was always much too busy to talk to people whom he could see at home every morning and evening. The day at the shop belonged to that sacred person, the customer.

When he wasn't counting the sovereigns which he tipped out of the little carriers that came whirring along on over-head wires, or looking with keen eyes at his domain, he was in his office surrounded by ledgers and stock books, or making a personal tour of every department, appearing silently behind his counter assistants, listening critically to their salesmanship, enjoying the way they nearly jumped out of their skins when they became aware of his presence. He was an awe-inspiring figure to them. That was how he was so successful, Mamma said. He kept everyone on tenter-hooks.

The small Beatrice, no higher than the shop counters, didn't know what tenterhooks were. She only knew that she, personally, wasn't afraid of Papa. He was an imposing figure with his snapping black eyes and black mustache, and he never made a secret of his disappointment that she wasn't a boy, but he could be jolly in the brief times that he put business out of his mind. She loved him because there was no one else in her life to love. Mamma, who changed her dress at least six times a day, and spent an inordinate amount of time at her mirror, was really only a body dressed in expensive clothes.

By the time that she was ten years old, Beatrice had developed a canny sense about money, perhaps because Mamma spent it like water. When the enlarged Bonning-ton's proved to be a great success Papa was at last per-suaded to build a house in a fashionable part of Hampstead, near the Heath. This new house was quite a change from the small old-fashioned one in which they had previously lived (in a common street in Kentish Town). Mamma was entitled to put on airs as she watched the dark-brown carpets laid and the dark-brown curtains hung. This was such a smart and fashionable color, and so practical, too, con-sidering the constant smoke from coal fires, and those dirty-yellow fogs in winter. The heavy oak furniture Mamma had persuaded Papa to buy looked very grand, as did the ornate Victorian silver, candlesticks, chafing dishes, trays, tea sets. An extra servant had to be engaged to clean it all, and to polish the long mahogany table after a dinner party. Mamma was beginning to fancy herself as a hostess. It was important that people should come to the house, since Beatrice was growing up, and must begin making friends. The first step toward this, of course, was to find her the kind of school where she would make the most suitable friends. After all, they were a prosperous family now. If Papa's ambitions were realized, they would be rich.

So, when she was twelve years old, Beatrice, rescued from

the clutches of a succession of patronizing governesses, found herself less happy at the snobbish dame school Mamma eventually found.

She had always been a lonely child, introverted and shy, except with people whom she liked. She had no friends of her own age. Her favorite outings were still those made to Papa's shop in the busy heart of London, where shoppers jostled on the pavements and stared at window displays, and the road, deep in mud in winter and chokingly dusty in summer, was a tangle of horse buses, carriages, tradesmen's vans, wheelbarrows, and street vendors with their movable stalls.

She was playing a part, of course, but it was a much happier part than that forced on her at the horrid dame school where she was supposed to make the right friends and get herself invited to the important houses on the Heath. Not houses that were wealthier than her own, but older, mellowed, part of history and inhabited by gracious cultured people.

Mamma, once a lady's maid (though this was never mentioned nowadays), had acquired, by working in them, a taste for such establishments and was overambitious for her only child.

However, even at the Misses Faulkners' school, Beatrice contrived to go her solitary way, although learning to play the piano, to sing in an agonized gruff voice, to dance the waltz and polka, to identify wild flowers and to paint watercolors, to speak French and German and to make polite conversation at a dinner table.

All this, she privately thought, was a complete waste of time, since what she needed was a practical education to fit her for taking over Bonnington's one day. There was nothing she wanted to do more, except marry for love. Since the latter did not seem probable—she was absolutely realistic about herself, and knew that no young man was going to fall passionately in love with a plain girl with a head for figures—she didn't allow herself to dwell too much on the thought. Her mother, of course, insisted relentlessly that there was only one aim for a girl and that was marriage. Papa agreed, but eyed his quiet, unspectacular daughter thoughtfully.

Lately she had been making some deuced good suggestions about the shop (opening the Indian room, for instance, so that trousseaux could be provided for the many young women going to India to marry or to seek husbands).

He had come to the conclusion that little Bea had an excellent practical brain, almost a masculine one, and it would be rather wasted on a husband and a purely domestic life. However, the girl's mother was right. She must marry. A woman without a husband was a poor half-thing. Like Miss Brown with her drainpipe figure in Ladies' Fashions.

It was possible, of course, that, once married, Bea might come into the shop. That thought Joshua Bonnington kept secret. Which was a pity for Beatrice. It would have improved her spirits had she known it.

It seemed, as it happened, that Mamma had been laying the right foundations for Beatrice's future, for when she was fifteen she was invited to one of the grandest houses on the Heath. Overton House, a small but beautiful Queen Anne house built by Captain Rufus Overton (who had made a fortune trading in the China seas) and subsequently occupied by his descendants, all of whom had followed distinguished careers in the army and the navy.

Beatrice, on her way home from school, had often stood at the gates of Overton House and looked up the steps to the white doorway and warm red-brick walls. She had seen the daughter of the house, Caroline Overton, pretty, delicate, insufferably haughty, whisked home by carriage, or escorted on foot by a maid, and had felt like the poor people in the Bayswater Road, pressing their noses against Papa's shopwindows and vainly longing for what was within. Caroline, although her classmate, scarcely ever deigned to speak to her, since Caroline was a snob of the first water and Beatrice belonged to that unmentionable class, trade.

Beatrice actually didn't care a pinch of snuff about Caroline, but Overton House exercised a fascinating spell over her. It glowed beyond the lime trees, a warm and gentle fire. She had a feeling for beauty and harmonious lines that neither her mother nor her father understood. Their own house, so solid and prosperous, filled her with gloom. Since babyhood she could remember nothing but dark walls, curtains drawn against the sunlight, claustrophobic, crowded interiors.

The color and opulence of certain departments in Bonnington's gave her this same feeling of fulfillment, but

there the goods were constantly sold. The treasures of
Overton House were permanent. If only she could get inside she thought that she would be bathed in light and
beneficence.

It seemed too good to be true when the opportunity
actually occurred.

It was Caroline Overton's fifteenth birthday and she
had made the request that her whole class at school be
asked to her party. It was a well-known fact that Miss
Caroline's requests were never refused because she was so
delicate.

So twenty girls (among them Beatrice Bonnington,
achieving her dream at last) played childish games like
drop the handkerchief and follow-the-leader in the sunny
walled garden, and later had tea in the music room, a long
room which ran the length of the house and was also used
as a ballroom. It was light and sunny, with French windows
opening onto a stone-flagged terrace. It pleased Beatrice
very much. But there were other more beautiful rooms, she
had heard, including the yellow drawing room, and the
famous mirror room where it was said some notable court-
ships had taken place.

Beatrice, tongue-tied but with her watchful eyes missing
nothing, sat at the tea table being waited on by two maids
in immaculately starched caps and aprons, while Caroline
at the head of the table gave orders with her nauseating
airs and graces.

Later, Caroline's mother, a small dainty woman with a
pretty pink and white face, like painted china, came in to
meet her daughter's guests, and apologized for her husband
not making an appearance. He was a retired general, a
good deal older than his wife, who now suffered indifferent
health. His temper was precarious, and Mrs. Overton asked
anxiously that there might not be too much noise, otherwise Papa would begin thumping with his stick.

Caroline's health had been adversely affected by living
in the extreme heat of Delhi and Cawnpore as a child. Nor
was her younger brother, the heir to this lovely house, as
strong as could have been wished. It really looked as if the
first winds of winter could blow the entire Overton family
away, like leaves. Beatrice had seen the large vault in the
churchyard just across the road from Overton House, which
held various Overton remains. All the family, including

those here today, she thought morbidly, would eventually be neatly put away like the bales of goods kept on shelves in the basement at Papa's shop.

The ancient church itself, part of it dating from the Conquest, was full of Overton memorials. The precise white slabs shone out from the spider-gray walls.

Colonel Rufus Edwin Overton killed in action while storming the Heights of Abraham. . . . Midshipman Charles Edwin Overton died of wounds received at the Battle of Trafalgar. . . . William Rufus Overton died of fever in Calcutta in the service of the East India Company. . . . Lieutenant Colonel Charles Henry Overton cruelly murdered by mutinous Sepoys in Delhi. . . . Major William Overton seized and killed by brigands while traveling in Afghanistan. . . .

And the women, the wives of these loyal and adventurous men, Caroline Sarah, sorrowing widow of Charles Henry Overton. . . . Mary Susan, widow of Rufus Edwin Overton and adored mother of ten children. . . . Elizabeth, dearly loved wife of William Edwin Overton, died in childbirth leaving an only son, William Rufus Charles, who has erected this memorial to his parents. . . .

The only son referred to in this memorial was, Beatrice knew, Caroline's father, General Overton, covered in honors for his outstanding services to his queen and country in the Crimea, Afghanistan, the Punjab and the Sudan, and now somewhere upstairs listening testily to the shrieks and giggles of twenty young ladies in their best party dresses.

Like the family vault, this house, with its arched and pedimented doorways, its wonderful flying staircase, its smell of beeswax and potpourri, was much more solid and permanent than its inmates had ever been. Beatrice responded strongly and intensely to it. Not long ago her father had told her that he was getting rich, rich enough to buy her anything she wanted. But he had been thinking in terms of clothes and jewelry, a new carriage and a pair of grays, a holiday abroad at that place the Prince of Wales had made so popular, the French Riviera.

If she had said she wanted none of these things, but only to own a house like Overton House, he would have given his great roar of laughter. Such houses couldn't be bought, even by self-made millionaires. They had to be married into. And it was scarcely within the realms of even her mother's most ambitious dreams that Beatrice should become an Overton wife and bear Overton children (eventually to be tidied away into that solid everlasting vault).

Nevertheless, Beatrice had a stubborn nature. During that birthday tea, where she felt like a nervous little goldfish in polar waters, she toyed with the thought of living in this charming house. That desire might have to remain a fantasy, but at least, while she was here, she was determined to see more of the house.

When tea was over and Caroline asked her guests to come into the garden again, Beatrice deliberately lingered behind. Presently, unnoticed, she slipped away and ran up the lovely flying staircase that curved into a dim passageway overhead.

If she encountered anyone, she would say she was looking for the bathroom.

The stairs were covered with a leaf-green carpet that extended along the landing at the top. It was like walking on a well-cut lawn. Portraits of dead and gone Overtons dressed in all the splendor of military and naval uniforms hung over the staircase; the walls were papered in a fascinating design of leaves and branches, the same bosky green as the carpet. The sun shining through the window at the far end of the passage was like light filtering into a forest.

All the doors were closed. What rooms did they conceal? The yellow drawing room would be on the ground floor, but one of these closed doors might lead to the mirror room or the china room. Her heart beating rather quickly at her temerity, Beatrice made a wild guess and opened the door on her right.

Instantly, out of the gloom a tremendous voice shouted, "What the devil do you want?"

Jumping with fright, Beatrice hastily retreated, only to be commanded to come back.

"Are you a new maid? Did my wife send you?"

Beatrice stood within the doorway, blinking until her eyes became accustomed to the gloom, and she was able to see the red-faced gentleman with the white mustache sitting up in an enormous bed. He was fitting a monocle into his left eye, so that he could observe his visitor more clearly. He looked very bad-tempered, his bright-blue eyes gleaming as sharply as glass between wrinkled eyelids.

Appalled, Beatrice found that she had stumbled into the general's bedroom, and there he was sitting up in bed in his nightshirt. She could not have been more embarrassed if he had been naked. What an absolutely appalling thing to have done.

"Well, speak up, girl! Who are you?"

"Excuse me, sir, I was only looking for the b-bathroom." Then, recovering partially from her shock, Beatrice realized that this terrifying old gentleman still thought her a servant. Indignation made her lift her chin.

"I am one of your daughter's friends," she said. "I don't see how you could possibly mistake me for a servant."

There was a silence, giving Beatrice time to wonder what new horror she had perpetrated. She refused to lower her chin, however, and the two stared at each other, the choleric invalid and the girl, plump and dumpy and dressed in an expensive but not beguiling dress of plum-colored velvet. (Miss Brown, who always dressed Miss Bea, was quite unaware that her middle-aged taste was unsuitable for a fifteen-year-old girl going to a party.)

The silence ended with the general abruptly giving a loud guffaw and making Beatrice nearly jump out of her skin again.

"Come here, where I can see you. What's your name?"

"Beatrice Bonnington, sir."

"Bonnington? Haven't heard that name. Who's your father?"

"He's Mr. Bonnington of Bonnington's Emporium."

"Bonnington's Emporium!"

"A shop," Beatrice explained, since the old gentleman seemed genuinely puzzled. He screwed in his monocle more tightly, to look at Beatrice again.

"Then why doesn't he call it a shop, instead of that damn silly fancy name?"

Privately Beatrice agreed. She thought "emporium" was pretentious, too. "I know what you mean, sir. When the shop's mine I intend to call it just Bonnington's. But Papa thinks customers like an emporium. It sounds more important. He says the turnover has nearly doubled since he put up BONNINGTON'S EMPORIUM over the front entrance."

"Then if you take it down, and revert to being simply a shop, are you going to lose all this trade?"

"Oh, no. I don't think so. But I do like to call a spade a spade."

"I can see that," said the general.

Beatrice was a little provoked. "How, sir?"

"By the way you look, young lady. Plain dress. Hair tidy but not fussed over. Good straight eyes. No looks to speak of, but they may add up into something one day. Or they may not, but either way it could be an advantage. I know what I'm talking about. I've studied enough women. So you're one of my daughter's guests. And I'll wager she's frilled and primped and curled, and made to look like a delicious nosegay."

She was. And Beatrice had spent most of the afternoon both envying and scorning her.

"Don't you like delicious nosegays, sir?"

"Adore 'em. But they're deuced expensive, and deuced irritating, too." Now was he talking about his daughter, or his pretty china doll wife? "There's plenty of room for the plain ones. They often wear better. Don't scowl at me, my dear. You'll remember what I said one day, and you'll agree with me."

Would she? Beatrice wondered, with grave doubts. Just at present she had to defend her appearance as much as she could.

"I look like this because Miss Brown from Ladies' Fashions in my father's shop dresses me. Mamma says she would be hurt to the bone if she weren't allowed to. I expect she'll dress me for my wedding, too."

"Of course she will. You can't go about hurting people to the bone. If you marry a man of any sense he'll realize that."

"And not mind me looking dowdy?" What an extraordinary conversation!

"Certainly not. If he does I recommend you to waste no time in seeing your solicitor and getting an annulment."

"I think you're making fun of me, sir."

The general leaned forward, looking like an old tired eagle. His open nightshirt showed a skinny corded neck. All at once he was not in the least alarming.

"Believe me, my dear, that was the very opposite of my intention. I was simply giving you some advice, and I count myself quite a worldly fellow. I've known enough women with plenty of looks, but when their petals begin to fall off there's nothing there, not even a seedpod. They're empty husks, and you're damn tired and your heart gives out." He leaned back against his pillows, looking very tired indeed. The monocle had fallen out of his eye, taking the piercing-blue light with it.

Beatrice was dimly aware that she had seen one of the last revivals of a fierce and hardy spirit.

Chapter 2

Three weeks after Beatrice's exceedingly unorthodox encounter with General Overton, a letter arrived requesting her company to luncheon at Overton House on the following Sunday.

This was a very different affair from being invited as one of a gaggle of twenty classmates to Caroline's birthday party. It meant that she had been singled out as an individual, a fact that pleased her mother but puzzled her more practical father.

"There's something behind this," he said suspiciously. "Do they want extended credit or cut prices?"

"Oh!" Mamma exclaimed. "You think of nothing but trade and customers."

"What else should I think of, may I ask? I'm not in business to keep the swells."

"I know why I'm asked to lunch," Beatrice said. "It's because General Overton regards me as a friend. I saw him in his nightshirt," she added inconsequentially.

"Beatrice!" exclaimed Mamma. "What are you talking about?"

"I was looking for the bathroom and I opened the wrong door."

"Couldn't you have asked someone the way?"

"No, because I wanted to see the upstairs of Overton House. I went into the general's bedroom by mistake, and there he was sitting up in bed, and we had a conversation."

"What about, for goodness sake?"

"Things," said Beatrice vaguely, knowing she could never repeat that extraordinary conversation to Mamma.

Anyway, Mamma was no longer listening, for her eyes had got their too familiar scheming look.

"What about the son? Did you see him?"

"No, of course not, Mamma, it was a girls' party. Anyway, he sounds a milksop. He's too delicate to go to school, so he has a tutor, and his hobby is catching butterflies."

"Gad!" said Papa. "Tutors and butterflies!"

"He does sound awful," Beatrice agreed. "But I may go on Sunday, may I not? I do so want to see Overton House again. It's the sort of house I want to live in one day."

"What's wrong with this one?" Papa asked touchily.

"It's not pretty, Papa. It's not light and airy. It hasn't got a staircase that wafts upward."

"Like a damn butterfly, I suppose," Papa said sarcastically. "Well, I prefer solid comfort, sensible colors, modern sanitation. I expect they still have those old powder closets at Overton House."

"Perhaps they do, but they're not used for *that* purpose any longer. The bathroom I was in was just as modern as ours. The WC was decorated with garlands of flowers."

"Good Gad!" said Papa.

Mamma, Beatrice knew, was delighted about her interest in Overton House, and even more so in the Overtons' interest in her. But Papa was, as always, disappointed in her. She couldn't help not being a boy, but at least, being a girl, she might have been pretty, someone he could have displayed like goods in his shopwindow.

He puffed his lips in and out and finally said he supposed she could go to Overton House again. But he didn't want her getting silly ideas about those swells, and above all he drew the line at any nonsense like rushing over the Heath with a butterfly net.

"Goodness, Papa, do you think I would?" said Beatrice. But she did.

To her disappointment, she found that the general was not well enough to come down to luncheon, so she didn't see that wild red face, full of mingled hostility and friendliness, again. In his place she met the son and heir, Master William, aged fourteen years and extraordinarily good looking.

Beatrice had been prepared to meet a child, Caroline's young brother, still in the nursery, delicate, spoiled and babyish.

Far from that, she found herself being stared at by a pair of sparkling brown eyes beneath an umbrella of tumbling, curly brown hair. Rosy cheeks that dimpled when the young paragon smiled, perfect teeth, a slender body at least three inches taller than hers, and an easy natural friendliness that seemed to be extended to the whole world, herself in particular.

"Are you Caro's best friend?" he asked, embarrassingly, for Beatrice was well aware that Caroline seldom bothered to speak to her.

Beatrice found that, under pressure, she had more poise than she had realized.

"Am I, Caroline?" she asked airily, and Caroline hadn't the sophistication to carry off that direct attack.

"Don't be silly, William," she said pettishly. "You know very well that it was Papa who invited Beatrice today. I really don't know why, except that sick people do strange things, and have to be humored."

"Caroline!" Mrs. Ovtron said sharply. But the sharpness in her voice was manufactured. Beatrice knew very well that she agreed with every word her daughter had said. She also knew that William was laughing mischievously at them both, and enjoying himself no end.

"I'm sorry my husband couldn't come downstairs today," Mrs. Overton explained to Beatrice, with tardy but meticulous courtesy. "He had a bad night and the doctor had to be called. All this is the result of that dreadful Indian climate. We've all suffered from it, and really in the end one's country hardly appreciates it."

"Moral," said William, "don't enlist in the Indian Army, or you'll end up as a memorial in the village church. That's where you'll find all our family, Miss Bonnington. Died of wounds, died of cholera, massacred in a mutiny, drowned at sea."

"Then what do you intend doing, William?" Caroline asked.

"I shall be a gentleman," said William. "I shall drink and smoke and gamble and be gloriously idle. Shan't I, Mamma?"

"Apart from catching butterflies," murmured Caroline spitefully.

"Caroline, you mustn't sneer at William's hobby. You know he already has a famous collection. He's even given specimens to the British Museum, did you know, Beatrice?"

"Will you come on the Heath with me this afternoon,

Miss Bonnington?" William asked. "It's a perfect day. I nearly had a splendid peacock yesterday. We just might have the luck to get it today."

He was only a little boy, Beatrice told herself, in spite of his sophisticated manner. He was only interested in a sissy thing like catching butterflies.

But to her surprise she found that she wanted to go with him. It really was rather difficult to resist the friendliness of those sparkling brown eyes in which she could detect no trace of patronage.

They didn't, as it happened, catch a peacock, but Beatrice, after leaping over humps and hollows, caught a fluttering creature in her net, and William exclaimed excitedly that it was a rare swallowtail (*Papilio machaon*) and a much more desirable catch than a peacock.

Beatrice hated the crawling creepy legs of the struggling insect, but the delicate wings strongly marked with black had yellow patches like pale sunlight. Like spring primroses, she thought, and realized that it was the moment rather than the captured butterfly that was important. She knew that she was going to remember it for a long time.

"Well done," William said approvingly. "I must say, for a girl, you're rather jolly."

That, then, seemed to be the final accolade.

But it was not one she was always going to appreciate, she discovered as she grew older. Who wanted the epithet of being jolly when other girls were dressing in their silks and chiffons and wafting about at parties, like butterflies themselves? Beatrice Bonnington, in spite of the snob school she had attended, either didn't get asked to these parties, or, if she did, she had neither the gift for wearing pretty frilly clothes nor the ability to make flirtatious conversation.

Her school friends were going to Paris or Switzerland to finishing schools. Caroline Overton was going to Switzerland, also, but not to school. The summer weather had not cured her persistent cough. She must go to better purer air. A few months in a sanatorium in Davos, the doctors said, would do the trick.

So her mother, her painted china face now covered with a fine crackling of lines, prepared to make the journey with her precious only daughter. William, who was now a tall stripling, would be left at home in charge of his invalid father.

Overton House was a tragic house, overshadowed with illness. If Caroline were to die, the old general would probably give up his tenacious hold on life, too. Then young William, who wasn't much stronger than his sister, would be the master. And unless he followed some profession where would the money come from? It was rumored that one of the family portraits, a Gainsborough, had already been sold to pay for Caroline's sojourn in the Swiss Alps.

What the family needed was an injection of good healthy blood. And money.

Despite the expensive sanatorium and all the care lavished on her, Caroline Overton died. She was brought home for burial in the family vault. The house, sheltering the dying general and the bereaved mother, became more tragic than ever. William, who also benefited from a warm climate, was studying at the university in Perugia. He came home for Caroline's funeral, then departed again.

Beatrice, now aged twenty, still too plump but grown to her full height which was a meager five feet two inches, frequently walked past the high brick wall enclosing Overton House, and lingered at the scrolled iron gates. The house was still an object of seductive charm. If she walked slowly she could hear the doves cooing from the lime walk, and the wind in the leaves of the ancient black mulberry tree, planted in the reign of Queen Anne. A Judas tree topped the brick wall so that passersby in the road could see the rosy blossoms on its bare branches in the spring. Pink and white may, flowering along the wall, had a lush, hardy beauty.

Beatrice was well aware that she was having a love affair with a house. She knew that the charming graceful boy who had pursued butterflies over the Heath was part of it, although she had, as it were, met the house first. But since her encounter with William she had been completely uninterested in any other boy. And he and Overton House were inextricably bound. She could not have one without the other. It was a fantastic assumption that she could have either.

Her other desire was the shop. Bonnington's. This, too, had seemed a hopeless desire until the day she was twenty-one, when Papa surprised her by putting a large heavy key in her hand.

"It's yours, Bea."

Her heart gave a great jump.

"I can come into the shop? You've decided? Oh, Papa, I can't tell you how bored I've been lately, leading this idle life."

"No, love, you're mistaking me. I don't mean you to come into the shop. Except as an ornament, of course. No, the key's symbolic, so to speak. It means Bonnington's will be yours one day when I'm gone. In the meantime, you might be interested in my plans for enlargement."

"Oh yes, Papa!"

Gratified by her interest, Papa explained that he intended to open a restaurant.

"We'll have a high-class one, on the first floor at the back, so that customers have to walk through the shop to reach it. We might have an orchestra in the afternoons. Lure those idle rich women to tea."

"Like me?" Beatrice couldn't help saying.

"You won't be idle when you've a husband and family." Papa looked at her thoughtfully. "Mind you, if you haven't achieved that in say ten years—"

"Goodness, I'll be dead of boredom long before that!"

Papa gave his loud guffaw.

"Tell that to your mother. If she weren't so set against the shop I might just relent. I believe you have a good business head. But I expect your mother's right. You must find a husband. Then you can give me some grandsons for Bonnington's."

Beatrice weighed the key in her hand.

"In the meantime I put this in a glass case?"

"You're all I've got to give it to," Papa said rather sourly. He still hadn't forgiven her for not being a boy.

"But I really can do what I like with the shop when it's mine?"

"I won't be here to stop you, will I? All the same, don't be in a hurry to bury me, love."

Beatrice flung her arms around him. "Oh, I'm not, Papa. I apologize for my rudeness. I know I'm considered one of the luckiest girls in Hampstead."

"And you'll be one of the richest one day. So get a move

on, Bea. Find a husband. You mightn't have all the looks in the world, but you've got the cash."

When, the next year, General Overton claimed his place in the family vault, Beatrice had neither forgotten his fiery face, nor a word of their conversation. She felt she had lost a friend. Without telling her parents, she attended his funeral service, and sat at the back of the church and watched Mrs. Overton, on the arm of her son, follow the flag-draped casket up the aisle.

At that time she had not seen William Overton for four years. His back view, tall, slender and straight, was pleasing. His thick brown hair curled at the base of his neck. Papa would think it foppish, but it met with Beatrice's ardent approval.

The service was moving. When the hymn "O Valiant Hearts" was sung, Beatrice's eyes filled with tears. She remembered vividly the vital figure of the old man sitting up in bed in his nightshirt. She was deeply sorry that he was dead. Where his daughter Caroline had been a mothlike creature, disappeared before dawn, one would almost expect to hear the general's voice thundering angrily from the family vault.

"I will be buried there one day," Beatrice thought to herself suddenly and surprisingly.

When the little procession moved slowly down the aisle she gazed eagerly and hungrily at William's face. It was sober and sad, as one would have expected on such an occasion. His skin had a healthy tan from the Italian sun. He was slim, graceful and mature in his dark clothes, yet Beatrice was sure that he had only to look at her with recognition and he would again be the friendly boy on the Heath, excited over the capture of a butterfly.

By chance he did look straight at her. Her heart fluttered wildly, like the caught butterfly in the net, although she knew she must be unrecognizable behind the dark veil. She discovered, however, that she was as deeply infatuated as ever. This hardly surprised her, as she knew she was one of those dull women who loved only once and forever.

And what was she to do about that situation, she wondered, for now that her ally, the general, was gone, it didn't seem that there would ever be an opportunity to renew her acquaintance with the Overton family.

She was mistaken, however, for some time after the general's death a gilt-edged invitation arrived. Mr. William Overton and Mrs. Blanche Overton requested the pleasure of Miss Beatrice Bonnington's company at a soiree with Elizabethan music and dancing on Saturday, the third of May, at seven thirty.

Beatrice was not an adept at the art of enjoying parties. In fact, she dreaded them. She was unnatural, her mother said, and if she didn't make an effort to make herself a pleasant guest she was going to become a social misfit. However, to her mother's surprise, she accepted this invitation with every evidence of pleasure, although she wore the withdrawn dreamy look that meant she was dwelling on some private scheme.

In this case the scheme only amounted to a determination to dance with William, and when the dance was over, to lure him into the garden. She had always wanted to walk over those mossy lawns in the moonlight. William would be too well mannered to refuse her request.

It didn't turn out exactly like that however. In the first place, with her lack of interest in clothes, Beatrice allowed Miss Brown to overdress her in dark-green taffeta with a great many ruffles. Beatrice rustled expensively as she walked. She rather enjoyed this. It made her feel like a duchess, she confided to Papa, who had been persuaded to escort her to the door of Overton House.

He didn't approve of this party any more than he approved of her association with the Overton family. He was afraid the classy lot of guests would look down on his daughter and give her a miserable evening. Besides, he had been checking accounts and had found that Mrs. Overton and her precious idle son owed far too much to Bonnington's where they had been customers for some years. He might shortly have to send them a dunning letter, which would be embarrassing after Beatrice had accepted their hospitality.

However, he grumblingly agreed to walk her the short distance to Overton House. He would call for her sharp at midnight, he said.

"Like Cinderella," Beatrice said.

"Cinder—who?"

"Papa, you must read your fairy tales. Sometimes they even come true."

They didn't, of course.

Beatrice made that sobering discovery after she had handed her wrap to the maid and, exposed in all the importance (Miss Brown's word) of her stiff taffeta dress, had seen that everyone else was wearing floating chiffons and soft silks. She looked like a little solid dark fir tree in a summer garden.

Well, it didn't matter. She would be noticeable. That surely was the old general putting thoughts in her mind to give her courage, as Mrs. Overton, in trailing misty gray, took her hand and murmured something inaudible. Then William came with his warm smile.

"Miss Bonnington! I'm so glad you could come."

He spoke with such apparent sincerity, and looked so handsome that excitement and pleasure made a corkscrew of pain twist through her stomach. She hadn't known one loved with one's vital organs as well as with one's heart, she thought dazedly. For this was love, she was certain. It had always been love.

But already William had left her and was the center of a cluster of pretty young women with ringlets and gauzy dresses. She, the unexciting little fir tree, stood at the edge of this gay plot of flowers.

Violins were twanging. The long music room, lit by hundreds of candles, had all the desired appearance of a fairy tale even if already, for Beatrice, the right atmosphere failed to exist. There were a lot of little gilt chairs around the walls. She sat on one of these and opened and shut her fan, thinking how ridiculous these affairs were, fans, beaded evening bags, dance programs, artificial chatter. When she was mistress here, she decided, indulging in her fantasy, parties would be comfortable cozy affairs with only one's best friends, and at last she would learn to be a good conversationalist.

"You must let me show you my butterfly collection before you go, Miss Bonnington. I remember you used to be interested."

That was William's voice as he paused a moment, before moving on with an entrancingly pretty young woman on his arm. A moment later the violins burst into full sound and the dancing had begun.

Somehow the evening passed. Beatrice danced several times with strange young men (sent, she guessed, by Mrs. Overton who was a painstaking hostess), and at last with

William who whisked her around efficiently, then said, "Oh, excuse me—awfully sorry—I think the next is the supper waltz and I've promised—Is someone taking you to supper?"

"Yes," Beatrice lied, and prayed for Papa to arrive.

There was to be no moonlight walk in the garden. Determination, she realized, wasn't enough. Neither was the hopeless love that she hid behind an impassive face. She decided she would spend the supper waltz upstairs, and once again wander from room to room. Why not? Nobody would miss her.

The house could not reject her, as William did.

This solitary occupation had its own reward. She found that William had moved into the general's bedroom. She knew this because there was a cabinet of butterfly slides where the general's writing desk had stood. The top one was pulled out and she could study the fragile iridescent insects imprisoned beneath the glass. Painted ladies, red emperors, fritillaries, a rare swallowtail. She was pleased that she could recognize them. She had read a great deal about moths and butterflies since that long-ago afternoon on the Heath. A happiness as fragile as the butterflies filled her. It came partly from memory, partly from stubborn anticipation.

One disastrous party had not ruined her hopes. She was not the kind of person to give up because the young man she loved was thoughtless and insensitive, though in the most charming way. Everyone had faults. She had enough herself. Besides, he wouldn't behave like this when he knew her better.

The old general was no longer there to encourage her, but another significant thing did happen. Two middle-aged women had emerged from the bedroom next door and were absorbed in the kind of vaguely malicious conversation that went on at parties like this. Beatrice could hear every word they said.

"If he doesn't marry money they'll be in a fix. Poor Blanche has confided in me."

"Then Laura Prendergast won't do?"

"Goodness me, no. She's got even less money than the Overtons. Anyway, she's only one of William's flirtations. He's a most disgracefully fickle young man. I hardly envy the girl he marries, in spite of all that devastating charm."

"I'd choose money any day, rather than charm."

"That's what poor William will have to do."

The two ladies rippled with laughter.

"You know, they say that Beatrice Bonnington is the richest girl here tonight."

"Really? That badly dressed girl with no looks? I wondered how she came to be invited. Although if William must marry an heiress, one would have thought he could find one in his own class."

"He's not that much of a catch, Millicent. Poor health, idle, a reputation for being a philanderer. Besides, an important heiress would want a bigger house than this. It's charming enough, but it's really not much more than a pretty cottage."

"Really, Etty, what a snob you are."

"No, I'm merely stating facts, Compare it with Syon House or Osterley Park, or Kenwood. Now those are great houses worth cherishing."

"So is Overton House, in its way." Beatrice agreed strongly with Millicent. "It's a perfect example of Queen Anne architecture, and goodness knows, in the future there may be few enough houses like this left, considering some of the monstrosities our generation is building. So ugly. Pretentious without being pretentious enough, if you know what I mean." Papa would not agree with Millicent. The house she described was exactly the kind he had built, and with which he was entirely satisfied.

"Anyway," Millicent went on in her confident carrying voice, "we weren't talking of preserving houses so much as preserving the Overton family. Wasn't there that rumor that the general wanted his son to marry the little Bonnington? Something about the family needing an injection of healthy blood. After all, the Overtons have practically bled themselves dry for their country."

"So the little Bonnington is to produce more cannon fodder?"

"Perhaps. But money's the first essential, I believe. Of course, if the girl's a romantic, she may well refuse William. She'll see through that kind of proposal."

"Don't you believe it. Haven't you noticed the way she was looking at him tonight? She hasn't even learned to dissemble."

"Then I say, poor little fool. I can't see Blanche being happy with a daughter-in-law like her."

"She may have to be."

"I'll believe you, my dear, when I see William having the last dance with the little Bonnington. I daresay he'll do as he's expected to."

He did. He danced several times with Beatrice before the evening was over, performing his duty with courtesy and charm. If he were only pretending sincerity he was a remarkably good actor. She was almost certain that he enjoyed her company and her conversation. Finally, he asked permission to escort her home. When she said that her father was coming for her, he said could he not walk on her other side. She had two sides, hadn't she?

Yes, thought Beatrice, she had, one that was highly suspicious of William's sudden dedicated attention to her, and another foolishly flattered and delighted one, which was going to suspend all common sense indefinitely.

"Now, Bea, love," said Papa when they were at home, "that young man we've just said good night to. His intentions aren't honest, you know."

"Papa, how can you possibly tell? You scarcely know him."

"Don't get on your high horse. Does William Overton know you frequently ride a high horse, for instance? No, he thinks you're a meek little mouse ready to kiss his feet because you've been invited to the big house and he's paid you a few compliments."

"Papa, I'm not exactly a fool."

"No, you're not, and that's my point. Young Overton thinks you're stupid enough to be taken in by flattery. All he wants is your bank account. Your mother knows it, and I know it. The difference between us is that your mother doesn't mind, but I do. What about you, Bea? You'd have more pride, wouldn't you?"

Desire was much stronger than pride. Didn't Papa know that? Or was he so immersed in business that he recognized only people's avaricious qualities?

"I think you're jumping to conclusions," she reproached him. "Just because I was invited to a party at Overton House doesn't mean that tomorrow I'll be wearing William Overton's ring."

"But you would like to be. Come on, love, confess."

"Yes. If he ever wants to put a ring on my finger I'll let him. Whether it's for my money or not."

"Good Gad!" Papa began stroking his mustache in a helpless way. "And I always thought you had plenty of sense. Supposing I decide to cut you out of my will?"

Beatrice was alarmed. "You wouldn't Papa! Promise you won't do that. It isn't that I want the money for myself—"

"But for that idle young man. Do you really think you could be happy in that kind of marriage?"

"Yes," said Beatrice. "Because I would make it a real marriage," she added, after a pause.

"Well, it hasn't happened yet."

"No, but it will." She knew, suddenly, that this was so. Her eyes, a soft moth-wing gray, had a glint as steely as that of her father's. He recognized this, for he gave a short unamused guffaw.

"Good Gad! I believe Master Overton may be getting a package he doesn't expect."

"And for my wedding," said Beatrice, "Miss Brown must be more careful. This dress was quite wrong for tonight. I looked a frump."

Papa's knowledgeable fingers felt the material of her dress.

"That's the best Macclesfield silk. Can't see how you could be a frump in something as good as that." His eyes had a wry look. "Don't let that lot patronize you, Bea. You're my daughter, and I'm not a nobody."

"I'm not a nobody either," Beatrice said.

It did seem that William was serious in his intentions, for from that night he began an assiduous courtship which even Joshua Bonnington could not criticize. Although the word "love" was never spoken. Beatrice didn't want it to be, for that would make William a hypocrite. She guessed that, pressed by the family solicitors and his mother, he had accepted the situation reluctantly, but since he had accepted it he meant to carry it through. He was a man of honor. And he would not be the first gentleman in straitened circumstances who had made a marriage of convenience.

When finally marriage was a certainty Blanche Overton, William's mother, took Beatrice on a tour of Overton House. Beatrice had longed for this. She wanted to absorb everything about the house and took such a gratifying interest that Mrs. Overton, who didn't consider that the marriage contract meant she had to feel any fondness for her daughter-in-law, relaxed a little of her polite hostility.

They progressed from the long music room to the yellow drawing room, then to the china room (the Overtons had always been collectors of beautiful things) and the mirror room, a frivolity of an eighteenth-century Overton who was said to have had some strange habits. Whatever riotous parties had taken place in this room in his day, it had later become more respectable, and was the traditional place for romantic proposals of marriage.

To Beatrice's regret, William had not made his proposal there. He had chosen the Heath, where the open spaces and the soft balmy air of a perfect summer day had improved his spirits and given him enough recklessness to commit himself.

All the bedrooms on the first floor had quaint octagonal powder closets adjoining. They were used now as dressing rooms. If there were to be a large family of children in the house, they would make perfectly adequate bedrooms for nurses or governesses.

The top floor was divided into much smaller bedrooms, servants being a species who didn't need much space, having few belongings. This was where Cook, two parlormaids, Mrs. Overton's personal maid, and two very young maids of all work slept. Beatrice made a mental note to claim the room at the end for Hawkins, whom she would bring with her. Mamma was willing to let her go, and Hawkins herself was eager. She was only four years older than Beatrice, and devoted to her. It would be nice to have an old friend in her new home.

After the inspection of the upper floors, Beatrice insisted on viewing the kitchen, the pantries, the still room, the storage room, and the long stone-flagged passages in the basement. She opened cupboards and inspected marble-topped benches and scrubbed wooden tables, and admired the shining black-leaded stove, big enough to roast a whole lamb. Her mother had taught her to cook, she said, so she would be quite critical of Cook's ability.

"Mrs. Jones is an excellent cook," Mrs. Overton said stiffly.

"I'm so glad. I wouldn't care to begin by dismissing servants. Do you know that Mamma and Papa began their life with only a very stupid girl called Polly? I remember her quite well. She had chilblains all the year round, and was scolded a great deal because she had never been properly trained. Now of course we have too many servants." Beatrice sighed a little. "I sometimes think Papa got rich too quickly."

"I hope you won't make remarks like that at dinner parties," Mrs. Overton said, giving her light rippling laugh.

"It's only the truth."

"The truth doesn't always need to be aired."

"No. Perhaps not." Beatrice sighed again, then added, with a rush of feeling, "But I do love this house."

"Not more than my son, I hope?"

Beatrice was startled. Was Mrs. Overton, this painted china woman with her carefully repressed hostility, speaking the truth herself, for a change?

"Why do you say that?" she asked.

"Only that—well, my dear, no one is pretending this is a love match. Come now, if you profess to speak the truth you must admit that you're longing to live in this house."

"I know I am. But for all that, on my side it's a love match," Beatrice said with intensity. "And it always will be."

Nothing, from then until her wedding day, had shaken her on that point.

"Take some interest, Beatrice." It took the sharpness of Mamma's voice to penetrate her consciousness and bring her back from her daydream. "Really, the trouble we're taking and you look as if you're a million miles away."

"I was, too. I was thinking how I came to be here today, getting dressed for my wedding. I've been going over my past like a drowning man."

Miss Brown gave her abrupt tittering laugh.

"Goodness me, far from drowning, Miss Beatrice! I only hope you won't be too grand to make your weekly visits to the shop."

"That isn't fair! You know nothing would keep me away."

"Except a husband, perhaps," Miss Brown murmured wistfully.

"Not even a husband. Anyway, I'll be bringing him with me."

Privately, however, Beatrice doubted this. William was

happy to have Bonnington's as a source of income, but he wasn't likely to get proprietorial about it. She knew already that it bored him. She had once begun a discussion about the merits of French goods as opposed to English. Bonnington's richer customers, she said, thought that if a hat hadn't a Paris label it wasn't worth buying.

The look of polite boredom on William's face had made her stop in midsentence. She never talked about merchandise again. Instead she studied his interests—music, poetry and art, painting and sculpture, butterflies. Soon she would be able to talk about such subjects with an assumption of ease. She intended to encourage William to take her regularly to the theater. She would read the latest books. She might even attempt to take up piano playing again, although she had no gift for music.

But she would *try*. She knew that she and William would be excellent friends. He would treat her with kindness and affection and she would not allow herself to embarrass him with displays of her deep devotion, even though she knew there would never be a time when she did not respond to his ebullence and gaiety, his wit and courtesy and good looks. He was one of those people intended to decorate the world. She gladly accepted him as such and hoped she would never be responsibile for dimming his spirit.

And long before they were ready to be laid in that gloomy family vault, and in spite of their disparate natures and interests, she would have made him love her. . . .

Then that whole awkward business of the money and her being an heiress would matter less than nothing.

Chapter 3

They were catching the boat train to Dover, crossing by ferry to Boulogne where they would spend the night, then on to Paris the next day. Beatrice would adore the Champs-Elysées, the Rue de Rivoli, the famous restaurants. Funny little unsophisticated thing, she had never been out of England.

An endearing thing about William was that he regarded all women as delicate dainty creatures to be protected and pampered. He had been accustomed to the delicate women in his own family. Beatrice didn't want to emphasize her good health or point out that her sturdy body was the opposite of dainty. Also, lack of sophistication was not the reason for her never having traveled abroad. It was simply because she had parents who, like most of their class, were suspicious of all things foreign.

So Beatrice's childhood holidays had been spent at Brighton or Bournemouth, splashing in the chilly sea, or joining her parents who sat in deck chairs, Mamma wrapped in rugs and Papa wearing his stout tweed overcoat and grumbling that he would rather be behind his haberdashery counter than paying good money to freeze at the seaside.

Beatrice remembered a particularly ugly bathing costume she had worn, striped yellow and black, like a wasp. The other children had laughed at her, which had made her feel extremely lonely and vulnerable. She had been even lonelier than usual on holidays, partly because of her nature, but more because Mamma would not let her associate with children of a better class because they were so enclosed by a hedge of nannies, nursemaids, and hovering mothers or aunts.

When she had reached her teens the annual holiday had

become a much grander affair, with a first-class sleeper on the train to Scarborough where Mamma had decided it was fashionable to take the waters, and where Papa walked briskly on the sands all morning and snoozed in a cane chair in a corner of the ornate Palm Court lounge in the afternoon. They all had to dress up for dinner and pretend to be people of importance from London. Papa did look important with his glossy black mustache, his glittering forceful expression, the heavy gold watch chain hanging across his stomach. Mamma never escaped gentility. Beatrice was simply uneasy, awkward and bored.

Holidays had always been desperately boring.

But nothing could be more different from this one, for which Hawkins had packed so carefully.

At the last minute it had been decided that Hawkins should accompany them. How could Beatrice, who was so careless about clothes, make the elaborate toilettes her husband would expect if she didn't have a maid?

William thought it an excellent idea, and only hoped that Hawkins was a good sailor. He was a splendid one himself, and he was sure his wife would be. So it would be too bad if they had to look after a seasick servant.

Hawkins said she was sure she would be fine, but whatever happened she wouldn't lose sight of the baggage.

To Beatrice's unsophisticated eyes they seemed to be taking far too much, three trunks, three valises, two hatboxes, her jewel case, traveling rugs, William's umbrella and her parasol, William's heavy fur-trimmed greatcoat (because Channel steamers were notoriously chilly) and her long mohair cape with matching hood. Her trunks, so carefully packed by Hawkins, contained handmade nightgowns and chemises, petticoats, peignoirs, shoes and slippers, gowns for all occasions, a sewing box equipped with materials for every eventuality, and a small medicine chest similarly equipped, books (because she cherished the idea of reading aloud to William while he lazed in the sun), sketching materials, in case she should feel like sketching on an Italian lakeside, her bathing gown in the event of really hot weather, opera glasses (they might go to the opera in Paris or Milan), a picnic hamper with Crown Derby porcelain, silver-handled knives and forks and small silver flasks for tots of rum or brandy.

Really, Beatrice thought, Mamma's extravagant forays

into the lower-middle-class wealth of Scarborough were nothing compared with this. They might have been preparing for an absence of years.

Papa hooted with astonishment at the variety of the baggage. Did they think they were going to some benighted African continent where there was no civilization? Mamma said briefly and crushingly that as Mrs. William Overton their daughter had a position to keep up. William merely said that Beatrice seemed to be bringing too many dresses. After all, he would want to choose some things for her in Paris, the home of fashion.

Mrs. Overton added in her sighing voice, "And perfume, William. She must have perfume."

Did she smell badly? Beatrice wondered furiously. She knew she should have been pleased by William's thoughtfulness, but two thoughts raced through her head. The first was a strong suspicion that he didn't like the clothes she was wearing, and the second, that it was her money he was proposing to spend.

Before the marriage there had been endless legal discussions, with the Overton solicitor, a gray, suave, shrewd man, on one side, and Papa's solicitor, less polished but equally clever, on the other. Papa, backed by his solicitor, persistently refused to transfer any real property into William's name. Bonnington's was to be Beatrice's absolutely. What she did with it when he died was her affair, but that wouldn't be for a long time, and by then she would know how this humiliating marriage had worn.

All Beatrice thought was how stupid and blind Papa was. Why would she be different and harder in, say, twenty years? She would still be a woman, she would still be in love.

It was a long time to wait to give William all that she wanted to give him. Although twenty years was a hypothetical time. It might be less, or it might be more. Certainly at fifty Papa looked the picture of health and vigor. One could imagine him reaching the age of eighty without any effort at all, which meant that when William was fifty, he would still be living on Papa's generosity. Which fact made it all the more important now to insist on her husband's independence. He must have a generous allowance, which would be paid annually into his own bank account.

"He mustn't feel dependent on me," she urged. "That would be too humiliating."

"That's my word exactly," Papa said sourly. "A thousand a year?"

"Generous," said his solicitor.

"Oh, *no*, Papa! At least two thousand. And I must pay the upkeep of Overton House. Please, Papa. We are family."

"You are," Papa corrected. "So this young man is to get two thousand a year to fritter away."

"To be a gentleman," said Beatrice in her quiet stubborn voice.

"Poppycock!" Papa exclaimed, crashing his fist on the table. "You're nothing but bedazzled and besotted. Time will bring you to your senses and then you'll thank us for our caution."

The solicitors exchanged pained glances. Men themselves, they thought the recent Married Woman's Property Act was loaded unfairly against their sex. For after all even an heiress went into marriage with her eyes open. And it looked as if this quite ordinary young woman was getting a pretty good bargain, a handsome young man from an illustrious family, as well as an ancient house. One would have thought old Bonnington would have been smug about it, instead of suspicious and outraged.

Finally, protesting all the way, Papa was prevailed on to add his signature to what he called an infamous document. William Overton Esquire got his two thousand a year. It seemed he had no desire at all to own a thriving drapery emporium. He was well content with the cash—and the Emporium's daughter.

Even if it were her money William intended spending in Paris, Beatrice knew that she must forget that fact once and for all. How else could she enjoy his generosity? It would be the greatest fun and happiness to have him choose clothes for her.

"M'sieu Worth, I think," he said.

"Poor Miss Brown. I must never let her see me wearing them."

"Why not? She might learn better taste."

"Oh! Don't you like my going-away coat and skirt?"

"Going away is what it is, my dearest. We'll give it to

the first suitably sized chambermaid. You must never wear
that particular shade of green again."

Beatrice laughed uneasily, her confidence diminishing.
One would have thought the gold band on one's finger and
William's hand possessively on her elbow as he helped her
board the train would have been enough to give her a soaring and permanent confidence. But it wasn't, she found.
She was too newly a bride. Time would take care of this
situation. She would grow less vulnerable.

Humiliatingly, it was Beatrice who was ill on the little
Channel steamer. She was furious with herself. The swell
was barely noticeable, but she could not bear to look
through the porthole at the lazy up-and-down sea. She
suffered Hawkins' ministrations with a nasty yellow basin,
while William hurriedly disappeared to stretch his legs on
the deck.

She was *not* seasick, she kept insisting miserably; yet
even when on dry land in France she remained stricken
with nausea and dizziness.

William must be revolted by her. She was far from being
his jolly girl pursuing butterflies. His remark about the particular shade of green she was wearing came back to her
and, her sense of humor feebly returning, she chocked on
a sudden snort of laughter. William thought it was a sob.
He gallantly took her clammy hand in his.

"You'll be better when you've rested. You're only overtired."

His expression was kind and gentle. He was happier now
that he had discovered she had feminine frailty after all. It
must make him feel pleasantly superior. He certainly looked
very handsome in his traveling clothes, and she loved him
with a sensation as sharp as pain.

At the hotel he insisted on her going straight to bed. He
would order a little light supper to be sent up to her. He
himself had a magnificent appetite and intended dining
downstairs. He knew this hotel from the past. It had a
superb chef.

"But wait until I take you to Maxim's in Paris," he said
enthusiastically. "Thank God it's got back its prewar splendor. That Prussian siege was barbarous. It's a great pity the
Germans are so under the influence of Bismarck, or we'd
have taken a trip up the Rhine. But I detest all this militarism. One hopes when Prince Frederick becomes emperor

things will change. He's far from being a warmonger, they say. You must ask my mother to tell you about the Princess Frederick. She met her on various occasions when they were girls, although I believe she preferred Princess Alice who was less clever and opinionated."

Hobnobbing with royalty, Beatrice thought hazily. Not that she wouldn't like to. It had always been Papa's ambition to have the palace patronize Bonnington's.

"I would like to go to Germany one day," she said politely.

"So you shall. We'll go to Vienna, too, and Budapest, and St. Petersburg. I've always traveled in the Latin countries, for the sun, but why shouldn't we broaden our itinerary?"

"The Grand Tour," Beatrice murmured, thinking again how unbelievable it was that this should be happening to her.

To be realistic, however, at this moment she only wanted to be back in England where the walls didn't spin and her stomach behaved itself.

Hawkins diagnosed her sudden illness as nerves.

"That's all it is, madam. It will pass. What shall I unpack? Your nightgown and robe with the blue ribbons?"

But that was for her wedding night, she thought, then nearly burst into tears as she realized that this was her wedding night. Fancy being so weak and dazed as to forget, even for a second, that after he had dined William would be coming to keep his part of the bargain that had been begun over the solicitor's desk, and completed in God's hearing before the altar this morning.

He would keep it because he was honorable. But how much, or how little, did he want to?

It was all very well to dream of her ability to make him love her; it was quite another thing to face this task in reality.

Beatrice sipped a little clear soup, then asked Hawkins to take the tray away and leave her.

"Couldn't I brush your hair, madam?"

The anxiety in Hawkins' face told Beatrice that she was looking her lamentable worst. But when her hair was loosened and brushed it was glossy and abundant. Her husband, who had never seen it like this, was going to be agreeably surprised.

However, Beatrice was not in the mood for feminine

wiles. If their marriaige were to be a success it must begin
now with absolute honesty. She wouldn't try to be seductive, hiding behind a curtain of hair. She would be herself,
honest, quiet, loving.

And if ever she were the type for blue ribbons on a
nightgown, it wasn't tonight.

She undressed, washed, put on a simple white lawn nightgown, and plaited her hair into two plaits. She was sitting
by the dying fire when William returned.

He said at once, "Why aren't you in bed, resting? I
thought you'd be asleep by now."

"Asleep?"

"Dearest, you can't think I'd want to bother you tonight
when you're so poorly. One must have the right time, and
all that."

Beatrice stared at him. Was he so experienced?

"It's really quite important, I assure you. So I've taken
another room for myself. You go to bed and get a good
rest. I only looked in to say good night."

He came to kiss her on the brow. There was nothing but
solicitude in his face. Yet, right time or not, she had to say
what she intended, what she had sat up in her plain nightgown in this hard chair, to say.

"Don't go for a minute, William. There are some things
I do want to say."

His eyebrows lifted.

"Curtain lectures already?"

"Don't be silly. I only want to say that I know you're
not in love with me. I've been afraid to mention this before in case it made you change your mind about marrying
me. And I did want that so badly, because I've loved you
ever since the day we caught that butterfly together. Do
you remember? The swallowtail. *Papilio machaon.* I even
remember it's Latin name."

She looked at him anxiously. Was he bored?

"But even if you never love me, I'll love enough for both
of us and our marriage will be all right. I should think lots
of people start less happily than this. What I'm really trying to say is that you don't have to pretend. I always want
us to be honest with each other."

She stopped when she saw that he was laughing.

"But, Beatrice, my absurd little wife, of course I love
you. Only not tonight. Tonight isn't for either love or long

speeches." He yawned. So he *was* bored. "And don't you dare make a speech when I'm in bed with you." He bent to give her another brief kiss. "Sleep well. Tomorrow Paris, heigh-ho!"

He was gone. Like one of his butterflies, light and exquisite of touch. Not wanting deep thoughts or emotions. Not wanting to search his heart, or hers. She knew she had learned her first lesson. He didn't care for intensity or plain speaking. He preferred to gloss over uneasy matters, pretending they didn't exist.

Perhaps he was right and she was wrong. She had to be thankful that he had this ebullient nature, for if he hadn't he would surely never have married her, even for the sum of two thousand pounds a year and the knowledge that his family home was secure for the next generation.

All the same Beatrice wept a little into her lacy wedding handkerchief. She suspected that he had been relieved to have an excuse to escape her bed that night.

But perhaps it was merely that he, too, was tired from the long, long day.

Chapter 4

The next day the weather was cloudy and damp, and William was catching a cold.

He apologized, saying that he caught cold with ridiculous ease. He hoped Beatrice didn't mind too much.

Their roles were reversed, for she had woken feeling completely recovered, with all her healthy optimism back.

However, she found her husband, flushed and bright-eyed and undoubtedly miserable, infinitely appealing. She wanted to smother him with love and care. She had enough sense not to do this, but after the long train journey and their arrival at their Paris hotel, she insisted on his retiring at once.

"Tonight, we will both eat upstairs," she said. "Can we ring for a menu?"

"You're the experienced traveler already," William said, and she flushed with pleasure.

"But you must order the meal. I haven't the courage to do that. My French is too awful."

"Then let us send for the maître d'hôtel."

They ate delightfully in the privacy of their room. Even Hawkins was not permitted in to unpack Beatrice's clothes. Tomorrow would do for that, when Mr. Overton was feeling better, Beatrice said.

It was fortunate that the room was equipped with another bed, for William refused to allow her to sleep beside him and catch his germs. In spite of his good spirits over their dinner, his cold was worsening.

It was the exasperating weakness in his family, he told Beatrice, only repeating something that Beatrice had always known. The Indian climate which was so cruel to children had left him with permanently delicate health. It

42

had also left a more subtle legacy, as Beatrice discovered
that night, when William moaned and cried in the grip of
a nightmare.

She leaned over him, holding a night light, and calling
to him to wake up.

"What is it, my darling? Are you in pain?"

His fever-bright eyes opened and stared at her as if she
were part of a remembered horror. Then slowly he came
out of the dream that had made him cry out and toss the
blankets into a tumbled heap.

He smiled weakly with relief.

"Oh, Bea! It's good to have you here." He gripped her
hand hard and pleadingly, as if asking her to keep these
familiar dragons, whatever they were, away.

She would do so, too. If this role were more maternal
than wifely she didn't mind at present. It was so wonderful
to find that he needed her.

"Was it a nightmare?" she asked.

"Yes. It usually comes when I'm ill. I've had this particular one since I was a child, since that day—"

His face tightened and she sat on the edge of the bed,
saying, "Tell me, my darling." Endearments, of which she
was a little shy in the daytime, came so easily in the night,
in these circumstances.

"It was a quite horrible experience," he said. "It happened in India when I was only seven years old. I was being
taken for my usual morning's drive in a gharry with my
amah. The driver had taken us to the outskirts of the town,
where we shouldn't have been, anyway, and we came without any warning on the scene of a massacre."

"You mean . . . dead people?"

"Yes. Several Indians, and someone I knew, Sergeant
Major Edwards. He was a jolly good friend of mine. He'd
taught me to shoulder arms and play cricket. He was a big
broad-shouldered fellow with blond hair and an enormous,
drooping blond mustache. Actually, it was only his mustache
that made me recognize him. There was a great deal of
blood, and his eyes had already been pecked out by kites."

"How dreadful! How appalling for a child!"

William smiled wanly.

"I see you understand. I think my mother did, too, but
my father didn't. He said that if I were joining the army I
was never too young to get accustomed to sights like that.

Actually, that was when I decided that nothing on earth would make me join the army."

"But it was mainly because of your bad health, dearest."

"No, it was my cowardice. I've been a coward ever since that day. I have an absolute aversion to any kind of violence or ugliness. My father, poor old boy, was pretty disappointed. He thought his only son was a namby-pamby. Which was true. Is still true." The hot fingers clutched Beatrice's. "I also have a fear of death and dying. I run away from it, if I can. I went to Italy when Caroline was dying. And I kept out of Father's room as much as I could when he was near the end. Are you going to despise me, Bea?"

"Never! If you ask me, your father was enough to scare any child."

"You weren't scared of him."

"I was a bit."

"No, you weren't, or he'd have known. He always knew."

"Well, he wasn't my father. That made a difference."

"Perhaps it did. How comfortable you are."

"I always want to be."

"Thank you, dearest."

"Will you be better tomorrow?"

"I think so."

"I'm so glad. We can start doing things, shopping, sightseeing. I keep reminding myself that we're in Paris. Do please remember that there are more beautiful than ugly things in the world."

"I do. That's why I spend my life seeking them out. Bless you, Bea." His lips touched her fingers gratefully. "I believe you do understand."

The next morning William felt a great deal better, almost recovered, in fact. His spirits were improved, as if relating that nightmare had lifted a weight from his mind. He called out to Beatrice as she came in, rosy-cheeked, from an early morning walk.

"Where the devil have you been?"

"Just out for an early morning walk. You were sleeping so soundly I thought I would take a quick look at the shops."

"The shops!"

"That big store, Bon Marché. It's quite good, but not as

good as Bonnington's. Papa will be delighted to hear that."
She was pulling off her gloves, and laughing at his indignation. Had she found a department store so much more interesting than her ailing husband?

"It's my first trip to Paris. I couldn't resist going out. Now I'm starving. Can we have breakfast? You look so much better. If you tell me you have an appetite, I'll be completely happy."

William allowed himself to be coaxed into amiability, and an admission that he felt much recovered.

"All the same, Bea, you must develop an interest in art galleries as well as department stores."

"Oh, I will! There'll be time for everything, won't there?"

"Certainly. Let's attend to your wardrobe first. I suggest a visit later this morning to M'sieu Worth's salon. Then, if we're both strong enough after luncheon we might take a drive and see the sights."

Sadly, it was all too good to last. For when they returned to their hotel that afternoon, with William still a little invalidish and ready to rest until dinner, the telegram addressed to Mrs. William Overton was awaiting them.

Beatrice tore open the yellow envelope (although not without taking a moment to reflect on how pleasing her new name looked), then exclaimed in shocked dismay, "Oh, how terrible!"

"What is it?"

"Papa! He's dangerously ill."

"Let me see!" William snatched the ominous yellow form from her and read, "Your father had apoplectic seizure. Return at once. Mamma."

They looked at each other in dismay, Beatrice suddenly painfully aware of how much Papa, impatient, hot-tempered, noisy, exasperating, vital and virile, a great storm always blowing through her life, meant to her, William looking uncertain, as if he were wondering whether his marriage of convenience had been unnecessary, after all.

Beatrice was already too clever at reading his thoughts.

"Bonnington's will go on, of course, whether Papa is there or not. We'll never need to be poor. But one can't imagine—oh, William, forgive me, we'll have to go home."

"Of course, my dearest."

"If Papa is going to die—But he won't. He's so alive.

God wouldn't dare. Where's Hawkins? She must be told to pack. What times does a train go?"

"I'll attend to that. There'll be one later this evening, but we may have to spend some chilly hours waiting for the morning ferry."

"I ought to go alone," Beatrice said distractedly. "You're scarcely over your fever. And what about those dress fittings? They'll have to be canceled." Her lips trembled. "I may have to wear mourning."

She found, however, that for one private reason she was glad to be going home. She had always wanted the consummation of her marriage to take place in the old general's bedroom at Overton House, where many other consummations, happy or unhappy, must have taken place, as well as numerous births and deaths.

Hotel bedrooms carried only the most superficial memories, the dimmest ghosts.

She could scarcely believe her eyes when she saw Papa propped against pillows looking almost as well as he had been when she had kissed him good-bye three days ago. A closer look, however, showed a certain dullness in his eyes, and one end of his luxuriant mustache seemed curiously tilted downward. Also, he put out his left hand in welcome.

"I'm glad to see you, Bea."

"Mamma said you were dangerously ill."

"I told her to say that. Wanted to be sure you'd come."

There was a hint of pathos in those last words, and Papa's voice had trembled slightly. Beatrice knew that he would be fiercely ashamed of that tremor. He and the old general—really, what had she done to be caught between two such men?

"Papa, tell me truthfully how ill you are."

Papa subsided against his pillows, and allowed the animation to leave his face. Then he did look ill and disturbingly old.

"Doctors never tell you anything," he grumbled. "You hand your damn body over to them and the rest is silence. I had this collapse after your wedding, that's all. Gad, I still had those stupid tails and striped trousers on. They put me to bed in 'em as far as I know."

"Yes, Papa. The whole truth. What did the doctor say?"

Bleakly his eyes met hers.

"That I'd had a slight stroke. Me, in the prime of life! I said I'd never heard a more mistaken diagnosis. But the truth is, Bea—you wanted the truth?"

"Yes."

"Knew you would. You face things. Different from your dreamy husband. You'll have to carry him, as well as the shop."

For a moment she thought he was wandering. What was he talking about?

But his eyes, even if dim, had not lost their intelligence.

"The truth is, Bea, I'm a bit shaky on my right side. Arm and leg. Can't get out of bed without the help of that damn fool nurse. Humiliating. Otherwise I'm as merry as a cricket."

Beatrice moistened her lips. She had to keep calm, but inwardly she was trembling as much as she had trembled in the lobby of the Paris hotel when the telegram had been in her hands.

"Is this permanent?"

"No, by God! No! You won't see Joshua Bonnington on crutches. But it's going to take time. I've got to be a prisoner here for a few weeks. That's all. Only a few weeks. But long enough for those bastards—sorry, Bea—to play havoc at the shop."

"Is there trouble, Papa?"

He nodded. "It blew up just before your wedding. I wouldn't have told you. Nothing to do with you, anyway, except that Bonnington's is yours now. Gave you the key, didn't I?"

"That was for when you died, Papa. Not for a long, long time."

"It's getting a bit nearer, Bea. Can't deny that." He made an attempt to move his right arm and failed. "The thing is, you'll have to take over."

"Me!" She was incredulous. Nevertheless, her heart had given an excited leap. Life was too ironic. Why should this opportunity, which once she had longed for, happen at such an inopportune time?

"And why not?" Papa said. "You've married a husband you have to support, you're going to run a house that's far above our level of living. Not that your mother doesn't spend money like water, but this is a bit different from that grand place where you're going to live. Bonnington's will be bled to keep that up. However, you chose it, so now it's up to you to keep it going."

"Surely I couldn't do that, Papa."

"Yes, you could. You're a Bonnington, aren't you?"

"You've always said I'm only a woman."

"More's the pity. But you're my daughter so they'll all have to listen to you. I might as well tell you that I made a bit of a misjudgment a little while ago when I took on an assistant manager."

"Mr. Featherstone?" Beatrice said, remembering the man. She had thought him sharp, clever and unlikable.

"That's right. Have you taken much notice of him?"

"No, but I know Miss Brown doesn't care for him."

"She's always against new blood, of course. But in this case she was right. He wants her to go, although she doesn't know it. Says she's old-fashioned. He wants to re-model several departments. I find he's been countermanding my orders, going behind my back, getting his toadies. And he's not honest. I established for certain a few days ago that goods were disappearing. I intended waiting until after your wedding before having a damned good row with him and getting rid of him. Instead, I was struck with this illness. And that scoundrel's singing praises about it, no doubt."

"Papa, this is a terrible situation!"

"That's what I'm telling you. You've got to put it right. Go down to Bonnington's and call a meeting and say you're in charge until I get back. Just hold up your head and talk firmly and they'll all be behind you." Papa smacked his good hand on the coverlet. "Bonnington's is yours and mine, and it's not going to be ruined by an ambitious scoundrel. You've got to stop that, Bea."

Papa was looking very tired, suddenly. He could hardly finish what he was saying. Something about her hurrying up and having a son to inherit.

"We've got to keep the business for him, Bea. So will you do it? Will you go and talk to them?"

"Yes," she said slowly. "Yes, I'll do that. But later—"

William would have to understand. This wasn't going out early to look at Bon Marché. This was a real emergency.

"You know I've always wanted to be part of the shop. But now, when I'm just married and have a house to run, and William hasn't been well—not ill like you, but with a very nasty chest cold—"

She stopped as she noticed the dampness around his eyes. He rubbed at them furtively, grumbling, "Eyes weak, that's all. Gad, why did this have to happen?"

"Because you've always worked too hard. And if I promise to go to the shop—"

"When, Bea? Tomorrow?"

She nodded, because she could see that there was no alternative. Nor, if she were to be honest, did she want one.

"But I'm not going to work eighteen hours a day, like you have. And you must promise to behave yourself, to do as you're told, and not be rude to the nurse—"

Papa was looking perky and alert again. "Now, Bea, don't get bossy with me. Save that for that rascal Featherstone tomorrow."

Chapter 5

Blanche Overton had given up her usual place at the table to her daughter-in-law.

Beatrice had eaten often enough at this table, first as a gauche schoolgirl, and later as a nervous fiancée. But never before as a wife. She was sure that when she was a wife in the full sense of the word she would feel she had more right than she had at this moment to oust Mrs. Overton from her place.

Mrs. Overton, wrapped in her familiar exquisite gauzy scarves, subtly patronizing, reluctantly making the best of a bad bargain, was deliberately doing nothing to put Beatrice at her ease.

She'll have to live somewhere else, ran the random thought in Beatrice's head. It is my house now and I don't intend to be patronized.

Shocked at her ruthlessness, she looked across at William, certain that he must read her thoughts.

But he was occupied with his meal. He looked a little flushed and weary. His cold was not better yet. A chilly Channel crossing hadn't helped it. He had already made the observation that it had been selfish and unreasonable of Beatrice's mother to summon her back, since her father seemed to be in no imminent danger of dying. He had traveled when he was not fit to do so, and although he remained kind and sympathetic, he had let her be aware of his mild displeasure that their honeymoon had been ruined.

But if William were disappointed that the consummation of their marriage was not to take place in a romantic city like Paris, Beatrice was still glad that it was to be in their own home and, most appropriately in the old general's bed.

In spite of her uneasiness at the dinner table, a strange violent joy kept ebbing and flowing through her. She thought that dinner would never end.

"Beatrice, whatever are you thinking about? I've spoken to you twice," Mrs. Overton said petulantly.

"I'm sorry. What did you say, Mrs. Overton?"

"I was asking you if you had had time to shop in Paris." Mrs. Overton's critical eyes rested on Beatrice's dinner dress, another of Miss Brown's choices, modest and perfectly correct, but definitely lacking in dash and style.

What did it matter, really what *did* it matter, since soon enough all her clothes, and those of her husband's as well were going to be discarded, lying in an untidy heap on the floor. . . .

"If you would like me to go on giving orders," Mrs. Overton was continuing in her high well-bred voice. "Beatrice! Are you listening to me? Just until you have time to settle down, of course, and have become accustomed to this kind of household."

Nothing could have been more tactful.

"No, thank you," Beatrice said uncompromisingly. "I will begin at once."

She would have to go into Bonnington's tomorrow morning, and several mornings afterward. The journey to the Bayswater Road took about an hour by carriage. William must be persuaded to allow her to take the carriage.

But it was her carriage as well as his. Indeed, more hers than his, since she was now paying the wages.

"As you wish," said Mrs. Overton. Her good manners forbade showing any sign of offense. "But you mustn't go on calling me Mrs. Overton. Must she, William?"

"No, Bea, you goose."

That slight upright little creature, delicately boned, petal-cheeked, fading but still exquisite, a mother, a maternal creature? One could never imagine her having been swollen with a baby.

I'll be broad, big-breasted, big-hipped, when I'm pregnant, Beatrice thought. Will William begin to love me then?

"Very well," she said politely. "I'll call you Mother if you wish. I hope you don't mind me wanting to start giving the orders. I must learn, mustn't I?"

"I understand perfectly," said Mrs. Overton.

There mustn't be many more of these dinners *à trois*, Beatrice thought with her new ruthlessness. They simply wouldn't do.

The general's room caught the first light of the sunrise. Beatrice was awake early enough to discover this. She lay for a while watching the pencil of light at the window, then crept out of bed to draw back the curtains, but only an inch, in case she woke William. She had slept very little that night, yet felt deeply refreshed. She wanted to walk about the room looking at things, as wide-eyed as the schoolgirl who had once stood in the doorway staring at the old man in the bed.

This same bed, with the Chippendale posts, which was now hers.

It was all so incredible that she wanted to laugh, to exclaim, to talk, to communicate genuinely for the first time with William. During the whole of her courtship and then her wedding and the strange out-of-joint journey to France, she had been nervous, distrait, in a dream.

But now, in this spectacularly lovely dawn, with the early sun stroking shadows over the lawn, the doves stirring in a flurry of white petticoats in the distant dovecotes, the little pointed cypress trees still as black as night, she was wide awake. She wanted to talk, to laugh, to coo and flutter starched petticoats, like the doves.

But William was still asleep. She hung over him, thinking how peaceful but how lonely sleeping faces were. William's was pale and remote, as if he had never belonged to anyone but himself. Who, looking at him now, could guess at his sensuality?

Or hers, she thought, glancing furtively at the mirror, her cheeks growing warm with remembered pleasure.

If William had expected a modest wife, his first touch on her bare skin had sent all chances of that to the winds. The astonishing thing was that she had never known she would have this lack of modesty, this sheer physical desire. William's skillful hands on her breasts had done something extraordinary to her. Her wild trembling had communicated itself to him, and very shortly she had made the surprising but satisfactory discovery that the consummation of a marriage was far more exciting than the vows taken at the altar.

No one had told her this would be so, not even her

mother. But Mamma, with her obsession for clothes and household affairs, and Papa utterly absorbed in business—she was certain it could never have been like this for them. If it had been, some of their tenderness would have been obvious, even to a child. How would she and William be able to disguise their tenderness for each other today?

The curtains, drawn back another six careful inches by her impatient fingers, showed blue sky, and the top of the Judas tree, and William was stirring at last, opening his eyes and looking at her.

And in a mere second Beatrice's euphoria had gone.

But euphoria, she had always known, was not a lasting emotion. A good thing that it wasn't, for one couldn't live permanently at that pitch of excitement.

For William's eyes rested on her with a look of surprise, first as if he had forgotten he had spent the night with a woman, and then as if he were disappointed the woman was her. Coming fully awake, however, the revealing moment had gone and he had assumed his usual pleasant amiable expression.

She hadn't realized how much she had hoped that that impersonal courtesy could not have survived the night. Didn't she deserve something more now? A look of love, for instance? But he did put out his hand and take hers in a light caressing clasp.

"Morning, dearest." He began to cough. "Sorry. I usually have a hot drink early to stop this cough."

"I'll ring for one," Beatrice said at once. "What do you like? I'd suggest lemon and honey which is very soothing."

"Is it? Then I'll try it." He sat up, in pleasant anticipation. "Bless you, you're so thoughtful."

"That's a wife's duty."

He looked boyish and young and charming against the pillows.

"What a word to use. 'Duty.'"

Had it been a duty he had performed last night? Then how clever he was, to do it so well. She hoped he didn't notice that she was trembling now, and hastily pulled on a robe over her nightgown. The one Hawkins had put out for her, white lawn threaded with blue ribbons to match her nightgown. Her honeymoon nightwear and really only suited to candlelight.

Surely she had always known that civilized people didn't

talk of what happened in the night. Such conversation belonged to the darkness.

Looking at her husband's boyish face, concerned only with the anticipated comfort of the hot drink, she found that she had plenty of courage to tell him about her promise to go into Bonnington's that day. She hoped he would allow her to take the carriage, she said. Indeed, she would be very happy if he felt inclined to accompany her.

He was astonished, more offended than amused.

"Are you proposing I learn how to be a shopwalker? No, no"—seeing her expression—"I was only joking. But is that why that crafty old devil, your father, brought us home? To make us earn our living?"

"Me. Not you, William." She found she could be coolly astringent. Love hadn't made her too soft and silly, thank goodness. "You know very well that Papa has had a stroke and it's most important that he shouldn't worry, otherwise he may have another. He wants me to clear up an unfortunate situation and I have promised to do so. That's all it is."

"What is this unfortunate situation?"

"It would take too long to tell you." She had no intention of risking his boredom. "It's merely that, being Papa's daughter, people will listen to me. I'll put matters in order and be home in time for luncheon. You must have a late lie in. Rest. Get over your cold."

He lay back on his pillows, enjoying her solicitude.

"Yes, perhaps I'll do that. But this won't become too much of a habit, will it, dearest?"

"Going to the shop? Oh, I shouldn't think so. To tell the truth all Papa wants is for us to have a son who could learn—"

She stopped as she saw William's face, momentarily as set and stuffy as his mother's.

"Darling, Papa's sick. You must let him have his dreams."

"Our son," said William, "will be expected to be a soldier, I'm afraid."

"But you don't like soldiering. Would you really inflict a career that you personally hate on him rather than let him be in trade?"

Her voice was aggressive. She couldn't stand him having that stiff snobbish look of his mother's.

"Dearest, stop bouncing about like that. You make my head ache." He was smiling again, obviously not caring enough for even this small seed of a quarrel to develop. "Are we going to argue about an imaginary person who may never exist? Come and kiss me."

She went, after the smallest hesitation, not wanting to be less spontaneous in her forgiveness than he was. Besides, she had wanted him to kiss her ever since he had opened his eyes.

"But he will exist," she murmured.

"Who?"

"Our son."

"I hope so." He kissed her again. "My little shopkeeper." Her body ached with love. But he had slipped back on the pillows again and was saying in a matter-of-fact voice, "Of course you may take the carriage. I seldom want it in the mornings. I'll stay at home and inform callers that I have sent my wife out to work."

"William!"

"Dearest, just to please me, develop an appreciation of my jokes."

"Is that what that remark was meant to be?"

"I'm afraid so."

"Oh, William, you're an awful tease. I'll be home at one sharp. I'll give Cook orders before I leave. Promise to drink your hot lemon and honey, and have a lazy morning in bed." She wanted to add, "I love you very much," but refrained. She sensed that the night was not to be mentioned. Anyway, William was already looking drowsy, and anxious to be rid of her too energetic company.

Beatrice was very well aware of the looks of surprise when she walked into Bonnington's. She purposely had not sent word of her intended visit. She didn't exactly expect to find Mr. Featherstone with his hands in the cashbox, but he was where she had thought he would be, in the gilt cage of the cash desk, perched on Papa's stool, surveying the shop as if he already owned it.

Her blood began to boil. This was Papa's shop, her shop, and this impertinent man was an intruder. He had come with excellent references and one could easily have been taken in by his ability.

Her feminine intuition, however, would have warned her

of the danger signals immediately. She had known for some time that she was a better judge of character than Papa who was apt to think that hard work must go hand in hand with honesty. He had been fortunate in his staff in the past.

"Yes, madam?" Mr. Featherstone said, mistaking her for a customer. Then he recognized Beatrice and hastily slid off his stool. "I beg your pardon, Mrs. Overton. I wasn't expecting the honor of a visit from you."

"I don't suppose you were," Beatrice said briskly, enjoying the effect of her surprise tactics.

However, in a moment Mr. Featherstone had overcome his shock and was saying suavely, "And how is your poor father, Mrs. Overton?"

"My father is getting on splendidly. He'll be back in the shop in no time at all."

"Ah, not too soon, I hope. These things can't be hurried. I remember my poor mother, well one day, alas, gone the next."

"My father has absolutely no intention of following your mother's example, Mr. Featherstone."

"One hopes not. One hopes not. But the Almighty—"

Beatrice had had enough of this sort of creeping Jesus talk. How could Papa have engaged a man like this, except that he was so clever? But not clever enough not to look down his nose at this little person and dismiss her as of no account. She was not only female, but had allowed herself to be married for her money.

"I'm afraid I don't agree with your pessimistic outlook, Mr. Featherstone. It's bad for the shop. But we'll talk more about that in my father's office. I want a meeting of buyers in half an hour. Will you arrange it for me?"

Mr. Featherstone allowed various expressions, surprise, a certain apprehension, and finally a calculated meekness to pass over his face.

"Certainly, Mrs. Overton. I'll arrange it at once. I'm sure everyone is most anxious to hear how your father is."

"I haven't come to present a bulletin of my father's health."

Beatrice found that she was enjoying herself. Giving orders was a heady business, and especially agreeable when a man like this was forced to obey. She felt six inches taller already.

She had one of the messenger boys, a cheerful curly-

headed lad called Johnnie Lundy, arrange chairs around
the heavy oak table in Papa's office. From now on, she
decided, she must observe every employee, from the humblest upward.

She sat in the elbow chair at the head of the table, one
hand resting lightly on each arm. She hoped she looked
the picture of composure.

Presently they all came in, led by Adam Cope, the head
buyer, who had been with Papa for ten years, and was an
utterly reliable, serious sober person. Then there was Mr.
Crowther from Linens and Damasks, Mr. Mortlake from
Gentlemen's Wear, Mr. Lang from Footwear, Miss Simpson
from Haberdashery, Mr. Seeley, the head bookkeeper, and
several others whose faces, although not their names, were
familiar to Beatrice.

Dear Miss Brown, who had worked for Papa since Bonnington's had been a one-floor shop like a village store,
selling everything from petticoats to cough drops, was so
overjoyed to see Beatrice that she kept saying, "Thank
heaven, thank heaven," in an audible voice, obviously
meaning Mr. Featherstone to make no mistake about her
meaning.

"Will everybody sit down, please," Beatrice said quietly.
Her nerves remained in admirable control. "I have asked
you all to come here to discuss the future. I daresay you're
surprised that it's me doing this, since I'm only a woman
and rather young and newly married. But I'm Bonnington's,
my father says, so I must deputize until he is well. And
that, I may say, knowing Papa, won't be in the very distant
future."

There was a polite murmur of relief.

"I have a great deal to learn, of course. I will want to go
through the department figures, the stock books and the
outstanding accounts. I propose to do that tomorrow
morning."

"Mrs. Overton—" began Mr. Featherstone.

"I think," said Beatrice pleasantly, "that when I'm in the
shop I would like to be called Miss Beatrice as I have always been. Yes, what were you about to say, Mr. Featherstone?"

"Only that for someone as inexperienced as yourself—"

"Oh, I'm not inexperienced, Mr. Featherstone. Far from
it. I've always had a gift for figures. My teacher said that it

wasn't a very feminine characteristic. Apart from that, I've
listened to my father talking business ever since he judged
I was old enough to be interested, and that's been for a long
time now. So I know a great deal of the tangible side of
buying and selling. The intangible side—pleasing the customer—is one that I think a woman knows quite as well, if
not better, than a man."

She gave her friendly smile. She was conscious of a very
pleasant sense of power.

"I have several ideas in that connection already. For instance, I would like the area around the front doors made
more attractive. And I do think there's a great deal of
room for improvement in our window dressing. It's really
rather old-fashioned, and I intend to speak to my father
about it. Why don't we have a special display, whenever
there's a birth in the royal family, for instance? Lots of
patriotic red, white and blue, and a slogan such as 'Every
infant is royal to its mother.' "

Miss Brown clapped her hands. "Brilliant, Miss Beatrice!"

"Then you must watch for happy events in the royal
family, Miss Brown. A royal wedding, of course, could be
a perfectly splendid occasion. We could advertise bridal
gowns for weeks ahead, and get in extra dressmakers, if
necessary. But I'm digressing. Just let me tell you my immediate plans. While my father is ill I intend to come in as
often as possible, probably every morning. This is an
emergency, and I've called you here to ask you to cooperate
with me. I'm sure you are all my friends."

There was an instant murmur of assent.

"That's all I want to say at this moment, so you may go
back to your positions. Except I would be obliged if you
would stay, Mr. Featherstone. I won't keep you more than
a few minutes."

They all filed out, Miss Brown lingering to press Beatrice's hand in an excess of emotion. Beatrice doubted if she
would ever be anything but "little Miss Beatrice," and a
child, to Miss Brown, but one thing was certain, Miss Brown
would be absolutely loyal.

Mr. Featherstone was another matter.

"I'm afraid I must ask you to go," Beatrice said, when
they were alone. There was no tremor in her voice to show
her distaste for what she had to do. "Those are my father's

instructions and I've come here this morning to carry them out. I don't want you to say anything because it will be a waste of your time and mine. Just get your things together and leave. Mr. Seeley will be instructed to pay you a week's wages which, under the circumstances, is extremely generous treatment. I hope you will never set foot in Bonnington's again. If you do, my father might be compelled to take out a writ against you for certain items of stock which have disappeared."

She stood up. She didn't want to watch the man's suave confidence turning to a particularly unpleasant abjectness. Papa would have been pleased with her, she thought. She had proved that women were not too emotional to be given authority. She could act with ruthlessness when necessary. Her gaze was as steely as Papa's.

"You were very foolish to ruin your chances here," she said. "My father is a generous employer to an honest person. But we won't waste time talking about what you have lost. Just take my advice and be more honest in your next employment."

"Surely I will be given a reference," Mr. Featherstone said, in a displeasing whine.

"Weren't you listening to me, Mr. Featherstone? I was speaking of honesty. How is my father to write a genuine reference about someone who has behaved as you have?"

The man turned without another word and went out, and it was over. Now she could tremble if she wished.

She remained perfectly calm, however. She was reflecting on the advantages and disadvantages of power. One could inflate or diminish a person by a few words. It was a dangerous thing. She must use it with discretion.

She was glad to seek out Miss Brown in her little den behind the screen of bonnets and hats and lace caps flowering from slender gilt stands.

"I thought you would like to know, Miss Brown, that Mr. Featherstone has just left."

"Oh, thank heaven! That dreadful man! We were all so worried. Fancy you, Miss Beatrice, dismissing him!"

"I'm perfectly capable of doing things like that. From now on, I intend coming in every morning until Papa is better. I can't make it a whole day because I don't think my husband would care for that. I have to think of him as well."

"Dear Miss Beatrice! You with a husband." Miss Brown allowed herself a moment of romantic reflection before saying more practically, "Won't he object to you coming into the shop at all? You such a new bride."

Beatrice said airily, "Goodness me, no. William and I are a very modern young couple." She looked at the silver watch that hung from a chain around her neck.

"If I leave now I'll have time to look in on Papa on the way home. I must set his mind at rest about this morning's affair. Oh, no. I don't think my husband will object at all to my morning occupation. He isn't strong and I'm insisting that he rise late. Besides, he's planning to begin his book on art. He's had it in his mind for a long time. He's very knowledgeable about paintings and sculpture. So he will be happily occupied while I am here. I think a great many married women could benefit from some extra occupation."

"Goodness me, how you've changed, Miss Beatrice."

"How have I changed?"

"You're so alive."

"That's because I'm happy."

"Bless you, my dear. I hope it will last a long time."

"It will last forever. I'll make it."

I'll make Bonnington's the best store in London, and I'll make William fall in love with me . . . she thought buoyantly.

"We must employ more women, Papa," she said, at Papa's bedside.

"Nonsense! I've never trusted 'em. Their nerves are too unreliable. They have attacks of the vapors."

"They understand their own sex, though, and since the majority of our customers are female, it's logical."

"I don't agree," Papa growled. He was sitting up in bed looking decidedly alert. Ever since Beatrice had come bursting in, pushing aside the twittering nurse in the passage, he had grown livelier by the minute. He had been pleased with her. He had said, "Well done, Bea. Now you can go home to your husband."

He was watching her carefully, however, and visibly relaxed when she said that she was on her way home now, but that she would be back in the shop tomorrow morning. He must know that the presence of the owner was vital for the morale of staff and customer alike. Besides, she had some ideas she wanted to put into practice. The façade of Bonnington's was too drab. Shoppers, especially women, could be persuaded to indulge in impulsive spending if the right atmosphere were present. As a beginning she suggested a banked display of hothouse flowers at the main doors to give an appearance of luxury. And something must be done about the banal style of window dressing. She would like to find a bright young man with originality who would help carry out her idea about introducing a theme of historical events into their window displays. There was always something happening in the far-flung empire. It wasn't enough to have an Indian room to outfit all those streams of women who set out for Calcutta or Delhi either to join their husbands or to find husbands. There were other countries constantly in the news. The discovery of diamonds on The Rand. Or the Zulu wars. Or the occasion of a royal wedding. With the old Queen's numerous grandchildren there were plenty of those. And it was high time Bonnington's received the royal warrant.

"Good Gad!" Papa said rather faintly. "You'll turn the place into a museum."

"No, you don't understand, Papa. We merely keep up with the times. Or we anticipate them. For instance, if Queen Victoria lives to celebrate her golden jubilee we must prepare for it months in advance. We must have all the society ladies buying their ostrich feather fans and their imperial purple at Bonnington's."

"That's several years ahead. Are you planning to be still there, Bea? Managing the place over my head?"

Beatrice pressed his hand.

"I expect I'll be somewhere about."

"I believe you will. I've started something, I can see. If you go on like this, who's to say what you'll be like in ten years."

"I told you, Papa. Women are better for selling women's things. Cheaper, too."

"Not in the end. They go off and get married as soon as you've taught them to measure a yard of ribbon correctly."

"And come back as customers."

"They upset the male staff."

"Miss Brown doesn't."

Papa gave his hoarse chuckle. "They won't all be old

Brownies. There'll be a fair percentage of the ones who get themselves into trouble. Then I suppose you'll want to run a nursery."

"No, but I intend finding a suitable house for the young girls to live in. They can sleep in dormitories. There will be a housekeeper and a cook. Then we can bring nice honest country girls to London and train them and make sure they're looked after."

"Gad, why didn't I consult you years ago?"

"I always wanted you to, Papa."

"But what's Master Overton going to say, losing his bride to trade? I can make a guess what old lady Overton will say. But that's nothing to you, I suppose, in this mood with that deuced determined look. What's happened to you? You were always a quiet little thing. And you've only been married five minutes. There's nothing wrong, is there?"

A small smile rested on Beatrice's lips.

"No, Papa. Nothing at all. William is the most understanding person in the world. But he hasn't a strong physique, and I have too much energy for him. I bounce about like a rubber ball, he says. So it would really suit very well if I have to be away for part of the day. There are plenty of servants at Overton House, and you know I was never a person to sit about with needlework. Besides, William understands how important it is for you to have peace of mind while you're recovering from this illness."

"I don't suppose he gives a tuppenny-damn about me. But I expect he has a thought or two as to where his income is coming from."

"Papa!"

"All right, I'm not criticizing. I'm simply stating a fact that we both know. Don't start manipulating your husband too soon, Bea, no matter if he is a good-natured chap."

"Papa, I'm not manipulating him!"

"Still, you reflect on that, love. You've always had a lot of private thoughts going on in your head. Haven't you, now?"

"If wanting to be part of Bonnington's is one, yes, I have. Do you know, there have only been three things in my life that I have passionately wanted, and now I have them all? A husband, a beautiful home, and Bonnington's. Isn't it unbelievable! And I'm not even pretty!"

Her sudden explosive happiness had to find a physical

outlet. She spun around in the bouncing-ball act that gave William a headache, then flung herself laughing into her father's arms.

She noticed sadly that his right arm could not fold itself tightly around her.

It was a reminder that everything was not perfect, not full of hope. . . .

"Come along, none of your smoodging," Papa grumbled. "Let's get down to business since you seem to have appointed yourself manager in my absence. Tomorrow I would like you to bring in the stock sheets for linen and damasks. We were low and I want to check orders. Those people in Dublin are a bit slow on deliveries. We might go to Boone's in Limerick. And let me know if that line of French brocade is moving. It was priced a bit high for our customers, I fancy."

"Then we must get richer customers."

"Think you know it all, don't you?"

"No. But I'll learn. So that by the time my second son is old enough he'll have a good inheritance. My first son will have to go into the army, I'm afraid. For the old general's sake. You understand, don't you, Papa? And after that I'll have a daughter for myself."

Papa gave his great guffaw.

"Gad, Bea, your boys may all be girls. All wanting expensive outfits at Bonnington's. Bankrupting us. Better go now, love. I'm a bit tired. I'll take a nap."

He looked so relaxed and peaceful that Beatrice knew she had provided the right medicine. Earlier this morning William had looked like that, too, deeply relaxed, at ease.

It was wonderful to be a woman, to minister to the varying needs of men, to be full of this quiet power. . . .

"Is this," said William over the luncheon table, "to be a pattern of the future, dearest?"

"While Papa is ill, yes." Beatrice's voice was quietly firm. She would have preferred not to discuss the matter in front of Mrs. Overton, who was already looking astonished and shocked, but perhaps it was as well to get an awkward task over.

William was giving his amiable smile. It was going to be very difficult ever to quarrel with him because he smiled most of the time. It made life civilized, certainly, but it also made the deeper places of his mind secret and unknowable, and Beatrice wanted to know every smallest thing about him. She was greedy for knowledge. She knew how his appearance, his voice, his humor, his gentleness, pleased her senses. She knew him physically, since the long beautiful night last night. Wasn't that enough in the meantime? She must contain her greed.

"And how long do you think your father's illness will last, dearest?"

"Perhaps two or three months. The doctor says recovery varies from one patient to another. But knowing Papa's will to get well, it shouldn't be too long."

"Three months!" Mrs. Overton was exclaiming, unable to keep silent any longer. "Beatrice, this simply won't do. You have a husband and a house to run."

"I gave Cook all the necessary orders before I left this morning," Beatrice said. "Is there anything wrong with the food?"

"The fish is excellent," said William. "Were you complaining, Mother?"

"You know very well that isn't what I meant," Mrs. Overton said sharply. She didn't share her son's placid nature. She was quick, tense, outspoken, disapproving. She looked at Beatrice as if she were slightly inferior goods being offered to her for purchase by one of Bonnington's saleswomen.

"You must realize, my dear, that as my son's wife you have a position to keep up, social duties, people to meet, to be accepted by. How can you be hostess to someone to whom you might have sold a dozen yards of lace that day? I'm not exaggerating. This is a situation that could very well happen, and it would be horribly embarrassing."

"Be quiet, Mother," William said, his brown eyes dancing. He appeared to be enjoying himself.

"I won't be quiet. Beatrice is young and unsophisticated and she must be told these things. I simply can't let your marriage turn into a disaster, dear boy. Your wife going off to work, standing behind a shop counter. It would be scandalous. Preposterous. I'm surprised that you could be so unwomanly, Beatrice. And as for entertaining any hopes of being invited to a royal drawing room, you could dismiss them at once."

"I don't want to visit the palace," Beatrice said. "On

the contrary, I want it to visit us. I was telling Papa. It's
high time that at least some members of the royal family
shopped with us. I intend to see that this happens." She
looked at Mrs. Overton dabbing her lips with her table
napkin (Bonnington's best damask?) and repressed a sudden naughty desire to giggle. "Do you think that's preposterous, William?"

She was deeply relieved that he hadn't got the set stuffy
look he had had earlier that morning. He now seemed to
feel nothing but amusement.

"I think you'll find, Bea dearest, that my mother is only
worried that I am to be so plainly seen to be supported by
my wife. This should have been an invisible side of our
marriage. Although everyone knows it exists, of course.
And if we're happy about it, what does it matter what anyone else thinks? This is something you must realize,
Mother."

"It's all so utterly *unsuitable!*" Mrs. Overton exclaimed
helplessly.

Beatrice was looking at William anxiously. "You are
speaking the truth when you say you're happy about it?"

"Oh, perfectly. Except that I will miss you when you're
at the shop," he added courteously. "And this doesn't make
me an eccentric, Mother. It only means that I'm not a
selfish, demanding husband."

He was a unique husband, Beatrice's fond glance told
him. And anyway, Mrs. Overton had no need to be quite
so scandalized. This was 1881 and women were emerging
from the extremely sheltered life they had lived since Queen
Victoria came to the throne and set her example of stifling
domesticity to the nation. They were becoming famous
writers, explorers, teachers, even doctors.

She wondered if her mother-in-law were aware of this
fact.

But not shopkeepers, Mrs. Overton would say. Trade!
That was something unmentionable, like a nasty disease.

"Mother, don't take it so seriously," William said in his
coaxing voice. "Bea has to do it, don't you, dearest?"

Beatrice looked at him gratefully.

"How do you know?"

"Because I know your devotion to your father, and I
have already discovered your passion for department stores,
or emporiums, or whatever fancy name you like to call

them. Do you know, Mother, she even deserted me in my sickbed in Paris to go and look at Bon Marché? Now if it had been the pictures in the Louvre. But a shop!" He gave his teasing impish smile. "Never mind, dearest, I intend to be a model husband, tolerant and understanding and long-suffering. Within reason, of course?"

"What do you mean by that?"

"If I want you I will expect you to be here."

"Oh, but of *course!*"

"Then it's settled. I'll tell Dixon to bring the carriage round every morning. What time would you like it?"

"Oh . . . about nine thirty, I think. But—"

"No buts, dearest. I said it was settled. On second thoughts, I believe a brougham would be more convenient than taking the carriage into town every day. We might arrange to get one. It would only need one horse, too. It would be quite economical."

Strange economics, Papa would say in his scathing voice. A new brougham and another horse, as well as keeping the carriage and the two nicely matched grays they already had.

Was William attempting a subtle form of blackmail?

No, of course he wasn't, he was merely being practical, and his suggestion was full of good sense. She must make sure that Papa understood this when she asked him for a check.

Chapter 6

Ten weeks later Joshua Bonnington made his first visit to the shop since his illness. The journey tired him aggravatingly, and he was able to stay only a short time. Long enough, however, to see his daughter ensconced in the cash desk, looking severely proprietorial as if she had been accustomed to sitting there for years. In her high-necked gray dress she looked like a damned governess, he thought ruefully.

Yet Joshua had to admit that he had had a good deal of satisfaction from discussing Bonnington's affairs with Bea. She had a remarkable grasp of affairs, and besides, one could trust one's own flesh and blood. There also seemed to be such a thing as a woman's touch, even in business. The shop was looking bright and attractive, with its new style of window dressing, and all those expensive tubs of flowers at the entrance. Little Bea certainly got things done.

Joshua could not say he admired the few sparse though choice items monopolizing all the valuable window space. He believed in showing as much of his stock as could be crowded into a window, piles of sheets and table linen, bolts of silk and Indian muslin and flowered cotton, smocks and aprons and petticoats, ribbons and lace, handkerchiefs, cravats, socks and stockings, and hats and bonnets like an overgrown garden, all clearly marked with the price. But Bea had found a young man, an aspiring artist, or a penniless artist, which was the same thing, and he had preached the modern doctrine that a window display should be like a fine painting, with not too many riches to confuse and distract the eye. A lady's lacy gown with a matching parasol and a casually dropped bunch of violets. Very French, very Rue de Rivoli, very chic.

But who was to know about the immense stock of Irish linen and other goods indoors? Joshua complained. He had to lean on his stick as he walked, and he was a bit breathless. But it was high time he was back in charge, he could see.

It was no use Bea confounding him with figures. Replicas of that lacy dress displayed in the window had been ordered eight times in the space of one morning. Christmas was approaching, of course, but there was no doubt a certain amount of trade was moving from other stores. Beatrice flourished new names among their customers. Lord McNeill's eldest daughter Amelia, going to India to marry a captain of Hussars, had ordered a complete trousseau, which included six of every kind of underwear, cambric chemises, hand-embroidered chemises, hand-embroidered lace-trimmed nightgowns, linen knickers and lace-trimmed knickers, petticoats of every variety, crepe de Chine, satin, Indian gauze, either lace-trimmed, hand-embroidered or both, also silk dressing gowns and muslin dressing gowns, half a dozen extravagant ruffled tea gowns, boudoir caps, blouses, stockings, and dresses for apparently every hour of the day. Amelia McNeill was going to put up the best possible show in English society in Delhi.

So that undoubtedly Bonnington's of the Bayswater Road, London, would be talked of even in that faraway place, and home-coming ladies, anxious to renew wardrobes ruined by the hot climate, would hasten to Miss Brown and her bevy of dressmakers.

Women! said Joshua Bonnington wonderingly. This was a market he had scarcely tapped.

His prosperity had been built on practical items, like boots and shoes and overcoats and household linen, and his business had been aimed at the lower-middle classes. This change was happening too quickly. It confused him. Having to please fashionable and vain women wasn't in his line at all.

"But I will do that," said Beatrice. Hadn't she obtained the order for a wedding dress and twelve bridesmaids' dresses for Flora Atkins, an old schoolmate (which showed that Mamma's snobbish school was succeeding in a way she hadn't envisaged)? Flora had come in to gape at Beatrice, and had remained to shop. With the new emphasis on women as the nation's spenders, Beatrice was expecting a flood of orders for evening gowns and wraps for the theater and the opera and other festivities in the coming season. She had instructed Miss Brown to hire more dressmakers and several young apprentices. Blanche Overton's friends were widespread, and the Millicents and Ettys, like Flora Atkins, would be coming to gaze on the intriguing spectacle of young Mrs. William Overton perched in the cash desk. She didn't at all object to being a spectacle if the gapers remained to spend money.

She said she could hear old General Overton's raucous chuckle as the sovereigns rattled into the till.

Anyway, they needed the extra trade, didn't they, because her new brougham, a very smart affair, shiny black picked out with green, had been rather expensive?

It certainly had been, Papa grumbled. But he hadn't been allowed to complain about that, considering how remarkably well young Bea was managing. She certainly had the bit between her teeth. One wondered if her husband, even with that handsome allowance, would eventually rue the day he had married her.

At present all seemed to be well. Beatrice was looking serenely happy and fulfilled. She said that William was quite undisturbed by all the gossip about her going to work, even though her mother-in-law was horrified by the spectacle she was making of herself.

This was true, although Mrs. Overton, while complaining endlessly to her friends, had to admit that she could find no fault with the running of the house. That maddening girl, her daughter-in-law, was up at the crack of dawn, and making sure that the servants were up with her. What was more, she had them eating out of her hand. One would have thought they might have had the sense to despise a mistress who went out to work, but on the contrary the exasperating creatures seemed to admire her for it.

Cook's opinion was that young Mrs. William was ever so clever, and what was more, since she worked so hard herself, she would understand what it was to get tired and have aching feet. She noticed when the parlormaid's chilblains were bad, or when Cook didn't do her best with her famous light pastry because of a scalded hand. She sent Ted, the knife boy, home when he had a nasty cough, then discovered that he and his mother and three younger brothers all lived in one room in Kentish Town, and gave orders that the lad

was always to be given leftovers from dinner to take home.
Cook was to see that there were leftovers. And none of the
younger maids was to carry coal scuttles too heavy for her.
It might damage her innards, especially for having children.
Not many mistresses stopped to think about a housemaid
being able to have babies safely when she married.

Of course, when Mrs. William got in the family way herself, what would happen about all this going to work? Then
the smart brougham drawn up at the front door sharp at
nine thirty every morning, with Dixon in his long overcoat
and top hat, in the driving seat, would have to remain in the
stables.

It would be a pity, in a way, because Mrs. William so
clearly enjoyed driving off, her face glowing beneath her
little tilted hat, a warm cape around her shoulders, the tartan
carriage rug over her knees. She always looked, Cook
thought privately, as if she had got up from a warm cozy
night with the master in the old general's bed.

And good luck to her. She was not one of those idle
fashion plates. She was a nice simple, kind little body with
thought for others. *'Uman,* said Cook.

Young Mr. William seemed happy enough. One suspected
he thought his wife a funny little thing, a bit of unexpec-
tedness, but he had an easy nature and enough self-
confidence to be quite undisturbed by malicious gossip.

He was a fortunate young fellow, getting up for his
leisurely breakfast, his prolonged luxurious bathing and
dressing, and then his writing or his cataloging, or his walks
on the Heath with a butterfly net.

And on Sundays the three of them, Mrs. Overton, William and Beatrice, attended church, walking across the road
and past the tilted gravestones as the bells began ringing. To
all outward appearances they were the most affectionate of
families.

In church Beatrice sang ardently in her gruff tuneless
voice, thanking the Lord for her happiness.

Afterward, they sat down to Sunday luncheon, soup, fish,
roast beef, Cheshire or Caerphilly cheese and fruit. Later,
if the weather was fine, Beatrice and William went for a
walk on the Heath; if wet or cold, William dozed and she
indulged in her favorite occupation of wandering from room
to room, lingering in the dusky-yellow drawing room, the

mirror room with its vaguely haunted atmosphere, the library where William's work lay spread on the desk.

She had everything. Or almost everything. If not yet her husband's love, at least his affection and faithfulness. That limpid look in his brown eyes, and the casual touch of his hand sent her blood racing. If he didn't turn to her in the big bed as often as she could have wished, she blamed herself for too much desire. It was not ladylike and she must conceal it. He would find it a little overpowering. Until the time came when he shared it.

In the meantime, with Christmas approaching, she could dissipate her boundless energy in hard work.

She had plans for turning the shop into a festive fairyland. Carol singers, tinsel, snowmen, trees of holly, every purchase wrapped with extravagant yards of red ribbon, and an unlimited supply of pennies for the beggars and the shivering waifs who pressed hungry faces against the windows.

She knew that she was getting talked about, and not always flatteringly.

The thing was that if she were talked about, so was Bonnington's.

"Beatrice," said Mrs. Overton, surprising Beatrice at breakfast, a meal which she liked to have downstairs alone. "This simply won't do."

Beatrice looked at the small erect figure, wrapped in soft white lacy wool. That wrap had not been bought at Bonnington's, but it was rather desirable; one might do something about stocking such articles of feminine luxury.

"What won't do, Mrs. Overton?"

"You've been married for two months and you haven't done a single thing about entertaining. That's rather bad manners, my dear. You and William have been out to dinner several times"—stuffy awkward occasions, when Beatrice had known she was looked on as an oddity—"and you've done nothing about returning hospitality."

"I haven't had time. I expected people to realize that. When Papa is better and able to take charge at the shop—"

"But since you're becoming such a dedicated shopkeeper, when will that be?" Mrs. Overton's voice, with its high bright tones, was perfectly polite. "I'm afraid William and I can't wait. I've taken it on myself to send out invitations for a soiree on Saturday week."

"In my name!"

"In yours and William's names, of course, dear. And don't worry about the organization, I will undertake that." She looked at a businesslike list in her hand. "I've asked the Marshes, the Prendergasts, the Andersons, Lord and Lady Tyler, the Caxtons, Colonel and Mrs. Mainwaring, Sir Humphrey Bowles, those pretty Morrison girls. You know them all."

The decorative Laura Prendergast, Beatrice thought. Hadn't she found a husband yet?

"Does William know about this, Mother?"

"We've discussed it. We didn't make a definite plan."

"Is he . . . has he told you he was feeling bored?" She risked the word, "Unhappy?"

"A little neglected, dear."

"But it is so important to keep the shop going, to pay the wages, everything. I thought he realized that."

"For a short time, of course. But not forever. Life doesn't depend entirely on the price of French brocade."

"If William is unhappy—" Beatrice muttered, and hated showing her uneasiness to Mrs. Overton.

"We would be the only house on the Heath not to have a party before Christmas," said Mrs. Overton with her pretty smile. "That would seem mean, to say the least."

Left alone to drink her cooling coffee, Beatrice gnawed at her lip resentfully. Who, she thought sourly, was going to pay for all this festivity, for all the champagne that undoubtedly would have been ordered, for the cold salmon and turkey, the hothouse strawberries and asparagus?

She pulled herself up sharply. Those might have been Papa's thoughts. They were unworthy of her who loved her husband. Mrs. Overton was perfectly right. It was high time she did her duty as a hostess.

Only one would have preferred to select one's own guests.

Whom? Miss Brown? Adam Cope, who lately had made no secret of his admiration for her? Adam wouldn't have objected to a shopkeeper wife. She didn't have other friends. She had had first her long dream of William, and her dream of Bonnington's, and now both of them in reality. She didn't need friends.

One thing was certain, if there were to be a party in the music room she wouldn't skulk upstairs this time, out of sight. She would be in the center of it all, the hostess, the wife. She would shine.

William was relieved that she was taking it so well. He had been a little nervous when his mother had first suggested it. He had thought Beatrice ought to be consulted. But there had never been an opportunity. She was always out of the house.

Not entirely true, Beatrice thought. She said nothing; she was too happy that William was being close and loving. He was saying that she must wear the cinnamon lace ordered in Paris. She had had the final fittings at Worth's Bond Street salon, and the gown had hung unworn in her wardrobe ever since.

It was snowing a little that night. Some of the ladies arrived in a nervous state, saying the horses had slipped on ice, and there had been near accidents. Hawkins was busy upstairs with warming possets, and smelling salts.

Laura Prendergast, having shed her wraps, was the first to come running downstairs, her curls dancing. She was dressed entirely in white, and looked fragile and insubstantial as a snowflake. William's eyes were warm with admiration. He didn't bother to conceal it. He had always admired pretty women. Besides, as his mother had said, he was starved for gaiety. Could this be a dangerous state for a young man not entirely in love with his wife?

Beatrice decided there and then to reduce her involvement with Bonnington's. Money was important for the purpose of showering luxuries on her husband, but personal attention might be more important.

She could begin now by proving that she could be a good hostess.

After the first half hour, however, she had the sensation that the guests (damn swells, Papa would say) were sweeping over her, taking possession of the house as if they owned it by right, and as if she were dumb and invisible.

It was her own fault, she told herself. She should have taken the trouble to get to know William's friends. But it was Mrs. Overton's fault, too. One suspected deliberate malice in that lady for inviting all the most arrogant people who could be relied on to make remarks such as, "So this is William's bride at last! Now *where* have we seen you before?"

It was easy enough to counter that sort of thing.

"Behind the counter in my shop," Beatrice answered one lady composedly. "Aren't you the person who wanted the Venetian lace? It's made on the Island of Burano, you know. I am having a special order sent over. Do remember to inquire for it in a few weeks' time."

More difficult was the way William kept disappearing. But then she should not watch him so closely.

Be polite to people, she admonished herself. Make small talk, if you can. Arrange for the music to begin.

Mrs. Overton had engaged Elizabethan players and wanted madrigals, but Beatrice serenely told the musicians to play Christmas carols. After all, it was Christmas, wasn't it?

Soon the carols were being sung lustily (proving how wrong Mrs. Overton had been about her silly old madrigals) and while the guests were enjoying this diversion, Beatrice took the opportunity to go in search of William.

She found him in the mirror room, with Laura Prendergast in his arms.

That beautiful, small, self-indulgent room of another philandering Overton, with the slender white form of Laura and William's dark shadow blotting out the reflection of the candles. They were ghostlike. There was nothing ghostlike about their kiss. By its very length it suggested unmistakably warm blood.

Beatrice stood transfixed until William's laugh, that short tender husky sound, made her step back hastily into the passage.

She must not let him find her here. If he thought she were spying on him he would never forgive her.

She knew immediately that the forgiving would have to come from her. In the space of a few seconds she had to lose whatever complacency she had had, and become wise, far-seeing, disciplined, patient.

Pressed back against the wall, clenching her fists in agony, and resolving never again to wander during a party in this house, she slowly disciplined her chaotic thoughts.

William had never kissed her in the mirror room. But then she had never worn a romantic white dress and drifted like a snowflake. It was wiser, too, with her short figure, that their embraces were not reflected by candlelight in dim glass. They would scarcely look poetic, would they?

She was trying hard to be sensible and realistic. She had been told constantly that the man she wanted to marry was a gay philanderer. Accepting that, she had married him. So why did she now think she had cause for complaint?

Only that she had hoped that marriage had contented him. Those embraces in the old general's bed, weren't they enough?

She knew now that they were not.

There was nothing to do at this minute but to be practical once more, to walk quietly away, return to the guests, behave as if nothing had happened. And never mention it. Never let the accusation cross her lips. Never, in her marriage, resort to the disaster and destructiveness of quarreling.

But her lovely world had shivered and cracked. It had been as fragile as one of those treacherous Chippendale mirrors. Now it must be put together somehow, the cracks papered over.

When William woke the next morning with a sore throat and some difficulty in breathing, Beatrice sadly recognized the pattern. He was always going to be ill when he was upset. Her hope that the scene she had glimpsed had been only lighthearted flirtatiousness vanished.

William was fretting for the lovely Laura, and regretting that he was tied for life to so dull a bride.

"I'm sorry, dearest, I seem to have caught a cold. It's damned tedious for you."

"For you, too," said Beatrice. "You must stay in bed today. I'll ring for a hot bottle, and hot drinks. No, I'll go and make a hot drink for you myself. I can't trust Lizzie to do it; she's a very stupid girl."

"Won't that make you late? Don't keep Dixon waiting. That new cob is a bit fidgety."

"I won't go to the shop this morning," Beatrice said.

"Why not?"

"Because I prefer to look after my husband." She felt his forehead for fever, then kissed it lightly. "Do you object?"

William looked surprised, then sleepy and contented.

"You know that I adore being pampered."

Beatrice fancied the heaviness in her heart lightened a

little. Being an adored nurse was better than nothing. It was a crumb to ease her starvation.

"And then I have had a brilliant idea. Why do we need to spend Christmas in England? You know how bad the damp and fogs are for your chest. Why don't we go and find the sun?"

William was up on his elbow.

"Bea! Do you mean that?"

"Of course. I've never spent a Christmas abroad, as you very well know. I hadn't been abroad at all until we went to Paris, and I've never made up to you for having to end that trip so suddenly."

"You don't have to make up to me."

"I may not have to, but I would like to," Beatrice said earnestly. "It came to me last night. I've spent so much time at the shop, and neglected you, and you've been so sweet and uncomplaining."

William's eyes had narrowed.

"What about the shop, if we go?"

"Oh, Papa's better. He's almost well again. With the staff Bonnington's has now he can manage perfectly well. So where is the best place for your chest, my darling? Egypt, perhaps?"

"I've never been to Egypt," William said animatedly, and she knew the battle—not a battle, only a skirmish, something the old general would regard as elementary— was won.

"But one thing, William," Beatrice said later, as she stood by his bedside, with a steaming hot toddy, "when we come back, I think your mother would be much happier if she had her own establishment. After all, if I am not to go to the shop, two women would fall over each other, in a house this size."

"Once you thought it was a palace."

"Once."

He reached out and patted her hand. He was profoundly selfish, her William, but when it came to loving him, she had no sense at all.

"I understand, dearest. Mothers-in-law can be the devil. I thought mine was better than most, but you see it in a woman's way. Well, if we can run to two establishments—I don't honestly think the mater will mind."

They would have to make those new ideas at Bonnington's work, Beatrice was thinking. Otherwise Papa was going to be furious about the additional expense. First the brougham and cob, then the trip to Egypt, then the small tasteful house for Mrs. Overton in a fashionable part of London. And was Papa fit to take over again?

"It's a matter of priorities, Papa," she could hear herself explaining. "William is the most important thing to me. I can even sacrifice Bonnington's for him. . . ."

Chapter 7

Money was the gist of all Papa's letters. Grumbling endlessly, he had paid for the trip to Egypt, but he had drawn
the line at buying a house for that vain demanding woman,
Blanche Overton. They must finance that themselves. If
Bea so badly wanted to get rid of her mother-in-law, she
must persuade her husband to sell one or two of the family
treasures. A couple of pictures, a piece or two of furniture.
Some of that Chippendale or Louis XIV stuff. It would
fetch a price in a salesroom.

Although Mrs. Overton protested, saying quite openly
that surely William's marriage had been to preserve the
treasure, she capitulated quickly enough. The idea of her
own establishment appealed to her. She had a small private
income which would be enough to run it. She was not finding her daughter-in-law either sympathetic or congenial,
and the Overton House was full of memories of happier
days when Caroline had been alive.

So somehow the money was found for the small house
in Hans Crescent in Knightsbridge. Beatrice added to the
sum required by announcing that she intended selling the
new brougham and cob. She wouldn't be needing it anymore since she had given up going to the shop.

But Papa must promise to keep to the new style of window dressing. It was proving such a success. And Adam
Cope must be given more authority. He was honest and
capable, and understood Beatrice's wishes. Miss Brown, while
retaining her status, must nevertheless be gently persuaded
to listen to the advice of younger women. If Bonnington's
were to be given the royal warrant, and that was the ultimate aim, they must take all the right steps.

Finally Papa had said exasperatedly, "For heaven's sake,

girl, get your trunks packed and get out of the country. Then perhaps I can prove I can keep Bonnington's afloat without the assistance of your particular genius."

All the same, one of his letters, reaching Luxor two days after Beatrice and William's arrival there, had its note of triumph:

> *Today Princess Beatrice with a lady-in-waiting came in unannounced and walked about for half an hour or so. I told old Brownie and Adam not to get excited, just to treat them with the same courtesy we treat all customers. In the end, the P. made only a piddling bit of a purchase, several yards of black braiding. I believe she said something about smartening up an old dress. I thought royalty never kept old clothes, but there you are. We will hardly qualify for the royal warrant on that performance, but it's a beginning, and I thought you would be pleased to hear about it.*

He added as a wry afterthought, "I related this to your mother, hoping it might be an example to her, but she thought it a bit shocking. Said what would the poor do if all the gentry wore their clothes to rags. If some of your mother's recent purchases have gone to the East End, there will be some mighty dressed-up housewives, and I daresay that will cause a riot, so who is doing good to whom?"

Sitting in her hotel room, with the shades drawn against the heat, and William stretched out on the bed dozing, Beatrice answered the letter at once.

> *Dear Papa,*
> *   That's truly interesting news about Princess Beatrice. My namesake, too, don't you think that's significant? You were right not to make a fuss when she came in. I have always heard that the royal ladies don't care for attention to be brought to them when they are on private shopping expeditions. What I would really like would be for the Princess of Wales to outfit her children at Bonnington's. Because she will eventually be queen, and then we could really apply for gracious consideration to be given to the grant of a royal warrant. Imagine if we were given the order for Princess May's wedding to Prince Eddy. I know*

*this is dreaming, but all achievements begin with a
dream.*

*I have been keeping my eyes open while here for
a reliable supplier of Persian carpets. The carpets are
good quality, but the suppliers less so. William and I
do not find the Egyptians at all an honest people, but
one has to realize that they have different standards
of behavior to us, and there are some likable characters among them. I do not agree with William that
they are all rogues.*

*We went on an expedition to the Pyramids by
camel. Very uncomfortable. William showed far more
facility in riding these ugly rocking beasts than I did.
I was very thankful to arrive back at our hotel with
no more damage than a sore unmentionable part of
my anatomy.*

*William is now in splendid health, which proves
our wisdom in wintering here.*

*You omitted to give me the January figures when
you wrote. I expect they are not anything to get excited about. January, following on all the spending at
Christmas, must always be a poor month. But by the
time we are home, by the end of March I hope, things
will be in full swing for an excellent spring season.*

*Have you taken my advice about commemorating
historical events in our window display? We are quite
cut off from news here, but I am sure various important things are happening in the empire. What about
that strange powerful man, Cecil Rhodes, in Africa?
Or India always provides some drama, and is popular
with the queen.*

They returned home at the beginning of April, Beatrice
very gladly, she had been homesick for some time, William
less willingly as he was an addicted traveler.

There was no question, however, of Beatrice going back
to Bonnington's, except as a visitor. She was expecting a
baby.

She was delighted, and so, she said, was William. They
had had pleasant and amicable travels. The constant change
of scene had prevented William from boredom. As far as
Beatrice was concerned, there was never any question of
her being bored with William's company. It was only the

hot dusty towns, the endless sand, and the squalor outside their comfortable hotels that had wearied her. Also, toward the end of their stay, she had been pregnant, and feeling decidedly queasy. She found the food nauseous, and failed to appreciate William's comment that she would never make a successful traveler if she couldn't eat the food of the country.

However, he was considerate and kind, and made no objection when she suggested returning home. He certainly would not risk harming the baby by having its mother under any physical strain.

"We'll go home and cosset you, dearest," he said, and she loved his tender concerned look. She loved him more than ever. It was hopeless, almost. No, it wasn't. Because no two people who were not true friends and companions could have got on so well, under various trying circumstances of heat and sandstorms and frequently wretchedly uncomfortable beds. Surely this amounted to some sort of love on William's part. On her part, it was simply complete love.

The baby, William said, would be a boy, a splendid strong little fellow destined for a great future. Different from his father.

"I'd be happy if he's like you," Beatrice said. She seldom allowed herself statements like that. If she were now more sure about her marriage, she was still afraid of wearying her volatile husband with her devotion.

The baby was born early on a summer morning in the big bed with its slender Chippendale posts. It was small but healthy and well formed. It should thrive.

The only trouble was that it was a girl.

When she was strong enough to face the disappointment, Beatrice said that now she understood how Papa had felt about her. The important difference, however, was that she had been an only child, whereas this daughter would have brothers.

The birth had not been easy, in fact it had been hellish, and the baby had had a painful journey into the world. When Beatrice saw the bruised head she had asked that William not be shown his daughter until her looks had improved. She knew William's almost pathological dislike of ugliness and pain. He would really prefer to believe the childhood story that a stork brought babies, beautifully pink and white and unblemished.

He looked very young and endearing himself when he bent over her, assuring her he was delighted that they had a daughter.

"It's your father who's going to read you the Riot Act, dearest. He thinks there's some sort of curse on the Bonningtons that they can't beget sons."

"Not on the Overtons, I hope," Bea said, putting up fingers to trace the loved face.

"Well . . . until you and I can prove otherwise—" William gave his merry laugh and kissed her fingers. He had kissed her forehead, too. Not her lips. Hardly surprising, since they were still dry and cracked and bitten. Darling sensitive William didn't care for either bitten lips or screams.

"When can I see the little puss?"

"In a day or two. I'd really prefer you to wait until she's beautiful."

"Just as you say. I'm sorry it was so bad, poor Bea."

"Not that bad. I've forgotten it already."

"Nurse tells me you were splendid. My capable girl."

Capable? Of course. She was always that. Who wanted flowery phrases?

"William, go and get some rest. You look much too tired."

"Been up all night with you, dearest."

Not flowery phrases, just that matter-of-fact statement. It was more than enough to set the warmth flowing in her heart.

The baby was called Florence Alexandra, Alexandra after the Princess of Wales, because that, Beatrice thought privately and with more than a touch of superstition, would bring them luck. (Bonnington's had not yet achieved the distinction of having the princess as a customer.) The christening ceremony became quite an affair, because William insisted on it.

Beatrice suspected that William only wanted an excuse for a party, but that was understandable. He was far more addicted to parties than Beatrice was.

Now she no longer had the excuse of the shop, or of pregnancy, she must begin giving dinner parties and musical evenings. Privately she winced at the thought. Her idea of a thoroughly congenial evening was a leisurely dinner alone with her husband, then preferably a bundle of reports from Bonnington's to study while William worked at his book.

Couldn't they always spend their evenings like that?

No, of course not. She had got her figure back and William had bought her some elegant new clothes. So now they must be gay. It was the prerogative of their class.

From the beginning little Florence was put in the care of a nurse, a sensible middle-aged person recommended by Hawkins. Beatrice visited the nursery several times a day, but found she did not want to linger long. Small babies were uninteresting creatures, and William, whose chest was troubling him again, absorbed so much of her emotions. Not that the baby wasn't an engaging little thing, even though she hadn't inherited the Overton good looks.

She looked just like her grandfather Bonnington, Mrs. Overton said. The little face with the too-long chin was old Bonnington over again. It was ludicrous and very unfortunate that one's first grandchild looked like a tradesman.

Sometimes it seemed to Beatrice that even Hans Crescent was not far enough away. Mrs. Overton gave elegant little soirees in her charming drawing room—"only big enough for a mouse," she said gaily—and although Beatrice was expected to attend, William was too kind to insist that she do so. By Christmas he was even making things easy for her by saying, "I know you'd prefer to stay at home with the baby. I'll make your excuses." Or he was telling her not to order an elaborate dinner because he did like to dine at his club now and then. A husband and wife in each other's pocket constantly were not a wise thing. There was a publisher, a member of his club, as it happened, who was interested in the book he was writing, which showed the importance of regularly attending one's club.

Beatrice, repressing the thought that sometimes William protested a little too much, tried to occupy herself with household affairs. The servants were too well trained, however. There was remarkably little for her to do. She didn't sew, she didn't play the piano, she didn't execute clever little watercolors. She could nurse the baby when she woke, but even that was with Nanny's jealous eyes on her. Nanny Blair was beginning to show the failing of most dedicated nurses; she was growing too possessive of her charge.

So who in the world really needed her? Beatrice wondered.

Laura Prendergast was married. Someone had told her that. Anyway, she wasn't in the least suspicious of William's absences. Only a little grieved by them, and so overanxious not to look reproachful that she often retired and pretended to be asleep when he returned. It was just possible that he took advantage of this, for his arrivals grew later, and this was disturbing, since his health would suffer. But what could she do? She couldn't turn into a Nanny Blair and cosset him too obviously. But she certainly must do more to keep him entertained at home. How?

As it happened, the problem was more or less solved by her becoming pregnant again. She stopped fretting for the shop, and worrying about William's absences, since now it was plain that she couldn't accompany him everywhere. She simply made herself accept facts as they were, and waited for her son.

The baby wouldn't dare be another girl.

Edwin William Overton was born at the end of November, in the middle of a particularly vile fog that had blotted out the Heath, and the street gate and even the steps up to the front door, and had laid his father low with a nasty bronchial attack. No escape to a sunnier climate had been possible this year because of Beatrice's condition, so in a way William's serious illness could be laid at his son's door.

Who could tell whether even a creature as innocent as a newborn baby were affected by anxiety, or whether the poor child had simply inherited his father's delicacy? Whatever it was, Edwin's first six weeks were a struggle for survival, and when it did seem more certain that he had arrived on the earth to stay, his grandfather, that inconsiderate old man, had a second stroke.

There was nothing for it but that Beatrice must go back to the shop.

She had never been away from it, if one were to speak the truth, William said. Not angrily, but with a little more tetchiness than was usual for him. He was still a semi-invalid, from that nasty attack of bronchitis, and could be forgiven his irascibility.

Beatrice, weak herself from another difficult birth (it seemed that for all her cozy roundness she was not an ideal shape for childbearing), tried to establish a peaceful formula for running the house.

Nanny, with a new and delicate baby to care for, required

an under-nurse to help with the solemn just-toddling Florence, and now the house was really too small. The mirror room, said Beatrice, would have to be turned into a day nursery. It was a pity, but it had always been a charming folly, and quite useless. Now, with a son in the nursery, she had the best excuse for selling the collection of mirrors and having the room redecorated. She had known she had been waiting a long time for the opportunity to do this.

Mrs. Overton was outraged and said so. The mirror over the mantelpiece was said to have belonged to Marie Antoinette. She had used to look into it and imagine it was the face of a lost queen that she saw. Privately, Beatrice didn't believe that Blanche Overton had ever seen any face but her own. Sentimental arguments had no effect on her. The mirror room, together with its uncomfortable memory, was going.

If Mrs. Overton did not approve of that, she did approve of her grandson. She thought him quite adorable, so much better-looking than his sister, a true Overton.

Which might have been the reason for Joshua Bonnington wearily closing his eyes when the baby was shown to him. Or it may have been genuine weakness, for the second stroke had been cruel. It had deprived him of speech, and left severe paralysis down his right side. He could communicate only by an occasional awkwardly scrawled message on a slate. A Harley Street specialist had been called in but this great man held out little hope for him.

At least he had lived to set eyes on his grandson, Beatrice comforted herself. If he saw too much Overton in the baby, and guessed that this child was destined for a military career, Beatrice was very happy about little Edwin herself. She saw all William's good looks in the tiny face, and fancied that the angry yell, for he was a fretful baby, was an echo of the old general's.

As well as falling naturally into her old routine of going to Bonnington's every morning, she found time to spend hours at Papa's bedside. She was never sure how much he heard, or remembered, but she told him everything about the shop, and her new arrangements at Overton House.

If only he could see how cozy the new nursery was, with the walls stripped of their shabby silk wallpaper and painted a nice fresh green, a red Turkey rug in front of the fire, a comfortable rocking chair for Nanny, and smaller chairs and a low table for the children. William's old rocking horse had been brought down from the attic. There was a dollhouse for Florence, and a fine collection of toy soldiers for Edwin when he was old enough to play with them.

The room had come alive. There were no more leering ghosts in old mirrors, no chance of glimpsing reflections of stolen kisses or other more daring indiscretions.

Papa indicated that he wanted to write something on his slate. Beatrice put the chalk in his fingers, and he scrawled feebly, *"Two households to support, Bea. Don't forget your mother is . . ."* Here he paused for a long time. Then he wrote *"extra-"* and paused again. The word, thought Beatrice, was meant to be "extravagant" but it had proved beyond poor Papa's spelling ability. Presently he substituted, *"spendthrift like your husband."*

That was Papa's last message to her, for he died that night.

Laid out for burial, he had a stern majestic remoteness that appalled and terrified her. She knew that she had lost the two strong men in her life, Papa and the old general. Now she had to be strong herself. There were so many people dependent on her, William and their children, Mamma, all the servants, all of Bonnington's staff. It was too much. No, it wasn't. She could manage.

After she had made her sad farewell to Papa, lying in his unwanted majesty, she walked home alone, and went into the churchyard opposite Overton House. The iron gates of the Overton vault were locked. Standing outside them was not like kneeling before a grave. Nevertheless Beatrice talked earnestly to the general, asking him to help her to have courage. "You and Papa, you get together in heaven and help me," she admonished him sternly.

They were both responsible for what she was. Were she and William to have a similar profound influence over their children? The thought was unnerving. Innocent lives, shaped by the character, behavior and circumstances of their parents. . . .

It was a gray, cold February day. The copper beech and the Judas tree lifted skeleton arms over the brick wall enclosing Overton House. There was no wind, no birds calling. Time seemed to have come to a stop in this empty afternoon.

But it hadn't, of course. Beatrice suddenly lifted her head

with brisk purpose. William, summoned from Venice, was
arriving tonight. She would go herself to meet him at
Victoria Station. She must be sure to take the warmest
carriage rug, and the stoneware bottle, filled with hot water,
for him to hold in his hands. He would be exhausted after
the long journey. Returning to such inclement weather, he
must not get a fresh chill. Neither did she intend to allow
him to attend Papa's funeral tomorrow. She only wanted
him home, in the house, to bring it to life, to comfort her.

Chapter 8

Fortunately Mamma was kept contented after Papa's death by being provided with a companion, a thin and anxious spinster called Miss Finch whom she could bully, and with enough money to spend. She liked to see her grandchildren occasionally, Nanny Blair or Lizzie wheeling them down Heath Street in their perambulator, and spending an uneasy half hour in Mamma's dark overcrowded drawing room. If the baby cried or Florence grew restless they were sent off at once.

What Mamma enjoyed most were shopping expeditions, dressing up for dinner in elaborate gowns, and spending the evenings after a too heavy meal playing whist or solitaire, while directing rambling monologues at the silent Miss Finch.

She had solved the problems of widowhood more successfully than Mrs. Overton with her frenetic gaiety had. Beatrice prayed with intensity that such problems would never be hers. Whenever William was ill, or when weariness gave him that look of extreme fragility, a shaft of fear struck deep into her heart.

She would always have Bonnington's, of course. Unlike Mamma and Mrs. Overton and most other women, she had a powerful interest outside her home and family.

She would also have her children.

But what would these be without her adorable butterfly husband, her dearest love? Everything in her life was for him, and would be valueless without him.

That spring two fantails came to the garden and spent the sunny mornings flirting and preening in the honeysuckle outside the library window. William begged Beatrice to come and admire them. He stood with his arm around her waist, in his easy affectionate manner, and Beatrice loved the pretty creatures for being indirectly responsible for this embrace.

"They're like your butterflies," she said.

"Are all butterflies mine?"

"They always make me think of you."

"We must have a day on the Heath with our nets. We haven't done that for a long time."

"No, we haven't. I thought you had lost your enthusiasm for catching butterflies."

"Not a bit. I was only going through my slides the other day. You know, a trip to Madeira might give us some fine new specimens. Why don't we do that?"

"Oh . . . there's nothing I'd like more. But is it possible? The children—"

"Take them with us."

Her elation was already dying, killed by common sense.

"William, you are the most impractical person. Think of the luggage. And Nanny Blair would have to go, probably Lizzie, too. Besides, Edwin is too small and delicate for traveling."

His face, a faint tentative frown between the warm brown eyes, hung over hers.

"If I am the most impractical person, you are surely the most practical. Dear Bea!" He had left her and gone closer to the window to watch the flitting fantails. His profile had a sudden disturbing melancholy.

"Besides, of course, there's Bonnington's," he said.

"Yes," Beatrice replied evenly. "Though I wasn't making that an excuse."

"Be honest, Bea. You were, in your mind."

She admitted that, reluctantly. So soon after Papa's death, it was the worst possible time to be away.

"William, you must realize, without Bonnington's—"

"The children would starve and your idle husband would be a beggar."

"Darling, don't exaggerate so. Besides you're not idle, you're always occupied with your book. It's only that it's too soon after Papa's death." *Two households to support.* . . . Those words seemed to have been written on her brain.

"I understand perfectly." William's voice was equable. "When I make a great deal of money out of my books

we'll be able to snap our fingers at ladies' corsets and all
that fiddle-faddle and go off to China or Timbuktu."

"Of course."

"In the meantime perhaps we can have a day on the
Heath. Bonnington's could spare you for that."

"Whatever day you suggest," she said eagerly.

"But I must go back to Italy to finish my studies of
Botticelli and Tintoretto. You won't mind that because
you know how the classics bore you. Before the heat of
the summer, I thought."

"If you must." She refused to suspect him of a subtle
form of blackmail, and hoped the desolation did not show
in her face. She was afraid he would never again ask her
to accompany him abroad.

Now that there were children in the house, Beatrice
found that it was not quite so easy to fall into her old
routine of leaving for the shop by nine thirty. It meant
rising earlier, taking care not to disturb William who
needed his sleep, what with his delicate health and his
reluctance to come to bed at nights. He was naturally a
night owl, where she was not. She lived in dread of the
day when he announced that he would move into the
blue room next door, which he occupied when she was in
the last stages of pregnancy. He would regard that as
an eminently sensible arrangement. After all, he had only
to open a door and cross the room if he wanted to join
her. She knew that many marriages, especially among the
aristocracy, were conducted in this way, but she was un-
ashamedly lower class, and knew of no more ineffable
delight than the warmth and comfort of her husband's
body beside her own.

Another of her acute pleasures was to look at his
sleeping face, after Hawkins had called her in the morning, and she had crept quietly out of bed. Sometimes the
bath that Hawkins had run for her was almost cold by
the time she got into it. She had been standing dreaming,
she said.

By the time she was bathed and dressed, however, there
was no more time for dreaming. Annie had her breakfast
on the dining room table sharp at a quarter to eight. There
was just time to eat her eggs and bacon and deviled kid-
neys, and drink her coffee, and to glance at the morning
newspaper before visiting the day nursery where the chil-

dren would now be, Florence in her crisp white pinafore sitting at the table eating her porridge (she was a quiet well-behaved child) and Edwin in his high chair banging his spoon and being extremely vociferous.

"He's having his tantrums, ma'am," Nanny Blair usually said, in some despair. Edwin had tantrums all too often, though nobody knew why. It was certainly not because of spoiling. Nanny was far too strict for that. He was highly strung, she said, and he was also greedy. He wanted everything. Fair screamed for things, she said. Then, when he smiled, he looked like an angel. Miss Florence now, she behaved like an angel, yet, because she was such a quiet little thing, she hardly got noticed.

After her morning visit, Beatrice could leave the children without any qualms and go down to the kitchen to discuss the day's meals with Cook. She would then hand out the stores, give the instructions about the day's duties to the housemaids, see that Tom, the gardener, and little white-faced Ted, the knife boy, had arrived punctually, and return upstairs knowing that the house would run smoothly while she was absent at the shop.

She had resisted getting a housekeeper. She wanted to be a real person to the servants, not one of those haughty and frankly lazy women who never descended below stairs but merely sat in the drawing room ringing a bell even for so small a thing as adding a lump of coal to the fire. Besides, she loved her home and would willingly have polished furniture and stair rails herself. She prayed she would never be reduced to filling in time by reading library books and paying tedious calls. That kind of life had been abandoned forever, thank goodness, when she had become absorbed in Bonnington's.

It was already in her mind that if William took that proposed trip to Italy in the early summer she would spend longer hours at the shop. She could profitably put in a ten-hour day there. There was so much to do, so much to plan. The morning was never long enough.

They had had a tremendously successful window display of redcoats with swords, and Zulu warriors brandishing spears after the Matabele rising in Africa. It had been very expensive having the dummies and the uniforms made, but it had brought flocks of people to the shop. They were to ignore that Regent Street shopkeeper, Mr.

Liberty and his aesthetic movement with William Morris and Burne-Jones and all those willowy, unhealthy young men and drooping women, Beatrice said. Bonnington's theme was to be patriotism. Whenever there was an opportunity to display the flag it would be displayed. Their Indian department was a gratifying success, so why not start an African one? With the discovery of gold on the Witwatersrand and diamonds in Kimberley they could stock bush outfits for the men, and strong sensible clothes for the intrepid women who set out for a pioneer life in the Cape Colony. Indeed, why not begin by importing some of those Kimberley diamonds?

Beatrice was amused and pleased when it came to her ears that Bonnington's Emporium was being called Bonnington's Empire, and she herself its queen. "A certain store in the Bayswater Road reigned over by an extraordinary little woman, Queen Bea," one newspaper wrote.

Beatrice sent the clipping to William in Florence, and he answered that he hoped she would descend from her throne when he came home, as he had no intention of being prince regent. There, he was taken for an English milord, and was often a guest in wealthy Florentine villas. "They do things in immense style, we couldn't begin to match them. Wine out of solid-gold goblets! I was entertained by a prince and princess in their small but unutterably beautiful pink marble palace in the Tuscan hills. But I still refuse to be a regent myself!"

"Not regent but king," Beatrice wrote back firmly. "And don't be one in exile for too much longer, please."

Though she really hadn't time to be lonely, except in bed at night when sometimes a fearful shivering desolation came over her, and she told herself she was crazy for the way she was living her life. She should be in Italy with William. She should never let him out of her sight.

Only then he might really want to run away. She had always sensed his necessity for freedom. And after all, if she idled abroad, who would buy the babies' shoes? Who would pay the servants' wages, keep the carriage and horses, provide Mamma with a new gown a week (and not one too many, Mamma insisted)?

Morning always brought back common sense, and the day fell into its familiar pattern. Although Beatrice had made one important alteration while William was abroad.

She stayed at Bonnington's most of the day, and had her lunch with Adam Cope and Miss Brown. They sat at the quietest table in the restaurant beneath one of the potted palms, ate absentmindedly, and discussed business for an hour or an hour and a half. These meetings were satisfyingly producitve. Adam Cope, an elderly thirty-nine years, unmarried, with no life but Bonnington's, a fact Beatrice thoroughly appreciated, provided the balance between Beatrice's wilder ideas, and Miss Brown's old-fashioned caution. Compared to her sparkling William, Adam was a dull-gray stone of a man, but his ability and integrity and loyalty were qualities for which she was always grateful.

He had bachelor rooms somewhere in Bloomsbury, but one wondered if he ever occupied them, for one never saw him arrive at the shop or leave it. He was simply always there.

Miss Brown lived with an aged mother in Doughty Street. She, too, spent very little time at home. Perhaps the old mother was too querulous. Once, when she was small, Mamma had taken Beatrice to visit there, and they had sat in a small stuffy front parlor eating sticky cakes, while old Mrs. Brown related how she had once used to watch Mr. Dickens coming in and out of his house opposite. Miss Brown always carried faintly the stuffy smell of that parlor about her person. This worried Beatrice a little, with the fastidious noses of customers in mind, but she decided it was too small a matter to mention. Miss Brown's sensitive feelings would be hurt, and fortunately she didn't hang over customers. She had excellent dressmakers and fitters to do that.

Beatrice was shrewd enough to see that the stiff old-fashioned figure of Miss Brown in her high-necked black dress with a cameo brooch at her throat was a personality, and a part of Bonnington's. She had almost forgotten that once William had said that she ought to go. Dear William was quite ignorant of the different facets of successful shopkeeping, and she was glad this was so. It would dim his radiance a little for her. He was, and must remain, quite above moneymaking.

William returned home in the late summer, then went off to Germany (he wanted to look at the Gothic castles, which he thought ugly but interesting). He wrote, "Prince

Wilhelm still thinks of nothing but playing soldiers—he should have been an Overton! It's said that he can't wait for not only the truly ancient emperor but his own father to die so that he can get on the throne and turn Germany into a military power. He is encouraged by that old warhorse Bismarck, of course. I shall never like the Germans. Their stolidity is suspect. It gives way to emotionalism and hysteria too quickly. Take Wagner, for example. And as for German women. . . ."

Beatrice imagined that unfinished sentence meant contempt, but William had surely never gone abroad to study women. Had he?

She seemed to be always seeing him off at Victoria Station, or, more joyfully, meeting him, espying his debonair figure in the distance and flying toward him. They were fresh to each other again. The reunion with the children, when they all sat cozily around the nursery fire, was so heartwarming that the separation seemed worthwhile.

Beatrice's secret plan for a trip to Madeira at Christmas came to nothing because Mrs. Overton was ill. At least, that lady said bravely, she was only a little poorly, her silly heart was misbehaving. She must curtail her activities and lead a terribly dull life sitting quietly at home and entertaining not more than two or three people at a time. William and Beatrice and the children must visit her on Christmas Day but perhaps they wouldn't mind making their stay fairly brief as she found the dear children a little exhausting. Unless William cared to stay on for an hour or two to help her stave off loneliness. He could follow Beatrice and the children in a cab, couldn't he?

Mrs. Overton, frail and almost transparent in her exquisite lacy shawls, as vain as ever, but with a bleak look in her faded-blue eyes, had Beatrice's reluctant admiration. She must have known that death was approaching, and she, with her birdlike brightness and love of company, would be terrified. But she intended to keep her standards of behavior until the end. She would be gracious, charming, witty and gay, and never, never commit that most deadly sin of being a bore or a burden.

So Beatrice took Florence and Edwin home to spend the remainder of Christmas Day with Mamma.

After eating heavily of roast turkey and plum pudding, Mamma had dozed over the fire most of the afternoon.

She was wearing one of her elaborate ruffled and braided dresses and looked like a vast sofa. Edwin screamed in her company, as he had also screamed in Mrs. Overton's, and Florence, who could be an aggravatingly uncommunicative child, made no sound at all.

It was not a successful Christmas Day. And in the dreariness of a cold and foggy January, William began to wheeze and cough and said he must get away to the Swiss Alps. It was not a long journey. The doctor had assured him that his mother might live for several more years, but if there happened to be a deterioration in her health he could be home in twenty-four hours.

Beatrice recognized the familiar pattern. Dear William, with his extreme sensitivity, hated illness, and death appalled him. He must put distance between himself and such calamity. Besides, he was not exaggerating his own symptoms. He breathed as if he were continually climbing uphill.

She clung to him at Victoria Station.

"My darling, do take care of yourself."

"I always do. You know that." He was growing more cheerful. He always became animated in the midst of the bustle and noise and billowing smoke of Victoria Station. "I'm sorry you've got such a useless fellow for a husband, Bea. And you're such a superlative wife."

Superlative? An intimidating word. Was it meant to be flattering?

"Then you truly don't mind me being a businesswoman?"

"It makes you happy. So that's perfectly splendid."

And absolves you from feeling guilty about your absences? Beatrice wondered. Then she observed how the suffocating smoke from the engine was making him choke, and, forgetting her treacherous doubt, was filled with her constant anxious tenderness.

"Darling, button up your coat. Don't go on deck without your scarf. And try to sleep on the train."

"Stop fussing, Bea," William said, pleased nevertheless. He was the most charming invalid.

The guard's whistle blew. He kissed her quickly, his lips cool against her own. She shivered slightly. It was a bitterly cold day. "Don't work too hard, Bea. Kiss the children again for me."

He was on the train and leaning out as it moved off.

"Good-bye," he called. "Good-bye, dearest."

The slender handsome figure in the caped greatcoat dissolved into the grimy smoke. She was left standing alone, as she had been too often. Never mind, she would make a brief call at Bonnington's on the way home. They had been unpacking a consignment of rugs from Persia and Samarkand. Colorful and romantic, and, although expensive, eminently salable. She could pretend today that they were flying carpets that would carry her to the Swiss Alps, and another honeymoon with William.

They had always promised themselves another honeymoon, though, with William turning to her in bed less often (it was his poor health, wasn't it? she told herself, as she lay awake, restless and longing), he probably now regarded honeymoons as something they had completely outgrown.

How did he occupy his evenings in those handsome and luxurious hotels he frequented?

Well, never mind.

Florence had invented a new game, of packing her bag, an old wicker basket of Nanny's and catching a train. She was being Papa going abroad. "Good-bye, Queen Bea. Good-bye!" Now wherever had she heard that?

She adored her Papa, which was rather a pity, Nanny Blair confided to Lizzie, because he didn't take too much notice of her. She was too quiet and self-effacing, and had no looks to speak of. A crime in *this* family. Master Edwin was another cup of tea; he looked like a cherub though he seldom behaved like one. All Nanny's famous discipline was lost on that child who was chronically naughty.

Nanny, suffering from a sense of failure, talked darkly of absentee parents (as if they were the same as those infamous absentee landlords who caused so much discontent in Ireland), and said the children, bless their innocent hearts, were suffering from a lack of love. Not that the mistress wasn't a good woman, but she had too many other matters on her mind. Running a big store, indeed! If she had wanted to do that, why had she bothered to marry and have children?

One occupation or the other but not both, thought

Nanny Blair, and resolved to find another position in the spring.

Mrs. Overton died suddenly before the spring and William had to come hurrying home to attend the morbid ceremonial of opening the family vault, and having a new slender casket laid within its dark recesses. He was overcome with grief. His eyes were red with weeping. This family was haunted by death, he declared. Bea must promise never to die. The children must never die. He lay in her arms the night after the funeral, clinging to her almost as if he were a small boy and she his mother. Just as she felt she was unable to bear her hungry desire any longer he made love to her with a violence he had never before exhibited. As if he were expressing a desperate defiance against death. At last not having to conceal her own passion she responded fiercely, sharing the soaring heights and the joyful release.

It was a haunting and beautiful night, and it seemed entirely right to Beatrice that she should have conceived her third child. William agreed with her. Between them, they had achieved a victory over death, and this child could not help being remarkable, with more beauty than Florence and more stability than Edwin. Florence, of course, might improve in looks as she grew older, and Edwin would certainly learn to master his tantrums. Nevertheless, the new baby was to be everything.

It was a great pity that in the fourth month Beatrice miscarried. Indeed, it proved to be a tragedy, for the doctor told William that it would be unwise for his wife to attempt to have more children. Beatrice was bitterly angry with that stupid old-fashioned interfering Doctor Lovegrove. If she wanted to risk her life it was her own affair. She did want to risk it. For how otherwise would she ever bring William willingly back to her bed?

He had been repelled by her miscarrying. Now he would think her unhealthy and unwomanly, and avoid her. He would be afraid he might be the cause of her death.

So how was she to face an eternity of lonely nights?

William would go abroad again, and this time she would be in torment, certain that he now felt legitimately free to seek the company of other women. Even her suggestion that she should join him was politely but firmly dismissed.

Dear Bea, what would Bonnington's be without their queen sitting on her little throne inside the gilded cash desk? You can't abdicate now, Bea. Besides, you would be miserable without your figures and your sales reports, and your new merchandise. I know you, Bea, totting up figures in your head *all* the time.

He scarcely ever called her dearest nowadays.

But she went on loving him. That was a condition she could change even less than she could change the natural satisfaction profits and growth in the shop gave her.

She was enormously pleased when at last William's book, after five years of research and work, was finished, and sold to an eminent publisher.

William, who had found the loss of his manuscript a physical deprivation, intended to fill in time before publication date by going on an ambitious trip to South America to catch butterflies. He said there were fantastically beautiful specimens there. If Bea was lonely, perhaps her mother would like to come and live with her. And, since Nanny Blair had also decided to leave (she preferred small babies, she said), weren't the children old enough for a nursery governess?

Mamma permanently in Overton House, Beatrice thought in high indignation. Overeating, looking at the lovely rooms with her empty eyes, spoiling the children, complaining. How could William suggest such a thing! But the nursery governess was a good idea. She would attend to that.

So they had another farewell at Victoria Station, again on a raw January day, with a yellow fog swirling about and, as usual, making William choke. Beatrice was fighting tears. She never cried in front of him, she knew how much it embarrassed him. He wouldn't have minded the tears of a young and pretty girl, but of his sturdy sensible Bea, goodness, no! Besides, if she began to cry, she would sob, and that really would be embarrassing. People would think he was ill-treating her.

"What shall I send you from Rio, Bea? Silks? Native carvings? No, I won't, you'll only want to start selling them in Bonnington's."

She shook her head, making herself smile, asking anxiously, "You'll be back in the summer?"

"I'll be back in July for publication date."

"Shall I arrange a party?"

"You don't like parties."

"I'll like this one. I'll be so proud of you."

He kissed her forehead, then her lips, briefly.

"Don't wait for the train to go. It's so cold, Dixon will be having trouble with the horses. Tell him to be careful with ice on the roads. Heavens, I'm glad to be leaving this filthy winter."

He waved from a distance, his face radiant with his eagerness to be gone. She lifted her gloved hand in response, then tucked it back in her muff, and turned and walked away, a cozy figure in her fur-trimmed coat and skirt. An attractive figure, some men might have said. Her eyes were bright with the stubborn unshed tears, her cheeks rosy from the cold. She had gained poise with maturity. She had a pleasant frank look without any coquettishness. And a nice air of quiet authority.

But her husband, interested only in stepping onto the train, hadn't noticed any of this. He really hadn't looked at her with any true observation for a long time.

Chapter 9

For some time Beatrice had personally interviewed all new applicants for jobs at Bonnington's, from the humblest messenger boy to the haughty top buyer shamelessly lured from other big department stores such as Whiteley's, Debenham and Freebody's or Swan and Edgar's. She prided herself on being a judge of character, and also of being a good employer. The young girl who stood before her, gauche and terrified, need have no fear if she did her work honestly and well. She would see to the girl's welfare both in and out of the shop. She had been known to call at the lodgings of a young dressmaker's apprentice to find out why she arrived at work with a tear-stained face, and every appearance of malnutrition. She had also made arrangements for the birth and adoption of illegitimate infants, although this calamity did not happen often. Bonnington's girls had the reputation for being good girls. They knew that if they were caught cuddling and kissing the errand boys or the junior salesmen or even the grander senior salesmen (who should certainly know better) they would be dismissed immediately.

No part of the shop, even the packing department, was secure from Miss Beatrice's perambulations. She would come walking down the aisles between counters, a robust little figure in her nunlike gray dress, with its stiff white collar buttoned to her chin, and her eyes missed nothing. The youngest shopgirl measuring ribbon half an inch too short, or too long, the customer who had not been offered a chair, an undusted counter or the carelessness of a display.

Kept you on the hop, did Miss Beatrice, new employees were warned. She was a good sort; if you did your work properly she appreciated it. And she always remembered who you were and where you came from. Her brain must have been full to bursting with information about people and prices and sales figures and stock, and what was going on in the whole of the British empire.

They had had a magnificent window commemorating the death of General Gordon in Khartoum, with laurel wreaths, and a lifesize dummy of the handsome martyred general. The tableau had been written about in the press, a fact that pleased Beatrice enormously. Since then there had been an Indian window and an African window, and then an Australian one with stuffed kangaroos and other queer mammals.

But the great event had been when the Princess of Wales had brought her prospective daughter-in-law, Princess Mary of Teck, to shop. This was done quietly, without any fanfare. Beatrice met the royal customers at the door, and personally escorted them through the shop. The young princess ordered three hats, and two evening gowns, and the Princess of Wales found some French kid gloves and a Cashmere shawl that she liked. Miss Brown had had to sit down and sniff *sal volatile* afterward. She was weeping with delight, as if the triumph had been entirely hers.

Everyone was whispering about the royal warrant; it was surely a *fait accompli* when the Prince of Wales came to the throne. But of course old Queen Victoria might live for many years yet. She was not yet seventy.

Beatrice's flair for selecting staff at the shop did not desert her when it came to domestic matters. The employment agency had sent five young women to be interviewed for the post of nursery governess. Beatrice had no hesitation at all in deciding on the most suitable.

Miss Mary Medway, aged nineteen years, was an only child and recently orphaned (her mother had died when she was fourteen, and her father, a country doctor, a few months ago). She had been well educated and had lived the life of a gentlewoman until her father's death. Then it was found that his affairs were in a deplorable muddle, and there was no money left to support his daughter. He had been gentle and saintly, the girl told Beatrice, but his generosity to the poor had left his own daughter impoverished.

Beatrice looked at the slight figure in the dark-brown

muslin dress with white ruching at neck and wrists. Miss
Medway had light-brown hair loosely framing her face,
and a mouth that trembled easily. Her eyes were full of
tears. She was gentle and sensitive and the children, especially timid Florence, would be happy with her. Her
references were impeccable.

It would be a tremendous help, Beatrice said, if she
could commence her duties at once.

"But you've decided so quickly, Mrs. Overton!"

"I always do," said Beatrice. "I pride myself on reading
character. Would you like to come and meet the children?"

The children, Florence in particular, took to Miss Medway on sight. Edwin capitulated when she successfully
pleaded that Edwin be allowed to play with his grandfather's famous collection of lead soldiers. These had been
kept safely behind the glass doors of the Chippendale
bookcase in the library, but surely, at four years of age,
Edwin was old enough to marshal them in rows, and not
to suck the lead.

So, under Miss Medway's supervision, the regiments of
the British, French and German armies fought the Battle
of Waterloo, the Russians marched to defend Balaclava,
and a contingent of sepoys in colorful turbans opposed the
British redcoats in the Indian Mutiny. Even at such a
tender age Edwin was absorbed, though one didn't know
whether he was beginning to be fascinated with the ancient
game of war, or whether he just liked the clever little
figures. At any rate, the old general would have been
pleased with his grandson.

Florence played with her dolls and professed contempt
for warlike games. She was a little jealous, though not too
much, for Miss Medway had time to make dresses for her
dolls, and always told Florence that she was pretty. No one
had told her that before. Little sourpuss, her grandmother
called her, and Mamma sighed over her long straight hair
which stubbornly refused to curl, even after a night spent in
knobbly rag curlers.

As for Papa, one knew that secretly he would have
liked a much prettier daughter, but he was nearly always
away.

However, he was coming home for the publication of
his book, and the party Mamma was arranging to celebrate this occasion.

His book was going to have a *succès d'estime*, people said, whatever that meant. And, fancy that delicate William Overton, he hasn't been wasting his time and living entirely on a rich wife, after all. Florence, who had a gift for overhearing things, had heard both those remarks. She liked overhearing snippets of conversation, although Mamma had once caught her at the drawing-room door and scolded her severely, saying that eavesdropping was a nasty habit, and frequently painful to the listener.

However, Florence did know what Papa had written to Mamma, just before announcing that he was coming home, because Mamma read the letter aloud to Miss Medway, laughing. *Who is this paragon you have in the nursery? I suspect you have the word wrong, and she is really another dragon, like Nanny Blair.*

Florence said, "You'll like our Papa, Miss Medway."

"Will I?"

"Oh, yes. He's very pretty."

"He buys us presents," Edwin said.

"That's called cupboard love," Miss Medway said.

"He always comes to the nursery and plays with us," Florence went on. "He says, 'How you've grown.' And Mamma buys us new clothes for when he's coming home so we'll do him credit. She gets a new dress, too, and Grandmamma gets six. Miss Brown says Grandmamma's girth is something to be wondered at."

"Florence, I don't think you should talk about your grandmother like that."

"Horses have girths," said Edwin. "I heard Dixon saying he'd have to tighten the girth. Does Grandmamma have hers tightened?"

Florence didn't have a quick humor. She said quite seriously, "Don't be silly, Dixon doesn't harness her into the carriage," and Edwin began to giggle so much that Miss Medway said sharply, "Children! That will be enough. Come and begin your reading lesson."

Florence was making great progress with her reading. Edwin was much slower, which was surprising, for he seemed to be a clever child in other ways. But they both had considerable improvement to demonstrate to Papa.

The next thing was the preparation of the blue room. Apparently Papa had written saying that he was sleeping badly, and didn't want to disturb Mamma, so he would prefer to occupy separate rooms. Besides, she knew how the damp English air would be sure to make him cough again.

So the carpets of the blue room were taken up and beaten, new curtains hung, and all the woodwork washed. Then Mamma had the slides of Papa's most colorful butterflies put in glass cases and hung on the walls. They looked very striking. Miss Medway said so. Florence heard Mamma explaining, with a little laugh, that perhaps if Papa's eyes could feast on his butterflies every day he would not have such a desire to travel so far to find more. Mamma had been very quiet during the whole of the renovation of the blue room, as if she would really rather have Papa sleeping in her bed as he had used to do. Although that must be very uncomfortable for two grown people, Florence thought. Didn't they kick each other?

The last thing of all was Mamma's going to a shop in Bond Street called Worth's to order her dress for the party, and, by doing so, deeply offending Miss Brown. Weren't her own dressmakers good enough for her? Miss Brown asked indignantly. Did she imagine herself better even than Princess Mary?

Mamma was too fond of Miss Brown to be angry. She said that it happened her husband had always liked Mr. Worth's creations, and she wanted to please him. However, she had been rather crafty; she had had a word in private with Mr. Worth's head dressmaker and it was just possible she might be lured to Bonnington's. Wouldn't that be a triumph?

"You're always thinking of Bonnington's, Miss Beatrice," Miss Brown said, not entirely mollified.

"And my husband," said Mamma.

"Two birds with one stone," said Miss Brown. "You are clever at that, aren't you, Miss Beatrice?"

The new dress was white lace over rosy pink taffeta. It had a low-cut bodice and a spray of moss roses falling down the full skirt.

It was delicious, Florence thought. It made Mamma look really pretty, and not old at all. She had begun to seem old beside Miss Medway, but Miss Medway had only a modest dark-blue dress for the party because she was still in half mourning for her father. So Mamma would be the person people looked at.

Anyway, although Miss Medway would certainly wear her party dress, she would spend most of her time with the children who would be permitted downstairs for only a short time before retiring to the vantage point of the stairway, and then to bed.

The great day of Papa's return arrived at last, and Mamma, with a rosy spot of color in each cheek and her eyes shining, climbed into the carriage and Dixon whipped up the horses, and they were off to Victoria Station.

The children had never been allowed to share the excitement of actually meeting Papa at the railway station. Once when Florence had begged to come she had been told kindly but firmly, "No, darling, Mamma likes to have Papa to herself just for an hour. Then we'll all sit round the nursery fire as usual."

"I want to see the train," Edwin had whined and Florence had slapped him spitefully. "If you're not a good boy Papa won't bring you a present."

Edwin's noisy tears had somehow relieved the need to shed any of her own.

But she didn't behave like that now Miss Medway was here. She wanted so much to please and to be loved. Mamma had had Papa and she had only had horrid Nanny Blair and Lizzie. But now she had Miss Medway so actually she would never need to be naughty again.

Both she and Edwin were dressed in their Sunday clothes, feeling uncomfortably scrubbed and tidy, and Miss Medway, although still in her neat brown day dress, had tied her hair back with a black velvet bow which made her look different and festive. When Mamma, followed by Papa, came into the nursery, saying happily, "Here he is, children. Here's Papa," Florence knew that Papa had seen the bow in Miss Medway's hair at once. Indeed, he stared rather hard at it, and didn't look at the children at all.

Florence didn't criticize this. She was not a child who expected attention, and she was glad that Papa obviously liked Miss Medway. It would make things so much safer. Miss Medway wouldn't go away and perhaps Papa wouldn't either. She was really only alarmed that Edwin had rushed at Papa and rudely demanded his present.

Nanny Blair would have sent him up to the night nursery on the instant.

But Miss Medway didn't. It was Mamma who remonstrated, "Edwin! Where are your manners? William, don't scold him. He's so excited to have you home."

"To see what's in my pockets, the young rascal," Papa said, swinging Edwin into the air. "I say, he's a handsome little devil. And this is Florence. How she's grown!"

Really, the same things said, except for that bad word "devil." Nanny Blair would have been scandalized. Miss Medway just pulled in her lips as if she were trying not to smile, and Mamma said, "This is Miss Medway, William. You remember, I wrote to you about her."

"Ah, the paragon. I can see that you were right, Bea, not I." Whatever that meant.

Papa and Miss Medway shook hands, and Papa said that he hoped she was happy here. She said thank you, she was, very.

"That's capital. Why don't we all sit around this splendid fire? We could have tea in here, couldn't we, Bea?"

Florence clapped her hands with pleasure. Mamma, not looking quite so pleased, probably because she had ordered tea in the drawing room where she and Papa could be alone, said by all means, she would ring for it.

Florence allowed herself to touch Papa's hand shyly. He really was so beautiful with his smiling brown eyes and his glossy hair and he had grown a neat little beard. It was clear that Miss Medway thought he was beautiful, too, for she kept giving him quick sidelong glances. And Mamma had that adoring look on her face that she kept only for Papa.

All in all, Florence decided with the wisdom of her nearly six years, it was one of Papa's happiest returns. Perhaps he would never go away again.

When he had left the nursery with Mamma an hour later, she turned eagerly to Miss Medway and demanded, "Don't you think our Papa is a pretty man? Isn't it true what I told you?"

"Yes," said Miss Medway in an absent sort of voice. "He is pretty. You did tell me the truth."

Chapter 10

Young as she was, Florence had already discovered that realization seldom lived up to anticipation. The longed-for happening was never quite as wonderful as one had expected it to be. Even the happiness of Papa's homecoming had ebbed away into disappointment and secret tears when it became obvious that his visits to the nursery were to talk to Miss Medway rather than to Edwin and herself.

She had so hoped he would think her not too big to sit on his lap, as she had done occasionally in the past. But of course she was a great girl of six now, as Lizzie frequently said, and too old to sit on a gentleman's lap, also too old to shed those silly tears.

The trouble was, as Lizzie said again, she got too excited by half. Her face was inclined to turn paper white and her stomach to close into a small tight space that refused food. So it was lucky, in a way, that Papa was so interested in Miss Medway, where she had come from, what her family was, how she liked living at Overton House, and looking after his brats. For no one noticed that Florence couldn't eat her tea, and sat hopefully invisible at the far end of the table, while Mamma plied Papa with cups of tea, and Miss Medway answered his questions in her soft pleasant voice.

That small tea party passed without any disaster, but the big party for Papa tonight, which she had so much looked forward to, was not going to do so. Florence realized that as soon as she had eaten the sugarplum that Grandmamma had given her.

The music room was looking lovely, with bowls of late-summer flowers everywhere, and all the candles in the shining Waterford crystal chandeliers alight. Mamma had

said that there was to be no gaslight on this occasion, and
Annie and Mabel had been kept busy first with the long
lighted tapers, then with the snuffers. Groups of chairs
were placed around the walls so that the center of the
floor would be free for dancing later.

Edwin, who was not at all shy, wandered among the
guests, giving his angelic smile (which didn't deceive anyone who knew him, Florence thought bitterly), while she,
in her usual self-effacing way, sought the refuge of Grandmamma's side, and the treachery of the sugarplum offered
by Grandmamma's fat stubby fingers.

Soon afterward the room began to blur. Mamma, in her
beautiful dress, Papa with the candlelight glinting in his
well-brushed hair and his little well-groomed golden beard,
Miss Medway neat and unobtrusive in her half mourning,
talking a little, but mostly keeping a wary eye on Edwin
who was showing off—these familiar figures disappeared
into the queer blurriness of the room, and Grandmamma,
an immense rustling figure above her, was saying in a loud
voice, "Miss Medway! Bea! You'd better come here. This
child is going to be sick."

It was all too humiliatingly true. Florence's unreliable
stomach had closed up again, and was about to reject the
carelessly eaten sugarplum. The only thing to be thankful
for was that, whisked away by Miss Medway, she reached
the bathroom in time. Imagine if there had been a disaster on the beautiful shining parquet floor on which the
guests' expensive skirts were brushing. She would never
have been able to show her face in public again. She
would have asked to be a nun and spent the rest of her
life saying prayers. Perhaps she should do this anyway,
since she had this uncooperative stomach and was such
a failure in society.

"I always do the wrong things," she wept, in the haven
of the bathroom where Miss Medway was washing her
face with a cool cloth.

"Nonsense," said Miss Medway. "You just get too
nervous. You'll get over that."

"Will I?" Florence pleaded.

"Of course you will. In two or three years or less. I
promise."

"Papa will hate me tonight."

"Not a bit of it. He's much too kind. Much too kind,"

Miss Medway repeated the words in a reflective way, as if she enjoyed saying them.

And, as it happened, she was right, for shortly afterward Papa came up to the night nursery to see Florence in bed, and patted her cheek and said, "It could have been worse, old thing. Don't worry. Are you all right now?"

Florence was filled with tearful gratitude for Papa's thoughtfulness, even though he only stayed a moment. Then he took Miss Medway's arm and led her out of the nursery.

"Send Lizzie to her," Florence heard him saying. "You're not to miss all the fun."

"Oh, but should I? And I think it's time Edwin came up to bed, too."

"Isn't Lizzie capable of seeing to that? Come along. I want you to enjoy yourself. By the way, no one's told me your first name."

Miss Medway's voice was lowered, almost inaudible.

"It's Mary."

"Then come, Mary. . . ."

Dear Papa. He always wanted people to be happy. He loved happiness. He was not made for sorrow, Mamma had once said.

Mamma stood over her later saying, not unkindly, "Florence, couldn't you have had more sense than to let Grandmamma stuff you with sweets? Now you've had to pay for it. Never mind, I'll ask Papa to slip up for a minute."

"He's been," said Florence drowsily. "With Miss Medway."

"Oh," said Mamma, after a pause, and from what seemed a long way off. "Didn't Miss Medway stay with you?"

"Papa wouldn't let her. He wanted her to dance, I think."

Then Florence's heavy eyelids closed and in the darkness she imagined she could see the figures of Papa and Miss Medway twirling around and around, growing smaller and farther away, until they were lost from sight.

I'll have to speak to her in the morning, Beatrice thought. If one of the children is ill it's her duty to stay with them. But if William had ordered her not to, through sheer

kindness, of course, one supposed she would have to obey.
Though he might have thought of his daughter's comfort,
rather than Miss Medway's.

However, there was no mirror room now, and Mary
Medway was a quiet little thing, not the kind to appeal
to William. Besides, it had been such a successful party
and he had had so much adulation, no wonder he wanted
everyone to share in his happiness and triumph.

He had proved he was not an idler, after all. He had
another dimension now, as an authority on art. He was
already receiving invitations to speak at various functions,
and also, he told Beatrice after the guests had gone, and
they were alone in the music room, he thought he would
begin adding to the collection of paintings and *objets d'art*
begun by his ancestors. The china room was lamentably
short on early English porcelain, and English painters had
been shamefully neglected in their own country.

It seemed that Miss Medway had a considerable knowledge of eighteenth-century porcelain.

"We were in the china room, if you wondered where we
had disappeared to," he said with his charming ingenuous-
ness. "I hope you didn't think I was neglecting our guests."

"I only thought Miss Medway might have stayed with
Florence," Beatrice said calmly. "It's most unfortunate
about that child's delicate digestion. And Mamma will
persist in thinking that children should be stuffed with
food. But it was a nice party, wasn't it?"

"Capital, Bea. Absolutely capital."

He hadn't said she looked well in her new dress. He
hadn't seemed to notice that her shoulders were very
pretty, and quite her best feature, though now he touched
them in an absent manner.

His eyes were shining. He seemed curiously preoccupied,
though happy.

"They all think the book will get good reviews. Well,
we must wait patiently."

"Oh, I'm sure they'll be good," Beatrice said enthusiastically. "Actually, I had a long talk to Mr. Aberconway.
Aren't publishers nice people!"

"I've no idea about the remainder of the profession, I'm
sure some of them are robbers, but I grant you, Aberconway is pretty decent. What did you talk to him about?"

"I suggested doing a window display of your book in

Bonnington's. I thought we could back it up with repro-
ductions of some of the paintings you discuss. Rembrandt,
Fragonard, Titian. It would make a lovely display."

To her surprise, William's face closed.

"I didn't know Bonnington's had a book department."

"They haven't, but—"

"Then how can you sell books? Besides, I detest re-
productions of great paintings."

"But, darling—"

"No, Bea. This time I can manage without Bonnington's.
It knows as little about art as, forgive me, its owner. Now
admit it. I'm only speaking the truth. Museums and art
galleries bore you to death."

Beatrice was deeply hurt. He had never spoken to her
like that before, as if she irritated him unbearably. Perhaps she had been stupidly clumsy in her suggestion. He
must have thought she was trying to steal his thunder,
when in all truth she was only wanting to share it.

"I'm sorry, William. Forget I suggested it."

"You and your precious shop," he said, but more amiably. "Me and my humble effort. We wouldn't tread on
holy ground."

"Now you're being absurd. Actually Mr. Aberconway
didn't think it was such a bad idea, but never mind. Will
you come to bed now?"

He yawned. "Presently. I'm tired but I'll never sleep.
Sorry I seemed so ungrateful. I don't deserve you to be
so good to me." He kissed her, an affectionate but brief
kiss, scarcely touching her lips. "You go on up. Don't
wait for me."

She hesitated, wanting to say she would stay with him
until he was ready to sleep. It was almost morning. They
could walk in the garden and watch the dawn.

But in the end she said good night quietly, not even telling him she loved him. She acted from intuition, as always,
but she was less sure now that her intuition was right.

She knew he would not join her in her room that night.

Lately Beatrice had instituted weekly meetings in her
father's office of all the department buyers.

The buyers were encouraged to express ideas. After all,
who knew the desires of customers better than those who
dealt directly with them? All ideas were discussed around

the table, some were adopted, some dismissed. Quiet but effective innovations had been made in this way. More important, the buyers developed a much stronger interest in the welfare of the store. Beatrice was always generous with appreciation, but caustic when her time was wasted by high-flown or plainly foolish suggestions.

Since everyone was encouraged to speak his mind, Beatrice wondered who would be caustic with her when she put forward her new idea this morning.

As she might have anticipated, it was Adam Cope. He was the only member of the staff who was not in awe of her, and also the one who had to be convinced that any change was desirable. Old stick-in-the-mud Adam, but always honest, always capable, and always there. Loyalty. A characteristic perhaps more important than brilliance.

"I presume you know the profit on books, Miss Beatrice? We would need to sell large numbers to make this venture profitable, and that means a lot of space. Besides, books aren't part of our overall design."

"We can make them so," Beatrice answered. "A counter on the ground floor next to haberdashery. The jackets would provide a nice note of color. After all," she said with gentle sarcasm, "we do have the sort of customers who can read."

"Popular novels, Miss Beatrice?"

"Of course. The customers who wander about the shop are usually ladies of leisure. Bored ladies. They'll buy the latest novels. But I also have in mind more serious books. Dictionaries, travel books, atlases, art books. Children's books make a colorful display. And of course a selection of religious books, which are infallible sellers. You all know how successful our mourning department has been. I believe religious books and Bibles will sell in the same way."

"This sort of thing will need to be run by a specialist," Miss Brown said.

"Of which there must be plenty about. I can speak to my husband's publisher. He'll be able to suggest a suitable person, I'm quite sure."

She was perfectly aware of the thoughts going on behind the polite faces. Was Miss Beatrice's canny business sense being pushed aside in the desire to please her husband? But why should books not be a part of Bonnington's? She thought of the shop as a well-stocked house, and every fashionable house had a library.

"So I plan to move handbags and umbrellas back, take a yard or two off haberdashery—you could manage with a smaller space, couldn't you, Miss Perkins?"

"My girls—" Miss Perkins began, then thought better of disagreeing with the boss. In spite of the candor of these meetings, when it came down to it nobody did really disagree with Beatrice. She had a way of making her proposals sound such good sense, and indeed they almost always were. Besides, she had that quiet but immensely strong will. No one underestimated her.

So Miss Perkins gave a small sniff and giggle. "Actually, my largest girl, Miss Oates, is going to be married soon, so perhaps we could make a point of engaging a rather small one when Miss Oates leaves. I must say that girl has been the clumsiest creature I ever knew."

Adam Cope, who had a limited sense of humor and took every statement seriously, pointed out, in his meticulous way, "Surely it's not so much the salesgirls as the goods we have to consider."

"The goods we sacrifice in haberdashery," Bea said, "will be more than compensated for by the sales on the book counter. I'm convinced of that. However, we must wait and see."

* * *

A month later, with remarkable speed, the book department, a small bright area of colorful books, was opened.

It was only the nucleus of what it would eventually be, Beatrice said. But it was a beginning. And William, although he was disappointingly lacking in enthusiasm, was much too courteous to refuse to go to the opening. After all his own book was prominently displayed, and he had agreed unwillingly to sign a few copies.

Beatrice was not quite sure whether he hated publicity, or just publicity in Bonnington's. He had certainly shown every pleasure in the good reviews the book had received. When, however, she had told him what she had planned he had said in some distress, "But why, Bea? Why? There are plenty of bookshops to sell my book."

"Because this is my husband's book and I love him," she said. A simple statement which he seemed to find embarrassing and unanswerable.

The children, too, were present at the opening ceremony. Florence enjoyed every minute of it, especially seeing the fuss made of Papa by all sorts of smart and gushing women. Papa, however, looked as unhappy as Edwin did when too many large-hatted women cooed over him, and was clearly relieved when it was all over.

Afterward, when they got home and were back in the nursery with Miss Medway, there was a delightful surprise. Papa came in with presents. Something for everyone. A doll for Florence, soldiers of the Gordon Highlanders for Edwin, and a length of red satin ribbon for Miss Medway.

"It's time you wore something gay," he said. "You can't stay in mourning forever."

Miss Medway flushed very becomingly and said Papa was very kind. Papa put her at her ease by saying flippantly, "Do you realize, I'm spending the first money I ever earned in my life. It's a remarkably satisfying feeling. Now I believe I understand why my wife enjoys working. It's for the pleasure of hearing those sovereigns chinking. Shall I tie that ribbon in your hair?"

Miss Medway blushed harder than ever and said oh, no, she could do it herself.

"You will?"

"Oh, yes. On a suitable occasion. Thank you, Mr. Overton. Children, did you say thank you to your Papa?"

Edwin was highly delighted with his kilted soldiers, but Florence was reflecting that everyone gave her dolls. She already had sixteen. No one had ever asked her if she liked them. They all said that Queen Victoria had been such a great girl for her dolls, and had used to make all their own dresses. Nanny Blair had taught Florence to be a clever little needle-woman before she was five years old. Which didn't mean to say that she must spend the rest of her life sewing.

And where was Mamma's present?

When she asked Papa, he said, "Don't be inquisitive."

Florence winced inwardly. She hadn't cared for the impatient tone of his voice, and therefore she didn't dare pursue the subject when Mamma arrived home, pink-cheeked and happy after the success of the afternoon.

Mamma came straight to the nursery, knowing that was where she would find everybody. They were gathered around the fire, Papa, too, while Miss Medway read to them. Miss Medway hadn't waited long to wear Papa's gift. She had her thick dark hair tied back with the red ribbon, and she looked demure and very pretty.

Mamma never missed anything. She noticed at once Florence's new doll, the new toy soldiers, and the ribbon in Miss Medway's hair.

"Well," she said. "Is it everyone's birthday except mine?"

Papa jumped up and kissed her on the cheek.

"I've been having fun spending my own money, Bea. That seemed the best cause for celebration. And you're not forgotten."

He took Mamma's arm and led her out of the nursery, so Florence didn't see the gift she received.

It was a choker of pearls, made fashionable since the Princess of Wales had begun wearing them in that style. It must have cost a great deal.

Beatrice was angry with herself that her total pleasure in the expensive gift was spoiled by her practical mind. In the first place, William was foolishly extravagant. In the second, the red ribbon in Miss Medway's hair seemed to have a greater intimacy than this formal circlet of pearls that was already living up to its name. When around her neck, it gave her a slightly choking feeling.

But she thanked her husband warmly, and said that although they were only dining at home she would wear them that evening.

Before William left her—he never stayed in her room very long—she said abruptly, "Darling, sometimes I wonder . . . is Miss Medway a quite suitable choice for the children?"

William paused at the door.

"Seems first rate to me."

"Oh, I know she's kind, but is she perhaps too gentle? I mean, for managing Edwin who is still a most difficult child. And perhaps she's a little melancholy, which she has had reason to be, of course."

"Then it's our Christian duty to cheer her up."

"With red ribbons?" Beatrice quizzed.

"That's one way, dearest."

Dearest. . . . Beatrice's heart leaped. How long since William had called her that?

But pearls and endearments. . . . Had he possibly got a guilty conscience?

She wouldn't ask; she couldn't anyway, for he had gone.

And the trouble with a governess in residence was that the wretched young woman had to share the dinner table with them. Mrs. Overton, critical and antagonistic, had been one thing. This quiet creature with her downcast eyes was another.

All the same, she had the good sense not to wear that ribbon down to dinner.

And surely Beatrice's suspicions were merely the creation of her starved emotions. William's taste had always been for the gay, the lighthearted, the effervescent. Someone as quiet as Miss Medway must depress him. The gift had been simply an act of kindness, as he had said, to try to cheer her up.

One couldn't dismiss her, for one had no reason, and the children, especially Florence, were devoted to her.

Things must go on as they were. And one very happy thing was that William had announced his intention of spending Christmas at home. He was remarkably well, he hadn't had a cough or a cold since he had returned from South America, and he intended to prove that he could withstand the perils of an English winter.

So, Christmas, for once, would be as gay as it was intended to be.

Except for Beatrice's deep secret unhappiness. William had settled himself so comfortably in the blue room that he rarely came to her bed. After the doctor's warning, he was simply afraid of making her pregnant again. That was all.

Chapter 11

There was an influenza epidemic just before Christmas. Half the staff at Bonnington's were away ill. Miss Brown had just recovered when Adam Cope went down, then Miss Perkins and two other buyers. Those who were left were frantically busy. Beatrice had ordered that Christmas decorations were to be as lavish as usual, indeed more lavish, to combat the gloom of a fogbound December and all the coughs and colds. The match sellers and other ragged beggars at the door were invited inside for a cup of hot soup and a few minutes of warmth. Beatrice had created a small curtained alcove for them for privacy. She didn't want any of her customers to misinterpret her kindness as a sales promotion idea.

However, word got around the East End, and the daily influx of shivering, ragged people, some of them mere children, became something of a problem.

"You can't run a shop as a charity," Adam Cope said gloomily.

"I won't have anyone turned away," Beatrice answered, and engaged a pleasant middle-aged woman solely to deal with the hungry supplicants. It was understood, however, that this generosity ended at Christmas.

Inevitably the newspapers did get hold of the story, and to Beatrice's chagrin there was an article about "the irrepressible Queen Bea with her alms to the poor. Does she think the child beggars of today will be the affluent of tomorrow? Or has she a canny eye on royal favors? Whatever her motives, one must applaud this Christian act, this thought for the needy, in a season when a few have too much, and a great many too little."

"You're mad, Bea," said Mamma, settling her bulk onto

one of the slim gilt chairs, the faithful Miss Finch standing dutifully behind her. "What would your father have said?"

"He would have approved," said Beatrice, knowing indeed that he would not have. Gad, Bea, turning the shop into an almshouse, he would have roared.

"That's as may be. I imagine you're inviting me for Christmas."

Mamma had become much less genteel in her old age. Some hitherto concealed coarseness had found its way to the surface.

"Of course, Mamma. Surely you know that's taken for granted."

"I suppose you intend that Miss Medway to sit at table with us."

"Certainly. Mamma, talk to me on Sunday. I'm busy just now."

"You're mad," said Mamma again, and this time Beatrice didn't know whether she was referring to the queue of beggars, or to Miss Medway, an orphan who had no family, being naturally invited to eat dinner with her small charges. She didn't inquire. One never knew what bee Mamma had got in her bonnet nowadays. She and that broomstick who followed her about, they invented things to relieve the dullness of their lives.

Actually, it was a fortunate thing that Miss Medway was there, for on Christmas Day Beatrice was feeling feverish and headachy, and knew that she was sickening for the influenza. How infuriating. One could only be thankful that she had survived the last hectic week at the shop, and that in her quiet way Miss Medway was most efficient at organizing the day's festivities. She and William and the children had decorated the Christmas tree very cleverly, and had been for a long walk on the Heath to gather holly branches which now adorned the hall and stair rail. Overton House had not looked so gay for a long time. It should have been the happiest of Christmases. Even Mamma, drugged with turkey and plum pudding and brandy, was in the most amiable of moods. And Miss Medway had finally laid aside her mourning, and wore a charming dress that made her look remarkably pretty. Even Florence was happy enough not to be stricken with one of her bilious attacks.

But Bea surveyed it all through the haze of her headache. After dinner, which she had made only a pretense of eating, she said apologetically that she would have to retire to bed. No one was to worry about her. The children were to be allowed to stay up to play with their presents and make as much noise as they liked.

Later, from her bedroom, she heard shrieks of laughter. The children must be putting on their paper hats. Then, after an interval, there came the sound of carols being sung around the Christmas tree, the pure soprano of Miss Medway rising above the children's piping, and Mamma's grumbling tones.

She fell asleep to the melody of "Silent Night," and awoke in the night, hot and uncomfortable, to wonder if anyone had been in to see her. Or had they forgotten all about her?

She reached for the little porcelain bell at her bedside, and Hawkins came hurrying to answer her ring.

"How are you feeling now, ma'am?"

"Poorly. Would you build up the fire, Hawkins? And get Annie to make me a hot toddy. She knows the one my husband likes when he has a bad chest."

"It's midnight, ma'am. Everyone's in bed. I'll go down and make your hot drink myself. Is there anything else you'd like?"

"No, thank you, Hawkins. Fancy it being midnight."

Has anyone been in to see me? she wanted to ask. Has my husband been?

But he must be kept away from her, he caught germs all too easily.

Anyway, Hawkins had gone down to the kitchen, and the house was silent. No, not quite. A board creaked in the passage outside her door.

Her heart quickened. William was coming to see her. She must tell him to come no farther than the door. She sat up to do so, but the door remained closed, and there was no more sound.

Hawkins had made a mistake when she had said everyone was in bed. Unless it was just the house creaking in the night, as old houses did.

The modest but satisfying success of his book had given William an attractive maturity. The charming boyishness

that had always delighted Beatrice had gone, except at
times when he romped with the children. He didn't even
do that very much now. He had grown strangely quiet,
even with a hint of sadness.

What was the sadness for? A marriage that still went
against the grain? But they were happy. Or as happy as
most couples. He hadn't wanted to go away at all this
winter. He had seemed quite content at home, as if the
roving were out of his system. Sometimes, however, Beatrice caught him looking at her reflectively, and that was
when she imagined a certain lonely thoughtfulness in his
eyes.

If only they could talk, she thought longingly. But any
attempt on her part to begin a more intimate conversation
was almost always thwarted by his adroit slightly flippant
wit. She didn't care for that flippancy, which was also a
recently acquired habit.

Her constant possessive love made her unduly sensitive
about small things. Such as feeling a usurper when she
went into the nursery and found William there, contentedly
listening to the children's story read by Miss Medway in
her soft clear voice, or to Miss Medway playing Chopin
ballades on the piano that had been bought for Florence
to have music lessons.

Apart from five-finger exercises, Florence must learn
an appreciation of the best composers, William said, when
it was plain that it was he who enjoyed Miss Medway's
playing. She seemed to be quite an accomplished pianist.
Beatrice was no judge since her own knowledge of music
was meager. Which was another barrier between her and
her husband, she thought regretfully.

As the tender light of spring lingered in the sky, and she
wandered in the garden to breathe fresh air after the
stuffiness of the long day in the shop, it seemed that the
slightly melancholy echo of Chopin ballades always haunted
the air, mingling with the evening bird cries. The early
primroses and snowdrops were over already, the Japanese
cherry tree had a froth of blossom, the air was sweet, free
at last of the horrible sulfurous winter fogs.

She loved Overton House and its quiet walled garden
more and more. Sometimes she rose half an hour earlier
in the morning to walk on the dewy lawn and listen to the
cooing of the doves and the starched-skirts crackle of

their wings. She was never lonely then. But she was frankly lonely in the evenings when William seemed to prefer the company of the children and Miss Medway's storytelling or piano playing to walking in the garden with her.

It was so wonderful, she told herself stoutly, that William had been contented to stay at home for so long. She wanted his happiness above all. So she deliberately shut her mind to her occasional unworthy suspicions. Anyway, they just weren't possible. For Miss Medway was no flirtatious, vivacious Laura Prendergast. She was really extremely dull. She seldom opened her mouth at the dinner table. It made them an awkward trio, and conversation difficult and tedious.

As soon as the children were old enough Beatrice resolved to send them to boarding schools. Then one would be happily free of the inhibiting presence of a governess. And perhaps William would talk to her again.

In the meantime, a vaguely disturbing thing happened.

She came home a little earlier one evening to find the children alone in the nursery, and quarreling furiously. At least Edwin was making all the noise, while Florence stood white-faced and stubborn, a drooping willow wand in her hand, refusing to obey his commands. It seemed that they were playing Zulu wars, and Edwin refused to take turns at being a Zulu. He much preferred to be the dashing British cavalry officer shooting Florence, armed only with her poor willow wand spear, down.

"Mamma, it isn't fair that Edwin should always win," she cried passionately. "Why can't I be the British sometimes?"

"You can't ride a horse," Edwin said contemptuously.

"That's only a pretend horse, you silly little boy," she retorted, pointing to his wooden hobbyhorse.

"Children, children, be quiet," Beatrice ordered. "Where's Miss Medway?"

"She has a headache, she's lying down," Florence said. "She walked too far today, that's the trouble."

"Why, where did you go?"

"Papa took us on the Heath to catch butterflies. He said it was warm enough, the first ones might be out. But then he made Edwin and me stay by the pond because we were too noisy."

"By yourselves?" asked Beatrice.

"Not for long, Mamma. Only Edwin was very naughty, he got his feet wet. He put them in the water with his *boots* on! And Papa was cross, and they hadn't caught any butterflies. So we came home."

Florence was getting priggish, Beatrice thought with one part of her mind. The other part was swooping into those happy past days, so far past and so few, when she and William had pursued their fluttering prey on the Heath. How dare he do those special things of theirs with Miss Medway. How dare he!

Anger was soaring through her veins. She rang the bell, and when Lizzie answered it she said sharply, "Lizzie, I came home and found the children quite alone."

"I'm sorry, ma'am. I was in the kitchen attending to their tea. I thought Miss Medway was with them."

"Then go and bring up their tea. I believe Miss Medway is lying down. Tell her, headache or not, I want to see her in the morning room."

"Mamma," said Florence timidly, as a flustered Lizzie bobbed and departed, "please don't be cross with Miss Medway. It was Edwin's own fault he got wet feet and ruined his boots. He's old enough to know better."

"Perhaps," said Beatrice. She ruffled Edwin's curls absently. He was her darling pretty boy. "But it was Miss Medway's fault for leaving you. Now, Florence, don't pout. A most unbecoming habit. Help Edwin to pack up his soldiers so Lizzie can put the tea on the table."

"But he won't allow me to touch them," came Florence's wail as Beatrice left the nursery, walking briskly down the passage to the morning room.

It had been in the papers this morning about the adultery and the subsequent disgrace of the leader of the Irish party, Charles Stewart Parnell, with a woman called Kitty O'Shea. A formidable scheming woman, one had no doubt.

Now why was she remembering that at this particular moment?

Ten minutes later Miss Medway stood before her. She was wearing the demure high-necked brown dress in which she had arrived at Overton House nearly a year ago. She looked young and vulnerable and she had been crying. It was certainly no headache that had made her eyelids so red.

Beatrice, after seven years of dealing with men and women of all ages, knew guilt when it was presented to her so plainly.

She also had a moment of cowardice. If only she could have ignored this, if only the three of them could have gone on as peacefully as they had done for the last few months, pretending nothing had happened, pretending that William had genuinely got over his wanderlust and preferred staying in England for no other reason than that he was devoted to his home and family. . . .

But she had been deliberately shutting her eyes for too long. She realized that all too clearly. She had ignored the hints and signs, and now she must pay for her self-induced blindness. It was a great pity, but Miss Medway would have to leave.

"Florence tells me that Edwin has ruined a pair of boots in the pond on the Heath, Miss Medway. Do you realize he might have caught a severe chill, quite apart from the danger of his drowning? I must hold you to blame."

Her voice was quiet and controlled, but tinged with the icy adamant note which the staff at Bonnington's had come to respect. She was ashamed of her sensation of grim satisfaction when the slight figure standing before her trembled. It was foolish to think that the grief which would overwhelm her shortly could be assuaged by punishing this wicked young woman.

Wicked?

Even her anger wouldn't truly allow her to think that. Of course the little fool was likely to fall in love with William. One had to suppose that she couldn't help herself.

But had William encouraged her?

That was where the source of the pain lay.

Miss Medway lifted large swimming eyes and bravely looked Beatrice in the face.

"I'm sorry, Mrs. Overton. I admit I am entirely to blame. But I—we—didn't think the children would come to any harm for a little while. There was something—" Then her composure vanished and she couldn't continue. She pressed her hands to her face and began sobbing so desperately that Beatrice had to overcome her own involuntary sympathy.

"Come now, Miss Medway. Whatever has happened

can't be that terrible. You've fallen in love with my husband,
I imagine."

The bent dark head moved in assent.

"Well, I suppose I can't altogether blame you for that."
Beatrice was holding onto her pain and anger. "I love him
very much myself, and have always thought that no one
could not love him. You are only human, as I am sure
you will tell me presently. But of course this means you'll
have to go. You know that, don't you?"

"Yes, I do know that, Mrs. Overton. I do, indeed."

"The trouble is, you're expecting a baby." Beatrice heard
herself speaking from some unfailing feminine intuition,
every word rasping as if her throat were on fire.

"No! At least . . . I never meant you to know. I was
going to leave as soon as I had found somewhere to go.
Only today, on the Heath when I told Will— I mean, Mr.
Overton—"

The faltering voice stopped altogether and again Beatrice's alarming intuition supplied the words. William had
refused to let her go. He had said he would talk to his
wife.

He would, indeed!

"Mrs. Overton, can you ever forgive me?"

Beatrice didn't allow herself to see the desperate appealing eyes. She was done with sentiment. At this moment she never intended to be sentimental again about
anything, not even her deceiving husband.

"No. I'm surprised you'd even ask me such a thing."
Her strange harsh voice went on talking as if she were a
judge in a court looking down from a superior height at
this wretched guilty witness.

"But you're not the first this sort of thing has happened
to. I've had various girls at the shop whom I've had to
help discreetly, and I may even help you when I get over
being angry with you. Just now, I want you out of this
house tonight. So go and pack your bags at once. I'd prefer
you not to say good-bye to the children, or my husband. I
will make the necessary explanations."

Then, of course, as one might have expected, the girl
fainted. She was stretched flat on the Turkish carpet, her
face colorless except for the long black lashes lying on her
cheeks. In that moment of unconsciousness Beatrice was
painfully aware of the fragile prettiness that had apparently

been so irresistible to William. Though who was to know
which had been the seducer, her volatile husband, or this
demure quiet creature with her deceptive air of innocence?

The old classic melodrama, she thought disgustedly, the
master and the maidservant. Above all, the servants must
not be called. She was quite able to cope with a faint. She
was never without a bottle of smelling salts in her bag, as
shopgirls had been known to do the same thing in her
presence.

The acrid smell in her nostrils brought Miss Medway
back to consciousness. She struggled up, apologizing at
once for her foolish behavior.

"I'm not usually as weak as this. Only today has been
so difficult. Tonight we were going to tell you—"

We?

Beatrice had no intention of having a three-cornered
conference. She would talk to William alone.

"Good Gad!" she exclaimed in Papa's tone of voice.

Miss Medway's sharp wince brought her back to self-
control.

"I'll have some tea sent up to your room, and then I
hope you will feel well enough to pack. I'll come up later,
and tell you where I have arranged for you to spend the
night, or the next few days. Don't look surprised. I'm not
an ogre. I don't throw people out in the street, no matter
what the provocation."

And the provocation was severe. William and this scrap
of a girl with their clothes thrown off, performing that
intensely private act of marriage, of which she herself was
too often deprived. The image in her mind was so vivid
that a moment of dreadful weakness came over her. She
thought she was going to mingle her tears with Miss
Medway's.

I married my husband determined to make him love
me, but he never has, so who is to blame? she wanted to
burst out.

Fortunately she controlled such devastating honesty. She
had always prided herself on her honesty, but from now
on she was going to be more clever, more subtle, more
devious. She would somehow manage this deplorable situation without losing William's friendship. She hadn't yet his
love to lose, but at least she would see that it hadn't all
been expended on a flighty governess. That would be too

incredible to believe. William's infatuations were passing affairs. This would blow over. Even the difficulty of the baby would be resolved. If necessary, she would personally find good adoptive parents for it.

But Miss Medway must leave tonight. One had better send a message to Dixon to have the carriage ready.

She saw the girl hadn't attempted to move and said in a voice that rasped, "Come now, Miss Medway. You're quite strong enough to do as I tell you. Go and begin your packing—"

"Oh, no, Bea. Just a minute," came William's voice from the door. How long had he been there? How much had he heard?

"Mary isn't leaving this house," he said.

Mary! That must have been the moment when the terrible reality of the situation came home to her, for she was conscious only of appalling misery as William stood beside Miss Medway and put a protecting possessive arm across her shoulders. His face was full of a loving, radiant tenderness, never, thought Beatrice bitterly, bent on her.

"Why don't you look like that for me?" she cried compulsively, and knew that in that moment of weakness she had lost command of the situation.

William looked at her with genuine remorse, after all he was the kindest of men. Miss Medway, too, had the gall to look at her pityingly. She was strong enough now that she had William's arm about her shoulders.

One advantage remained to Beatrice, however. She could twist the wedding ring on her finger and, recovering something of her self-possession, say, "Miss Medway will have to go, William. You surely can't deny that."

"But she can't, Bea. She's going to have my child."

"And so?" said Beatrice stiffly. "This unfortunate situation is hardly a new one. It can be coped with, I imagine."

She was realizing suddenly that William himself had only today heard the disastrous news. That accounted for his emotional tenderness. His first reaction would be to want to protect the girl he had wronged. And he should do so, too. He was a gentleman, after all.

Too much of a gentleman, indeed, for it seemed that he was proposing to marry Miss Medway.

Beatrice could scarcely believe her ears.

"So you intend to commit bigamy?"

"Now, Bea, don't pretend to be a fool. You know that I would have to ask you to divorce me. I intended to do that this evening, since Mary only told me today—"

"And what do you propose living on?" Beatrice interrupted, with an air of deep interest.

"Oh, I'll continue writing. Aberconway has already offered me a fairly substantial advance for my next book."

"Remembering that your first took seven years," Beatrice murmured. "Is he offering you enough to live on for seven years?"

"Don't be sarcastic, Bea. I have some royalties. And I'll do other things. You and the children must remain in Overton House, of course. I'm willing to transfer my title to you in trust for Edwin."

Once he had been willing to make the sacrifice of marrying a plain young woman whom he didn't love in order to keep his treasured home. What alchemy had this wretched governess worked on him?

But stick to reason, stick to the practicalities.

"With your style of living, my dear William, you won't be able to exist for months, let alone years. You'll be poverty-stricken. I really couldn't allow that to happen. After all, we married for that very reason. Had you forgotten? We both made a pact. I believe in keeping pacts, especially legal ones. So," she said with finality, "there will be no divorce."

"You're speaking from shock, Bea. When you've thought it over—"

"You have my answer now," said Beatrice.

"But Mary and I love each other!"

His devastating simplicity was almost unanswerable. It was the first time she had ever heard him speak of love.

"I'm afraid that particular emotion wouldn't survive under these circumstances, William; you really must be more practical. I mean what I say about no divorce. So to avoid a scandal I hope you won't be doing anything so foolish as leaving the house tonight. We must make some constructive plans about this infant. When is it expected?"

"Sometime in September," Miss Medway said faintly.

So the lovemaking had happened at Christmas when she was ill, when her feverish fancy that the passages had rustled with nocturnal meetings had indeed been no fancy.

And how often had it happened since?

"Then we have five months," she said briskly. "Being a small person, Miss Medway, it's likely you won't show your condition too much for another two months."

"I don't know what you're getting at, Bea," William said. "But this is my child and I simply don't intend to give it up. Neither will I desert Mary."

Beatrice recognized the stubborn note in his voice. But she also thought she detected deep uneasiness beneath his determination. She knew him all too well. He hated trouble. He so much preferred the easy path. His troubled frown showed that he was well aware of what was ahead of him if he stuck to his noble principles. A hole in corner life with a woman he was not free to marry, a child born out of wedlock, poverty, being ostracized by his friends and asked to resign from his clubs, the permanent loss of his luxurious travels abroad.

Not to mention that he would probably be dead in five years of chronic bronchitis.

She simply could not allow these terrible things to happen to her gentle, sensitive, adorable, faithless husband. She would fight every step of the way, and she had all the weapons.

Except love. . . .

And the agony of his white face tearing at her.

She had to win, but she knew that she was willing to make almost any concession to ease his pain.

Actually, her logical mind had already realized that there was only one concession possible. The enormity of it appalled her. Would she be capable of making it? She must speak quickly, before cowardice kept her silent.

"Now listen, both of you. This is a deplorable situation, but it isn't irretrievable. There's one practical thing we can do to avoid a scandal and protect the child. You and I, William, must adopt it. No, more than that." She was improvising as the fantastic scheme grew in her mind. "It must *be* our child."

Miss Medway was as still as a ghost, listening. But William's chin had a stubborn implacable tilt.

"Bea, you're a famous organizer, we all know that, but you can't give birth to another woman's child."

"Of course I can't. However, I could seem to. And it wouldn't be the first time this sort of thing has been done." *Though surely only by women who love their errant hus-*

bands beyond all reason. . . . "We would have to go abroad, to begin with."

"We?"

"Miss Medway and I. Everyone knows I have difficult pregnancies. It wouldn't be so strange if my doctor suggested that I spend the last three months abroad in a quiet pensione in Switzerland or Italy. It would be quite simple, really."

"Bea, you can't be serious?"

"Indeed I can." She met his incredulous gaze sadly. "You speak of love. I speak of love, too. If this would make you happier, the child would be born an Overton. Because you simply must understand that I will never divorce you."

William made no answer. He stood rigid in his dilemma, and only came to life when Miss Medway suddenly broke into noisy sobbing. Then he put his arm around her again, tenderly, and rested his lips on her hair.

He had no shame, Beatrice thought furiously, nor any thought for her feelings. It was only this wretched Mary Medway whose feelings must be protected. This girl who had seduced him with a red ribbon tied in her hair, with her Chopin ballades, her soft voice. . . .

"If I am not to leave here tonight, neither is Mary," William said at last, quite mildly.

Beatrice nodded.

"I agree. If we're going to give this scheme serious consideration, Miss Medway will need to be in the house for another two months. She must get some fuller gowns, and so must I. What a pity the fashion for crinolines has gone out. They were such a wonderful camouflage."

"You want everything, Mrs. Overton! Everything!" Miss Medway burst out with sudden passionate spirit.

"I can assure you I don't want this situation," Beatrice retorted.

"Then don't stand in our way," William begged. "Have a little compassion."

"Compassion!" Beatrice exclaimed. "Gad, I can't stand any more of this. Would you prefer to find some old crone in the back streets of Paddington, with a knitting needle?"

"*Bea!*"

"Well, don't you both deserve that remark? Isn't it more practical than high-flown words like 'compassion'? I assure you I have plenty of compassion for deserving people. But just at this minute, it's too much to ask of me."

So the long night had to be lived through. Did she lose her husband, or did she acquire another and very unwelcome child?

And what about poor Mary Medway? Poor, indeed! The sin was hers, she must suffer.

All the same, who could resist William at his most beguiling? He had never had to beguile his wife because she had fallen too readily into his arms.

Perhaps that was the trouble.

But at some time, in the long vista of the years ahead, he would seek her anxiously and lovingly. Time would achieve this desirable state.

She had to cling to this long-held belief. Otherwise her life would be a desert, an emptiness, a null and void state, a bankruptcy, which simply did not bear contemplating.

At eleven o'clock Hawkins tapped at her bedroom door.

"I didn't ring for you," Beatrice said.

"No, ma'am, but Annie said you hardly touched your dinner. I was wondering if you were feeling poorly."

The anxious devoted face was too faithful to be dismissed. One had to appreciate faithfulness, above all.

"I've had a worrying day, Hawkins, that's all. I think I need a holiday."

"Oh, ma'am, you do. We were only saying below stairs the other day—"

Beatrice cut that off sharply. "I hope you were not gossiping."

"Oh, no, ma'am. We were only anxious about you, working so hard."

"Well, then, you'll be pleased to hear that I am contemplating a long holiday."

"I'm so glad, ma'am."

"But only contemplating. I may think better of it in the morning."

"For your sake, ma'am, I hope you don't."

How would Bonnington's survive without her for three months? It would have to, that was all. She would have three idle months abroad in which to write long letters to Adam Cope and Miss Brown, and that very young man, James Brush, who was so clever at window dressing. She would tell him to do an elaborate maternity window, ha-ha! He would do so, anyway, she suspected. If the birth of royalty was to be commemorated, surely the birth of a child to the owner of Bonnington's deserved the same attention.

All this fuss would be made for a little bastard who was to grow up an Overton and probably be the most successful soldier of them all! Would the old general approve of her action? She rather thought so. Strategy, he would say. But give the child a sensible upbringing. Stamp out any weaknesses it might inherit from that governess who was not even one of his pretty nosegays, but just a common brown sparrow.

Which made it all the more humiliating. . . .

Toward morning Beatrice thought she heard the sound of a piano playing, but that must have been imagination, for dawn was breaking. Apart from that dream-filled doze she had been awake all night.

She rang for Hawkins at her usual time and handed her a letter she had just written.

"Tell Dixon to deliver this to Mr. Cope," she said. "I won't be going into the shop today."

"Ma'am, you are sick!"

"No, I am not, Hawkins! I have simply decided to take a day at home to attend to my wardrobe."

"Your wardrobe, ma'am? What's wrong with it?"

"Nothing, except that I seem to be putting on weight. I want to decide what gowns can be let out."

She saw the flicker in Hawkins' eyes, and knew the hint had registered. In no time at all, there would be whispers below stairs.

Lord, I am like that old Tudor Queen Mary with her false pregnancies, and just about as unhappy. . . .

Though whether she could conceal the real truth from Hawkins with her sharp devoted eyes was another matter.

An hour later William knocked at her bedroom door and, with a formality that was one more wound in her vulnerable breast, asked permission to come in.

He didn't approach the bed where she was propped against pillows finishing her breakfast. He stood at the window with his back to her, and said wryly, "Have you begun the first act already, Bea?"

"The sooner the better. Isn't that right?"

"Yes." His head was bent, his voice almost inaudible. "Mary has finally persuaded me. She spent all night doing it. It's for the child, she says. She knows you're a good mother."

"And you a good father," Beatrice said evenly.

"What the devil does that matter!"

"It matters a lot." She was terribly afraid he was crying. "William, Mary's right. This is the best way. Indeed, it's the only way, because, believe me, I wouldn't be happy to see a child of yours lost."

"Oh, blast the child!" he muttered. "You might as well know, Bea, that even though it seems I have to lose her, I'll never stop loving Mary."

"You think so now—"

He lifted his head, showing the embarrassing tears on his cheeks.

"I'll think so until the end of my life. I love her, Bea. Don't you understand the meaning of that word?"

"Yes. I understand it."

"Well, it's something there won't be much of in this house in the future," he said, and abruptly left the room.

Chapter 12

Their unavoidable intimacy began in their cabin on board the Channel steamer. With a sigh of relief Beatrice undid her skirts and flung off the padding she had been wearing around her waist. Instantly she felt light and slim, as if she had indeed given birth to a baby.

Miss Medway, on the other hand, could now lose her modesty and show the bulge in her stomach as much as she pleased. For the last month Beatrice had insisted that she did not leave the house, that she wear voluminous skirts and shawls to conceal her increasing size, and that apart from giving Florence and Edwin their morning lessons in the nursery and making an appearance at dinner at night (this last merely in order to avoid servants' gossip) she keep to her room.

She could occupy herself usefully with sewing and knitting for the baby. She was a beautiful needlewoman, and Beatrice acknowledged that this infant would be more exquisitely dressed than either of her own had been. The story told to Hawkins and relayed to the rest of the staff was that Miss Medway was proving so useful that Beatrice had chosen her for a sympathetic companion during her exile abroad.

"Exile" was a funny word to use. She could see the faint bewilderment in Hawkins' eyes.

"Any time spent away from my family is exile," she said.

How much Hawkins guessed she didn't know. The dear creature was so loyal it didn't really matter if she did guess, except that Beatrice would never get over the pain of admitting her husband's infidelity. She wished that no one in the world needed to know about that.

One person, however, had had to be taken into her confidence. Miss Brown.

No one but she could organize the clever padding to wear over Beatrice's stomach, and discreetly acquire the disguising garments for Miss Medway. Also, plans had to be made for her absence from the shop, and only Miss Brown with her sharp eyes and forbidding manner could quell possible gossip. Finally, Beatrice would never have succeeded in deceiving so old a friend, and one so full of anger on her behalf.

"That little slut!" she had hissed on hearing the disastrous story. "Oh, poor Miss Beatrice!"

She never said a word against William, a fact for which Beatrice was grateful. Though what she thought privately was another matter. She had always made it clear that she considered no man worthy of Miss Beatrice. Indeed, she hadn't too high an opinion of men in general, and this episode only served to prove how right she was.

The last eight weeks had been the longest and most difficult in Beatrice's life. She had found long ago that the only way to cope with mental perturbation and anxiety was to keep endlessly busy, even with the most trivial things. So, although she had to curtail her time at the shop in order to give credence to the story that her health was indifferent, she filled in the long hours at home with setting out in detail new plans for Bonnington's with adding accounts, with sorting out clothes, with discussions with Cook and the gardeners, and with interviewing applicants for the post of nursery governess. A plain girl, this time. A good sensible, unimaginative creature who would bore William on sight. For one had to be realistic about this hazard even though she was certain William would never allow himself to get into such an embarrassing situation again.

He was too susceptible, that was all.

She had already forgiven him for Miss Medway, and had told him so.

"When I come back from Italy, everything will be the same as it always was," she had said in the forthright brisk manner she used to hide emotion.

"Hardly." He scarcely spoke to her nowadays, but he had to make some acknowledgment of this apparently unwanted generosity.

"But it will be, because I haven't stopped loving you,"

she said earnestly. His haggard and haunted appearance had been giving her the greatest anxiety.

His lips quirked, though not in a smile.

"Haven't you? One day I expect you'll add up these things against me."

"Will you care if I do?"

"I don't know." His voice was flat, indifferent. "I suppose I will. I like to be loved. That's my trouble."

It was a crumb of comfort to which she clung.

Florence's and Edwin's lamentations were another thing.

"Mamma, Miss Medway won't take us for walks on the Heath anymore. Why won't she?"

"Because Lizzie is perfectly capable of taking you."

"But we'd rather have Miss Medway, Mamma. Edwin hates Lizzie. So do I, rather."

"You must simply make the best of her, my darlings, because Miss Medway is coming to Italy with me."

"But *why?* Why are you so unkind to us?"

Florence was becoming a nagging child. Beatrice had to speak sharply to her, and then was remorseful when Florence winced, and her face closed. Now she was in danger of making an enemy of her daughter.

What that deceitful governess had to answer for!

Finally, William had said a polite good-bye as she had stood in the hall surrounded by luggage. His lips had barely brushed her cheek. What form his farewell of Miss Medway had taken, she didn't know.

She doubted if he had smiled since the day he had agreed to what he now privately called her monstrous plan. His haggard look had increased and his eyes showed a deep sadness that sometimes made her shiver, fearful that it would be there forever.

But he couldn't have so deep a love for this reticent pale-faced girl. It wasn't possible. She simply had to be right about that. She told everyone that he was not well, that his chest was troubling him, and that he would probably have to spend the next winter abroad. But in the meantime he would remain with the children until she sent for him to accompany her home with his new child.

It was a difficult time for everybody, but it would pass. In three months Florence would have got over her unfortunate devotion for Miss Medway. Edwin almost certainly would have, since he was not a sentimental child. And

William, realizing life had not ended, would sometimes smile again.

Dear heaven, wasn't she making a big enough sacrifice to deserve his smile?

Lake Maggiore was a beautiful lake. In the early autumn mists hung over it until the sun rose, then it was a sparkling blue, and the Borromean Islands floated in a gentle haze. They stayed in a small austere but comfortable pensione on the lakeside. They had exchanged names and were Mrs. Overton and Miss Medway in reverse. When the baby was born it would be registered as an Overton. Beatrice had had to discard her wedding ring, and Miss Medway had had to wear one, a thin gold band she had produced as soon as they had arrived. Where she had got it Beatrice didn't ask. She refused to think that William had slipped it on that thin fragile finger. Though he probably had.

On arrival a doctor who spoke sufficient English and who had a kindly manner had been found. He had immediately ordered a nourishing diet for Miss Medway. The patient, he said, was much too thin and delicate for approaching motherhood. Her English doctor had shown good sense in ordering her abroad to a beautiful sunny place like this, where she could rest and build up her strength. He personally would see that the bambino was born strong and healthy.

Beatrice's ruthless honesty made her examine her feelings about that. Did she want a strong healthy child? Wouldn't she have preferred it to be stillborn? If it were extremely delicate, would she try hard to rear it?

She endeavored to put these disturbing thoughts out of her mind, but knew by the expression in Miss Medway's large luminous eyes that she was well aware of them. She knew also the young woman's desperate uphappiness, although after two or three weeks in the relaxing sunshine, she seemed more composed. She liked to go for walks alone, and to sit in the garden alone. Once, unknown to Beatrice, she hired a boatman to take her across to the little island of Isola Bella with its famous formal gardens, made for another lonely much-loved woman. When she came back she talked about the white peacocks, the statue of the unicorn, the little pointed cypresses and the camphor trees, the monks in brown habits, the peace. There had been a species of butterfly she had never seen before. It had black wings edged with a coquettish white frill.

At once she wished she hadn't mentioned the butterfly. The flash of alarm showed in her eyes. But Beatrice said composedly, "I'd like to have seen it. Perhaps I'll go with you the next time.

They didn't seek each other's company. The enforced intimacy of mealtimes was enough. The endless weeks were not so much torment as excruciating boredom. Beatrice had not been able to sustain her hate for this hapless creature. Her nature was not revengeful. The girl had made a tragic mistake and was now paying for it to the best of her ability. She was also being honorable, for she wrote no letters and none came for her.

The packets of mail were always addressed to Mrs. William Overton, and although the formality of handing them to Miss Medway (the pseudo Mrs. Overton) had to be made, Miss Medway immediately passed them over to Beatrice and then discreetly vanished to let Beatrice read the letters in peace. She was adhering strictly to her part of the bargain, and for this she had Beatrice's respect.

But what had made William love this gentle quiet person, he who had always admired the spectacular, the vivacious, the witty? That was the torturing question that nagged at Beatrice. And did she imagine that sometimes Miss Medway looked at her with pity? She certainly hoped she imagined it, otherwise the stiff conversations they had at the luncheon and dinner table would cease altogether.

It was Mary Medway who was to be pitied. It was she who had lost William.

One didn't know how to make the endless time pass. Beatrice read books and wrote numerous letters and thought of plans for Bonnington's. One day she hired a carrozza to take her to Como to visit the silk manufacturers. She wanted to inquire into importing of Italian silk which was expensive, but superior to that which she had been buying from Macclesfield in Derbyshire. There were leather goods and shoes which also might be imported with profit. A foreign department stocked with luxuries from different countries? The notion stimulated her. She must write to Adam about it. She was keenly missing the

shop, and the excitement of creative ideas. It had become
a necessity to her, a drug, perhaps.

The night away, the business which had fully occupied
her mind, and the escape from Miss Medway's inhibitingly quiet company, cheered Beatrice up. She returned
to the pensione to find Mary more animated too, although
there was a blurred look in her eyes that suggested recent
tears.

She had had a letter from England! Beatrice's alarming
intuition was operating again. William had broken his
word. He had written to his lost love.

Carefully she kept her voice even.

"And what have you been doing while I have been
away?"

"Oh, I've been to Isola Bella again. I sat in the gardens
all morning watching the peacocks. The sun was shining,
and it was so peaceful. I'm sure all that peace is good for
the baby."

"Peacocks are vain creatures. Perhaps you will be making the baby vain."

Mary smiled faintly. "Surely not. But I was wondering
if I have the right to suggest that if the baby is a girl she
might be given the name of a flower. There are so many
flowers in this beautiful spot. Don't you think Azalea
would be pretty?"

Pretentious, Beatrice thought. And what is giving you
these sudden romantic thoughts?

"Shall we wait and see what the baby's sex is? Did the
English mail come yet?"

The barest hesitation. "Yes. There are letters for you."

And for you, Beatrice thought, more certainly than
ever, noting the averted gaze. My dear vulnerable husband
has been swearing his undying devotion, and you are finding that enough to live on at present, you romantic little
fool.

However, a more worthy impulse made her refrain from
asking questions. Must one grudge everything, even the
name of a flower for the unwanted child? In a few weeks
she would say good-bye to Mary Medway forever. At
least let her distinguish herself by a little generosity.

"If you'll excuse me, I'll go and read my letters."

Florence wrote in her small tight unchildish writing:

"Edwin and I don't like Miss Sloane. I am sorry to tell you that Edwin kicked her on the ankle. Yestidy I went into Papa's study and he was crying. Lizzie said I imagined it because men don't cry."

Beatrice dipped her pen in the ink and wrote to Miss Brown, stabbing the nib into the paper.

"I have ordered several bales of silk for delivery in the spring. It is of very fine quality and we must advertise it as desirable for gowns for Easter weddings and summer garden parties." As always, work was the panacea, shutting out a little that loved haunted face with the red-rimmed eyes in the library.

He *couldn't* have been hurt that badly, not her dear ephemeral, flirtatious William. He was simply bored and lonely, having to remain at home with the children until she returned.

"Darling Florence and Edwin," she wrote, "you must obey Miss Sloane whether you like her or not. Comfort Papa if he's lonely. . . ."

She thought a long time before she began the third letter.

MY DEAREST WILLIAM,

I have been visiting Como, to do some buying, among other things, and I have been put in touch, through an agency, with a German banking family living in Zurich who require an English governess. They sound eminently suitable, and I am writing to them today. So have no more worries about Miss Medway's future.

We both go on very well, but I miss you and the children more than I can say. . . .

The candle guttered in the stream of balmy air coming through the open window. The moon was sailing high in the sky above the lake, and no doubt Mary Medway was gazing at it, lost in her sad romantic dream. She was obviously the kind of person who thrived on dreams of the unattainable; otherwise how could she have been foolish enough to get herself into this situation?

Beatrice firmly closed her own shutters, and the candlelight steadied.

She must begin her next letter now, to Herr Gunter

Wasserman in Zurich, father of three children, and solidly wealthy.

If only that tiresome baby would hurry up and arrive. . . .

Her ardent longing must have had good effect, for two weeks later the birth began. It was long and exhausting, and at one stage the harassed Italian doctor was afraid he would lose both mother and child. However, he finally emerged from the sickroom crying triumphantly, *"Bella bella bambina!"* and a little later Beatrice went to see the child lying in its cradle beside its mother's bed.

It was small, with minute features, and a girl. It had been born in all the sighing beauty of an Italian evening as the sun dropped over the lake.

"It's not an azalea," Beatrice said gruffly. It was hers now, she told herself. She was going to have to love it. Surely it would be easy to love a baby. "More like a daisy."

Mary raised herself to look at the baby. For a moment her guard was down and her white exhausted face had a shining radiance that made Beatrice realize in a painful flash why William had fallen in love with her. She must have looked like that for him.

"Call her Daisy if you want to," she said softly.

"Yes, I believe I will. It will be easier for Florence and Edwin, too. They would never have got their tongues round Azalea." She sounded too brisk, too practical, for this darkened room with its just finished drama. But life went on, hopefully without any more such dramas.

And one day William would forget that lustrous radiance in a face he scarcely remembered.

When he met her in Milan three weeks later, Mary Medway had already set out for Zurich, and Beatrice had engaged a young Frenchwoman, Mademoiselle Laurette, to care for the baby. She was coming to England with them. Everything was organized. William had no need to look so surprised. Didn't he know he had a capable wife?

And the baby's name was already decided on.

"Daisy? Isn't that a bit ordinary?"

He had already spent more time hanging over the cradle than Beatrice would have wished. He certainly hadn't shown that much interest in either Florence or Edwin, but he had been younger then, and perhaps less ready for fatherhood.

"Her mother has agreed to it. I hope you don't think I have been too heartless, William."

Surely he had some appreciation of her generosity. Didn't he think it was generosity? When he didn't answer, she persisted recklessly, "I'm sure not many wives would have behaved as well as I have. The baby will be properly brought up, and Miss Medway has gone out into the world without a blemish on her character."

But with what scars on her heart? Beatrice had to drag that slight figure boarding the train at Milan railway station back into her memory. Now she was glad William didn't look at her, for she was afraid she would see too much desolation in his eyes. He really had aged distressingly in the last three months. The last trace of his attractive boyishness had gone.

When he spoke at last it was not to express any appreciation of her behavior but to say, "I'm not happy about that German family. You know I have never liked Germans."

She repressed her exasperation.

"If Miss Medway doesn't care for them she doesn't need to stay there. But it's a start for her. I found her a good position as I promised to do." Her voice was brisk and determinedly cheerful. "Now we must do our part and give Miss Daisy Overton a good upbringing."

Chapter 13

Florence didn't believe that Mamma was bringing a baby home, although Edwin said that it was true. An Italian baby, too. There was something funny about that. Would it look different from an English baby? Florence wondered. She suspected that it would, because of the expression on Lizzie's face.

"Innocent little creature," Cook called it, and Lizzie tossed her head and said, "Innocent!" in a peculiar voice, as if the baby had been caught red-handed in some crime.

"Then why did she have to go to foreign parts to have it?" she demanded.

"To rest in the sun, as you very well know," Cook said. "She had enough trouble with the other two. But that was before your time, of course."

Lizzie sniffed and said, "She looks the breeding type to me."

"Appearances don't always speak the truth."

"I daresay. But why couldn't she have gone to Harrogate or Bath or somewhere civilized, and at least give the poor mite the chance of being English?"

"What's so wrong with Italians, then? They're all right. Opera stars and such like."

"I've never been one for foreigners," Lizzie said and spun around, as if she had eyes in the back of her head. "Miss Florence! Master Edwin! What are you doing down here, you naughty children? Back to the nursery, quickly! Really"—she sighed to Cook—"it's been bedlam ever since they heard their mamma was coming home. And that Miss Sloane is worse than useless. Says now that Master Edwin bit her hand. Fancy! He can be a bit of a terror, but he isn't a wild animal."

142

Florence, lingering long enough to hear that choice piece of information, trailed back to the nursery. She still hadn't heard what she so longed to hear. Was Miss Medway coming back with Mamma?

If she were, horrid Miss Sloane would go, and Edwin wouldn't cry so much. He had turned into a terrible cry-baby since Miss Medway had gone to Italy with Mamma, not only because he disliked Miss Sloane, but because he loved Miss Medway. So had Florence. But no one had consulted them when it was decided that Miss Medway should be Mamma's companion on the journey to Lake Maggiore. "Who is Majory?" Edwin had asked pitifully, and Florence had snapped, "Don't be such an ignorant lout. It's not a person, it's a place."

Children, Florence had discovered, were never consulted about major upheavals in their lives. They just had to suffer them, and use bad language occasionally, like "ignorant lout" (which she had heard Cook call the butcher's boy). Even though one was slapped for it, it was a more satisfactory way of easing one's sorrow than by crying.

She suspected Papa was doing the same. He must miss Mamma very much. Once, when he had been ill for a few days, he had looked very lonely in his narrow bed in the blue room all by himself. "Like a monk," she had heard Annie murmuring under her breath.

However, in spite of his loneliness, he hadn't seemed too overjoyed when Mamma's letter had come saying they had a new baby daughter, and would he come and fetch them both home.

"Crossing the Channel in this weather," he had grumbled. "Why couldn't the child arrive at a more seasonable time?"

No one had said why Miss Medway couldn't help Mamma home with the new baby. Nor, indeed, why this poor little foreign baby seemed so unwelcome.

"When I come home to you," Mamma had written to Florence and Edwin, "we will all be happy together again. I hope that you have been good children and kept Papa company while I have been away."

Almost as an afterthought, the letter had finished, "I will be bringing a new little sister for you, whom you must learn to love."

Why *learn?* Florence had wondered pedantically. One just naturally loved a baby.

Papa had left for Italy a week ago. Traveling by steamer and train, he and Mamma and the baby were due at Victoria Station at three thirty this afternoon. Dixon was meeting them. They would be home an hour or so later, Dixon said. With those fast grays Papa had bought (because he was so miserable while Mamma was away, he had had to find something to amuse him), the journey might take less than an hour, providing there wasn't too much traffic on the roads, and that the mistress didn't want to stop at Bonnington's on the way home.

She would hardly want to do that with a new baby, and tired after the long journey, Cook said. But Dixon said you could never tell with the mistress. After three months away she would want to see the shop just as much as she would want to see her children.

"If there's one thing wrong in one of the windows she'll notice it. And she'll have me trying to hold the horses quiet while she goes in to raise hell. That's the whole trouble, if you ask me," he added darkly. What trouble? Florence wondered miserably. "And another thing, she'll have the accounts sent up this evening, come hell or high water. Can't blame her, can you? These pair of nags has to be paid for, for one thing."

"Seems unnatural, a woman at business all the time," muttered Cook. "But if the master . . . if things were other than what they seem to be—now get on with you, Dixon, gossiping here. It isn't safe. That Miss Florence has ears that can hear through a six-foot wall."

It wasn't a six-foot wall, it was an open window, Florence thought contemptuously, and anyone could hear through that. She intended to slip away before Lizzie found her, but she was too late. Lizzie pounced on her, scolding that her sash was untied and her fingers black with soot from the windowsill.

"Listening *again,* Miss Florence. You are Miss Inquisitive, and no mistake. You'll hear all the news soon enough without trying to hear what Cook and Dixon have to say."

But that was just the trouble. She wouldn't hear. No one told her anything. They just passed her scraps of information that she had to try to fit together and make sense of. The object of all her listening had been to discover whether

her dear Miss Medway was coming back. It was a question to which she still had no answer.

At half past four, almost on the second, the carriage rolled up. Florence, who had been at her habitual place at the nursery window, shouted, "They're here! They're here!" and was down the stairs like a thunderbolt, Miss Sloane calling vainly to her to behave like a little lady. Edwin was only slower by virtue of his shorter legs, but both children were at the front door when it opened and Mamma came in, followed by a strange woman carrying the baby swathed in shawls. Papa slowly, and somehow reluctantly, brought up the rear.

Mamma was dressed in her familiar bottle-green traveling cloak, her round rosy cheerful face framed by her sensible black bonnet. It was possible that her face was a little less rosy and cheerful than usual, but Florence scarcely noticed this since she was so disappointedly aware that the woman carrying the baby was not Miss Medway.

"Well, children," Mamma said, "how well you are looking. Florence, you've grown quite two inches. And Edwin, my baby. Are you happy to have Mamma home? Laurette, show the children the new baby."

The young woman obediently parted the swathing of shawl, and displayed the little face, squeezed up in sleep.

It didn't look much of anything, Florence decided. Not even as interesting as one of her dolls. By the brisk way Mamma had spoken to the woman called Laurette, Florence suspected she felt much the same, as if babies were more of a nuisance than anything.

But, to her surprise, she realized Papa felt quite differently. For he was looking down at the little face with a dreamy expression on his own face, as if he already loved this pale-pink crumpled little thing. Had he looked like that when she and Edwin had been as small as this? Florence wondered. She wished she could remember. Because now he never took much notice of them.

"Oh, the children, of course," she used to hear him saying to Miss Medway. "I suppose they must come."

He thought they ran about too noisily, and disturbed the particular butterfly he might be stalking, Miss Medway had once explained. But even when they sat down in some quiet part of the Heath to have a picnic, he would say, "Can't you two find something to amuse yourselves with? Go and look for birds' nests, Edwin. Florence, can't you pick some flowers for your mother?"

He wasn't a man who cared much for children, Cook had said once, when Florence had confided in her. Some men were like that. Wait until she was a young lady. Then her Papa would take the greatest pride in her.

Even if she wasn't pretty? Florence had wondered agonizedly.

This new baby wasn't pretty, to her way of thinking, but somehow Papa looked as if he was going to have far more patience with it.

Of course it might cry a lot, and then he would lock himself in his study out of hearing. "He's a very selfish man, the master. Charming as he is, and all." That was another of Cook's remarks.

"And what's going on in that head?" said Papa to Florence, now, in his joking voice. He had once said Florence had a head like a dictionary. She quite clearly knew more than he did. That remark had been made when she was in one of her frowning thinking spells, which was often enough. He was probably hoping the new baby would never think at all.

"Isn't the baby jolly?" he went on, as if he thought someone ought to be talking. "She's like a little kitten. Now, Bea, wouldn't that be a better name for her? Kitty."

"She already has a name," said Mamma.

"What is it, Mamma?" Florence asked eagerly.

"It's Daisy. Papa thought it a little too simple, but I don't agree. There are some very beautiful women called Daisy. The Princess of Pless. The Countess of Warwick. It's by no means a servant's name, as Papa seemed to think."

Then something strange happened. Papa's eyes horrifyingly filled with tears. He turned away quickly, saying in a stiff voice, "You must be tired after your journey, Bea. Why don't you go up?"

Then the baby began to cry, and Mademoiselle Laurette exclaimed in very strange English, "She is 'ongry, madame. And tired. Where is meelk, and her bed?"

"The cradle! The cradle!" shouted Florence. "We got it out."

Mamma opened her mouth, then closed it, without saying anything. It seemed she had been about to object to the baby being put in the cradle, but Papa said firmly, "That means the family cradle, Laurette. I believe four generations of my family have slept in it. Florence, show Laurette the way to the night nursery."

Florence was delighted to charge up the stairs, leading Mademoiselle Laurette to the nursery and the cradle, complete with its sparkling white mattress and pillows, which Lizzie had prepared. It gave her something to do, and made her temporarily forget Mamma's strange behavior, and dear Miss Medway's absence.

Mademoiselle Laurette had a plain sallow face, and a most unbecoming hat. She looked tired and harassed, but not too tired to stare inquisitively at Florence and comment that she had expected a daughter of M'sieu Overton to be more petite, more ravishing, if Florence understood what she meant.

Florence understood all too well. She pushed her long limp hair behind her ears, and said, defiantly, that the baby wasn't very pretty either.

"Ah, but that is all you know of babies, mademoiselle. She is going to be a beauty, that one. That Mademoiselle Keetty!" Mademoiselle Laurette, who obviously already much preferred Papa to Mamma, went into a strange whicker of laughter.

"Are you going to stay here?" Florence asked apprehensively.

"Stay! *Mon Dieu*, no! I came only to assist on the journey. I will leave Mademoiselle Bébé in your care, Mademoiselle Florence. How is that, eh?"

Florence looked at the baby lying quietly in the cradle, and something did begin to stir in her heart. Something grown up and motherly. This was her little sister. It was her duty to look after her and protect her. Edwin, for instance, a great rough boy, should not be allowed near her. And it would be fun to dress her in pretty clothes. Mamma would take her to Bonnington's, and all the staff would gather around, reverently, to admire her. Miss Brown would bring out the most exquisite baby clothes. Florence would push the perambulator. She believed she was going to enjoy having a sister, after all.

"Will her name be Kitty?" Florence asked Mademoiselle

Laurette, and Mamma, unexpectedly behind her, answered in a cool firm voice, "No, Florence, it will be Daisy. That's already settled."

"And will Miss Medway come back to help me look after her?" Florence asked impulsively, mentioning that dear name at last.

But it was a mistake, because Mamma's face went stiff and she said coldly, "No, Florence, she won't be back. And I think I asked you once before to put her entirely out of your mind. She has other children to look after now, and you have Miss Sloane. I will be wanting a report on your lessons later."

"But, Mamma—"

"Silence, miss! You heard what I said."

Chapter 14

The journey home had been sufficient for Beatrice to discover that William was already daft about the baby.

He had never shown much more than a polite paternal
interest in Florence and Edwin. But with this new child
he was as fussy as a woman. Beatrice found the sight irritating beyond endurance. She realized that there were all
too many difficulties ahead.

But she would overcome them. She had the patience and,
she hoped, the wisdom. Eventually William must realize that
she was the kind of woman who would wear much better
than that governess whose name she was now determined to
forget.

The immediate crisis was past. All in all, it had gone
very well, considering its stupendous problems.

It was wonderful to be home again. Running her hand
over the glossy stair rail as she climbed the stairs to her
bedroom, Beatrice paused to look down into the hall with
its black-and-white tiled floors, its bowls of glowing autumn
leaves and chrysanthemums, its well-polished furniture,
and the good paintings on the paneled walls. She allowed
herself a moment of possessive pleasure.

She had come such a long successful way since her first
visit to this house. She had proved that what one wanted
enough one could get. Though at a price, and it was a
little disconcerting to find that the price kept increasing.
One thought it paid and the future secure, then a crisis
such as this one occurred and the bill mounted. But she would
never be bankrupt. She knew the resilience of her own
nature, and her total refusal to be defeated.

She would not discourage the pleasure the baby gave

William. It was even possible she would join in the baby
worship herself. Though unlikely.

Her immediate object was to have a husband again,
and none of this nonsense of separate rooms.

But that much-desired state of affairs might take a little
time and tact to achieve. In the meantime there was a great
deal to do and to discuss at the shop. On her visit this
afternoon (travel-stained and weary, and with William
fidgeting in the carriage), she had only hurried in and out.
But even in those brief moments she had seen that the
displays were a little tired and unimaginative, two elderly
well-dressed customers had not been offered chairs, a
young assistant at the glove counter had extremely untidy hair, the moss-green carpet was surely more dusty and
foot-marked than it should be by midafternoon.

After her long absence her eye may have been too critical.
But it was clearly time she was back. Tomorrow morning
Adam Cope would meet her in her office with a complete
set of figures for the last quarter's trading, and later she
would call a general meeting of buyers. She wanted that
Italian silk unpacked and displayed well in advance of
Christmas. She hoped young Mr. Brush had some clever
suggestions for Christmas window dressing. And no doubt
there were numerous staff problems.

It was good to be home. Soon she and William would
find a great deal more to talk about than they had done on
the journey. Anyway, she was much too busy to be lonely.
It occasionally occurred to her that where other women of
her age had many friends she had none. This, however,
did not unduly concern her. She had her family, her loyal
staff at Bonnington's, Hawkins who would have laid her
broomstick body across the threshold of her bedroom, if
necessary. What did she want with idle gossiping friends?
The life of desperate boredom her mother lived convinced
her of that.

"That baby doesn't take after you, Bea," Mamma had
said in her outspoken way. "She's going to be a beauty."

"Yes, she looks like William," Beatrice answered calmly.

It was true that the little thing did. The sparkling brown
eyes were a replica of William's. And the charm. Even
at ten weeks of age Baby's face lit up with smiles when an
admirer bent over her cradle. And there were too many

admirers. She was already well on the way to being shockingly spoiled.

Florence, unfortunately, was going to be put in the shade. The years had a way of going by, and one day, unless she had made her own life by then, it seemed certain that Miss Daisy Overton was going to outshine her elder sister.

"We'll meet that problem when it arises," Beatrice murmured to herself in the vulnerable hours of the night when doubts did assail her. Sometimes she wondered if it wouldn't have been better to have had the baby adopted at birth by strangers.

And lost William?

Although hadn't she already lost him, behind the firmly closed doors of the blue bedroom?

Patience, she said to herself yet again. I am right. I *must* be right.

Charles Stewart Parnell, ruined by a woman, was dead. Young Willie of Prussia, nephew of the Prince of Wales, was on the throne of Germany and William was uneasy about it. He didn't trust that young man. In a country that esteemed physical perfection above everything, the young prince had had to try so hard to compensate for his withered arm that his character had become warped. He was too ambitious, he admired that old warmonger Bismarck too much. Although his grandmother, Queen Victoria, still seemed to retain some affection for him. She, poor thing, stiffer than ever with rheumatism, had lost her precious youngest daughter and ewe lamb, Princess Beatrice, to a handsome husband. Bonnington's had had a hectic and stimulating time outfitting guests for that wedding.

The new Italian silks had been a triumphant success, and it was rumored, though it had not yet actually happened, that the elegant Princess Louise was coming to examine them and order a gown. The old queen got all her mantles from that haberdasher at Windsor, and was too old and too little interested in clothes to change her custom now. But it was said—this was another rumor—that she had much admired certain of the Princess Beatrice's wedding gifts in Italian leather, and Venetian glass, and had wanted to know where they could be obtained.

So Beatrice's foreign department was successfully established. Now, with Mr. Brush's clever help, she was plan-

ning a theatrical display with its theme those very successful operettas of Mr. Gilbert and Mr. Sullivan. *The Mikado*
provided material for the most colorful Oriental extravaganza of multi-colored silks, kimonos, Chinese porcelain
and jade. Even William commented on it.

"You're becoming a virtuoso, Bea," he said, and her
pleasure was quite out of proportion to the compliment.

"I deserve success, don't I?"

"You do."

"Then shouldn't we have an evening at the theater to
celebrate?" She had spoken impulsively, and now was
thinking quickly. She would wear that lovely Worth gown
hung away for too long, and this time William would
notice it, since there would be no rival to take his attention.

"By all means," William said amiably. "Why don't we
give Florence a treat? She's old enough to stay up, isn't
she?"

"I expect she is," Beatrice answered reluctantly, the
vision of their tête-à-tête evening gone. And Florence had
that deplorable tendency to be sick with excitement. But
if it pleased William to have his eldest daughter with them,
then his wishes must be indulged. It was enough that he
had agreed to go.

Finally, the theater outing became a family party, for
Mamma thought she would like to go, too, and this meant
the inclusion of the faithful though sadly bullied Miss
Finch.

It wasn't exactly what Beatrice had intended. However,
with William spending so many evenings at his club, this
was better than nothing.

They took a box, and rustled into it importantly just
before the curtain rose. Florence was put on one of the
little gilt chairs in the front so as to get an unimpeded view
of the stage.

She was deliriously happy. She had thought for a long
time that she was old enough for a night out, and it was
doubly gratifying that Edwin was to be left at home. She
promised him patronizingly that she would show him her
program.

She had a white dress trimmed with tiny pink rosebuds,
and a blue velvet cape. Her long fine hair, released from
knobbly rag curlers, looked very pretty spread over her

cape. She had just made the intoxicating and very feminine discovery that if you felt beautiful you were beautiful.

Everyone said that one day Miss Daisy would put Miss Florence's nose out of joint, but she had nothing to do with Florence's triumph tonight. Baby was fast asleep in her cradle, and Florence indulged in the fantasy that she was the prettiest child in London, at least, if not the world.

She sat on the edge of her chair and drank in the scene, the ladies with their bare shoulders and their sparkling jewels, the gentlemen in evening dress, though none more handsome than Mamma in her lovely lacy dress, and Papa looking smiling and happy as he hadn't done for a long time.

Grandmamma rustled in the background. Whenever she moved she creaked mysteriously, as if her bones were breaking (it was only her stays, Lizzie said). She was eating chocolates out of a box which Miss Finch held. Florence had been forbidden to eat any, in case of dire consequences, and neither Mamma nor Papa cared for them. Grandmamma, enormous in her rustling black taffeta, was probably glad that she could have the entire box to herself. The older she got, the greedier she got, saying frankly that she might as well enjoy her favorite food while she could still digest it. It was a pity she had chosen to enjoy it at the theater, for the sucking noises she made were irritating. But when at last the curtain went up and the glittering stage was spread before her dazzled eyes, Florence was aware of nothing else. She was in a trance of delight. She knew that she was going to remember this evening all her life.

Even though its happiness was to be so brief.

For in the first interval, Grandmamma suddenly said, "That Miss Medway. I thought you said she was with a family in Germany, Bea."

"In Switzerland, Mamma."

"Well, she isn't. I saw her in Flask Walk this morning." Mamma turned sharply.

"You must have been mistaken."

"Oh, no, there's nothing wrong with my eyesight. Is there, Finch?"

"No, Mrs. Bonnington, your eyesight is remarkable."

"There she was in that brown dress and a little bit of a bonnet. She always did dress neatly, I must say. She looked as if she was coming down from Overton House. Had she been calling?"

"No!" said Mamma in an explosive whisper that sent a queer tremor down Florence's spine. "You've made a mistake, Mamma. Miss Medway is in Zurich. Isn't she, William?"

Instead of answering, Papa did something quite extraordinary. He got up and walked out of the box, closing the door behind him, quietly, as if he didn't want to disturb anybody.

"Now what did I say to offend him?" Grandmamma grumbled. "Really, Bea, William is ridiculously touchy. He's not ill, is he?"

Before Mamma could answer, the curtain went up, and all the magic of the scene was there again. Papa was missing it. He really must hurry back or the play would be spoiled for him. When he didn't return, it was obviously spoiled for Mamma, and for Florence, too, for she could no longer concentrate on the stage. Her acute senses told her that something was very wrong, Papa mysteriously disappearing like this, and Mamma sitting stiffly with both her hands gripping her pretty feather fan. Beneath these worries, there was the fearful excitement that perhaps Grandmamma was speaking the truth, and Miss Medway really had come back.

If she had been outside Overton House, why hadn't she rung the doorbell and come in? Had she been too afraid of Mamma, for that mysterious reason never told to Florence and Edwin? But in that case, why come near the house at all?

When the lights came up at the end of the second act, Mamma said quietly, "Excuse me a moment. Florence, stay with Grandmamma," and she, too, left the box.

She had gone to look for Papa, of course.

"Men!" Grandmamma was muttering. "Self-centered wretches! Finch, isn't there a strawberry-flavored chocolate in this lot? Well, I hope they come back before the lights go down."

Mamma came back alone. She said to Florence, "Papa wasn't feeling well and has taken a cab home. We must wait until the end, otherwise we'll miss Dixon."

She said this in a voice of restrained impatience, as if she were afraid the third act would last forever.

"How do you *know* about Papa being ill?" Florence whispered agonizedly.

"The doorman told me he'd called a cab. He left a message for us."

But Florence, who sometimes, regrettably, was forced into telling lies, was fairly well able to detect lies in others. She knew Papa hadn't left the theater because he was ill. He had gone to look for Miss Medway. In the dark. And now they were both lost.

"She's overtired, that's all," Mamma said to Lizzie, handing over the damp sobbing Florence. "The excitement has been too much for her. Get her into bed and make her drink some hot milk. It was a mistake to take her, I'm afraid. She's still too young for the theater."

Not a word about Papa being lost. Not a word about Dixon driving home with four ladies, and Papa's seat empty. Florence's sobs had swollen her throat so much that she couldn't speak. Anyway, by this time she was in such a nervous state that she was afraid to ask whether Papa was home, or whether his bedroom, like his seat in the carriage, was empty.

"It will all sort itself out in the morning," Lizzie was saying cheerfully.

Papa going away with Miss Medway? That was the fear that made Florence cry so much. Because she had known for a long time that Mamma would never allow Miss Medway in the house again.

Soon after her return from Italy with the new baby, Florence stubbornly had raised the subject again, but the answer had been chilling.

"Florence, I am asking you and Edwin never to mention that name again." Then Mamma had added more calmly, "It's hurtful to Miss Sloane, being always reminded that someone else was your favorite governess. Now don't look so tragic. These things happen in life. People come and people go."

The more reasonable voice hadn't erased the shock of Mamma's first sharp not-to-be-disobeyed order. Florence had only been able to conclude that Miss Medway had done something bad. Although obviously Papa didn't think so, or he wouldn't have gone in search of her tonight.

Would he ever come back?

Florence's tears trickled into her pillow. She heard the crackle of Lizzie's starched apron, and the hissing of the little spirit lamp as the milk was heated. Safe familiar nursery sounds that made her aching eyes fall shut.

Perhaps this had all been a dream, the theater, Papa's disappearance, everything. At least, she thought with glum satisfaction, she hadn't been sick.

In the early hours of the morning the door of the blue bedroom banged shut. By then the servants had long ago been sent to bed, told that the master had gone on from the theater to his club, and only Beatrice, lying sleepless, heard that reassuring bang.

Like Florence she, too, had been afraid that William had disappeared, never to return.

Three o'clock in the morning was not an hour for wisdom. Anxiety and grief had taken its place.

Beatrice knocked softly at William's door, then louder.

"William, it's me. I hope your door isn't locked."

His voice came draggingly.

"For heaven's sake, of course it isn't."

She went in then, and saw him seated at his writing desk writing something by lamplight. She had meant to say, "Where have you been, what have you been doing?" but instead the suspicious words shot out, "What are you writing?"

"A letter."

"At this hour of night?"

He was still dressed in evening clothes. He looked achingly tired and hollow-cheeked. His eyes had a look of burning intensity.

"It's to a hotel in Rome."

He waved the sheet of letter paper at her, showing the heading in his fine handwriting. "The manager, Grand Hotel. . . ." The unspoken thought that it was not a letter to Mary Medway hung between them.

"Are you going away?"

"I thought so."

"Perhaps it's a good idea."

What *was* she to say, faced by his haunted eyes?

"Mamma could have been mistaken, you know," she said.

He nodded slightly. Then he said almost inaudibly, "It would be the baby she came back to see. If she did come.

She wouldn't break her word otherwise."

"She has no right even to see the baby," Beatrice cried furiously.

He moved away from the light so that his face became shadowed, his expression unreadable.

"William, you must forget her!"

"Don't ask the impossible, Bea. I've done everything else."

"Only because she asked it. Not because I asked it. And not of your own accord." The bitter jealous words escaped, and it seemed as if he were never going to answer them.

But he did, eventually. And then she wished he had never spoken, for he hurt her unbearably.

"I thought you knew about love," he said.

She *did* know about love. But another kind from his, the strong enduring kind which had nothing to do with this romantic fancy from which he was suffering. That was all it was, a romantic attachment aggravated by deprivation.

He must not think her an unfeeling monster. She was only acting for the good of them all. Time, that slow-footed dragging old time, would tell. If only they were both ten years older and this agony dimmed and forgotten.

"It's best you go away, dearest," she said, with infinite tenderness.

A week later he left, and the very next day the new nursemaid, Hilda, told Lizzie a young woman had taken ever such a fancy to Baby when she had been wheeling her down Heath Street. The woman had stopped to look in the perambulator, and Baby had crowed at her, little angel that she was. But then everybody admired Miss Daisy. This event wasn't unusual enough to tell the mistress.

Which was a pity, because if she had done so, what followed might have been prevented.

Two days later Hilda, with Lizzie and Florence and Edwin, wheeled Daisy in her perambulator into the Heath where there was a little crowd gathered around the striped tent of a Punch-and-Judy show.

Fascinated by the little frenzied, gabbling puppets, the children pressed closer. Edwin clapped excitedly. When the performance was finished he wanted to stay to watch another one, and shrieked when Lizzie dragged him away.

"Little monster, ain't you?" she said good-humoredly.

Florence, a little behind in the crowd, thought Edwin shrieked again, but this time it was Hilda.

"Mother of Mercy!" she was crying in a distraught voice. "The baby's gone!"

It was true. The perambulator was empty, as if Daisy, not quite three months old, but very bright for her age, had clambered out and walked away.

Hilda might be inclined to go into hysterics, but Lizzie was practical and quick-thinking. She saw a policeman on the edge of the crowd and pushed over to him with her extraordinary story.

"The gypsies has stolen the baby!" she gasped. "Come quick, officer."

"Was the child left unattended?" the policeman asked, as he examined the perambulator, the cozy nest of blankets, the hollow in the pillow where Daisy's head had lain.

"We was only watching Punch and Judy," Lizzie said. "We only had our backs turned for five minutes."

"Time enough, it seems," said the policeman. "And what makes you think it's gypsies who have stolen your child?"

"She isn't my child, officer. She's Miss Daisy Overton from the big house in Heath Street. I'm only the nursemaid. This is Miss Florence and Master Edwin. They'll tell you we had Miss Daisy five minutes ago. And it's always gypsies that steal babies, isn't it?"

"Not necessarily, madam."

Lizzie gave a high-pitched giggle at being called madam, and the policeman waved back the crowd collecting curiously.

"Keep back, if you please. Now did anyone here see anything suspicious, such as someone making off with a baby out of this vehicle?"

Florence thought she heard a faint little cackle of laughter, an echo of the Punch-and-Judy show. Then an old man, very raggedly dressed and dirty, the sort of person Florence had always been strongly warned against, said he had seen a young woman carrying a baby. "A nice decent-looking young 'un," he said. "But it looked like her own babby she was cuddlin'."

"Where did she go?"

The old man pointed a disgracefully dirty finger.

"Toward village."

The cold winter sun shone through a mist on the innocent Heath. Florence was shivering, her feet were frozen. Hilda had overcome her hysterics but was still beyond speech. It was left to Lizzie, goggle-eyed but reasonably calm, to obey the policeman's orders and take the children home.

He himself was going to wheel the empty perambulator. He looked very silly, such a big man, in his policeman's helmet, pushing a pram. He was taking it down to the station, he said. He or one of his colleagues would be around to Overton House in a little while. Lizzie was to tell the children's parents to be available.

"The master's abroad," Lizzie said. "The mistress is at the shop."

"Then get her home, my good woman."

Dixon said he would drive hell-for-leather with the terrible news. Miss Daisy stolen! It wasn't to be believed. Who had been careless, Lizzie or Hilda, or both of them?

But who was to think you could lose a baby in broad daylight? Cook and Annie and Hawkins had never heard the likes.

"It can't be gypsies. That's just Lizzie's imagination. It's a deliberate kipnapping," said Miss Sloane, who seemed to know about such bizarre matters. "There'll be ransom money demanded. This isn't a rich house, such as the Duke of Devonshire's, for instance, but it's rich to a lot of people."

Miss Sloane had what Cook disapprovingly called "a touch of Socialism," whatever that was, Florence found that her numb toes and fingers had prevented her ability to think. She only wanted to cry for dear sweet vanished Daisy, though that would do no good at all, Miss Sloane said in her dry unsympathetic way.

The first thing Mamma said, when she burst out of the carriage and ran indoors, was that Papa was not to be telegraphed for. Not yet, at least. Daisy would be found in a matter of hours and Papa would have been worried for nothing.

Then she was shut in the library with two policemen for a long time, and when she came out she said briskly to the servants who were gathered in the hall, "We mustn't be too worried. We're perfectly certain Daisy is being well cared for by—by this woman. We don't think it's a kid-napping for money, just the act of some unbalanced person."

"Why would this woman take *our* baby?" asked Cook indignantly.

"She's probably childless, poor thing. Some women get a little strange about that. It's good of you all to be concerned, but now get back to your work. I have every confidence in the police. Baby will be home before night."

She was upset, though, for all her pretended calm. Her cheeks were bright pink, her eyes had an uncomfortable staring look. She saw Florence and Edwin because she spoke to them, but Florence knew all she was seeing, really, was that woman running off with Daisy in her arms.

"Miss Sloane, take the children to the nursery and read to them, or play games with them. Lizzie, you go, too. Turn on the lights. It will be dark, soon." A visible shudder swept over her, as if she were imagining poor little Daisy outdoors in the chilly misty dusk. Then she took Florence's hand and motioned her toward Miss Sloane. "Run along, dear. Do as I ask."

Her hand on Florence's was stone cold, like a dead person's. Like Grandmamma Overton's, which Nanny Blair had made Florence touch before the coffin was closed.

Fear shivered through her. She began to sob, saying in a loud grieved voice that she wanted Miss Medway, it wasn't fair that Miss Medway whom she dearly loved had gone away.

"B-baby would n-never have been stolen if Miss M-Medway was here," she stuttered.

"Be quiet!" Florence jumped at the anger in Mamma's voice. She obediently snuffled into silence. "Such nonsense!" said Mamma. "Go to the nursery at once."

Later Doctor Lovegrove, wearing his familiar frock coat and tall hat, came into the firelit nursery. Someone must have fetched him. He felt Florence's forehead, looked at the wreck of the battlefield where Edwin had been conducting a screaming battle, and said in his deep jovial voice, "I think small soothing drafts for you two whipper-snappers. A couple of drops of this in a glass of milk, Lizzie. Give 'em pleasant dreams."

"And Baby?" Florence asked quiveringly.

"Oh, Baby's been found, didn't you know? She's fine and dandy."

It was after midnight, but Beatrice was still sitting in the library struggling over the letter that must be written to William.

She would dearly like to have kept silent about the whole dreadful affair, but it wasn't possible. Her husband must come home, the police officer had said. He would probably be needed at the trial.

The trial!

Young woman charged with kipnapping baby with felonious intent. . . .

She had protested that she had only wanted the baby for a night, a few hours even. She had intended to return it unharmed. No, she had no children of her own. She was unmarried.

Mary Medway's tragic eyes glittering in her luminously white face came between Beatrice and the letter she was attempting to write.

Even in those dire straits Mary had kept to her peculiar code of honor. She had not betrayed William or given her child the brand of illegitimacy.

Beatrice guessed that she was simply torn to pieces by loneliness and longing. Her reason had given way.

But in the silent library, with the fire burned to ashes, Beatrice gripped the pen in determined fingers, and her mouth tightened. Here was no room for softness. The girl was mischievous, a felon, perhaps dangerous because of her unbalanced mental state.

She must be committed to an institution simply to save herself from some further crime.

Daisy, fortunately, had suffered nothing more serious than an overdue meal. She had been yelling angrily from hunger when found.

"The police were quite remarkably efficient in discovering where Miss Medway had taken our baby," she wrote to William. "She had been seen hurrying down Downshire Hill, and had gone into one of the small cottages at the bottom where she had taken a room. Several people had noticed her, since it is unusual to see a woman running with a baby in her arms. She wasn't as clever as one would have expected her to be, but perhaps it was scarcely surprising, in her confused mental state. Her one idea seemed to be to get Daisy to herself for a little while. It is all very sad and I am unutterably grieved at having to inflict this pain on you. However, it will soon be over. . . ."

It was not, of course. It was a wound that seemed as if it would never heal.

Mary Medway was committed to Holloway Prison for eighteen months, sentence to be reduced to one year on good conduct.

She was safely out of the way temporarily, Beatrice told herself, and one could only try not to be vicious and wish that she were removed permanently. Transported to Australia, or something.

Because no one except Daisy had been quite the same since that disastrous day on the Heath.

Nothing now would induce Florence to watch a Punch-and-Judy show; she was even nervous of going on the Heath for a walk, and clung to Lizzie, Lizzie said, like a regular limpet. She had never been a demonstrative child, but now she didn't seem to care for anybody, and was even jealous of innocent Baby. Why wasn't it her who had been stolen, she demanded, not a new baby whom Miss Medway didn't even know?

Edwin, who had never cared for discipline, grew more rumbustious as Florence became quieter, and it was obvious that he would have to be sent off to school in the near future. Seven was not a bit too young, his father said. Besides, he was backward at his lessons and one assumed he would respond better to a master than to Miss Sloane. It seemed that he could scarcely read yet, which was a deplorable state of affairs. Though Lizzie said he peered too closely at the pages, as if he couldn't see properly.

William, after the trial in the Old Bailey which had lasted only a few hours, to be sure, but which had seemed an eternity, had come down with a bad chest cold that later turned to pneumonia. He was dangerously ill, and in delirium kept calling out, "Don't let her go down those stairs!" Beatrice knew all too well what he meant. He had had to watch the melancholy sight of Mary Medway going down the stairs from the dock, leading to the cells, after being sentenced.

She had had a fair trial, and the services of a brilliant defense counsel, who had been engaged and paid by William, a fact which Beatrice knew, though did not comment on.

She didn't resent it. Indeed, it eased her own conscience. She, too, wanted to be absolutely fair.

Nursing her husband and coaxing him back to life and some sort of cheerfulness was an all-absorbing task that gave Beatrice no time to brood. Otherwise she might have wanted to curse Mary Medway for the unhappiness she had brought into their home.

All the same, with her usual uncomfortable honesty, she asked herself if the unhappiness were Miss Medway's fault entirely.

Hadn't the seeds been sown when she herself had so willingly and optimistically entered into a marriage of convenience, and then ruined its slender chance of success by being too overbearing, too confident, too possessive? Was she the kind of woman who should have confined herself solely to a career in business, for which she was eminently well suited? Had her strong and determined nature had the effect of killing love rather than nurturing it? Trying to shape someone to her will—were the far-reaching effects even going to harm innocent children?

Those thoughts were too disastrous to believe. She simply could not allow herself to believe them.

What about her understanding, her tact, her patience, her lack of recrimination, her uncomplaining loneliness?

Were these qualities which simply did not appeal to a man? Or were they too obscured by her "Queen Bea" tendency?

She must take stock of herself as factually as she took stock in Bonnington's. Unwanted characteristics must be thrown out, more appealing ones cultivated. She must mold herself into being the kind of woman who was acceptable to William's sensitive, romantic spirit.

At least she was humbly grateful that he did not seem to object to her nightly vigil at his bedside. Once he stretched out his hand and took hers in a hot dry clasp. He may still have been delirious, even though he murmured her name. But her natural ebullient optimism was rising. She took it as a sign of his not actually hating her. That was something. Under the circumstances, it was really a very great deal.

Chapter 15

After plunging into mourning for the untimely death of Prince Eddy, who had been betrothed to Princess Mary of Teck, only a year later Bonnington's was bedecked in flags and bunting. It had been decided to marry the Princess Mary to Prince Eddy's younger brother George, and the handsome, phlegmatic young lady had apparently made the adjustment without too much difficulty.

The bizarre situation suited Bonnington's very well. They had been able to sell not only a lot of mourning clothes, top hats, black veils, et cetera, but now had the more cheerful task of dressing wedding guests.

It was midsummer, and just the weather for royal panoply, with the trees in Hyde Park a lush green and the lawns like watered silk. It had been a wonderful summer for roses. A deputation from Bonnington's had been up very early that day and bought hundreds of blooms from the Covent Garden flower market with which to decorate the shop entrance. Mostly white, Beatrice had ordered. As symbols of purity, virginity, innocence and so on, though one wondered if the princess were full of rapture about her second attempt at marriage into the British royal family.

Beatrice, with no intention of leaving the shop to join the thousands lining the route of the wedding procession, nevertheless felt a sympathetic rapport with the stiff, shy royal bride. She would have liked to have told her that marriages for convenience could be a great success, although requiring patience and self-sacrifice. And, it need hardly be said, a dedicated and durable love.

Florence and Edwin had been permitted to go to watch the procession, so long as both Miss Sloane and Lizzie

164

accompanied them and never let them out of their sight. Baby, naturally, was much too young although she had begun both walking and talking at a precociously early age.

Beatrice hadn't discovered what William intended doing. He was so obstinately uncommunicative nowadays, and, in spite of all the small entertainments Beatrice arranged (she had never learned to enjoy being a hostess and only made herself sit cheerfully through the dinner parties and musical soirees for William's sake), he still wore his vague haunted air. So romantic, the ladies murmured. But why so *triste?*

At least, Princess Mary of Teck wouldn't have a Mary Medway in her life, Beatrice thought. Or one hoped not.

For a prison sentence came to an end, and then one would begin living on tenterhooks again, constantly watchful of Daisy, constantly looking for a slim dark-haired figure lurking in the streets outside Overton House.

Beatrice could not mention her fears to William, for it had become impossible to talk to him about anything except the most superficial things. It was not that he was not courteous and mild-mannered; simply that, behind his gentle smile and his handsome face, she could sense nothing but blankness.

She knew that he was happiest when dandling Daisy on his knee. That was a private pain about which she could do nothing. She refused to be jealous of a child.

Or to worry about William's frequent absences which he never explained. He was at his club, walking on the Heath, at an art exhibition, calling on his publisher, he indicated vaguely. He had another book under commission; he was doing research for that at the London Library and the British Museum.

In other words he was leading his own life. As she was, perforce, leading hers.

The last decade of the nineteenth century was a time of great prosperity for the middle classes. The cotton mills in the Midlands, the coal mines and the iron- and steelworks in Wales were showing handsome profits. More and more people had carriages and servants, country mansions, expensive wardrobes. They were the *nouveaux riches* whom fashionable stores cultivated. Of course there could be strikes in the mills or the mines, an uprising somewhere in the old queen's vast untidy empire, or a war on its bor-

ders that would spoil things a bit, but at present all was
well, and the sun could shine on the splendor of an important royal occasion.

Since little business was done on a day like this, Beatrice spent her time usefully down in the basement store-
rooms, discussing stock. She liked to have her finger on
everything. She walked between the piled-up shelves, a
decisive little figure inclined to plumpness. She was going
to bear quite a resemblance to Queen Victoria in a few
years if she kept putting on weight. Queen Bea. She had
a cold stare when annoyed or angry, but a warm sympathetic look when things pleased her, and a jolly laugh.
In her thirties, she was more attractive than she had been
in her twenties, having more confidence and poise, and
proving that in spite of her formidable abilities she could
remain pleasantly feminine.

Adam Cope thought her remarkable, as he had always
done. She was a phenomenon in modern society, a successful businesswoman and a wife and mother.

Not a popular phenomenon among men who regarded
her as having begun a new and dangerous fashion, and
therefore being a traitor to her sex.

It was only her husband who didn't seem to mind. But
then he had his pockets comfortably lined, hadn't he?
And he was an extravagant indolent fellow who liked the
best of everything.

He also had other ways of amusing himself, if rumors
were to be believed.

It seemed that he still had the philandering tendencies
of his youth, with one important difference. Now he sought
a different kind of woman. In other words, his taste had
become depraved. He was frequently to be seen in the
squalid areas of Balham and Wandsworth, driving his fast
cob in the phaeton which he preferred to a carriage and
coachman. That preference answered itself, didn't it? He
wanted to be alone; he couldn't have a family servant
knowing his destination.

Nor his wife, who had heard nothing of these rumors.
No one saw fit to tell her, partly from kindness, partly
because William Overton looked so infernally miserable
over his philandering.

But someone would tell her someday, if she didn't find
out for herself.

Well, the marriage had been an awkward one, and no one had thought it would be particularly happy.

At the end of that summer day Beatrice took home a large bouquet of the white roses, wilted only slightly by the heat. She would arrange them in a bowl on the dinner table, and perhaps the air of festivity would make William less withdrawn and preoccupied.

There was a letter awaiting her on her arrival home. It had been delivered by hand, Annie said. It was addressed in heavy black masculine handwriting, and just looking at it gave Beatrice one of her uncanny and accurate intuitions. She knew who it was from although the handwriting was unfamiliar.

She tore it open, and extracted the thick sheet of paper.

DEAR MRS. OVERTON,
This is to inform you that the prisoner Medway was released at 11 a.m. today. You asked me to apprise you of this fact when it happened, and I am so doing.
I have the honor to be, madam,
Your obedient servant,
J. J. BROWNE
Governor of Holloway Prison for Women.

"Is there something wrong, ma'am?" Annie asked.

Beatrice crushed the letter in her hand.

"No, Annie. Just a small business matter. Tell Cook to put dinner back half an hour. The master may be late."

Or he may not come home at all. . . .

Because she was almost certain a great many of William's absences could have been accounted for if she had liked to follow him on what she presumed were his fortnightly or weekly visits to Holloway jail.

She hadn't followed him and she hadn't asked questions. But this simply could not go on.

When dinner was announced at eight thirty, she went in and ate alone, watching the white roses shedding petals on the polished table. She was still sitting there an hour later when William came in.

He sat down, looking desperately tired, and said quickly

that she was not to ring, because he didn't want anything to eat.

"Please don't argue," he said, in a strange gray voice. "I know when I can eat and when I can't."

"But, darling, what is it? Are you ill?"

Anxiety for him, as always, had overridden her jealousy. She looked hard at his lips because they were so pale, not because they might have been all too recently kissed.

"No, it's not I who's ill, Bea. It's—" His lips trembled violently. "She's dying, dammit, she's dying!"

"Who?" Beatrice said stupidly, knowing without the least doubt what he would answer.

"Mary, of course. Who else? They released her today because they didn't want her to die in prison. That would have been a bit of trouble for them. So they pushed her out, and she can scarcely walk."

"Oh, William, how dreadful! Is there nothing we can do?"

"She's dying of consumption. She's known it for months. So have I. I've been visiting her every week."

"I know."

His haggard face shot up.

"You knew!"

"Never mind. I knew. Or I guessed."

"But you didn't say anything."

"Should I have? I thought you might feel I had inter-fered enough."

"But I've never blamed you. Only myself. Oh, God, this is hopeless!"

"Hopeless for poor Mary Medway, if what you say is true. Where is she now?"

"I've got her into a small nursing home. It's run by nuns. They seem kind. Anyway it isn't for long. A few weeks at the most. Tomorrow perhaps. It was that damned prison, the cold and the damp and the bad food. I've been appealing for months to get her out. Now they've let her out, but it's too late."

"William—"

He winced as she came around the table to him. "Don't touch me, Bea!"

She stiffened, in shock and anger. She wasn't his enemy. She was only intensely grieved for his suffering, and gen-uinely appalled by the tragedy of that slim gentle young woman who was to die so young. Yet a dreadful exultant feeling was rising in her. Was she wicked, and heartless, to be conscious of such exquisite relief at this moment? It seemed to her that God was ending this tragic story in the only way possible.

It was surely God, not she, who was slowly killing Mary Medway.

When she was dead, William would be able to weep for her, and then forget her. Dead, she would be so much easier to forget, than alive.

Chapter 16

For the rest of Florence's childhood (she regarded that as over when she became twelve years of age), Papa was mostly away. Which was a pity as far as Edwin was concerned, because he was in fairly frequent trouble at his preparatory school. He needed his father's firm hand, Florence heard Miss Sloane saying to Lizzie, and Lizzie answered, "Across his backside, the young devil."

Actually Florence knew that Edwin hated boarding school and behaved badly because he was unhappy. On one dreadful occasion he was almost expelled for cheating. The headmaster, because of certain mitigating circumstances, finally decided on a caning, and Edwin, much to his disgust, was reprieved. He had secretly hoped to be expelled.

Mamma said later that the mitigating circumstances were the medical report they had just had on Edwin's eyes. It appeared that he had never been able to see clearly because of shortsightedness. This was the reason for his perplexing slowness in learning. No one had suspected it. The poor boy had had to peer at a blurred blackboard, and been driven to cheating to get through his examinations.

Now he would have to wear spectacles, which was a disaster, not so much because they spoiled his handsome looks, but because it meant the end of his ambitions for a distinguished career in the army. He had badly wanted to be a soldier.

When he had come home on his last school vacation he had packed all his battered and shabby lead soldiers into boxes and put them in the cabinet with his grandfather's famous collection. The spectacles he wore seemed to have given him a completely different personality. An owlish little boy now, he stood gazing silently at the serried ranks of Grandpapa's British Grenadiers and Hussars, the French cuirassiers, the Russian bearskins, the Irish and Scottish Guards, the Gordon Highlanders, the turbaned Indian Sikhs and the squat strong Gurkhas, the war-horses and artillery, cannonballs, rifles, and sabers.

Edwin had been allowed to play with this superb collection twice a year, on his birthday and on Christmas Day. He didn't think he would want to play with it again, he said. He was tired of soldiers.

Florence supposed it must be disappointing to have to change one's life ambition, but Edwin didn't need to be quite so silent and miserable about it. Now he could go into Bonnington's and help Mamma. But it seemed that Edwin was deeply opposed to that. Somewhere, at that silly school probably, he had heard that gentlemen weren't shopkeepers, and Edwin was turning into a dreadful snob.

Besides, he couldn't add. He was catching up fast with his reading now that he could see properly, but he had no talent for figures. And he thought buying and selling the greatest bore possible.

Now that he was a schoolboy and imagining himself superior in every way, he refused to go near the shop, even when there had been that wonderful display for the queen's jubilee.

Mamma had spent thousands of pounds having dummies made to represent the peoples of the far-flung empire, Indian maharajas gleaming with jewels, warriors with spears from South Africa and the Gold Coast, Maoris in flax skirts from New Zealand, little brown Malays from Singapore, Egyptians from the Suez Canal area, and ebony natives from the British West Indies. The newspapers called it a tour de force, and there was a photograph of Mamma alighting from her brougham outside Bonnington's, captioned "Another monarch surveying her empire?"

Edwin told Florence that he was ragged terribly at school about it.

"You should have been proud!" Florence cried.

"Of being in trade?" Edwin said in his new supercilious voice. "If you want to know, I get ragged because my mother has to go out to work."

"Well, what of it? I intend to go out to work, too."

Florence had no such intention. She wanted only to be married and have as many children as possible.

"You'll probably have to," he said unkindly. "Who would marry you?"

Florence had to restrain herself from rushing at him and pulling his hair out. She was too old for that sort of thing now. But he really was odious, and who would marry him?

However, when Papa resolved Edwin's career by deciding that he should go to Winchester, then Oxford, and then into the Foreign Office, he seemed a little less unhappy about being denied the danger and glory of a soldier's life. But the sulky bespectacled youth was no longer Mamma's "pretty boy," and he seemed upset about that even if he was much too big for such babyish treatment. Florence could have told him that Mamma had always loved Papa better than either of them, and that they were extremely tiresome when they took up time which she would have preferred to spend with Papa. Yet they had not been allowed to keep Miss Medway, whom they had loved. Which had been bewildering and painful, but it was all a long time ago.

She was grateful that she had her small sister on whom to lavish affection. Daisy, small-boned, light-footed, capricious and enchanting, roused a strong maternal feeling in her. Since Mamma was out so much, and had as little time to spend with Daisy as she had had with Florence and Edwin, Florence privately decided to take over Daisy's upbringing. She instructed, scolded and adored. She didn't even resent Papa's obvious preference for his youngest child, since who could resist such an entrancing creature?

As Florence entered her teens and grew awkward, shy and diffident, and Edwin became more aloof and uncommunicative when home from school, it was little wonder that such a merry little thing as Miss Daisy was worshiped by everybody. Spoiled, too, except by her mother and, oddly enough, Miss Brown who had always been prepared to unreservedly admire any of Miss Beatrice's children. But Miss Brown was growing testy with age, and was quickly irritated by lively small children. She said that she was afraid Miss Daisy was quite unscrupulous about getting her own way, and someone would pay for that little habit someday.

It was true that all doors opened to Miss Daisy Overton. Even her father, no matter how important it was for him to stay abroad for his health or his work, always came home for her birthday. Which wasn't entirely fair, since he had been known to forget both Miss Florence's and Master Edwin's.

But Miss Daisy, the little foreign baby as the servants still called her (and she did sometimes seem foreign, with her chattering vivacity and her restlessness), brought her Papa home like a magnet.

It was galling to have to be grateful to a child, Beatrice thought more than once.

"It's your own fault, Bea," her own mother said frequently in her grumbling voice. "You spend altogether too much time at business. It's unnatural for a wife. Look at me, I scarcely left the house when your father was alive."

And grew as dull as ditchwater and drove Papa to his account books night after night. . . .

"I have a great many people to support, Mamma," Beatrice said mildly. "I have a hundred and fifty employees as well as my family. We're sending Edwin to Winchester and Oxford, did you know? And Florence must have a season. She wants it very much. She's completely conventional."

"And a very good thing, too."

"But it's a pity she hasn't better looks. However, one hopes that by seventeen she'll be greatly improved. Did you see that Princess Louise took the queen's drawing room the other day? She's quite the most elegant of the princesses. I believe the queen is failing quite seriously. It would be nice if she lived long enough for Florence to be presented, wouldn't it?"

"I hardly think it will mar the end of her life if she is deprived a glimpse of your daughter, Bea. But I'm glad you're doing the right thing by Florence. I was always disappointed you weren't presented after your marriage. But by that time your father had you in the shop, and there you were determined to stay. Are you putting on weight, child? You're beginning to look like a pincushion."

"I still have my twenty-four-inch waist."

"Well, don't let yourself go, dear. William wouldn't care for that."

If he ever noticed her rounded bosom and hips, her neat waist, and her clear skin. Some men did. Indeed she had an increasing number of admirers now that she had become something of a personality. She was no longer regarded with resentment as an intruder in a man's world, but as a deuced spirited little creature, and an amusing eccentric. That languid fellow Overton had done far better than he deserved, was the general opinion.

Added to these compliments which came to Beatrice in a roundabout way, she had recently received the biggest compliment of all. As the head of Bonnington's, she had at last been granted the royal warrant of appointment. It was high time this had happened, everyone said, considering Bonnington's many visible displays of loyalty to the throne, quite apart from the goods supplied to the royal household.

So now it was permitted that the royal arms be hung above the front doors. The erection of that plaque was one of the proudest moments of Beatrice's life. She kept wishing that Papa had been there to see it.

And William. But William was in Italy, and anyway he wouldn't have been profoundly interested. Disappointingly, Edwin wasn't interested either. He thought it a tradesman's sort of thing.

But Daisy clapped excitedly, because she always unfailingly sensed jubilation and high spirits, and Florence said that her best friend Cynthia Fielding was quite impressed.

William did write to congratulate her, however. He said he was very happy for her, it was so satisfactory to achieve an ambition, and that he would be home for Daisy's birthday. He was feeling extremely fit, he had progressed with his current book, and thought that he would spend the winter at home.

It was six years since Mary Medway's death.

On his first evening home William said diffidently that he was finding the blue room rather chilly, he didn't care for its northern aspect. Perhaps he would claim his half of their bed again. If she had no objection.

Objection!

Beatrice, overcome with surprise, burst out laughing.

"It must be because Mamma said I was looking like a pincushion. Not prickly, but too rotund."

"A charming pincushion, my dear," he said with his faint quirky smile. Sadness still lingered in his eyes, and he had a fine-drawn look that was moving and intensely exciting.

Beatrice found that she had to be flippant, otherwise her rapidly growing emotions would explode. She was so filled with pity for his shy tentativeness, with grateful love and surprise and joy, and, overriding all, her long-suppressed sexuality.

But she found enough remaining sense not to burden him with words of love.

"That is if the royal arms aren't affixed to the bedhead," he said.

"Come and see for yourself."

She was as light-footed as a girl on the stairs. Even Daisy was not lighter.

But in the bedroom, in the dusk, he only said, "I'm so lonely, Bea," and she knew that there was still a long way to go.

Yet not an impossible distance. He had turned to her of his own free will. He was in her arms again, and he found her physically pleasing. She had enough remaining sense to recognize that, too.

Chapter 17

"My father isn't strong," Florence told her friend Cynthia Fielding. "He's always had to spend a lot of time in milder climates. But it fits in very well because he has to do so much research abroad, in museums and art galleries. He's writing a book on medieval art. He's been working on it for simply ages. He hates finishing a book, he says. It becomes like a child to him. But that's a good thing, really, because it keeps him happily occupied while my mother's at the shop."

"Lucky you, getting all your blankets and table linen and things for nothing."

"Do we? I suppose we do. Sordid commerce!" Florence giggled. "Now I sound like Edwin whom I despise for being a snob. Cynthia, you will come to my ball, won't you?"

"Of course I will, if you ask me."

"I was only thinking . . . some people think we're just in trade, you know. But Overton House has been in Papa's family for generations, and the Overtons have mostly been terribly respectable. All those generals and admirals with their decorations. That cancels out the trade side a bit, doesn't it? Mamma says there hasn't been a real ball here since my Aunt Caroline died when she was only seventeen. She would have been a great beauty, they said. Daisy's supposed to be like her, but I'm not."

"You're a great rattle, Flo dear," Cynthia said.

"Only with people I know well." Florence sighed. "I get paralyzed in company, because I know I'm always being compared unfavorably to Daisy. How on earth am I to be a success at my own coming-out ball?"

"Shall I bring Desmond?"

"Your brother? Would you really? That would be the

greatest help because Mamma keeps complaining that I don't know enough young men."

"Desmond isn't good-looking. None of us Fieldings are, with our big noses." Actually that was one reason why Cynthia was Florence's friend, because she wasn't inhibitingly glamorous. "But he looks rather well in full-dress uniform. His regiment is leaving for India shortly, that's the only trouble."

"I expect he's a mad philanderer."

"Desmond! Oh, no, he has *ideals* about women! Isn't it killing! But he's only nineteen and regimental life will cure that nonsense, Papa says."

"I don't think it's nonsense at all. I think it's rather nice."

"Having ideals? Except for the women who have to live up to them. Does your mother, for instance? Because your father looks madly romantic and idealistic."

Florence frowned. She was anxious to be absolutely honest.

"I don't think Papa would have put Mamma on a pedestal. I mean, she's so practical, and she couldn't ever have been beautiful. Papa must have married her for her good qualities. And her money, of course."

Florence had once heard a customer in Bonnington's say to her friend, "If you could think of her without all that money she'd look like somebody's cook," and she had known indignantly that it was Mamma who was being discussed. Well, it was all too true that Papa liked spending money, but he was also fond of Mamma. Anyway, he was in his early forties, and so was Mamma. Who would be expecting romance at that age?

"Everyone says Daisy will be married for her looks," Florence went on, rather wistfully. "With me, it will have to be my money if Mamma gives me a decent dowry."

She hoped Cynthia would contradict her, but all Cynthia said was, "What about your brother?"

"Oh, he used to be a pretty little boy, but since he's had to wear glasses his personality seems to have changed. He's got moody, and he's always in trouble. He has terribly extravagant tastes, too. He spends money like water, Mamma says. He loves good clothes. And guns. Guns are horribly expensive. He has a friend at school whose parents have a shooting lodge in Scotland. Edwin goes there to stay. He says the army will be sorry they wouldn't have him because he's a crack marksman in spite of his bad eyesight. He could knock off a few Germans."

"Why Germans?"

"Because Papa says there'll be a war with Germany one day. He's always said that. He says Bismarck and now the Kaiser have made Germany a military nation, and naturally a military nation wants a war simply to display its prowess."

"But against England?"

"I suppose. They'd want to pick the strongest competitor. There wouldn't be much glory in only squashing little nations. Besides, the Kaiser is jealous of the Prince of Wales, and when he's King of England matters will come to a head."

"I didn't know you were so interested in history."

"Papa says countries ought to have foresight, not hindsight."

"Then Desmond will have to come home from India to defend us," Cynthia said flippantly. "Personally, I'd have more faith in Edwin. And anyway Desmond's colonel says we're going to have trouble in South Africa over the diamond mines. Wouldn't it be a pity to lose all our beautiful diamonds to those ugly Dutch women? Boers, or whatever they are. You and I can wear them so much better."

"Not me," said Florence. "I'll only have a small string of pearls, while Edwin's making Mamma foot his bills."

"I wasn't suggesting it should be your parents who bought you diamonds."

Florence blushed.

"Oh, that's different, I suppose."

"Only don't count too much on Desmond because he says already that he can't keep up with his mess bills."

Florence's blush deepened.

"Don't tease. I haven't even met your brother."

Florence had another reason for anxiety, although in this she was unselfish enough to keep quiet. One couldn't be rude to an old woman, could one? All the same, it was a great shame that Mamma had allowed Miss Brown to decide on Florence's ball-dress.

Miss Brown was so *old*, quite sixty, and although Mamma insisted that she couldn't be head of Bonnington's Mantles and Millinery without keeping up with current fashion, she was still hopelessly prim and old-fashioned in her ideas of what young girls should wear.

She smelled faintly musty, and sniffed a great deal, pinching her thin nostrils together. Her eyes were sharp and querulous behind steel-rimmed spectacles. Her own clothes should have been given to charity long ago; she had worn the same style of shiny black dress with stiffened waistband and high-boned neck ever since Florence could remember. It was true that she knew how to cajole and bully customers and that she never forgot a face or a waist measurement or a bank account. Apparently the great majority of Bonnington's customers liked this, but they were growing old with Miss Brown. There weren't many young ones coming in, Florence reflected shrewdly. Only the timid daughters of domineering mothers who thought it the thing to be dressed by Miss Brown of Bonnington's.

There was a story that Papa had objected to Mamma's wedding clothes chosen by a much younger Miss Brown. But Mamma had the greatest loyalty to people who had served her well, and Miss Brown would remain at Bonnington's until she decided of her own free will to leave. Her aged mother had died some time ago, and she lived alone in the dark and dismal house in Doughty Street. Florence and Daisy had sometimes been bidden to take tea with her on Sunday afternoons. Florence did so with a good enough grace, because she was a docile girl, but Daisy had to be bribed with the promise of a penny if she behaved herself. It was understandable that Daisy wouldn't care for an old stick like Miss Brown, but more perplexing why Miss Brown didn't care for Daisy. She made no secret of the fact that she regarded the child as spoiled and selfish, and in need of a good "straightening up."

Daisy who shone in that dark musty parlor like a newly lighted candle! Florence thought indignantly.

Florence, however, basked in Miss Brown's approval, and was grateful to someone for liking her best. Not many people did. Therefore she accepted the style of dress Miss Brown decreed, an organdy, white of course, with yellow rosebud trimmings and a discreetly high neck. "To hide those dear little salt cellars," said Miss Brown, her old dry fingers moving knowledgeably over Florence's bone structure.

The dress was childish, said Florence wistfully to Cynthia. Sweetly pretty, said Hawkins. Too *jeune fille* for words, said Edwin in the satirical manner he had lately cultivated. Exactly suitable for a debutante, said Mamma. Papa made no comment. Perhaps he was remembering Mamma's trousseau.

Daisy was another matter. She suddenly declared that she would not wear the dress Miss Brown had chosen for her, white muslin with a pale-pink sash. A *baby* dress, she said indignantly, and she was ten years old. She simply would not wear it. It was too humiliating.

Daisy, by dint of determination and her sunny charm, usually got her own way. However, it did not seem as if she were going to do so this time. Mamma took Miss Brown's side, and said Daisy would wear the white muslin or she would not have a new dress at all. Indeed, if she didn't have better manners she may not be allowed to come down to the ball. Daisy, who even wept gracefully, hid her face in her handkerchief and whispered that Mamma didn't love her. She had always known she was not loved.

This, to Florence, seemed to be the most outrageous statement Daisy had ever made. Why, she was everybody's pet. She was loved to distraction.

Nevertheless Daisy turned away and would not be comforted. If Mamma loved her she would care about her happiness. And who could be happy wearing that baby dress!

Finally Mamma lost patience and told her to go to her room until she had regained control of herself and was ready to apologize to Miss Brown for her rudeness. Daisy whirled away, now sobbing audibly, and then what should happen fifteen minutes later but that she should come downstairs, dressed in her outdoor things, and holding Papa's hand.

"We're off on a shopping expedition," Papa announced. "Now not a word, Bea. This young lady has a certain taste in clothes and I think it should be encouraged. You will all see the result shortly. You, too." He bowed with the faintest scorn to Miss Brown.

"Really"—Mamma sighed, as the front door closed behind them—"that child will be ruined. Her father dotes on her too much for her own good."

"So I have observed," Miss Brown said, her sharp eyes

snapping. "But I do think, Miss Beatrice, for an important occasion your daughters ought to be dressed by Bonninton's. I mean—"

"Oh, be quiet about it," Mamma answered, her good temper suddenly vanishing. "After all I, too, have been dressed by Worth."

"Surely he isn't taking her to Worth!"

"I said be quiet. If my husband has a whim to do this, it's really none of your affair, Miss Brown. Now don't be offended. We're very pleased with Florence's dress, aren't we, Florence, my dear?"

If she had made a fuss would she too have been taken to the fabulous Worth? Florence wondered. No, of course she wouldn't, because with her angular frame and plain face Papa would have thought the money wasted, whereas Daisy would look a dream, even at the very youthful age of ten years. This was a logical enough reason. Florence wasn't resentful. All the same, she couldn't help wondering what one of those alarmingly elegant women at the Worth salon would have chosen for her.

Well, she was doomed to organdy and yellow rosebuds, while Daisy came tripping home with exciting striped boxes containing a floor-length rose-colored taffeta dress, slippers to match, and the most darling white lace mittens that came to her elbows. She was so exquisitely pretty in her excitement that of course one forgave her her naughtiness and shared her pleasure.

She knew how to get things. One wished one had a little of that talent oneself.

Now this, thought Beatrice contentedly, three weeks later, was the happiest party she had known at Overton House.

It was a perfect mild midsummer evening, and the doors of the music room were open onto the terrace. Lanterns had been cunningly hung from trellises and tree branches, and were lighted by the gardener and his boy as the darkness grew. It looked as if a dozen small yellow private moons hung in the greenery.

The music room was full of roses and delphiniums and in the dining room the supper table, lavishly spread with one of Cook's finest cold collations, was decorated with trailing fronds of smilax and clusters of sweet peas.

The whole house was lit by candles because Beatrice said they were romantic. Privately she had thought the softer light more flattering to Florence who, through nervous anxiety, had seemed to shed pounds in the last few days. She really did have salt cellars above her collar-bones now, but she also had acquired a large-eyed ethereal quality that was rather appealing.

So much, she had declared passionately, hung on this ball. It was to be the acid test as to whether or not she was attractive to men. Or to one man, as the case may be. If she failed the test she was going to have a miserable season. Edwin had been urged to dance with her at least six times, if she appeared to be short of partners, and Papa also must lurk watchfully.

Daisy had said in her extravagant way, "Oh, Florence, you are beautiful! You truly are beautiful!" and one had to hope that either Florence had enough sense not to take her seriously, or else that the exuberant praise would give her some much needed confidence.

Daisy herself, dressed in that pretty but absurdly grown-up dress that William had bought for her, was flitting about with her air of radiant pleasure that most people found so irresistible. She just naturally assumed that she was created to be admired, which fact Beatrice found intensely galling. She herself had never been in the slightest danger of being taken in by Daisy's charms, but her prejudice was secret and deep-rooted and permanent.

It was too bad that even tonight the little minx was stealing Florence's limelight. Perhaps it was innocent and unintentional; after all she was only a child and could scarcely be aware of what she was doing, but it was happening.

Beatrice had promised that woman to bring up her child. She had not promised to love her.

The band was playing a waltz, the dance floor was full, and Beatrice had come outside for a little cool air. It was an emotional night whether she wished it to be or not, the coming out of her daughter, an Overton, in this lovely old house. She, the onetime usurper, had at least partly realized her dream.

It was realized more fully when William came out and joined her. Hadn't she longed for this once, William's hand on her arm as they strolled in the half-lit dusk?

"Everything seems to be going well, Bea. Florence is quite smitten by the young cavalryman."

"Desmond Fielding?"

"Is that his name? I remember dozens like him in the Punjab when I was a boy. Too fair-skinned for that climate. They suffered hellishly. Went brick-red with sunburn and liquor, or died of fever."

"I must say that's cheerful for poor young Lieutenant Fielding!"

"A fact. But with things the way they are I should think it's more likely he'll end up in South Africa. We're going to have a war on our hands there."

"William, not tonight?"

"Oh? Am I a pessimist?"

"Only about the Kaiser and Kruger."

"Well, it's all true, I'm afraid. But this is a good show tonight, isn't it? Thanks to you."

"Not thanks to me at all. Yours is the house, the background, the atmosphere of privilege. Mine's only the sordid money."

"But as necessary as the privilege, my dear."

"Perhaps. Florence seems to be doing nicely, doesn't she?"

"Surprisingly nicely. And Daisy is breaking hearts in all directions."

"Only because of that unsuitable dress which is much too old for her. I believe some of the young men believe she's in her teens."

William chuckled. "I did hear one of them swearing eternal devotion to her."

"Not really! That little scamp. I must call Lizzie. It's time she went up to bed."

"Nonsense, let the child enjoy herself. She has this captivating response to gaiety, as if she were making up—"

"Making up for what?"

William took his hand off her arm and moved away.

"Nothing, my dear. Aren't we lucky with the weather? By the way, I believe this young Fielding is in line for a baronetcy."

"I know!" Beatrice gave a short ironic laugh.

"Why are you laughing?"

"I was just thinking of what my father would say."

"Supposing he had lived to become grandfather to a

title? Really, you women, with your matchmaking. As far
as I know the young man has only danced with Florence
a couple of times. Shall we go in for some strawberries before our guests have hogged the lot?"

Beatrice took his arm gladly, forgetting Florence and reminding herself that her dream really had come true. At
an elegant party at Overton House. William Overton was
taking her in to supper.

"Do you go to a great many parties, Miss Overton?" Desmond Fielding asked.

"No, not a great many."

"I'm sure you will. Could we sit this dance out? Somewhere where it's cool. On the stairs, perhaps."

"I think you look wonderful in uniform," Florence said
shyly. "But I suppose it is rather hot."

"Hot! It's stifling. I can't imagine how I'll survive India,
dressed like this. Damned silly, really. Instead of full-dress
uniform there should be undress uniform, ha-ha! I mean"—
he ran his finger around his high collar—"something
sensible in the tropics."

"Don't let my grandfather hear you." Florence pointed
to the row of portraits hanging above the stairs. "He's that
one at the top. He was a great stickler for tradition, my
father says. My brother wanted to be just like him, but he
can't join the army because of poor eyesight."

"Hard luck! Though I don't know. He can stay comfortably in England. Can I ask you something, Miss
Overton? Will you write to me while I'm abroad? I'd appreciate it a great deal if you would."

"But you hardly know me!"

He laid his hand on hers, and she trembled. She had
been trembling inwardly with excitement ever since she had
danced with Lieutenant Fielding. He was the only guest
wearing uniform. This perhaps was why he made such
an impression on her. The scarlet tunic with the frogged
gold fastenings was immensely colorful. She tried to
imagine him in ordinary clothes, thinking that then his
long face with its pale-lashed blue eyes and blond mustache
would probably be quite ordinary. All the same, it was not
only his appearance, it was his courteous manner that
pleased her. Most heady of all, he seemed genuinely to

admire her, and as a consequence she knew that she looked unusually animated and perhaps quite pretty.

Bless Cynthia for having a brother, bless him for coming to her ball. How sad that he was leaving England so soon, but how wonderful that he wanted her to write to him. Did he really, or was he making the same request to every personable girl he met?

"I feel I do know you, Miss Overton. You have such a look of sincerity."

"Have I?"

"So do think of me scorching on those hot plains, and drop me a line occasionally. I'll be thinking of girls like you all the time, cool and elegant and English."

Girls! Her suspicion had been right.

"So you are collecting female correspondents, Lieutenant?" she said primly.

"No, I'm not, you goose. I swear you're the only one I've asked to write to me."

"I'll write to you, too, if you like, Lieutenant," came Daisy's voice, unexpectedly. She was looking through the banisters, her eyes sparkling mischievously.

"Daisy, you little wretch!" Florence exclaimed. "Have you been listening to us?"

"Only to Lieutenant Fielding calling you a goose. I wish I'd heard more."

The young man burst out laughing.

"Introduce me, Miss Overton. Who is this gorgeous creature?"

Florence repressed annoyance. Much as she adored Daisy, she could not have been less welcome at this moment.

"She's my sister. Lieutenant Fielding, Miss Daisy Overton."

Daisy came to the foot of the stairs to give her polite curtsy, and Lieutenant Fielding said, "That's a very kind offer of yours to write to me, Miss Daisy. I'll be happy to accept it."

"She's only a schoolgirl," Florence put in, a little crossly.

"But I'm sure she writes a dashing letter. You two sisters aren't at all alike, are you?"

Daisy, showing her dimples, said, "Florence is the good one and I'm the bad one."

"Well, that makes for a nice balance," Lieutenant Fielding said, and Florence, still irritated by Daisy's pertness, said, "You mustn't take her seriously, Lieutenant. She's a great tease. And isn't it time you went up, Daisy? It's nearly midnight."

"Papa said I could stay up until the clock struck twelve, like Cinderella."

"You're no Cinderella," said Lieutenant Fielding.

Daisy dimpled with her radiant pleasure.

"Does that mean I'll never have a Prince Charming?" she asked in pretended dismay.

"I should think you would have plenty of those. I might even have waited for you myself if I hadn't met your sister first."

"Oh, what a pity!" The little minx really was too precocious for words. "But I'll forgive you if you promise to come to my ball in seven years' time. Seven years! Oh, dear, do you think we will all live that long?"

"I certainly intend to, Miss Daisy, simply so that I may come to your ball."

Daisy gave her delighted gurgle of laughter. "That's perfectly wonderful. That makes eight men I have already. Now who else can I ask?"

She tripped off, and Florence exclaimed, "She's incorrigible! I must apologize for her."

"Quite! The modern generation! She's going to be a wonderful flirt. I fancy you're not a flirt, Miss Overton?"

His hand was laid over hers again, and her happiness had returned.

"No, I'm not. I'm much too slow-witted, for one thing. And I suppose I'm too honest."

"I like honesty. It's a bit rare, you know."

"I will write to you if you want me to, Lieu—"

"Desmond."

"Desmond," Florence said, her voice admirably calm. "And now I really think we ought to go back to the ballroom."

His lips only touched her cheek. It was a quick snatch at a kiss, and afterward she could only remember how unexpectedly soft his mustache was against her skin.

It could scarcely be called a kiss at all, yet it put the crown of success on the evening, and gave her a comforting memory to cherish for long afterward.

She needed something to cherish, for this kind of thing had its drawbacks. It meant that for the rest of her season she was profoundly uninterested in all the young men she met. She went to luncheon parties, tea dances and balls, and looked faraway and distrait, determining to show any hopeful admirer that her affections were otherwise engaged.

Actually, there were no other admirers because her aloofness was discouraging, and without animation her angular face and too long nose were distinctly plain. She refused to make any efforts to be attractive, to the exasperation of her parents and of Miss Brown (who had been hoping for an early and elaborate wedding).

"Florence dear, this young man in India," Mamma said. "You only met him once. You can't be in love with him."

"Why not? You said you fell in love with Papa the first time you met him."

Mamma bit her lip. "That was different. He wasn't going to disappear to a foreign country for several years. Don't you see that you're wasting all your youth?"

"I don't care."

"And you don't even know if he's serious."

"He writes to me," Florence said, having no intention of displaying the precious missives. She was a very private person. Besides, Desmond was not a gifted letter writer. She had to read between the lines, although she was perfectly certain what was written there.

"He writes to Daisy, too," Mamma pointed out.

That was another matter. Desmond's letters to Daisy were purely a lesson in history and geography. He was explaining a strange country and its customs to a schoolgirl.

"Florence dear, do you think he might be just homesick, and overromantic, remembering the night of your ball, and knowing he was leaving England and the things he loved? You told me that he was sailing for India immediately afterward."

"Yes, Mamma, he did. And I promised to write to him, and to wait for him—"

"You never told me you had promised to wait for him!"

"To myself I did. I made a vow."

"Oh," said Mamma. "That was rather foolish, surely. Rather precipitate." She reflected for a little while. "If you are determined on this behavior I think we must find you some occupation. I can't have you mooning about the house all the time. I don't approve of idle young women."

"Flo, Desmond is awfully stupid in some ways," Cynthia said. "Are you sure you love him?"

"Oh, yes."

"Lots of girls fall in love with a glamorous uniform, you know. I can tell you, some of those guardsmen are almost invisible out of uniform. And they're blockheads, too."

"I'm much too sensible to fall in love with a uniform," Florence said. "Really, Cynthia."

"You are a goose. After only one meeting!"

"Two." Telling nobody, Florence had gone to Waterloo Station to say good-bye when Desmond's troop had entrained for Southampton docks. He had been delighted to see her, but hadn't kissed her again. It was broad daylight and rather too public. But he had held both her hands and looked deeply into her eyes and said it was jolly decent of her to come to say good-bye. And she would keep her promise to write, wouldn't she, and not get bored with an absent friend? Friend, he had said. Not lover. But it was enough.

"One meeting or two, I think you're being much too romantic," Cynthia said briskly. "It was Desmond's last ball in England, you know, and the men in my family are inclined to sentimentality. It's a soldier's privilege, my father says. But that isn't to be interpreted as meaning a lot, you know."

"Isn't it?" Florence said composedly. "I do intend to wait and see."

It's damned hot, and it's getting worse. Even on parade I find my thoughts turning to cool green grass and girls in white dresses, like you that night we met. In my mind now, you seem like an angel. . . .

Florence locked the letters in a drawer of her writing desk, and hid the key. Every one was kept as a precious treasure.

There was a ball in the mess last night, a lot of army wives and sisters came, some of them very pretty, but this climate ruins their looks in no time. I much prefer you to be in England where your looks will be preserved. . . .

Preserved. . . . A slightly unfortunate word, since she was now twenty-one and officially without a beau. The old queen had died last year (in the arms of her grandson, the Emperor of Germany, much to Papa's disgust, who still disliked that braggart young man, as did his royal uncle, now Edward the Seventh of England).

But Florence had luckily had the honor of being presented to the stout, immensely regal, black-clad old lady with a little twinkling tiara balanced on top of her lacy cap, at a royal drawing room the previous summer. She was the daughter of William Overton, Esquire, most of whose forebears had been decorated for valor by their monarch. Nothing was said about her mother being a shopkeeper, and one of that new strange race of busy clever women of whom the queen strongly disapproved.

An elderly aunt of Papa's had emerged from some old ivy-clad house in the country, like a moth struggling reluctantly out of a dusty chrysalis, and did the presenting. She would do the same for Daisy in a few years, if she lived long enough. Daisy, she commented in her rusty voice, was a jolly gel and would make a bit of a splash when she came out. What was the use of Florence with her long nose and her absent beau, even though she did now have this invisible asset of having been presented, of having curtsyed to an elderly monarch shortly to die?

Mamma, who had always taken Florence's side against Daisy, probably to compensate for Papa spoiling Daisy so much, said that she had never met Aunt Sophie before and hoped she would not have to do so again. One should not think that age gave one the right to be rude. She was as arrogant as Grandmamma Overton had been, and Florence was to pay no attention to her.

All the same, it was a great pity that those letters from India inflicted such a paralysis on her social life.

"But I won't lecture you, Florence, because I loved your Papa for a long time, too. I know what it is to wait. We're too much alike, I think."

"But the waiting was worthwhile, wasn't it, Mamma?" Florence asked intensely.

"Oh, yes. Yes." There was no uncertainty in Mamma's voice. It was clear and strong, and consequently it was strange to hear the murmured qualification, "The trouble is, you find you're doing it all your life."

"What do you mean, Mamma? You and Papa have each other. What are you waiting for now?"

"Waiting? It becomes a habit, I suppose." Then Mamma said in her warm strong voice, "Yes, I have your dear papa. And if Desmond is half as good a man, then he is worth waiting for. But I think you'd better come into the shop, Florence, and learn a bit of Miss Brown's work. She could do with some help. She's getting old."

"But, Mamma, I wouldn't be any good, since my only ambition is to be married."

"We'll see," said Mamma kindly.

Chapter 18

When, as had been feared, war broke out in South Africa between the Boers and the British, Beatrice said with her habitual common sense, "We can't help our soldiers by crying, so let's show plenty of flags. We'll keep them flying every day until the war is over."

If a few unkind critics said that Bonnington's was now pretending to be an outpost of the British Empire, on the whole the patriotism was applauded. The triumphal array had to be taken down once, however, when Queen Victoria died. For a week, then, Bonnington's plunged into its biggest mourning display. The windows were hung with black and purple crepe, every employee wore a black armband, and at intervals funeral music was played on a phonograph placed discreetly behind the banked white flowers in the front hall. Young Mr. Jones from Gentlemen's Wear was stationed beside it to wind it up regularly; otherwise it wheezed to a melancholy halt. It was as if her Majesty were being buried from Bonnington's, Mr. Jones said privately. You almost expected to find her coffin among all those sickly white flowers.

Was it good for business? he asked, more boldly.

Prestige, Beatrice answered. That amounted to the same thing. She liked the younger employees to express opinions. She remembered the ones who asked intelligent questions. Youth must be encouraged. Miss Brown would soon have to retire. The poor old thing was creaking in every bone. And Adam was looking gray at the temples. She herself wouldn't be there forever, incredible as that seemed. She had hoped that Edwin might change his mind and become interested in the shop, but he showed no sign of doing so. Indeed, he made no secret of despising shop-

keeping. He was afraid of what his friends might think,
perhaps. Although he didn't seem to have many friends.

Edwin was causing Beatrice some private uneasiness,
although he was working hard enough at Oxford, and was
still destined for the Foreign Office, if that austere establishment would have him. He said he liked the idea of living abroad.

But it was obvious he would never live abroad on his
salary. His expensive tastes persisted, and bills from his
tailor, his shoemaker, his gunsmith, and his clubs (he already belonged to two, which was one more than necessary, Beatrice thought) kept coming in.

So far Beatrice had paid them without too much demur.
She felt guilty about Edwin. The bad news about his eyesight had come when she had been entirely absorbed in
the trouble that wretched Miss Medway had caused. She
had been able to think of nothing but saving William from
his folly, and preserving their marriage. She had sympa-
thized with Edwin, of course, but he was young and would
adjust to his disability and his disappointment about an
army career. Life had many alternatives for him. It held
none for her if she lost her husband.

Looking back now, she realized that this was when Edwin had withdrawn from her. It was a sad fact, but he
would understand when he was older and he, too, experienced an overwhelming love that shut out all else.

Besides, it was foolish to think that the boy had been
damaged. He had only grown uncommunicative and secretive, but didn't all boys get like that after they had gone
to school, and felt that they had outgrown their parents
and their childhood?

It was not only Edwin who was disappointing her.
Florence was still in her everlasting daydream about that
shadowy young man in India, although she had consented
to go into Miss Brown's Mantles department and try her
hand at fashion since she couldn't go on being a wallflower
at yet another season's balls. She might have a flair for
fashion, Miss Brown had said. She certainly had the right
sort of figure, tall and willowy, to show off the new models,
and her society background would bring in some new
custom. The trouble was, she wasn't interested, except in
spasms, when some color or quality of material excited

her. She hoped to have eight children, Miss Brown told Beatrice helplessly.

So it was left to Daisy, of the three of them, to enjoy growing up. Beatrice thought it exceedingly unfair that she, the little cuckoo, should be so well equipped for doing so. She had looks, a sunny temperament, vivacity, a quick wit, a talent for music, certainly a talent for dancing, for she moved beautifully. She had everything, that child, and she was disgracefully spoiled by her father and most of the servants. Though not her governess, for, since Miss Medway, Beatrice had kept a watchful eye on that sort of thing. Miss Sloane, she knew, was the kind of woman who sensibly never allowed herself to become emotionally involved with her pupils. She struggled perpetually with Daisy's pranks and high spirits, and hoped she was keeping the willful little miss in her place.

William had published his second book, once more to considerable critical acclaim. His health was still a matter of concern to Beatrice, but to her pleasure he spent less time abroad. He now quite enjoyed being fussed over by his wife, and if this wasn't the most satisfying relationship between a husband and wife, she was almost certain that William could now never do without her. She had imposed her own form of imprisonment on him.

Imprisonment? No, that was a cruel term. Domesticity was better. A gentle acceptable form of domesticity, which should be recommended to all husbands as the most comfortable way of living.

He was still a very handsome man, and he still flirted mildly with pretty women. Beatrice was quietly indulgent about that. That was her William, after all. She had never wanted to quench his spirit.

But she wished that vague shadow would leave his eyes. He had once had the sunniest of eyes.

She was glad that he had taken up his interest in butterflies again. He now had the intention of compiling a book of reference on European butterflies and moths. Apart from writing, and working with an artist on sketches of his own famous collection, he liked to take Daisy on long butterfly-hunting expeditions. They went much farther afield than the Heath. They caught trains into Sussex and Surrey and Kent, and came home sunburned and happy with their trophies. A Camberwell beauty (*Nymphalis*

antiopa), a particularly fine painted lady (*Vanessa cardui*),
a fearsome hawkmoth.

Daisy, he said, was the best companion he had ever had.
She was like a butterfly herself, skimming over the short
grass, her cheeks as rosy as the wings of a monarch
(*Danaüs plexippus*). What was more, she could quote
those awkward Latin names as well as her father could.
She used to put them in her monthly letter to Captain
Fielding (he now had a promotion) simply to fill up the
page. She grumbled a great deal about this chore; she had
long regretted her promise made at Florence's ball when
she was a silly child, but Florence insisted that ladies kept
promises.

Then she didn't want to be a lady, Daisy muttered. It
sounded a dull duty-ridden sort of thing.

And the letters Captain Fielding wrote back were full
of information about the natives and the villages and the
climate, and meant for a schoolgirl. Didn't he realize that
some years had gone by and she was hardly a schoolgirl
now? She was fourteen, and she was going to put her
hair up any day.

Papa, at least, didn't think her a child. When they went
on one of their excursions into the country, he took a
picnic hamper containing such delicacies as *foie gras* and
claret. He allowed Daisy to drink a small glass of the
claret, and when, one very warm day, she fell asleep
afterward, she awoke to find the summer grass tickling her
nose and Papa bending over her with an expression on his
face that could only be described as loverlike. Dear Papa.
She was glad that he had said she was not to go to a
stuffy girls' boarding school. She was to grow up to be
individual, like her mother.

Immediately he had said that he looked as if he regretted
it. But it was true, for Mamma, neat and brisk and commanding in her gray white-collared shop dress, was extremely individual. It was not how Daisy imagined herself
however. She wanted to wear romantic tea gowns and glide
about like a swan. She would end by being exactly like her
grandmother Overton, Mamma said impatiently, and did
she know what Grandfather Overton had called her? A
delicious nosegay. But he hadn't meant it as a compliment.
He had indicated that such women were vain, and without
depth, and faded quickly.

Who wants *depth?* Daisy demanded. She saw the disapproval in Mamma's eyes. They always went curiously frosty when they rested on her. They had for as long as she could remember. This perplexed her a great deal, but she no longer shed private tears about it. She simply accepted that for some reason Mamma didn't like her. Now she was old enough to understand adult things, she thought that perhaps this was because Papa liked her too much. Mamma was simply jealous. And that was very odd, being jealous of one's own daughter. Daisy never intended such a thing to happen to her. Her husband would adore her to distraction, and seldom pay any attention to the children. Actually, she didn't think she wanted children. Unless they adored her, too. She could never have enough love. She wanted her life to be overflowing with it, like sunshine, like music, like the scent of a summer garden.

"Life isn't like that, Daisy," Miss Sloane pointed out in her flat voice. "But I can see you will never believe me. You will only find out to your sorrow by living it, and being unprepared for trouble."

Soon, there was the frenetic excitement of Mafeking night, when at last that small town in South Africa at the center of the Boer War was relieved from its long siege. At last the end of the war came.

Papa was quietly triumphant about that old Boer Kruger's humiliation, and said that if the same thing could happen to the Emperor of Germany the world should be free from war, and Britain and its vast empire safe, for generations to come.

With the party-loving King Edward on the throne business boomed. Bonnington's Mantles department became inundated with orders for morning gowns, tea gowns, ball gowns, gowns for Ascot and Henley, for Badminton and Eton, the Derby and Goodwood, and the parties that followed these events, not to mention the entire trousseaux ladies required for country house weekends, The flood overwhelmed Miss Brown. She tottered about, her thin old body looking about to crack in half. Against her will Florence found herself getting drawn more into the running of the department. She had to admit it was strangely hypnotic, the chaotic rush that went on in the workrooms contrasting sharply with the soft-carpeted hush of the showrooms. There, the more affluent customers sat on couches and sipped a glass of sherry or champagne, while saleswomen, trained in a reverential manner, showed the latest models.

If Florence, like her mother, found herself concerned with the chilblains and the head colds and the sometimes severe cases of undernourishment of the girls in the workroom, cutting, hemming, basting, ironing, working on expensive materials that must not be ruined by the blood from a pricked finger, or an unwary drop from a clogged-up nose, she also got a thrill of satisfaction from making an important sale. Even more so from guiding a floundering customer (one of the many of the *nouveaux riches*, frequently accompanied by a portly husband) into good taste. So she must have inherited some talent for trade. However, she was only filling in time, as everyone knew.

Captain Fielding was due back in England any day. Actually any day!

She was twenty-three and Desmond had been away a little more than five years. He would be twenty-five and eager to marry. Would he still admire her? She would be humbly content with admiration at first. It would grow into love, with time. She herself could hardly wait to pour out her love on him. After all those letters she felt she knew him absolutely, his integrity, his sense of duty, his courage (although he frankly admitted to moments of fear), his ideals which included faithfulness to one woman. What was more, he had not minded her occupying herself in the shop. It kept her out of mischief, ha-ha, while he was away. But such a thing was not to be taken seriously, of course. She was naturally destined for marriage to some lucky fellow.

Of course he meant that he hoped to be the lucky fellow. Didn't he? Florence, with her diffidence, and her lack of confidence, had to overcome some anxiety. She did this by never being still, never allowing herself time to brood. She flew about like an animated broomstick, Papa said. But the tension suited her. Her eyes shone and for the first time in her life she had an attractive stain of color in her cheeks.

And one afternoon, without any announcement at all, Captain Fielding walked into Overton House, admitted by a flustered Hilda, who later said, below stairs, that he was so tall and handsome, and when he had heard that Miss Florence was at the shop and only Miss Daisy at home, practicing on the piano, he had said that he would enjoy whiling away an hour with Miss Daisy until Miss Florence came home. So what could Hilda do but announce him to Miss Daisy in the music room?

Miss Daisy had been singing one of her French songs. She was ever so clever with her French. But when the young gentleman had spoken she had stopped on midnote, jumped up, and in her impulsive way, almost flung herself into his arms.

A little later she rang for tea.

"We'll have it in here, Hilda," she said. She was sitting in one of the basket chairs near the French windows, and Captain Fielding was sitting opposite her. The sun shone through the overhanging creepers, making a curious green light, so that the two of them, the tall soldier in his smart uniform, and Miss Daisy, with her skirts spread about her and her thick hair with its rich reddish tints hanging over her shoulders, looked like something out of a painting. Ever so romantic, Hilda said.

Tea and plum cake and hot scones and strawberry jam. The captain, just home from India, must have an English tea, Miss Daisy said. She had such a way of putting her heart into everything, she made you feel that you were the one person she had most wanted to see. No doubt she was doing exactly that to Captain Fielding at this moment. It was a great gift. Though how she would manage all the followers she would be bound to have in two or three years was another matter. She would be thought a terrible flirt, no doubt, but anyone who knew her realized her friendliness came simply from a warm heart. All the same, the sooner Miss Florence got home, the better, Hilda thought.

On hearing the unbelievable news when she did arrive home an hour later, Florence rushed to the music room, bursting in with an impulsiveness unusual to her.

By this time tea was finished and Captain Fielding was leaning back comfortably in his chair relating some incident to Daisy who was listening with her air of entranced attention. When she saw Florence, however, she sprang up with an exclamation of pleasure.

"Flo dear, we've been waiting for you. Captain Fielding thought you would never come."

Florence held out her hand and had it gripped by Captain Fielding. A sudden paralyzing shyness made her almost unable to look at him. She only noted that he was taller than she remembered and that his luxuriant mustache seemed white against his brick-red skin. His high-bridged nose was arrogant, his eyes a gentle blue.

"In black?" he said, looking at her in surprise. "Are you wearing mourning for somebody?"

She was able to laugh.

"Oh, no. This is my working dress. I've been at the shop."

"The shop?"

"I told you in my letters. I got so bored doing nothing."

"Oh, of course. You've been selling buttons and pins and needles all day. How amusin'." Could he have been a good soldier if he were this vague? Or was it Daisy who had addled his wits?

"You didn't let us know you were coming."

"No. Our ship got in a couple of days early. Thought I'd give you a surprise, Miss Overton."

"Florence," she corrected. All those letters *"My dear Florence"* . . . and now he was talking to her as if she were a stranger. Perhaps he was as shy as she was. She always forgot that other people could be shy.

"Florence, of course. But would I be shockingly rude if I told you I don't care for you in black? Whatever you say, it looks like mourning."

"I'm going to change immediately. You can stay to dinner, can't you?"

"I hadn't intended that. I just dropped in—"

"Oh, you must, please. Mamma and Papa will never forgive you if you don't."

"And what about you?"

Florence was about to answer that neither would she when she realized he was speaking to Daisy.

"Of course, Captain Fielding. We all expect you." Daisy had contrived to shoot Florence the briefest glance, one eyebrow raised, one eyelid falling in the ghost of a wink. Florence knew that cry for rescue well enough. The foolish girl bent her ardent gaze on all and sundry, and then wondered why she couldn't escape them.

"Captain Fielding has been telling me fascinating stories about India, Flo. He'll want to tell them to you."

"I must say Miss Daisy is a capital audience," Captain Fielding said enthusiastically. "If I stay to dinner, Miss Daisy, will you promise to sing to me again?"

"You're so kind," Daisy murmured, with her grown-up air. "May I tell Mamma and Papa we have a guest for dinner, Florence?"

She had whisked out of the room before Florence could answer, and Desmond was saying admiringly, "I say, I couldn't believe how grown up she is."

"She isn't out of the schoolroom," Florence said, with a trace of stiffness.

"Well, you could have deceived me."

"She's not sixteen yet."

"She's going to be a beauty. She is already."

"Yes, she has all the looks in our family."

Captain Fielding tugged at his mustache, realizing his clumsiness.

"Forgive me, that wasn't very gallant. I've been out of society for too long. You have charming looks yourself. Except for that depressing dress, mind you. Do go and change it. I'll be quite content here. I'll wander in the garden. Smell some English air. God, it's good to be home."

"Is it?" Florence asked eagerly. He had said she had charming looks. . . .

"It certainly is. And I'm not expecting to be posted abroad again. Unless there's a war, of course. So I've the chance to settle down."

In spite of her impatience to be downstairs, Florence took a whole hour to dress for dinner. She borrowed Hawkins from Mamma, to do her hair and to button the twenty or so buttons down the back of her new oyster-colored lace, made especially for Desmond's homecoming. Of course she had looked depressing in black. She would never wear it again in his presence.

"A simple hairstyle suits you best, Miss Florence," Hawkins said.

"But I don't want a simple style. I want an elaborate one. I should think Captain Fielding is tired of simple old-fashioned styles. The ladies in Delhi wouldn't have had a Hawkins to do their hair."

Hawkins compressed her lips. "Being a flatterer doesn't suit you, Miss Florence."

"Am I so dull! That I must wear a simple hairstyle and have no feminine wiles, like flattery."

"I'm only saying it's always best to be yourself."

"Oh, no, it isn't. That's a complete fallacy."

Hawkins stood back, eyeing Florence's thin, strange elegance in the new dress. She could be something, when she was thirty. All the same. . . .

"You look as if you're going to Buckingham Palace, Miss Florence. And if that's suitable for a quiet dinner at home—"

"I'm not having Daisy upstaging me in a Worth gown this time, Hawkins. That's what."

But, although Daisy was wearing an unadorned muslin dress that was suitably young, she had chosen to put up her hair, without permission, naturally, and suddenly she was precipitated into maturity. She looked, Florence thought, shocked but helplessly admiring, exactly as Captain Fielding would have expected her to look in two years' time. The glossy topknot allowed tendrils to escape over her ears and the nape of her narrow little neck. She looked ravishing.

It was scarcely surprising that Captain Fielding didn't seem able to take his eyes off her, or to notice especially that Florence had taken a great deal of trouble to remove the image of herself in her black shop dress.

Mamma was angry with Daisy, that was obvious. Papa, however, as could be expected, gave his doting smile and said rather wistfully that his youngest daughter seemed in a hurry to grow up.

Edwin, back from his day's work in Whitehall (he was now a very junior secretary waiting for a posting abroad), ignored both of his sisters. He wanted to talk to Captain Fielding about his favorite subject, the army, and war.

Had he been in many skirmishes? Had he had to put down any local rebellions? What guns did he think the most effective, Mausers or Lee Enfields? Was the day of the cavalry over, as some military experts seemed to think? Would he be interested, after dinner, in looking at his grandfather's collection of model soldiers, to which he himself was now making additions?

"I picked up a dozen Meissen porcelain models at a salesroom today. They were ridiculously cheap."

"What regiment?" asked Captain Fielding.

"What do you call cheap?" asked Mamma suspiciously.

"An obscure Prussian one, and I call a hundred pounds for a 1740 collection dirt cheap."

Florence knew that Edwin had dropped this piece of information at the dinner table because Mamma couldn't make a fuss in front of company. He was either shrewd or cowardly, probably a little of each. He had outgrown his spotty schoolboy look and was almost as good-looking as Daisy, with his thick fair hair, his rosy skin and his bright-blue eyes. Except, of course, for the spectacles which he still considered humiliating and disfiguring.

Only half listening to the conversation, Florence was thinking vaguely about her family, how Papa looked distinguished and benign in his velvet dinner jacket and white silk cravat, how Daisy was obviously due to be the debutante of the year when she came out, how Mamma was silently disapproving of Daisy's precocious behavior and Edwin's extravagance although she was never upset when Papa bought a new picture or a piece of china to add to his collection. But then, she doted on Papa the way Papa doted on Daisy.

And I, thought Florence, blinking back sudden embarrassing tears, was only once in all my life doted on, for a very short time, by a governess called Miss Medway, who eventually came back to Overton House to steal Daisy. And now Daisy, whether she knows it or not, came the horrifying thought, is stealing Desmond. And succeeding very well, for he can scarcely take his eyes off her. He isn't listening to Edwin, or to me, not even to Papa and Mamma. He has lost his manners. He's being made a nincompoop by my fifteen-year-old sister. And I am sitting here like a dummy in this silly dressed-up dress that I will never wear again.

At Captain Fielding's especial request Daisy sang again, after dinner. When she had stopped there was a little silence, then Captain Fielding, with a struggle to remember his manners, politely asked Florence if she also would sing.

"I have no voice," she said. "I'm not in the least musical."

"Florence has other gifts," said Mamma.

"Of course. I know. Absolutely."

"And it's high time, Daisy, that you went upstairs," Mamma said.

"Oh, Mamma—"

"Not a word, miss. Do as you're told. And take all those pins out of your hair and brush it properly."

"Bea—" Papa began, instantly aware of Daisy's quick distress. He frequently thought Mamma too harsh toward Daisy, but couldn't he see now that in reducing her to her schoolroom status Mamma was merely trying to repair the damage done to Florence? If it were not too late. . . .

Chapter 19

It was too late. Captain Fielding had discovered that when he had been writing all those letters to Florence he had been thinking of her as a sister. He hadn't realized that at the time. It had only come to him when he found that although he admired and liked her no end, it was Daisy whom he loved.

More accurately, perhaps, he was bedazzled by Daisy, but as he knew he would have to wait at least two years for her (if she would have him then), that would give him time to sort out his feelings, wouldn't it?

After all, marriage had never been mentioned between Florence and himself. Her letters had been a great diversion and a comfort in a foreign land, but he had always intended to wait until he came home to determine his feelings about her.

So he wasn't being a cad. Was he? he asked anxiously. He was excessively sorry if Florence thought he was a cad, and he couldn't apologize enough. Though she had to admit that she had never made any declaration of love in her letters, either, so she surely couldn't have imagined herself committed to him. It was just bad luck for her that she had such a captivating sister.

"Oh, stop whitewashing your conscience," Florence snapped with an asperity quite foreign to her. She had anticipated this scene, and wondered whether she would choose anger or tears. It turned out that tears were quite out of the question. "I suppose you can't help it if Daisy has seduced you."

"Not seduced!" exclaimed Captain Fielding.

"Oh, don't be such a prig!"

Captain Fielding's mouth fell open.

"I say, Miss Overton, you have changed."

"Overnight," said Florence bleakly. She saw in his eyes relief at his escape from marriage to such a shrew.

"Flo, this is *terrible!*" Daisy cried. "I'm not in love with Desmond. To tell the truth I'm beginning to find him a great bore. He follows me about like a *shadow!* He's got the nerve, if you please, to inform me that he'll wait two years for me!"

Florence found that Daisy's flushed lovely face had no appeal for her. She would be sixteen in September, which was quite old enough to know exactly what she had been doing. Seeking Desmond's company constantly, listening with breathless interest to everything he said, dressing up for him, singing and playing the piano to him, picking early rosebuds for his buttonhole, attending constantly to his comfort. . . . If she thought this was behaving with complete innocence then it was time that she was disillusioned.

Quivering with misery and anger Florence turned a startling flow of recriminations on Daisy.

"Then why did you put your hair up? Why did you sing to him? Why did you seduce him?"

"S-seduce!" The word shocked even Daisy who liked to pretend sophistication. "But I never did! I only talked to him and entertained him as I would anybody."

"Any man, you mean? Why did you put your hair up?"

"Oh, you keep going on about that. It was just a lark. I detest being in the schoolroom still. I'm far too old for it. And you were dressing up, and you know I can never bear being left out. You and Edwin have always been so much older than me. I *hate* being the youngest."

"But you weren't too young to flirt with Des—with Captain Fielding. I've watched you. In the music room. In the garden. There used to be a mirror room in this house where people flirted, did you know? It would have been just the place for you two."

Out of the window Florence saw the Judas tree in flower, the rosy blossoms as warm as a fire against the bare branches. In an inspired voice she hissed, "You're a Judas!"

"Flo!" Daisy's voice faltered. "You look awful! I've never seen you look at me like that. I thought—"

"You thought what?"

"You loved me."

"So I did. Once."

Daisy pressed her hands to her eyes. She made little choking, sobbing sounds.

"I can't help it if I want everyone to love me."

"Why do you have to be so greedy? Everyone does love you."

"No, they don't. Mamma never has."

"Of course she does. Don't be such a little hypocrite."

"I'm not a hypocrite. That isn't fair."

"Well, you're jolly spoiled. You've been spoiled ever since you were stolen when you were a baby. Even that woman wanted you, you see. Mamma says she used to watch the peacocks in that Italian garden before you were born, and she thinks that's made you vain. I just think you're plain selfish, and it's time you realized what harm your thoughtless behavior causes."

"Oh, Flo darling!" Daisy cried in anguish. "You're talking as if I've ruined your life."

"So you have." Florence's voice was flat and cold. "Didn't you even know that?"

Beatrice was remembering the mirror room, too, when she went to the library to find William. Her thoughts were similar to Florence's. Although you could banish a room, it didn't seem that you could change the disturbingly repetitive habits of human nature.

And this house was turning into a museum, she thought with sudden uncharacteristic intolerance. There were those ridiculously expensive Meissen porcelain soldiers Edwin had just bought to add to an already overlarge collection of toys, for that was what they were, the pathetic toys of a soldier *manqué*. Because of this, she would pay for them, but in future Edwin, who now received a salary, must finance his own extravagances.

The charming little Guardi that William had bought the other day was another matter. It looked delightful, as did everything William found. His taste was so good, and it was right that he should add to the Overton House collection. She liked that, and she enjoyed giving William presents herself, watching his pleasure on the occasions when they proved to be an inspired choice.

However, today, William, bending absorbedly over his

butterfly slides, was suddenly irritating and disturbing. He was growing too wrapped up in his treasures. The butter-flies were dead, the pictures were dead, Edwin's soldiers were porcelain and would never raise arms and fire their muskets. It was not right to become so possessed by inanimate things. It seemed to represent an escape from a life not happy enough.

So perhaps there was a trace of merit in Daisy's thought-less but extremely lively behavior. Except that in a way she was a ghost, too. Although William didn't know what Beatrice was talking about when she burst out impetuously, "I believe that woman is still in the house."

"What woman, my dear?"

"Mary Medway. Who else?"

She still hated to say the name. William seemed equally to dislike hearing it, for he became very still, his eyes getting their blank opaque look. This she recognized as the familiar defense to conceal the pain he still felt, even after all these years.

"If you're referring to Daisy, call her Daisy."

The aroused pain gnawed at Beatrice, too.

"It seems to me that she's becoming her mother over again. She's ruined poor Florence's happiness."

William was carefully lifting a butterfly on its pin. The radiant spread wings, held up to the light, had gone dusty. He didn't look at Beatrice again.

"She can't help it if she's so much prettier than Florence. It's not fair to blame her."

Just as Mary Medway should not be blamed for the havoc she had caused?

"I'm afraid you're much too lenient with her, William. She wanted to be the center of attention, at no matter what cost to Florence. Now she has broken two hearts, both Florence's and Captain Fielding's."

"What, Captain Fielding's, too?"

"You must know she hasn't any deep feelings for him. She's far too young, anyway. She's simply been amusing herself. She has to learn she can't do that at the expense of other people."

"I always thought that young man was a dull stick," William said.

"Florence didn't. She has wasted five years over him.

William, will you listen?" He had seemed to disappear behind his bland façade.

"I am listening, my dear. I'm quite aware of Florence's tragedy. But she's young enough to recover, and you might reflect that Captain Fielding has proved to be rather fickle. Perhaps Florence has had a lucky escape."

"Not if she doesn't have another chance of marriage."

"Oh, come, Bea. Sheltering under Bonnington's roof, as she is."

"If you're suggesting I can buy her a husband—"

William came toward her, giving his tilted charming smile.

"Only teasing, Bea. But you must admit buying a husband is one of your capabilities."

"Only if the man is willing to be bought," Beatrice flashed, losing her temper.

She was immediately shocked at what she had said, but William had deserved it, with his gibes, which weren't teasing, by any means. One was not deceived by the soft voice in which he spoke his clever cutting words.

He didn't mean to quarrel, however. He never did. He hated that sort of destructive emotion. He had admirable self-control. So had she, mostly.

"And what is it you're about to suggest regarding Daisy? Isn't that what you've come to tell me?"

"Yes, it is. I've written to a finishing school in Paris, one that has been recommended to me where the discipline is strict. I think a year or two there is the best thing for Daisy."

"Isn't her father important enough to be consulted about such a major step?"

"I'm consulting you now. But you must see that it really is important that Daisy should be sent away. Florence has to have a chance. She's thrown away all this time on that faithless young man."

"She's so intense," William complained gently.

"And having a sister like Daisy doesn't help. You know that nobody looks at Florence when Daisy is in the room."

"If I speak to Daisy—"

"No. It's no use. She can't help herself. It's the way she's made."

"She hasn't any of you in her, Bea, that's the trouble."

"If you mean she should have more common sense," she answered tartly, "I agree that that is the trouble. However, she can't help her own nature, beyond making a real effort to correct her faults. She does little enough of that, I'm afraid."

"She's always fancied you didn't love her."

"Nonsense!" This was becoming a very painful conversation. "She's been treated exactly the same as Edwin and Florence. I've brought her up as I promised to do, and I'll see her properly launched. She can come out after her year in Paris. But then, if she goes on misbehaving, I'll wash my hands of her. I mean that, William. Because this has all been far more than I should have been expected to do."

When I bought myself a husband. . . .

William had turned back to his butterflies.

"I don't recall anyone asking you to do it, Bea. I had always regarded what we did as an order. From the commanding officer, so to speak."

His eyes were flickering with that bleak mischief again. His teasing was cruel.

"It was the only solution," she cried. "And don't go on putting me in the wrong."

"Was I, my dear? Then I'm sorry. I thought we'd got over all this long ago. I'm being a cad. It's just that you've upset me with these sudden plans. I'd like to have been invited to talk them over. You know that I'll miss Daisy infernally."

"Of course I know," Beatrice said, anxious now to make amends. If he could apologize, so could she. "But you can go to Paris to see her."

"So I can." William's voice was at once more lively. He was blessed with a charmingly resilient temperament. Already he was dwelling on pleasures ahead. "I can take her to the opera. Show her off."

"Not show her off, for goodness sake. What that young lady needs is a bit of obscurity."

"Well, you must admit that unless we put her in a nun's habit she's going to be noticed. How has she taken to this idea herself?"

"She hasn't been told yet."

"Then allow me to break the news to her. I can soften

the blow by preparing her for the excitements of one of my favorite cities." As an afterthought he added politely, "It's a pity we never got back there ourselves. You never saw anything but that store, did you? Bon Marché."

Typical, he might have added. But he didn't. Which was just as well, because he had said far too much already. It seemed so long since he had cried "I'm so lonely," and she had thought the victory hers.

"Are you not feeling well, ma'am?" Hawkins asked that evening.

Beatrice answered, sitting at the dressing table and pressing her fingers to her temple, "I have a litle headache. That's not like me, is it, Hawkins?"

"No, ma'am. You're the one in this house that's always strong."

Too strong. Was that the trouble?

"We've decided to send Miss Daisy to school in Paris, Hawkins."

"Now that will do her a power of good. You'll be happier with her out of the house."

Hawkins had never gone so far before. Sometimes she had made obscure comments, but this attitude was blatant. Had she known the truth from the beginning, or was she, like Miss Brown, immune to Daisy's charms?

"Tell me what you mean, Hawkins."

"She takes up too much of her father's time. It isn't right. And poor Miss Florence is always outshone. That's not fair since she has all your good qualities."

"And Daisy hasn't?"

"You know she don't resemble you at all, ma'am."

That was all that was said.

But Hawkins had spoken a certain amount of truth, for it was much better when Daisy's lively disturbing presence was out of the house. If more dull.

Accompanied by her father, and innumerable trunks, she set off in early September after the summer vacation. Only Florence knew that she had cried herself to sleep every night lately because she thought she was disgraced and that Mamma was discarding her forever. But since she was able to manage her radiant smile when she said good-bye, Florence hardened her heart. People like Daisy didn't need to be pitied. Besides, Papa intended to stay in Paris until she was happily settled, which didn't suggest that her disgrace was being taken too seriously.

When Papa returned it would be Edwin's turn to leave, for he had received a posting to the British Embassy in Berlin. Edwin was hugely pleased. He so admired the Germans' efficiency with guns. He was hoping to get a look at the Krupp iron- and steelworks at Essen, he said. And also to try his skill at one of the famous German sports, hunting wild boar in the forests. He would prefer shooting grouse, but the boar represented a challenge which he did not intend to evade, poor eyesight or not.

Funny, the killing instincts of the Overtons, he thought ironically. Papa sticking pins in butterflies, himself tumbling birds out of the sky. But with Grandfather, the general, and a few other jolly ancestors, it had been people in their rifle sights, or at the receiving end of a sword. Which made them all a murderous lot, if you could count Papa with his butterflies. Privately, Edwin thought him a bit of a milksop with his poor health and his harmless academic occupations, and he was relieved that Papa, who still found the Germans too uncivilized for his taste, didn't propose to accompany his son on his first trip abroad. Edwin had learned very early in life that it was better to be self-sufficient. Love, especially parents' love, was arguably a very unreliable emotion.

He did, however, pay a farewell call on Grandmamma Bonnington in her gloomy house where the curtains were scarcely ever pulled back, and the air in the drawing room was the same musty concoction smelling of camphor and unaired clothes and filthy coal smoke which had circulated there when he was a child.

He thought old age grotesque and Grandmamma a prime example of this, with her wheezing breath, purple cheeks, nasty yellowish hair, pouting, peevish mouth and figure of colossal size. That nervous bird Miss Finch (though more like a stork than a finch) hovered constantly in the background.

One could not say that love or even affection drew Edwin to this curious establishment. His motives were much more deliberate. He knew he was Grandmamma's favorite. She wasn't rich. She owned only this ugly home, some jewelry and a great quantity of terrible clothes. Her actual income, which would cease at her death, came from Bonnington's.

But the house would fetch a fair price, and Edwin had strong hopes of it being bequeathed to him. As a school-boy his visits here had always been rewarded with a half sovereign, and when he went up to Oxford these welcome gifts had increased suitably.

Grandmamma was an old sport the way she helped a fellow out. It was the least he could do to pay her a dutiful visit now and then, and entertain her with a few schoolboy jokes which she greatly enjoyed. In a way, he was quite fond of the old horror, and he liked being told he was a dear kind boy. Few enough people said that about him, or even thought about him. He couldn't talk to his sisters, much less to his parents. He had long ago dis-covered that even when Mamma was kissing him good night, she was listening for Papa's step. Not even Grand-mamma actually knew how lonely he was. He never in-tended anyone to find that out, since he regarded it as shameful, and sign of an inadequate personality.

But Berlin and the new friends he would make, and the boar sticking and so on would change all that. He wanted to meet officers of those elite squadrons who paraded their dueling scars.

With good eyesight he could have been as good as any of them. And if one day before too long he got the money from the sale of Grandmamma's house, he could cut more of a dash. It was degrading always having to beg for money out of Bonnington's coffers. And one needed some com-pensation for having to acknowledge that one's mother was a shopkeeper.

Florence had quietly continued at Bonnington's. She said very little except that she had no alternative, since how could a jilted young woman return to social life? She would never have been able to hold up her head.

So she went where she could hold her own. To the Mantles department which she now intended to run. Old Brownie wouldn't object, because she had always carried on a feud with the other candidate for her shoes, Miss Saunders, who had once been recruited by Miss Beatrice from Worth's, and who looked down her nose at everything in Bonnington's, except the handsome salary she was paid.

Miss Florence had real talent, Miss Brown said. If she gave her whole attention to clothes, as she now said she intended doing, she could achieve wonders. Shops had to move with the times. Miss Brown stopped denying that she disliked modern fashions, that she thought women displayed too much bosom and ankle, that her heart was no longer in business.

Presently she would go home and prepare to die.

But first she would get Miss Florence safely established, and there were to be no regrets about a marriage that hadn't taken place. After all, what happiness had marriage given Miss Beatrice, if she were to speak the absolute truth? Miss Brown was inclined to mutter mysteriously about cuckoos and faithlessness, and congratulate Florence on her escape from some sort of slavery.

Florence didn't know what she was talking about and wasn't interested. She was too absorbed in the development of her new hard, ambitious, unsentimental self. She would prove she could be somebody in the world without the aid of a husband, and she could soon forget that silly dream of eight children who were now to remain unborn.

Much better for them, poor little mites. Life could hurt too much. Who would voluntarily choose it, except charming little show-offs like Daisy with her too high spirits and too few morals. Daisy wanted to wear a real diamond tiara when she came out. A tiny tiny one, she said, but all her own. That was the height of her ambitions.

Chapter 20

At the end of the current financial year Adam Cope announced with satisfaction that profits were up by twenty thousand pounds. It was due a great deal to the cessation of the war in South Africa. People felt secure once more. They had a pleasure-loving king and they wanted to follow his example, spend extravagantly and enjoy themselves. At least that was the maxim for the majority of Bonnington's customers. Beatrice found herself inclined to overlook the ninety percent of London's population which could not afford to shop in a high-class store. Well, there were shops in less affluent areas for them. Bonnington's, now it had the royal warrant, was turning more and more from practical goods to luxury goods. Papa would have been anxious, he had never thought the rich were good payers, for one thing, but Florence, who had an instinct for quality and a surprisingly strong will, was implementing some of her extravagant ideas. Beatrice was a little uneasy about this.

"Stock necessities," Papa had always said, "and you can't go wrong." Russian sables were scarcely necessities, nor were those expensive French toiles. They meant a considerable outlay, and a long wait for one's money, if they were sold to some members of the aristocracy who were pretty close with their checkbooks.

Adam Cope saw this problem in the same way. He and Beatrice had always thought alike. But he was being fair, as he announced in his level unemotional voice, "Mantles have done particularly well, and we must give Miss Florence a good deal of credit for this. Initially I was against including furs in our range, but I'm happy to have been proved wrong."

"If we claim to dress a young lady from the skin out we

213

must have furs," Florence said calmly. Like her mother, she had adopted a uniform for the shop. In her case it was a severe black dress adorned only with a long gold chain on which she hung the pretty little enameled watch her parents had given her for her twenty-first birthday. She had only recently been admitted to these meetings of the heads of staff. Beatrice was still against it. She thought Florence much too young and inexperienced. However, taking into consideration what she had already achieved, she had to be acknowledged. And, to be fair, she had been no older herself when, just married, she had come into Bonnington's.

"I agree with Miss Florence to a certain extent," Adam was saying in his measured voice. "But I'm not sure this maxim includes sables."

"Who are we dressing, Mr. Cope? Debutantes or housemaids?" Florence asked.

Beatrice nodded reluctantly. She hadn't cared for that rather daring motto of Florence's, "From the skin outward," but Florence had insisted that no fashionable young woman was dressed without a fur of one kind of another, beaver, fox, Persian lamb, red squirrel, ermine, even plain rabbit. And certainly sables for the fortunate few.

So a salon for furs came into being. It was carpeted in powder blue and furnished with comfortable couches, where husbands or fiancés were persuaded to sit and sip champagne while Florence herself, with her tall flat figure and pale hair and eyes, modeled the luxurious furs with professional skill. Even the wives approved of her, because she had a plain face and was so remote, like some sort of animated doll. And she never had the bad manners to recognize an old friend unless that friend recognized her first. It was a long time since she had gone to the palace to curtsy to the plump old lady with the little twinkling coronet perched on her black-veiled head.

That sort of thing had definitely been a waste of time, Florence told herself. In these new changed times, if she didn't allow herself to lie awake at nights, she was happy enough. She was a Bonnington, not an Overton. Her business life was becoming more and more absorbing, and she had so many fresh schemes to put into effect. Just in the moment that Mr. Cope had announced the increased profits a brilliant idea had flashed into her head.

Everyone was going mad about the Russian ballet since

Karsavina had danced at the Coliseum. It was rumored that next year Count Sergei Diaghilev's ballet would be coming for a season at Covent Garden theater. Why not, when it came, be ready with a display of Russian culture? All those bizarre and beautiful things, such as painted icons, jeweled caskets and trinkets made in the workshops of the famous jeweler Fabergé, materials of barbaric color and design, wooden carvings and furniture. Perhaps a violinist could be engaged to play background music by Tchaikovsky and Stravinsky.

"It would be stupendous," Florence said, her eyes getting the strange arctic gleam that betokened enthusiasm. Could she begin working on the project at once?

Adam Cope was growing penny-pinching in his old age. Beatrice saw him scowling and pulling down his mouth.

"Fabergé! But he's jeweler to the czarina. Only empresses can afford his stuff."

"Then let's have imitations made," Florence said promptly. "I wasn't thinking of an exhibition. Everything will be for sale—paintings, icons, wooden shoes, furs, brocades. But I really don't see why we shouldn't have some real jewelry as well. We don't want to look as if we can't afford the grand gesture. Don't you agree, Mamma?"

Beatrice thought wonderingly that it was simply no time since Florence had been too timid to do more than beg a favor. Now she was demanding, indeed she was giving orders. What an extraordinary effect that broken romance had had on her. One feared she was soured for life.

"Don't let yourself get so carried away, Florence. This scheme may work, or it may not. It requires a lot of thought. I admit it would make a wonderful window display and I can see that Mr. Brush is licking his lips at the thought. Well, Adam, we can't be the only sticks-in-the-mud. I suggest that Florence be allowed to work out the idea thoroughly, find her sources of supply and get her costings done. Then we can examine the scheme again. But don't rush into it, Florence. Plan it carefully."

"We could have all those wonderful colors, violets, scarlets, sharp yellows, that the ballet costumes are made of," Florence said dreamily. "They'll make Mr. Liberty and his William Morris stuff look very dull."

She should have been looking like that for Captain Desmond Fielding, Beatrice thought. Well, it was something that she could be aroused to this gleaming excitement at all. Papa, one imagined, would have approved. He would have laughed and exclaimed, "Good Gad! You've produced a Bonnington after all, Bea."

It was a long time since she had been devastated by those milk-and-water Gilbert and Sullivan operettas, Florence thought. What a silly gullible, impressionable creature she had been. Ready to spend all her emotions on the most transient and unreliable things. She knew better now. She would never again allow herself to be so vulnerable. One simply occupied one's mind with all sorts of schemes. Buying and selling was fascinating. She enjoyed filthy lucre. That was obviously in her blood. And she enjoyed bending people to her will, bossy old dowagers, timid daughters, fluttering, silly fashionable women. . . . In a way, it was a revenge for her own uneasiness in their social world. She had found her niche. If she had married she would probably have made a terrible wife.

Not that she intended to forgive Daisy or Desmond Fielding. Nourishing that resentment was making her the strong person she was. Shortly she could foresee endless quarrels with Mamma, who was growing old and therefore old-fashioned. And who had always been a deplorable mother, if it came to that, wrapped up in Papa and the shop, in equal proportions. What chance had her children had?

Edwin was particularly fierce about that. Since he had gone to live in Berlin he corresponded frequently with Florence. They had developed a rapport they hadn't known as children. He had been exceptionally understanding of her difficulties with Daisy, and she was more aware of his own disappointments in life.

"A happy person is much too selfish," she wrote, and he answered, "It always surprised me how Mamma could have a flibbertigibbet daughter like Daisy. She takes completely after our father, and I have always thought him rather a milksop of a man, although I suppose he can't help his bad health. How I wish Grandfather Overton had been our father. The more I hear of the Kaiser, and the more I see of him (riding his splendid charger) the more I admire him. He has overcome his disability of a withered arm, so likewise I am determined to overcome mine, of poor eyesight. I mean, I can compensate for it in some way. Life in Berlin is immensely exciting. I know some people don't care for the Germans' love of militarism, begun by that old war-horse Bismarck, but I think it is splendid and inspiring. I would dearly love to be a member of the military elite. Alas, I can only watch and admire. Don't tell this to other people, Flo, it might be misunderstood. I am British to the core, but I do think we can be awfully ineffective, and never see things until they are pushed right under our noses. For instance, I have no doubt that war Papa has always predicted will happen. But it is more likely to be against France or Russia than England. At least I hope so, for I can't see Germany being beaten. If only you could watch the squadrons with their colors parading down the Unter den Linden. I confess to you a very secret wish, that I had a dueling scar down my cheek. To me it is the complete emblem of manhood.

"It really was filthy luck for you about Desmond Fielding and the machinations of one's charming little sister. But good luck to you and your plans in Bonnington's. Make plenty of money. We need it. I don't suppose you could persuade Mamma that my salary and her allowance are ridiculously inadequate for the life I am supposed to lead here? If she doesn't cough up, I'll have to write to Granny, and God knows how long the idea will take to sink into her ancient head."

Money. The increased profits, Beatrice said, must as always go toward improvements and expansion. That clever American shopkeeper, Gordon Selfridge, was building a large department store in Oxford Street. He was expecting to lure custom from the established stores by means of brilliant and extravagant publicity ideas.

Bonnington's had neither the wish nor the ability to trade on Mr. Selfridge's scale. They must remain what Beatrice, with the assistance of Adam and Miss Brown, had so painstakingly created from Papa's hotchpotch drapery, a shop of taste and quality catering for the better-class customer, and with a reputation for the best window dressing in England. People said that it was bettered only by shops in the Place Vendôme and the Rue de Rivoli. Even

William agreed that this was so. He said that it all stemmed from Beatrice's early morning visit to Bon Marché on her honeymoon!

With the kind of husband and children she had. Beatrice reflected, she would not have dared run a cheap or cut-price business. They would have looked down their disdainful noses. Neither could she have displayed the royal warrant, her own private medal, outside a vulgar establishment.

So let Mr. Selfridge beat drums and fill his vast floors with the curious. Bonnington's would go on in its usual well-bred way, and keep its customers. All the same, it might be that Florence's Russian exhibition had come at an opportune time. That was a point to be conceded to Florence without, one hoped, her triumph going to her head.

The profits simply must not slump because her family grew more and more expensive. Sitting at her desk in the morning room, Beatrice did her accounts over again. William's allowance had been increased because of rising prices, and because he must be allowed his extravagances (the little Cotman, the yellow-ground Worcester dinner set, the Chinese red lacquer chest which exactly matched the red lacquer grandfather clock in the hall). William had an instinct for color, as proved by his marvelous iridescent butterfly collection. These objects were heirlooms, as Beatrice fully recognized. Though for whom? That troublesome little cuckoo, Daisy?

Edwin, in Berlin, had not mended his spendthrift ways, either. It seemed that to get on in his career he must give elegant (he called them *recherché*) dinner parties with the best food and wines. To these he invited influential people, not only members of the embassy staff, but Germans, those smart young officers of crack cavalry regiments he so admired, and their women friends. He had twice mentioned a Baroness Thalia von Hesselman, but this may merely have been Edwin's habit of name-dropping.

William wanted Beatrice to wash her hands of Edwin now, tell him he was out on his own, make him grow up. "Don't let him be like me," he said, "I've always lived on you."

"That's quite different. Anyway, you work so hard at

your books, and that's a lasting achievement. If only Edwin would work as hard."

"Perhaps he'll marry a rich wife." William's voice had its tinge of irony. "I'd recommend it."

"Would you?" Her too eager response was unguarded. She saw his gentle polite smile. His manners were too good. Simply too good.

The bill Edwin had just sent her for a pair of eighteenth-century dueling pistols of exquisite and irresistible quality, if she could just help him out temporarily because Grandmamma had unfortunately refused, had provoked that conversation with William. Now Beatrice pressed her lips together and wrote emphatically:

"No, my dear boy, you must take the pistols back to the dealer you bought them from. I am not made of money. I have all too many commitments. Surely these objects are quite unnecessary to either your welfare or your happiness." (Were William's treasures necessary to his happiness?)

Florence, apart from her ambitious ideas at the shop, seemed to have few personal requirements. Too few. She lived unnaturally quietly when not at business. She had asked that the day nursery, the old mirror room (what an enormous pity Mamma with her lack of aesthetic values had once destroyed that), be made into a sitting room for her, and she spent all her spare time there, mostly alone. She was too young to live so serious and sober a life. But the hard flippancy she had assumed after her ruined love affair seemed to be permanent. Beatrice doubted if she would ever now know what her daughter was feeling or thinking. If indeed she had ever known. . . .

But Daisy, at her finishing school, was another matter. According to her father, she required a great many expensive extras, like music lessons, art equipment, riding and dancing lessons, and a remarkably full wardrobe for a schoolgirl. This was necessary because of the theaters, the operas and dinner parties, and apparently all the other pupils were the daughters of millionaires! Daisy must not be outshone, must she? said William in his doting voice.

Could she be? Beatrice retorted.

This finishing school idea seemed to have turned into

one long festive occasion for William and his favorite child.
He was constantly slipping over to Paris to beg the headmistress (whom he had obviously charmed) to allow Daisy
to accompany him to see the Prix de l'Arc de Triomphe at
Longchamps, or Sarah Bernhardt in a new play, or to go
riding in the Bois de Boulogne, or to dine at Maxim's.

Daisy was seventeen, going on for eighteen. She would
have to come home soon.

Beatrice was ashamed of herself for dreading that day.
She wished she could look at Daisy and not see her mother.
But it was impossible. The prejudice and the pain were too
deep, and ineradicable.

William would expect Daisy's coming out to be something in the style of minor royalty, that was certain. There
would be balls, parties, soirees, the old treadmill which
Florence would boycott, and which she herself once more
would have to pretend to enjoy. And at the end of it,
probably, a large expensive society wedding.

In addition to this coming expenditure of thousands of
pounds, Mamma was now a semi-invalid and required a
nurse in attendance, as well as the faithful Miss Finch.
The bills from the house in Heath Street had gone up
astronomically, and Mamma had developed senile miserli-
ness. She refused to pay any of the servants or tradesmen.
She was saving all her money for dear Edwin who didn't
care a button for her. She had also had sent from Bonnington's the most expensive white satin lace-trimmed nightgown they had in stock. It was for her funeral. She didn't
intend to be buried looking like a lady's maid.

This was all too much for one woman, Beatrice thought,
tapping her pencil absently, frowning in anxiety. Was there
another woman in England who carried so much on her
shoulders?

Overton House, for instance, at this time in its two-hun-
dred-year-old history, needed extensive repairs to the roof,
and dry rot had been discovered in the attics. There had
been workmen prowling about for weeks, and William had
had to lock away his work, and go off to Paris to escape
the annoyance.

Miss Sloane, after years of loyal but uninspired service
in the schoolroom, had gone, and so had the French mademoiselle whom William had insisted on engaging for Daisy
before she had been sent to school. Old age had forced

Dixon to give up working. He could no longer mount the steps to his coachman's seat, nor control mettlesome horses. A young man, Johnnie Greaves, had taken his place, but William was talking of getting rid of the carriage and getting one of the new motors. At least it wouldn't require feeding when not working, as horses did. It would surely be an economy, which ought to please Beatrice.

Lizzie, now that the children were grown, had stayed on as a housemaid. Cook, too, in her sixties, intended to stay until she could no longer beat an egg satisfactorily. Overton House was their home. Hawkins was the third servant who could not imagine life anywhere else or with any other mistress. She was a little younger than Miss Brown, and considerably fitter, which was a good thing, because Miss Brown's days at Bonnington's were numbered. Shortly she would have to lie in her bed in that dark lonely house in Doughty Street, her blue nose pointing at the ceiling, her breathing rattling and wheezing with the bronchitis she couldn't throw off.

There would be a handsome pension for her, of course. But she probably wouldn't require it for very long.

There were other pensions to be paid, too. Beatrice refused to neglect a loyal employee grown old or incapacitated. This philanthropy could be carried to ridiculous ends, Florence objected. If pensions were to be paid, one should begin by stopping a small percentage from the staff's weekly wages. Accumulated over the years, this sum should take care of them in their old age.

But one liked the personal touch, Beatrice said. "You just want to be Lady Bountiful," Florence said scornfully. Florence, it seemed, was always going to want a fair return for outlay. Which was good for Bonnington's future, of course. But not for the heart she ought to have.

Well, money had been the motivating factor in her own life ever since her courtship, Beatrice admitted. She had accepted that fact then, so she could hardly complain now that it seemed to grow into a more imperative matter each year.

She was only a little tired. She would keep going for another ten years at least. What would she do without her life at the shop, anyway?

William wouldn't want her at home day after day. Her presence would be an embarrassment and a bore. He con-

sidered that the nights were enough, side by side in the big
bed. Although there were a great many of these when
William was away, especially now that Daisy had to be
looked after in Paris. They didn't often touch as they lay
in bed. They were getting a bit old for that sort of thing,
weren't they?

Beatrice had long ago taught herself to be content (or
as near content as possible) with what she had, William's
loved familiar body beside her, the sound of his breathing,
sometimes his hand briefly in hers, sometimes a little
drowsy talk. His health had been surprisingly good over
recent years, but he still had a delicate look. When sleeping, with his worn cheeks and his little pointed beard
touched with silver, he had a frail monkish look.

She had poured out so much love on this face, this body,
this mind, this intangible spirit that was William Overton.
She refused to dwell on the fact that at fifty she was still
waiting for some of it to be returned.

In the late autumn it was obvious that Grandmamma
at last was dying. She kept asking for Edwin. "Where is
he, Bea? Is he like his father, chasing women in Europe?"

"Mamma!"

The gross shape heaved beneath the bedclothes in a sad
attempt at a chuckle.

"Did I speak out of turn? Sorry. Your father never
thought of me if he could think of the shop. I'd have preferred it to be a woman."

Then she seemed to wander. "Beatrice! There was a
bird—"

"Who do you mean? Miss Finch?"

"No, no, no. A cuckoo. I know. Old Brownie knows,
too. Safe as the grave, old Brownie."

Daisy, thought Beatrice. She's always known. Poor sad
old thing. Will my children know as little about me as I do
about my mother when I lie dying?

"Would you like a drink of water, Mamma? A little beef
tea?"

"Nothing. Nothing more in this world." The ghostly
chuckle heaved in the breathless chest again. "What a relief.
All that putting into one's stomach, and getting out again.
Tiresome things, bodies. Glad to—" She stopped speaking,
and seemed to sleep. A few moments later she opened her
eyes and said in an uncannily normal voice, "Bea, your

father always said money could do anything. Well, it produced Edwin and Flo and I suppose that naughty Daisy, too. In a different way, heh? Heh, Bea? But don't go on—"

"Don't go on what, Mamma?" Beatrice asked, bending over the suddenly collapsed face.

"Expecting it to bail you out of trouble. Tell Edwin."

"Edwin will be here tomorrow, Mamma. You can tell him yourself."

"All the same, when Joshua began making money I thought it was fine." Mamma's eyes, opaque gray and white marbles, stared sorrowfully at Beatrice. "But it doesn't make you happy. Have you found that out, Bea?" A quick panic passed over her face. "Don't let Miss Finch hear. I've kept it from her that I was a ser-servant." The hated word stumbled on her thick tongue. Before it could be spoken properly, she was gone.

A long expelled breath and there was just this gross body that had never succeeded in forgetting the long-ago hunger and poverty and humiliation.

I will have a ghost in me, too, Beatrice thought, gently closing the staring eyes. But everyone, if they have lived at all, must share their deathbed with at least one ghost. Poor Mamma's at least was innocent, and part of herself. Not another woman. . . .

Chapter 21

The will was to be read after the funeral, when Edwin had
arrived from Germany and Daisy from Paris. Beatrice
asked that this occasion take place in the drawing room at
Overton House. She didn't think she could stand the gloom
of Mamma's house, where the dark cluttered, claustrophobic rooms were still full of the musty stuffy smell of
old flesh, and uncleaned clothes with overtones of lavender
water that was so individually Mamma.

She had always hated that house, anyway, and in the half-
light of a foggy November day it would be insupportable.

An enormous fire burned in the fireplace of her own
drawing room. William, who hadn't gone to the funeral
because it was such a dank cold day and gravesides were
such famous places for catching pneumonia, was sitting in
his favorite armchair. He had grown noticeably older
lately, Beatrice realized with a pang. His look of interesting frailty was near to gauntness. But he was still the best-
looking man she had ever met, with his lively brown eyes,
his charming gentle smile, his air of courtesy and breeding,
even his look of quiet acquiescence to fate. He hadn't always had that look, but one tried not to notice it.

She herself felt that she could have benefited from a little of his frailty. She was altogether too healthy and in-
destructible, although sometimes she fancied Florence
looked at her speculatively at staff meetings. Florence was
turning into a coldly ambitious young woman. One could
see her ultimate objective would be control of Bonnington's, and that not too far ahead. If only she would find
herself a husband. One didn't want a Miss Brown in the
family, perpetually dressing other brides.

When Mr. Thorpe, the solicitor, arrived Beatrice found

herself studying her children instead of listening attentively to the contents of Mamma's will.

Her house to Edwin, her jewelry (ugly jet beads and semi-precious stones which Florence would despise) to Florence, except for one dismal mourning brooch to Miss Finch, which could only be regarded in the nature of an insult. Five pounds to her cook, and five pounds to the housemaid. The unlucky Miss Finch also got an ostrich feather stole, a tortoiseshell fan, and ten pounds, and had the hypocrisy to show pleasure. Was it genuine? Were some women as truly humble as this? Whatever her real emotions, her services to Mamma had been faithful and long-suffering, so it looked as if she would have to be found some niche in Overton House. At least she would not be obtrusive.

Daisy was not mentioned in the will. Mamma seemed to have completely overlooked her existence.

Edwin had begun wearing a monocle. Beatrice didn't care at all for the supercilious look it gave him. But then he had always hated his spectacles, poor boy. No doubt the monocle gave him more confidence. He was certainly a handsome young man. But strange, withdrawn, unknowable.

Even hearing of his grandmother's handsome legacy had brought no more than a small satisfied smile to his face. What was wrong with him and Florence? Had they no natural warmth or love for poor Grandmamma or their parents?

Daisy was the one who showed generous delight at Edwin's good fortune, and made a quick humorous *moue* of distaste when Florence received the ugly Victorian jewelry. She hadn't shown any distress when her own name failed to be mentioned.

But they taught good manners in that French school. Daisy's were noticeably improved. She was behaving with quiet decorum. And she looked touchingly wistful and large-eyed and demure in the black dress that had been quickly made for her in Bonnington's workroom. "Has she really got an eighteen-inch waist?" one of the seamstresses had been heard to remark.

She was going to be a raving beauty, there were no two ways about that. And how was one to cope with all the inevitable complications of that situation when they were not leavened by maternal love?

Get her married young, Beatrice said to herself. That should present little difficulty. There would be plenty of successors to the spurned Captain Fielding.

"I think some wine, my love," Beatrice said before dinner that night. "It's the first time we've been together as a family for a long time. Don't let's grieve for Mamma. She wouldn't want it."

"She wasn't fair to Daisy," William said.

"No. I suppose she wasn't. But Daisy wouldn't have wanted that hideous jewelry any more than Florence does. All I can say is, I hope Edwin doesn't squander the whole of his legacy too quickly. I think you should speak to him about the set he's getting in with in Berlin."

"What set? He hasn't talked to me about it."

"Only because you're prejudiced against Germans, and he seems to admire them a great deal."

"Then he has questionable taste."

"Perhaps. I think some of the Moselle, don't you? It is not too heavy for the girls. And really, William, Daisy does very well without Mamma remembering her. It won't damage her pride. She isn't sensitive like Florence."

But she was. Only she would never never let anyone be aware of it. Smile! she said to herself in her bedroom. Laugh! Be gay! Even in this horrible black dress. I wonder if the roof would fall if I went down in a pretty dress. If anyone besides Papa noticed, of course. Florence still hates me, Edwin has always been too full of himself to notice my existence, and Mamma doesn't approve of me. She simply never has. I think she secretly hoped that that day when I was stolen out of my pram I would never be found again. Sometimes I wish I hadn't been. The woman who took me must really have wanted me very much.

Muttering to herself Daisy pinned up her rich brown curls. There was the usual problem of their escaping from hairpins and tumbling onto her neck or over her brow. She wished she was back in Paris. No, she didn't. Unless Papa was there to bribe Madame with a box of her favorite bonbons, and consequently to be permitted to take M'selle Daisy out. It was appallingly dull and stupid at Madame's school, and some of the Swiss and German girls were pure bitches. There had, of course, been the brief excitement of her love affair with Antoine, the good-looking gardener. She had left notes for him in the greenhouse, and the strawberry bed, and he had responded with passionate expressions of adoration. But that had ended when she discovered that he had a wife and two small children. The false wretch. But he still admired her from a distance, his black eyes flashing, and she had by no means broken her heart over him.

One day she would break her heart. She longed to. It was part of living. She would grow romantic and pensive and speak in a low voice of lost love. She certainly wouldn't grow the hard flippant shell that Florence had.

But neither would she be unhappy forever, of course. There was no shortage of fascinating men in the world and she intended to meet her share of them. One of them would truly love her, and the secret gnawing loneliness in her heart would at last vanish forever.

And no one would ever remind her that once a fat selfish insensitive old woman had forgotten that she had a granddaughter called Daisy.

It was really terrible to be forgotten. It was like not existing.

At ten minutes to seven she tapped at Florence's door. "May I come in? Are you dressed?"

A mumbled assent came from within. Then Florence gasped, "What are you doing in that dress?"

Daisy looked from Florence's narrow-waisted black—she was like a burned stick—to her own primrose-yellow voile.

"Grandmamma didn't remember me, so why should I remember her?"

"It's only good manners. What Mamma will say—or the servants? It will be all over the Heath—"

"That Miss Daisy Overton danced on her grandmother's grave? Well, she deserved it. Anyway, I can't bear to be all black and dreary. You know that. Besides, by wearing a yellow dress I'm not impeding Grandmamma's progress to heaven. Why is it always assumed that peopde do go to heaven?"

"Don't change the subject. If you're going down in that dress you're going down alone."

"All right. I don't mind. Though I do think—" Daisy

suddenly advanced impulsively with her arms held out.
"Flo, are you *never* going to forgive me?"

"I'm always going to know what you are, if that's what
you mean."

"But I'm the same person you used to love. I was only
being civil to Captain Fielding. I couldn't help it if he
liked me better than you."

"You didn't have to throw yourself at him. And just to
amuse yourself. That's what I can't forgive."

"I was so bored in the schoolroom! Anyway, I only
played and sang to him."

"And held his hand and looked into his eyes and whispered and giggled."

"Not giggled!" Daisy cried, outraged. "I don't giggle. I
didn't do the other things either. I mean, not seriously. I
was only experimenting. Didn't you experiment with your
female powers when you were sixteen?"

"Who with?" said Florence bleakly. "Captain Fielding
is the only man who ever looked at me. But you, who
didn't love him, didn't even like him, I imagine, couldn't
resist experimenting, as you call it. And now," Florence
finished dramatically, "I'm a shopgirl!"

"Oh, Flo, you're always so intense. I can't help it if I'm
prettier than you."

"But you could have been a bit invisible. Couldn't you?
Are you going to see Captain Fielding again?"

"Oh, heavens, I hope not!" Daisy exclaimed spontane-
ously. "But I suppose it's possible I'll run into him at
balls."

Florence's pale-blue eyes rested on Daisy with detachment.

"Heartless, thoughtless, shallow, cruel. And you expect
me to forgive you. Life can't be made that easy for Miss
Daisy Overton just because she's pretty and charming.
What you need, my girl, is a taste of your own medicine."

With that unkind remark, Florence swept out of the
room, her black taffeta skirts rustling. With her hair piled
high, she looked like one of those terrifying sexless *ven-
deuses* in the Paris *couturier* establishments. What sort of
a wife would she make for Captain Fielding? Perhaps
Bonnington's and shopkeeping were her true niche after
all, Daisy thought, and was comforted. She hadn't liked
her year-long burden of guilt.

Papa could always be counted on to be on her side.

This evening he said approvingly that she brought a ray of sunshine to the table, which statement took Mamma's reproving words right out of her mouth.

So she sat happily in her yellow dress and attempted a little gay dinner table conversation. Edwin responded. He actually went to smart dinner parties in Berlin and had grown quite expert at dinner table conversation. He began to talk with increasing enthusiasm about German customs and the people he knew. Baron and Baroness von Hesselman's name kept cropping up.

"Who is this Baron von Hesselman?" Papa asked.

"He's a member of the aristocracy, Father."

"I'd assumed that."

"He's a close friend of the Krupps. He's also a Uhlan officer."

"Cavalry?"

"Yes, Father, of course."

"Your father isn't to know a great deal about German regiments," Mamma put in.

"But the Uhlan cavalry is famous, Mother. All the officers are crack horsemen and swordsmen. Most of them have dueling scars."

"And I never saw how that added to a man's good looks," Florence said.

"It does, I assure you. It has a sort of mystique of bravery and daring. Women love it." Edwin fingered his own smooth cheek tentatively. His monocle made him look foreign.

"Anyway, what I was saying about the Krupps, Father. Baron von Hesselman says he'll provide the courage and fighting skill if Krupps provide the guns."

"What for?" Papa asked, as if he were stupid.

"When they go to war, of course. They're bound to go to war sooner or later. The Kaiser's supposed to be obsessed with the Grand Plan that Schlieffen drew up. And he loves martial music. When the troops parade down the Unter den Linden it's quite a thing to see."

"I would prefer to watch our own Guards parading down the Mall," Papa said stiffly. "I can't think why you think these Germans better than them, Edwin. Give me a Coldstreamer to a Uhlan any day."

"I didn't say I thought them better, Father."

"It's those dueling scars," Daisy murmured. "Has the

baron some, Edwin? Is that what made the baroness fall in love with him?"

"How do you know she's in love with him?"

"I don't. I don't even know them. I'm asking you. Is she beautiful, too? I mean, of course, without dueling scars."

Edwin's monocle had fallen out of his eye. As it was anchored by a black cord around his neck it had not fallen far, but he blushed violently as he retrieved it. He could scarcely see across the table without it, and it made him squint. But it seemed he needed the confidence these affectations gave him.

"Thalia von Hesselman is quite attractive," he said offhandedly.

"For a German, I imagine," said Papa.

"Father, you're a little unfair."

"I hope I am, my boy."

"She's very loyal, too. She still wears that iron jewelry the German women were given in exchange for theirs during the Franco-Prussian War. It looks marvelous on her, I must say."

"The Iron Maiden," Papa murmured. "Daisy, a little more of the sherry trifle? I believe Cook made it especially for you. Bea, don't you think we can keep Daisy home for Christmas? She looks remarkably well finished to me."

"Except for failing to show respect to her grandmother," Mamma said, making sure of that reproof at last. "Well, we'll see. We must get Aunt Sophie up from the country, William, to discuss Daisy's season. If she thinks she can undertake it. One must remember she's quite an old lady now."

"Oh, there's nothing like a season to rejuvenate Aunt Sophie. She'll sail up with all colors flying. They tell me Queen Alexandra's a bit starchy."

"It's only because she's deaf, poor thing. Florence, you'll have to take over Daisy's wardrobe now that Miss Brown is unavailable."

"Oh, no!" cried Daisy apprehensively. "I mean, being dressed by one's sister—"

"Florence's taste is impeccable. She already has a great many recommendations, including two from duchesses."

"She'll make me look ugly," Daisy muttered.

"Perhaps I will," said Florence.

Papa looked from one to the other. But all he said was, "That would be an impossibility. Perhaps we might have one or two things from Worth, Bea? Just for variety."

"I'll sell the house." Edwin, as always, was totally absorbed in his own thoughts.

"The house? Oh, you mean Grandmamma's?" Mamma was uncertain. "I think you ought to take advice on that, Edwin. Don't you agree, William? It's a nice property investment as it is."

"I'll invest the proceeds. When I've paid off my tailor and one or two other small things."

"Edwin is of age, Bea. We can't dictate to him, whatever we may think."

Mamma's eyes had their thoughtful but steely look.

"Just so long as he understands that we don't finance him anymore. In future if you have debts, Edwin, they're your own affair. That's reasonable. Your father and I have done a great deal for you."

"Understood, Mother. Understood."

"Excellent. And now"—Mamma was as busy as a bee tonight—"let's decide what's to be done about Miss Finch."

"Oh, she'll fit into a crack in the wall," Papa said easily.

"It's what she's always done, I'm afraid. It would be nice if we could make her a little happier."

"All those employees in Bonnington's, Bea. Do you think about their happiness as well as their wages?"

"As much as I can. And Miss Finch deserves something better than Mamma's bullying. Florence and Daisy might share her as a personal maid."

"I don't want a maid. I pick up my own clothes," Florence said flatly. "If I'm to succeed Miss Brown at the shop I don't want any advantages she didn't have."

"Poor old Brownie," said Mamma. "It seems she has a little heart trouble now. We must all look after her, too."

That night William moved over to Beatrice's side of the bed, and waited for her to fold him in her arms. This she did lovingly and gladly. She knew what was troubling him. He hated death, not only poor Mamma's death, but all departures from this world. He was haunted for days or weeks by thoughts of damp cold churchyards and decay.

She hated it, too. But anything that brought her husband willingly into her arms could not be hated entirely.

So her thoughts, as she lay in the warm bed, listening to the wind outside, and to William's gentle breathing against her breast, were half poignant, half happy. She had forgotten the sharpened concern she had felt at dinner that night for the way her children were growing up.

"But you will come in with me!" Florence hissed, gripping Daisy's wrist savagely. "What are you scared of?"

"I hate illness. Smells."

"It's only humanly right that you go and see her. She's known you from a baby."

"But she's never liked me."

"Don't be silly! Come on!"

So Daisy was dragged into the dark small room where Miss Brown lay, conserving all her energy, so that only her eyes moved, and the tip of her nose twitched.

"Miss Florence—Miss Daisy—"

"We brought you some daffodils," Florence said.

"Ah! Back from Paris—"

"You mean Daisy? She's been back since before Christmas. Don't you remember?"

"Of course. . . . Coming out—"

"Next month," said Daisy, forcing herself to go close to the bed and smile at the skeletal face on the pillow. Such a narrow bed. Such a lonely bed.

But Mr. Charles Dickens had used to go in and out of the house opposite. One had to remember this highlight in the lives of old Mrs. Brown and her daughter. Everyone in this world had something to value, Daisy comforted herself. According to their standards, of course. She would want something more than Mr. Charles Dickens.

"What?"

"Pale yellow for her dance," Florence answered, anticipating the question. She didn't add that the pale-yellow chiffon over silk, like mimosa, came from Worth's salon, not from Bonnington's. A great deal, of course, was coming from Bonnington's.

"I do hope you'll be feeling better soon, Miss Brown," Daisy said, with all her natural warmth.

"Oh, yes . . . I shall—"

Before the girls went she managed another gasped sentence.

"Your trousseau . . . Miss Daisy—"

"All in good time," said Daisy gaily. "I'm still absolutely heartfree."

What a pity there was no giving in marriage in heaven, so that Miss Brown could have been happily engaged on preparing trousseaux for all eternity.

One had to remember her long life of loyalty to Bonnington's, Mamma said, and pay her the utmost respect at her death.

That was a pension saved, said Papa, but not unkindly. He even consented to go to Miss Brown's simple funeral, which was a great concession from him.

It was the end of an era, said Mamma sadly.

Now was the chance to modernize the workrooms, and do a new daring, fashionable color scheme in the showrooms, Florence said. Old Brownie had been fine in her day, but that day was long ago, and all the fittings were hopelessly out of date, and unsmart.

"Unsmart" was a word Florence had coined, and frequently used. It could never have been applied to herself.

Chapter 22

Fortunately for Daisy, King Edward the Seventh died the year before she came out, so her season was not spoiled by a cloud of black mourning over the summer scene. The coronation of the new king, George the Fifth, would make the next year a colorful one. It should be quite a year for Daisy.

The Kaiser, Edwin wrote, gave his empress a birthday present of a dozen hats. What a pity he didn't live in London; he would have made a splendid customer for Bonnington's. Even without his patronage, however, Bonnington's prospered.

Beatrice decided to get rid of their horses, except the cob which William liked to drive, and buy a very imposing Daimler motorcar in which she and Florence could drive daily to the shop. Daisy spent her time in a fuss and flurry of organdies and chiffons, and picture hats and tea gowns, and invitations to parties and balls. William announced his intention of staying in England for the whole of Daisy's coming-out year, and seemed completely contented to be at home.

Sitting up in the back of the Daimler with the hood down, Beatrice and Florence tied their hats on with long silk scarves, and decided they must stock a new range of goods called motoring clothes.

The young chauffeur Bates, engaged to drive the Daimler, wore a smart gray uniform and cap, very different from poor old Dixon's long coat which was designed to keep his ankles warm on the box of the carriage. Bates had no interest in horses. He was a man of this alarming new age, a time which, to Beatrice's dismay, seemed to be dominated by smelly, noisy engines. Although she had to admit the Daimler was faster and more comfortable than the now old-fashioned carriage. Florence had insisted that they must keep up with, or even keep ahead of, the times. She liked the picture she and her mother made, sailing down the Bayswater Road in the spring morning. Miss Bea and Miss Florence of Bonnington's. Let that American usurper, Mr. Selfridge, think they cared about his expensive elephant of a store. Admittedly, it was bringing in a great many customers. "But not ours," they said smugly.

That strange gifted Russian, Count Sergei Diaghilev, after his triumph in Paris, was bringing his ballet with his leading dancer Nijinsky to Covent Garden theater in the early summer, and Florence was deep in plans for her Russian exhibition. It was going to be exquisite, jewellike and unique. Mr. Selfridge's lilies and carnations, his string orchestra and painted backcloths depicting Watteau and Fragonard, were going to pale in comparison.

"But what are we going to sell?" Beatrice grumbled.

"Cossack hats, for one thing. *Petrouchka* puppets. I've found a toymaker who will make as many as we can sell. Ball gowns in *Firebird* colors," said Florence, whose own elegance was composed of subdued grays and fawns.

"It's a terrible gamble."

"I expect that's what Grandpapa used to say about your ideas," Florence commented.

Beatrice nodded grudgingly. But she smiled to herself, remembering her startling and successful innovations in window dressing. Poor Papa had had to submit to those changes because his poor health had taken away the energy needed for opposing that small determined whirlwind, his daughter.

She had both sufficient strength and energy to oppose Florence. But her fairness wouldn't allow her to do so. Give the girl a chance. She would make mistakes, of course, although so far she had made surprisingly few. In a way, she was simply carrying on the tradition her mother had begun. But it was a little galling to have to admit that she might be even more clever.

"It's the twentieth century now," Florence added, not for the first time. She knew it was the most effective way of putting her mother in her place.

But I'm not tired, Beatrice thought to herself, even if my daughter considers me to be a nineteenth-century woman.

I can go on for many years yet. I've lost Miss Brown but I've still got Adam's support. We represent Bonnington's solid success. Florence wants only the spectacular trimmings. But what else has she got in life, poor child? I'm so lucky, I have my adored husband.

Only, be honest, I'd be lost without the shop. It's a habit now. I'd be lost wandering about the house all day, keeping out of William's and the servants' way. The way William and I have lived, our marriage has been a most splendid success.

Except for Mary Medway.

Except for Daisy.

There had been no peace in the house since Daisy had come home. She was gay, restless, pleasure-seeking, delectably pretty and superficial. Although sometimes Beatrice caught her looking at her mother in a thoughtful way that hinted at some unexpressed feelings, which made Beatrice feel vaguely and unjustifiably guilty.

She filled the house with her friends, created a great deal of extra work (although the servants, doting on her, never complained) and was woefully extravagant. She needed a new gown for each ball, a succession of wide-brimmed flower-decked hats, parasols, ruinously expensive French kid shoes, tea gowns, heaven knew what, all to keep that exquisite little body suitably decked for the husband-hunting game.

Old Aunt Sophie, stiff-jointed, rice powder lying in the wrinkles of her face, a high choker of pearls constantly around her skinny neck (holding her head on, Florence said unkindly), but still completely in command of social affairs, kept her gay little butterfly in control. One had to say for Daisy that she had charming manners with the elderly. Aunt Sophie, who had suffered that stick Florence, was genuinely fond of Daisy. Indeed, she loved her, she admitted. "The child needs love," she had the impertinence to tell Beatrice.

As if she hadn't always been loved adequately! And look at the ball they were giving her, with champagne, Russian caviar, plovers' eggs, cold turkey, whole pineapples from Jamaica, wild strawberries, everything of the most expensive because William wanted it that way.

It was to be the most brilliant ball at Overton House

since the days when General Overton had brought home his little porcelain-faced bride.

Edwin was getting leave and coming home for it, but it was a pity that Florence had said she couldn't attend. Her Russian exhibition was proving more difficult to arrange than she had expected, and of all things, she proposed making a journey to Moscow and St. Petersburg to gather genuine articles of Russian culture. It was going to make the cost of the exhibition ruinous, but Florence was full of words like "prestige" and "originality" and "flair." James Brush was traveling with her, together with a woman assistant, to remove any hint of scandal from the venture. The only scandal was that she had arranged her absence at the time of Daisy's ball, simply because Captain Fielding, who still had stubborn though diminishing hopes of persuading Daisy to marry him, was coming.

One had to admit that it would have been humiliating and embarrassing for Florence to meet him, although she might just have endured it for Daisy's sake, instead of arranging this elaborate face-saving expedition.

Daisy was deeply hurt. She hated the never-ending punishment Florence was meting out. It was so unfair. One could only pretend not to notice it, and not let it spoil the lovely, exciting, shimmering evening when she was secretly hoping to fall in love. As didn't every girl at her coming-out ball? Even Florence had done so, though with disastrous consequences.

I won't have any disasters, Daisy thought. I will fall in love deeply and forever, and I will be loved back in the same way. I don't care who it is, rich man, poor man, beggar man, thief, so long as we love each other.

Disappointingly, it didn't turn out that way. Not that the ball wasn't a great success. It was dawn and the birds were singing in the garden before the last guests departed. Daisy had danced a hundred times. She had been complimented, flattered, adored, and kissed beneath the stairs, by a bold but embarrassed young guardsman. But no young man had made any shattering impact on her sense.

All those pink-cheeked, well-behaved young men had been so *dull*.

She made this remark to Edwin when they both sat in

the deserted ballroom, their feet up on the little golden chairs, now gladly vacated by the sleepy and exhausted chaperones.

Edwin said that in his opinion the girls had been dull, too.

"I would exchange all those blue-blooded Englishmen for one amusing Frenchman." Daisy sighed.

"Me, too, with the women, though I'd make mine German instead of French."

"Would you really? But I always thought German women were pretty dull, too. Fat, heavy *Fräuleins.*"

"Some of them. Not all."

Edwin looked self-conscious, and Daisy exclaimed, "Have you a special one? Oh, do tell me. Are you in love?"

Edwin blushed. He still blushed much too easily. He had also had a little too much champagne, and was less inhibited than usual.

"Yes, I am. For God's sake, don't tell anyone."

"Why? Would the parents disapprove?"

"Not only them. Everyone."

"*Edwin!* Are you having an illicit liaison?"

"Not exactly. I mean we haven't done anything. Except talk and hold hands. God, there's not much satisfaction in that."

"Is she married?"

Edwin hesitated, then nodded.

"*Edwin!* But you're mad. In your career—"

"A man even forgets his career when he's in love," Edwin said intensely. "You watch it, young Daisy. You'll find out one day. Do you know, I estimate that only one couple in ten, perhaps less than that, marry happily without complications or reservations, or plain dislike. Look at Mother and Father."

"But Mamma adores Papa. She's still absolutely besotted with him, even at their age!"

"But he isn't with her. You only have to have eyes in your head to see that. Poor devil, he's had to make a good show of it all these years. I tell you I wouldn't be like that, marry for money, or for any reason but love."

"Neither would I," Daisy agreed fervently. "All the same, if the complications are too great—"

"They can never be too great if your love is strong enough."

"Is that what you and this *Fräulein*—no, she must be a *Frau* if she's married—have decided?"

"She's not a *Frau*, she's a baroness," Edwin said stiffly.

"Edwin!" Daisy was shocked and intrigued for the third time. "Is she the one you talked about at dinner once? Thalia?"

"Yes."

"Is she very beautiful?"

"Very."

"Does she love you, too?"

"Naturally. Or I wouldn't be talking like this." Edwin's monocle fell out of his eye, and he left it out, and sat back looking suddenly boyish and sad. "But we didn't mention it until I spent a weekend with them, she and her husband, in their castle in Silesia. It was a hunting party. I happened to be the best shot there, and it was all great fun, and Thalia said what a great pity it was about my eyes preventing me having an army career. She said I'd have been a better soldier even than Horst—her husband—and he was one of the best. And then suddenly I found I was kissing her, and she wanted me to, and it all just happened."

"You mean . . . everything!" Daisy exclaimed.

"Oh, heavens, no, not that. I haven't gone that far." Edwin sighed. "Though I want to. And I shall if I'm ever given the opportunity."

"Oh, Edwin, do be careful."

"I'm careful. And I shouldn't be telling you this. Why am I?"

"I don't know. Because we've both had too much champagne, I expect. Oh, Edwin darling, I am so sorry."

He smiled faintly. "You're a warmhearted little thing, aren't you? Different from Flo. You haven't got frozen in this house yet."

"No. Though I feel cold sometimes."

Edwin nodded understandingly.

"It was only a warm house once, for a little while, when Flo and I had a governess called Miss Medway. You weren't born then. We loved her, but Mamma sent her away, and then it got cold again."

"I don't feel cold with Papa. Only with Mamma."

"I know. She never used to see us when we were children. Did you ever notice that? She thought she did, of course. Oh, well, who cares? Who cares?" He held out his arms. "Let's have another dance before we go to bed. It's been a good night. Though better if I had had Thalia and you had had your Frenchman."

Daisy went into his arms and began gently waltzing with him, humming to herself.

"He might not be a Frenchman. He might be an Italian or a Swede or a Turk or a Russian. I just don't think he's going to be an Englishman." She swooped dreamily in circles. "I never used to like you, Edwin. I never thought you were human. But you are, aren't you? I suppose falling in love has done it. But do be careful."

"Caution and love never mix."

"You look so handsome without that silly monocle. Not so awe-inspiring, but handsome."

"And I can't see a thing."

"You could never marry her, Edwin."

"Unless the baron died. We might fight a duel."

Daisy gave one more startled exclamation.

"You're crazy. It might be you who got killed."

"I told you, I'm a better shot than Horst."

"You're teasing me. You're not going to shoot him. Besides you could never afford a castle in Silesia."

"Aye, there's the rub. That's one thing Mamma's purse won't stretch to. Anyway, she says I'm in charge of my own fate now."

"Are you?"

"I'm going to have a damned good try."

Florence came home triumphantly with piles of baggage. "Like the Queen of Sheba, only there's no King Solomon," Daisy murmured wickedly. However, when the baggage was unpacked and, a month later, displayed in a splendid island on the ground floor of Bonnington's, Daisy was generous in her admiration. The effect was stunning. Florence seemed to have brought everything with her except the czar and czarina themselves.

What was more, Florence had pulled off another brilliant coup. The Russian ballet had just opened at Covent Garden in a glorious gala performance in honor of the coronation of King George and Queen Mary, and somehow Florence had persuaded some members of the cast, not the great Nijinsky, to be sure, but some impressive lesser names, to attend the opening. She was able to advertise this fact in all the morning papers, and to splash posters along the whole of Bonnington's façade.

"They're not coming in costume, I hope," Adam Cope said to Beatrice, in some apprehension.

"Oh, goodness me, no."

"I hear those tights they wear are embarrassing," Adam muttered. "We have to think of our older customers."

"Ballet is supposed to be a great art." Having made that concession to her daughter's efforts, Beatrice could add reassuringly that, dressed in ordinary clothes instead of the embarrassing tights, the dancers were going to look quite insignificant. No one would notice them.

However, she was wrong about that, in more ways than one.

The shop was thronged. It seemed as if the whole audience at Covent Garden theater, which had watched Nijinsky's brilliant *Petrouchka* the previous evening, had come to Bonnington's today to buy *Petrouchka* puppets and toy Cossack dancers, and the brilliant red-and-gold brocades, the fur-lined cloaks and those strange barbaric necklaces and rings. Florence excitedly reported the sale of one sable coat already (she had invested in six, as an experiment), and a certain very wealthy lord had been more than interested in a Fabergé gold and enamel box set with emeralds and rubies. It wasn't the Cullinan diamond, which Queen Mary had worn to the theater the previous evening, but it was a bauble that Beatrice would never have had the courage to stock. She still feared that they were getting out of their depth, although Florence insisted that they wait until the exhibition was over before they anticipated their losses.

Actually, it didn't seem as if there would be a loss, because it did promise to be the most spectacular and successful display they had ever had.

Even William had come. It seemed that Daisy had persuaded him, and here he was, smiling, and admitting that Florence had been very clever indeed. She also seemed to have taste, which was a blessing. But where were the famous dancers? Weren't they at least wearing Cossack hats so that they could be distinguished? Or perhaps they would execute an arabesque.

Daisy said, "Don't be naughty, Papa. If you wait here

I'll make a bet I find one and bring him to talk to you."

"You'll cheat. You'll ask Florence."

"I promise I won't."

"Then do make sure that he can speak English, otherwise we'll simply have to stare at one another."

"I'll use my instinct," Daisy said gaily.

And that indeed was what led her to the young man standing on the edge of the crowd, looking interested but puzzled. It was very obvious that he was not English. He had high cheekbones and long tilted, shining dark eyes that suggested Tartar blood. He was tall and slender with thick glossy hair as black as his eyes, and growing long down his neck. One could almost have tied it back with a ribbon. He looked alien and very exciting, and was certainly one of the visitors, but Daisy didn't entirely win her bet with her father because he was not one of the dancers.

"Aren't you?" Daisy said disappointedly. "I'm sorry, I made a mistake."

"But I am traveling with the ballet."

Daisy turned back eagerly. "Then you are a Russian?"

"Oh, yes."

"You speak awfully good English."

"I am an interpreter."

"You mean you interpret for the *corps de ballet*?"

"For all those who do not speak English or French. I also am scene shifting and carrying baggage and doing the bookkeeping."

Daisy said, "My mother would appreciate the bookkeeping."

"Appreciate?"

"Approve. She likes doing figures."

"Your mother!"

His tilted eyebrows lifted in surprise and perplexity, and Daisy began to giggle.

"My mother's good at figures. Are you a ballet lover?"

"Excuse?"

"A follower of the ballet?"

"Oh, yes. I even can dance myself, but not well enough to be a member of the *corps de ballet*. I am improving my English, which is why I am here in London."

He looked at her seriously, then something made him smile, and his strange eyes flickered and blazed, and Daisy felt as if a shaft of lightning had struck her. Or, if that was exaggerating, something pretty effective had struck her. She wondered if Edwin had felt like this when his German baroness had looked into his eyes.

"My father wants to meet you," she managed to say in a casual voice.

"Me! How is he aware of me?"

"He isn't. It's as a bet. Do you understand? A wager."

"No."

"It means—oh, just come."

He followed her through the crowd, but Papa was no longer where she had left him. A shopgirl touched Daisy's arm. "Excuse me, miss, your father asked me to tell you he's gone to have tea with your mother. You're to join them."

Up the stairs, beneath the towering potted palms, the orchestra was playing the *Nutcracker Suite*. The store blazed with light and color. It had never been so gay or so festive. It was the stage of Covent Garden theater, a piece of Eastern extravaganza.

"I'm so sorry, my father didn't wait," Daisy said to her companion. As those strange exciting eyes looked at her, she knew she had no intention of losing him. They could go up the stairs to take tea among all the dowagers with their sharp eyes and significant nods, but apart from anything else she could not imagine him sitting conventionally at the table with Mamma and Papa. It would simply spoil everything.

As she hesitated she saw Florence's cold blue eyes looking at her across the crowd. Florence, keeping a close watch on the Fabergé treasures, was not missing what her younger sister was up to either.

Then let's give her something to talk about.

"I say," said Daisy, "you don't want to have tea up there, do you? I know a place just down the street where we can get lemon tea. That's if you're thirsty."

"I am exceedingly thirsty."

"It's opposite Kensington Gardens. We can be back in half an hour if your friends need extricating from language difficulties."

"Magnificent."

Magnificent! What a splendid word.

"I'm Daisy Overton. Who are you?"

"Sergei Pavel."

He was looking at her sideways as they went out onto the street. "Is this how women behave in London?"

"Absolutely."

"Taking lemon tea with strange men?"

"Why not? I have always vowed never to be bored."

He laughed, with a sudden deep throaty sound. "I am not sure what you mean but I think I guess. You are already improving my English, Miss Daisy."

"Magnificent."

She had never been in that unpretentious little teashop before. It would never be unpretentious for her again. After today there ought to be a plaque fixed over the door, not exhibiting the royal arms like Bonnington's, but making the simple statement that here Daisy Overton had met Sergei Pavel from St. Petersburg.

If they hadn't got lemon tea she would teach them how to make it.

"Sir Gay," she murmured.

"Yes?"

"Nothing. I was just Anglicizing your name. It's gay."

"Gay?"

"Happy. Carefree."

His strange, brilliant slanted eyes were studying her again. "I was told Englishwomen were cold."

"I was born in Italy."

"Does that make a difference?"

"I think so. At least it has made me different from my sister. Where were you born?"

"In a village not far from St. Petersburg. Now I live in St. Petersburg."

Daisy nodded approval. "That's absolutely right. I see you against steppes, or old Byzantium, or something. I believe Florence brought you to London with her treasures. Are you for sale, Sergei?"

"Are you laughing at me, Miss Daisy?"

"No, no, no! Oh, please don't think that. I am only talking nonsense. Did you have an English teacher?"

"Yes. And my father has a small bookshop where I read very much."

"Tolstoy?"

"And Pushkin, Turgenev, Dostoevski, Chekhov. And I

listen to the music of Tchaikovsky, Stravinsky, Borodin."

"What are you going to be, besides an interpreter?"

"Oh, I will be a professor of English in a university. Poor, of course," he added, looking at Daisy's fur-trimmed jacket.

"Of course. Why not? What fun."

"Fun?"

"I was thinking of something."

"I know. Your eyes are telling me."

"I was thinking of that witch in Russian fairy tales. Baba Yaga. So deliciously fearsome."

"What a funny girl you are."

"I have an undisciplined mind. All my teachers have told me that. Sir Gay."

"Eh?"

"I think your name is fascinating."

"I like yours, too. Can we meet again?"

Daisy drew a deep breath. This had been meant to be a prank, nothing more. But it was more, already.

"Perhaps."

"I am free every afternoon there is not a matinee."

"So am I. Mornings, too."

"Then you are a society lady?"

"By birth but not inclination."

"Explain. You are rich?"

"Well . . . I suppose I'll have to tell you sooner or later. My mother owns that shop where we met."

They had been sitting close together. He moved away from her sharply.

"Now don't be silly. She isn't rich. I mean, not rich like the landed gentry."

His eyes had a gleam that looked like hostility.

"I understand what you mean by the landed gentry. That class in Russia causes much suffering to the poor. But why isn't it your father who is rich?"

"My father is a darling, darling, clever lazy man. He's a connoisseur of living."

"So your mother does the work in a big business. That is strange."

"It isn't strange at all for her. She loves it. She's never bored for a minute. I envy her. Florence has her talent, too. But I haven't. I'm like Papa. Lazy and opportunistic."

"Opportunistic?"

"That means doing things on an impulse. Like coming here with you."

He nodded, more intrigued than approving, she thought. Probably he thought she was a terrible fast creature. He had a long nose, a wide thin-lipped mouth, and that strange foreign face that was yet so sweet and ardent. It was something out of a Russian fairy tale, not the fearsome Baba Yaga, but the innocent who walked through treacherous dark woods unscathed.

I'll never look at those pink-cheeked brainless guardsmen again, Daisy thought.

"I expect I'd better go back now, though, before there's a hue and cry."

He smiled suddenly and unexpectedly, his wide mouth stretching, his eyes luminous.

"Would you like two tickets for the ballet tomorrow night?"

"Oh, how marvelous!"

"I would have to meet you here tomorrow to give them to you."

"Naturally."

"We would have more time?"

"Time for muffins as well as tea," Daisy said blithely. "What a lovely adventure."

Chapter 23

Those were the words she used when she went downstairs to dinner that night, ten minutes late, and breathless with lingering excitement.

"I have had such a lovely adventure."

It was not in her nature to be secretive. Besides, how could she hide the evidence of her glowing face?

"Well, I'm glad it was enjoyable," said Papa. "Your mother and I thought you had been kidnapped."

"Oh, no, no. But I have been promised two tickets for the ballet tomorrow night. You will come with me, won't you, Papa?"

"Perhaps we would like to hear who the donor is first," Papa said.

"Yes, Daisy, didn't you get the message to join us at tea?" Mamma asked. "Miss Smith assured us she had delivered it."

"She did, yes. But I had met this Russian who is with the ballet—he was one of Florence's guests at the shop this afternoon—and he didn't care about tea among all the dowag—I mean, we thought we would prefer a simpler and quieter place. They're very unpretentious people, the Russians. It was such fun talking to someone from such a different world. It was almost as if he had come from a star."

"I didn't regard Russia as remotely resembling a star," Florence put in dryly. "I thought it cold and uncomfortable, and there were far too many serfs or peasants or whatever they called them. With rags and idiot faces. It's obvious, Mamma, that Daisy is being romantic again."

Daisy looked quickly from Mamma's frowning face to Papa, her constant ally. To her surprise, however, he was not looking at all sympathetic, in fact he was disapproving. Had he forgotten about their lighthearted bet?

"Papa, don't you remember our bet? I found a Russian who could speak English."

"What's his name?" Papa asked suspiciously.

"Sergei Pavel. He isn't one of the dancers, he's an interpreter, he's going to be a professor."

"You've found out a great deal about him very quickly."

"But why not? I told him who I was and he told me who he was."

"Daisy," said Mamma, not unkindly, "for someone of your age and education, you are quite remarkably naïve. Now what you must do immediately after dinner is write a note to this young man telling him that you can't accept his kind offer of tickets for the ballet. We're all going on Saturday night, as you know. Once is quite sufficient. So do as I ask and Bates may take the Daimler to deliver your note personally. Now let us go into dinner. Florence must be worn out after her exciting day."

Florence nudged Daisy in an unusual gesture of friendship. Perhaps her heady success today had thawed her long chilliness.

"You don't tell everything in this house, idiot. Who's going to understand?"

But didn't they want to know more about Sergei? Daisy thought indignantly. Mamma had already dismissed him as just a Russian peasant, and Papa seemed so suspicious of her glow of happiness.

Well, in spite of their disapproval, she had every intention of meeting Sergei in the tea shop tomorrow. This was the first really big happening in her life and she wasn't going to let it just vanish. She would have to refuse the ballet tickets, but if Sergei wished it, she would see him whenever possible during his stay in London. If for no other reason than proving that she was grown up and in charge of her own life.

So what in the first place had been an intriguing adventure and only half-serious grew rapidly into something much more significant. Perhaps it would have, anyway. But there was something about secret meetings and limited time that hastened the process. Daisy found that she couldn't sleep all night, she kept starting up half-trembling with unidentifiable emotion. Sergei's voice and his deep throaty laugh kept echoing in her ears, and she could see his strange, vividly alive face all the time.

It was no use calling her romantic or dreamy or impulsive or simply reckless. Something very deep and important was happening to her. Even if she were never to see Sergei again, life had changed irrevocably. She had discovered for the first time the irresistible impact a man could make on her senses.

Even the night that they all decorously attended the ballet, and Papa kept looking sideways at her on the little gilt chair in the box, as if she might vanish from sight, into the dark gloomy forest of *Giselle,* she only half saw the magic on the stage. She kept thinking how near Sergei was. He had said he would be behind the scenes. The sad, swooning music ravished her, and every dancer, even the amazing Nijinsky, like a smooth taut-muscled panther, seemed to have tilted Tartar eyes, and a long curling mouth that smiled secretly toward her.

She was possessed. She had never met a man like Sergei before. Indeed, she could scarcely remember the faces of any of her escorts of the previous summer. She certainly remembered nothing of any conversation.

Every word spoken between her and Sergei was vital and important; every glance he gave her burned into her heart. During the next two weeks they walked the whole of Kensington Gardens several times, they had tea with muffins, with crumpets, with cream buns, with hot toast and with bread and jam (a nursery tea which amused Sergei). Sergei had even daringly come to Hampstead Heath one day and she had pointed out the spot from which she had been stolen as a child. He had listened to her story in surprise and sympathy. But of course anyone would have wanted to steal her, he said flatteringly.

He had talked a great deal about Russia, the great snowbound winters when the wolves howled on the steppes, but in St. Petersburg the sleighs glided along icy roads, carrying the rich fur-wrapped guests to glittering parties at the Winter Palace. In the summer the parties were at the summer palace, the beautiful Tsarskoe Selo where there was the little Chinese theater and the ballet was performed. The czar and the beautiful czarina (who wore dresses stitched all over with jewels) were ballet lovers. A new dancer, Anna Pavlova, was exquisite. Sergei, sitting on the

Heath beside Daisy, took her foot in his hand, and said that she had a long high-arched instep just like Pavlova's.

He bent his head and kissed her ankle, and she had to snatch her foot away to conceal her sudden violent trembling. She couldn't understand why she trembled so much nowadays. She was in love, of course. And the days were running out, and she could never let him go.

Supposing he didn't ask her to go with him!

Then she would simply propose herself.

"I will arrive in St. Petersburg for Christmas," she would say. And Saint Nicholas could fill her stocking with Russian presents.

They laughed so much and Sergei said that although she looked like a princess she could never be one, she was far too indecorous.

"You sound just like all my governesses!"

"But they punished you, I expect. I am awarding you the Order of Saint Nicholas for gaiety."

Then he kissed her, for the first time, very seriously, under a tree beside the Serpentine, in the hot white summer light, and two elderly gentleman stared, and muttered. Daisy winked at them over Sergei's shoulder.

"What is it?" he asked.

"Nothing." She had stopped laughing and seemed to be crying. "I think I love you, Sir Gay."

He kissed her again, his long sweet mouth possessing hers.

"I love you, too. Will you come back to St. Petersburg with me?"

"Of course. I was going to invite myself if you didn't ask."

"As my wife, of course."

"I know that's what you meant."

"What will your parents say?"

"Well. I'll just have to find out. But don't worry, Papa never refuses me anything in the end."

He did. He did. And it was terrible and unbelievable. He had sat hunched and tragic in his fur-trimmed dressing gown (he had been in bed for several days with a troublesome cough) and had said that under no circumstances would he consent to Daisy's marriage to this unknown foreigner.

He had used words like "impetuous," "childish," "bizarre," which had cut her to the quick. But what had hurt even more was that he had needed no prompting from Mamma for the attitude he had taken. One might have expected Mamma to oppose Daisy's plans. She had so little romance in her nature, and so little understanding of her youngest daughter. And at this time she was entirely engrossed with Papa, as was always the case when he was ill.

Edwin had once said that if one of them were drowning Mamma would never have time to save them if she were distracted by Papa's cough.

So Daisy could not be sure that her news had really penetrated Mamma's consciousness.

It had Papa's, however, all too disastrously, and he was adamant. He simply closed the subject. It was finished. It was not to be mentioned again. She was a minor by law, and she would obey her parents.

Daisy flew into Sergei's arms, in the park that afternoon, and sobbed her disappointment.

"Papa won't allow us to marry. He won't even meet you. He acts as if you don't exist. I never thought he would be so cruel."

"He loves you, I suppose."

"Selfishly! If he really loved me he couldn't do this to me. He would want my happiness. All he cares about is not losing me. If you lived in England he might be kinder, but Russia is so far away, so foreign."

"And I am a foreigner. I always heard that the English don't trust foreigners. Besides, I am sure your father would expect his beautiful daughter to marry one of the landed gentry you talk about. Not the sort of man I am."

"He hasn't even met you to judge!"

Sergei stroked her hair. His bony hand was so gentle, his solemn face concerned only with her feelings, not with his own bitter disappointment. No one except Papa (and now not even Papa) had cared about her feelings as Sergei did. That alone would have made her give him her loyalty forever.

"So what we will have to do, my darling"—he made the English endearment sound quaint and sweet—"is wait until you are old enough to marry without your parents' consent."

"Another eighteen months!" Daisy moaned.

"And then I will come for you and make you my wife."

"Sergei, you're too sensible."

"What else is there to be?"

Daisy pressed her cheek against his mournfully.

"I will write to you and you will write to me every day," Sergei said.

Letters. Once Florence had lived in that dreamworld of closely written script, page after page.

"I hate writing letters," said Daisy.

"Not to me."

"Sergei, I do truly and absolutely love you and I won't stop."

"I, too."

"So why do we have to part? I can't bear it."

He crushed her to him. She knew he couldn't bear it either. His whole body trembled. But he was older than she, more practical, more disciplined, for presently he controlled his trembling.

"Really, the time will go. We will be watching the ballet in the Hermitage theater in the winter next year."

Daisy blinked at her tears.

"Is the Hermitage far enough to go by sleigh?"

"If it were only ten steps and you wanted a sleigh, it would be far enough."

A flicker of eagerness possessed her. Perhaps it would be possible to wait and have none of this delicate starry happiness spoiled. She said, with all her heart in the words, *"Sir Gay. . . ."*

Papa had gone back to bed with a temperature.

"I'm afraid you upset him," Mamma said reproachfully. "He asked that you go and see him as soon as you came in. Where have you been?"

One could not say Mamma was either kind or unkind. She was in some neutral state where Daisy's behavior only upset her if it were going to have an adverse effect on Papa's health.

"I've been seeing Sergei, of course."

If only Mamma would open her arms wide and let her run into them and be comforted.

"Saying good-bye, I hope," said Mamma calmly.

"Yes."

"I'm glad. Do go and tell Papa. It will do him more good than any medicine."

Was her happiness to be sacrificed to a sick old man? Daisy wondered rebelliously.

Even though Papa did hold both her hands lovingly, and remarked tenderly on the traces of tears he could see on her cheeks, she still could not give him her whole-hearted affection. He thought the problem was over. With the ballet gone, stopping for a brief season in Paris, and then on its way back to Moscow, Daisy would soon forget her very young first attack of love and madness.

Her misery grew as he said confidently, "As soon as I am well enough let us go on a jaunt somewhere. I wonder where you would like. Somewhere beautiful and gay. Venice, perhaps."

"No, thank you, Papa."

"Oh, come now, I won't have you sitting at home brooding. A change of scene is the infallible remedy for a broken heart."

"How can you say that, Papa, when you don't know what a broken heart is? You and Mamma were able to marry."

To her utter dismay Papa's eyes suddenly filled and overflowed with tears. He couldn't speak for a moment. When he did he said, "You're too young to assume such things." He licked his lips and made a poor attempt at his whimsical smile. "Although I believe, clinically speaking, hearts do not break. Run along now, you might tell your mother I would like one of her hot toddies."

"You're not going down to dinner, Miss Daisy? Are you poorly?"

That was Miss Finch, anxious, meek, as narrow as a crack in the wall, as she stood in the doorway of Daisy's bedroom.

"I'm not hungry, that's all."

"A little light supper on a tray, then? I'll bring it up myself."

"Don't fuss, Finchie, please. I'm not Grandmamma. I can survive without my dinner."

"You're upset, Miss Daisy."

So the servants knew already. Of course they would. They knew everything.

"Yes, but there's nothing anyone can do about it."

"There have been several gentlemen callers for you, Miss Daisy. They have been most anxious to know where you have disappeared to lately."

I have been journeying on another star, Daisy thought, and suddenly the misery of loss sweeping over her was appalling.

"I just would be grateful if *you* would disappear," she managed to say, and Miss Finch had no alternative but to obey. "Tell everyone I want to be alone," she called after her.

If Miss Finch conveyed this message to Florence, Florence was not deterred by it. She knocked peremptorily on the door and came in without permission.

"Are you going to do what I did?" she asked. "Let him get away?"

Daisy stared in surprise at the cool pale-blue eyes, the unemotional face.

"What do you mean?"

"Exactly that. When I was your age I let Desmond Fielding go away, believing implicitly that a year or two would make no difference. Young girls are too romantic."

"But with Desmond it was my fault. At least you said so."

"And my own. For letting him go when he was hot."

"Hot?"

"Men go off the boil, if you'll excuse the vulgarity."

"Sergei—"

"Oh, he will, too, even with, or especially with, his Tartar blood. There'll be other girls close at hand. Tempting him. I advise you to catch the train to Paris tomorrow."

Daisy sat bolt upright, unable to believe her ears.

"You just want to get rid of me!"

"Perhaps I do. Perhaps I was thinking you could blackmail Papa. He'll be over to Paris to see you safely married quickly enough. If he finds he can't keep you here he won't have his pure little Daisy besmirched."

"Flo!"

"Is your Sergei to be relied on?"

"Oh, *yes*."

"Then what's stopping you? I never thought you'd be lacking in spirit."

Chapter 24

Beatrice tore open the yellow telegram.

DAISY AND SERGEI MARRIED THIS MORNING AT ST
CLOUD ARRIVING HOME TOMORROW AFTERNOON SEND
BATES TO MEET THREE THIRTY AT VICTORIA WILLIAM.

Send Bates, indeed! When had she not met William, if it
were humanly possible? This time it would be doubly important, for he would be heartbroken.

He had rushed off to Paris full of confidence that he could
prevent this desperately foolish runaway marriage and persuade Daisy to come home. Why would she have left that
note telling her intentions and her whereabouts if she did
not secretly want to be rescued?

Her flight was only a dramatic gesture, the sort of highly
colored romantic episode that any high-spirited young girl
might like to indulge in, simply so that she could boast of it
for the rest of her life.

Daisy had not climbed out of her window by the aid of
knotted sheets; she had gone quite boldly at midday with
no luggage at all (except her small diamond tiara which
William had been prevailed on to buy for her coming out)
and thus none of the servants had particularly commented
on, or noticed, her departure.

She had written in the note left on William's desk in the
library, "The crown jewel is my dowry. You wouldn't want
me to go to Sergei empty-handed, would you?"

The impertinence of the girl! Beatrice had wanted to
leave her to her fate. She had wanted this much more
strongly than she dared to say. But William had been in
such a state of sorrow and loss that she had not been able

to protest at his pursuit of that spoiled scatterbrained child.

She was afraid that he would hold it against her forever if she did so. So she had even offered to accompany him, but he had said he could manage perfectly well on his own. When had he not been able to sway Daisy to his wishes? She adored her Papa. She would never break his heart by some foolish escapade.

He had been wrong, Beatrice reflected, crumpling the yellow envelope.

She was sorry, as she was sorry for anything that hurt him. But she was also glad in the most fierce secret way. She had the sensation that only now had Mary Medway finally left the house.

All the same, she showed every solicitude to William, for he arrived home looking so old, tired and desolate that immediately his pain became hers. She couldn't bear his red-rimmed eyes, his drawn face, his silence.

She called Doctor Lovegrove to give him a sedative, and then lay all night listening to the heavy breathing of his drugged sleep. If only she could have wept for Daisy she thought that he would have taken her in his arms and they could have comforted each other. But her old awkward failing of honesty could not be overcome. She simply was not sorry that Daisy had gone. The little cuckoo had flown the nest. Their home was their own again.

The next day William gave the bare facts.

Daisy had worn a simple white dress that one of the ballerinas, Karsavina he believed, had given her. She carried a posy of pink and white daisies, apparently at Sergei's request, and looked like a simple village girl in an opera or a ballet. Utterly charming but not his daughter.

"Happy?" asked Beatrice.

"Oh, radiant," William said reluctantly. "She's living on a cloud. She looks bewitched, as if this young man is some kind of god. He just looks like a complete foreigner to me, with those high cheekbones and slanting eyes."

"But they're in love," Beatrice murmured.

"Oh, they're a complete Romeo and Juliet. I did my best, Bea, but I couldn't make Daisy see reason. She said that if I didn't give my consent to their marriage she would simply live in sin. And I believe she meant it!"

Of course she would mean it, being her mother's daughter. . . .

Long practiced in discretion, Beatrice didn't say those words. She took William's arm and said in her soothing voice, "Then let's wish them happiness. I know you will when you've got over missing Daisy."

"I'll never get over that."

"But, dearest, she would have married somebody. You couldn't have kept her forever. She isn't Florence. You wouldn't want her to be, would you?"

William grimaced.

"I don't want any more shopkeepers in my family, I grant you. But if only it weren't Russia. Such an uncivilized country. How can a delicate sensitive girl like Daisy survive there?"

"I really think, my dear, that Daisy is a good deal tougher than you give her credit for. And talking of Russia, you've never traveled there, have you? Perhaps you could make a journey next summer. Florence could advise you on it. Then, if Daisy finds she has made a terrible mistake, you can rescue her, can't you? I'm sure a divorce under those circumstances wouldn't be too difficult or too scandalous. I know that Edwin has friends in the British Embassy in Moscow who could help. Although, of course, this is just conjecture. I do sincerely hope she will be happy. Why don't we open some of that Veuve Clicquot you got in? We can at least drink to Daisy's and Sergei's happiness."

William took her arm in his. She felt the familiar pressure of his body against hers, his the frail tree, hers the rock. It was no use wishing that sometimes this position could be reversed. She had encouraged him to lean on her. He would always do so. At least he now did so willingly and gratefully.

Daisy's letters, infrequent (because of those atrocious Russian posts, William said), were as gay as the song of a lark.

"Sergei and I have two rooms above his parents'. From our bedroom window we can see, believe it or not, a cherry tree! And I adore Sergei's parents who are just like Tolstoy characters. I am trying to learn Russian quickly so that I can talk to them. Just at present we have to make do with smiles and sign language. I am also learning to make Russian dishes. Do tell Cook. She knows that I couldn't even beat an egg, which Mamma Pavel thinks is disgraceful ignorance. . . .

"It has begun to snow and Sergei has promised me my first sleigh ride. He is the kindest, most wonderful husband. How can I tell you what it is like lying under a warm quilt with my darling husband's head on the pillow beside me, and watching the snow pattering on the window? Sergei says it makes a sound like a fashionable English audience applauding with gloved fingers, as they did when Nijinsky danced. . . .

"Yesterday I saw the czar and czarina and their four daughters driving by. When I curtsied they all bowed in return, most charmingly, but Sergei says they do not command the respect that the British royal family do. The peasants have been so badly treated for centuries and there are alarming undercurrents. Also, he says, Russia is beginning to fear Germany's militarism. What does Edwin say about this? What is the news of Edwin? I very much fear he has cast me off because he thinks I have disgraced the family. He was always a fearful snob, with those barons and baronesses and the elite regiments and so on. If I have disgraced the family, Papa and Mamma, is it some comfort to you to know how blissfully happy I am?"

Florence was noncommittal about these undoubtedly light-hearted letters. She merely said that this odd marriage might be the making of Daisy, and returned to her arguments with Beatrice on the future policy of Bonnington's.

Florence, with her ally James Brush, who was to Beatrice's mind a thought too clever, wanted modernization. All that kowtowing to royalty was a bit out of date. Everyone said that with the death of Edward, the playboy king, and the retirement to the background of the still beautiful but stiff and invalidish Queen Alexandra, the grand days of monarchy were over. Oh, people were still loyal and waved flags, and the coronation of King George and Queen Mary had been an affair of superb pageantry, but the time had come when shops must appeal more to the masses than to the privileged few.

Bonnington's would still maintain its air of luxury, it would still, for instance, offer glasses of champagne to weary and wealthy (titled, preferably) customers, but it would begin stocking a wider and cheaper range of merchandise, such as cosmetics and artificial jewelry that would attract the young, who would be tomorrow's dowagers.

Florence also wanted to open a design room and get away from all those dressmakers faithfully carrying out "madam's" wishes and producing well-made but uninspired clothes. She had found a clever young designer who was daringly lowering necklines and lifting skirts above the ankle. His fashions were aimed at the young.

Miss Florence and James Brush, with his foxy, alert face. It had used to be Miss Bea and Adam Cope. It still was, except that dear Adam, capable, solid and utterly loyal to Bonnington's and to her, was unalterably opposed to new notions. Beatrice didn't agree with all Florence's ideas, by any means, but she knew that a closed mind meant a slow death, not only to business but to oneself.

Adam would eventually have to be retired, as Miss Brown had been. If it came to that, so would she, though as owner she was entitled to totter in and take her familiar seat in the cash desk until senility overcame her. Adam was not so fortunate and neither Florence nor James Brush was over-endowed with sentiment. Had they been told that Adam Cope, aged sixty, had loved Beatrice faithfully for nearly forty years, they would have giggled in mild hysteria.

It was not a laughing matter that love had so little value when it came from the wrong person. But one strove to be grateful for it.

The whole subject cut too near the bone, as far as Beatrice was concerned.

However, eventually Adam's health would fail or he would retire voluntarily, and then she would be outvoted on matters of policy by the younger generation. It was the way of life, as William would say.

William had grown quietly thoughtful and philosophic since Daisy's departure. He sought Beatrice's company more in the evenings, but that may have been because he found the house lonely during the day. She contemplated spending less time at the shop after the spring and summer season. It was not because she was tired, she was full of vigor, but she had had the thought that now, in their late middle age, she and William might travel with real enjoyment in each other's company. Daisy had recently written saying that she and Sergei were expecting a baby. Couldn't she and William travel to St. Petersburg to see their first grandchild?

It was an intriguing thought that grew on her after

Edwin's visit home for Christmas. He was in a strange, distrait, nervous mood that he said was due to his anxiety about the growing megalomania of the Kaiser. No one else seemed to take seriously the fact that Germany was trained and ready, not for some small-scale skirmish, but for a major trial of strength against one of the big powers.

"Russia?" said William uneasily.

"Perhaps. I think more likely Europe. A sort of Napoleonic conquest. Bismarck had always envisaged this and the Kaiser, after all, was his pupil. France, Belgium, the Netherlands."

"Good God! England couldn't stand by if that happened."

"No, that's my point. I don't think anyone here realizes the perfection of the German soldier. Particularly the officers."

Edwin held his head at an uncomfortably high angle, as if he were wearing a stiff military collar, and talked staring over his father's head. He added that in spite of all this he had no wish to leave Berlin. He found the city and the atmosphere fascinating, so virile and somehow fraught with destiny. He didn't mention women. Beatrice seemed to remember his once talking about a beautiful baroness. But now he was no longer a little boy who could be questioned. He was handsome, mature, and completely unknowable. He didn't even ask her for money nowadays. He must have grown more provident, though his dark-gray flannel suit, his pigskin gloves, his handmade shoes, were all of fastidiously high quality. Could the pay of a civil servant run to clothes like that? She noticed that he was using a gold cigarette case, too. Had that been a present? From some woman? It was maddening not to be able to ask. But even if she had ever had his confidence, she could not pry into the affairs of a young man approaching thirty.

When Edwin said good-bye, however, he gripped Beatrice's hand hard, almost, she fancied, with desperation.

"I am working hard, Mother, whatever you may hear about me."

"Oh? What am I likely to hear?" Beatrice looked up at the tall young man with the strangely chilling blue eyes, and thought again that he was a stranger. "Are you having an affair with a woman?" she asked lightly.

He gave a quick smile.

"Of course. Many." Even his voice had acquired a foreign tinge. "Good-bye, Mother. Wish me luck."

He must have known then about the scandal that was likely to break. He certainly was well aware of the tight-rope on which he was walking.

The year of 1913, however, was not all disaster. Daisy's news arrived in midsummer.

"Our baby was born on June 1, and is a girl. You should just see Sergei, he is puffed up with pride like a bullfrog. I don't know which he thinks the greatest miracle, the baby or me or himself. We have called her Anna because that is what Sergei wanted. He was thinking of his idol, Anna Pavlova. She is exactly like Sergei, with his tilted eyes. Although, he says, she has my feet and will undoubtedly be a ballet dancer.

"Sergei has kissed me a thousand times, and bought me a new dress. Next year he will be a full-fledged professor and we will have a house of our own. I have often wanted to sell my crown jewel to get a house, but Sergei says that must only be done in the event of dire disaster. And now, anyway, we want to keep it for our daughter."

A new baby, a new dress. Who would have thought that Daisy, who had had so much lavished on her, would be content with so little, the kind of things that even peasant women achieved?

So little? Beatrice blinked back tears, angry at her senti-mentality and her jealousy.

William had given her nothing more than a dutiful kiss on the brow after the birth of her children. One didn't dare think what he might have done to Daisy's mother had he had the opportunity.

"Well, Bea," said William, who was as pleased as Punch, "so we have one grandchild, at least, even if it is a Russian one. Now how about that trip to St. Petersburg? Shall I go and see my fellow and get some travel brochures?"

"I think so. Yes, do."

They looked at each other in a completely spontaneous moment of affection and anticipation. Beatrice felt her heart quicken with joy. She didn't say so, because it would sound ridiculous, but this strange exciting journey would be like a very belated honeymoon for her, even if William's purpose was primarily to see Daisy and his granddaughter.

The brochures were obtained and studied, the tickets ordered and the traveling bags brought out. And then the news arrived from Germany and, like delicate summer buds whipped off in a gale, their lovely journey had vanished.

Edwin was under arrest in the British Embassy in Berlin, and was to be brought to London for trial for treason.

Florence said bitterly and furiously, "Serve him right! He never had a conscience. Didn't you know that, Mamma? He would do anything to get things for himself. All those clothes and guns, and hobnobbing with the aristocracy— that's how he's been paying for them. The stupid fool! Those Germans set traps for silly little boys like him."

Handing over military secrets to the enemy! What military secrets would a minor embassy official be entrusted with? It simply couldn't be true.

But William, after he had made detailed inquiries, said that it could.

"You know Edwin's passion for the army. He'd made a friend of the British military attaché, for one thing. And then he's such a damn fine shot. He was accepted in circles that otherwise wouldn't have noticed his existence, and he got carried away by his enthusiasm for Prussian military superiority. We knew that. He told us so himself."

"That Baron von Hesselman," Beatrice said indignantly.

"*And* the baroness," Florence added.

"Yes," said William. "Thalia von Hesselman. You'll have to know, Bea, because it will come out at the trial. Edwin was having an affair with this woman. It was a plot, of course. To live up to her he needed plenty of money. He got into debt, as was anticipated, and then these people offered to pay"—William licked dry lips—"for any information he might be able to give them. Trifling, perhaps. But useful."

"A spy!" Beatrice whispered. "Our son!"

William straightened his shoulders.

"Yes, my father wouldn't have cared about it. We'll have to ride it out, Bea."

"But doesn't treason carry the death penalty?" Beatrice asked painfully. Edwin hanged in some horrible dank jail courtyard, and buried beneath the cobblestones! Was this her punishment for allowing Mary Medway to languish ill in jail? The wild thoughts raced through her mind, and she could hardly listen to William's grave judicial voice.

"It depends on the degree. I gather that the amount of information passed to the enemy has been pretty innocuous. Fortunately, the whole thing was nipped in the bud. I'm glad to say that at least the boy had no real talent for spying."

"He revered the Uhlans," said Florence. "I believe he'd have joined them if he could have. Surely that will go against him."

"Idealism," said William. "I've talked at great length with John Merton who has agreed to defend Edwin. We'll plead arrested development owing to his bad eyesight and his thwarted ambitions for an army career."

"With a first at Oxford!" Florence exclaimed.

"That's a strange form of precocity that apparently young men of Edwin's type can have. But he is, in fact, still mentally an idealistic schoolboy."

"Would this baroness"—Beatrice frowned with distaste —"have fallen in love with a schoolboy?"

"But she wasn't in love with him, of course," said William. "That's Edwin's tragedy."

Edwin was fortunate in having not only a brilliant defense counsel, but a reasonably lenient judge. Before pronouncing sentence the judge made remarks about a flawed personality, and lack of mental balance, as evidenced by his obsession for anything military. It seemed that the country which was most accomplished in spit and polish would have this unfortunate young man's admiration and even, regrettably, his loyalty. However, he had begun on his clumsy fumbling career as a spy and must suffer the consequences. He would be committed to prison for a period of seven years. The judge wound up his comments by an acid suggestion that in future the Foreign Office take more care in selecting its recruits.

And all the time Edwin stood in the dock with his head held at that high awkward angle, and the monocle his counsel had forbidden him to wear (it made him look too much like one of those Uhlan officers whom he aped) concealed in his pocket. Beatrice knew it was there because his right hand was constantly pressed against it. She hoped he would look across at her and his father when sentence had been pronounced, but he never varied that far-off stare, as if he were entirely alone in the world.

Since he had been brought back to England she and William had only been able to see him in his prison cell, in the presence of a warder. At these meetings he had remained almost entirely silent, neither defending himself nor admitting regret for what he had done. Even then he had had that terrible solitary look.

Now that the trial was over, Beatrice hoped she might get nearer to him. Perhaps he couldn't bring himself to confide in her completely, but surely he could show some feeling toward her, his mother. She longed to help him and comfort him. He was her only son. If she had failed in this kind of comfort before, it was because he had not seemed to need it. From such an early age he had had that self-contained aloofness.

One knew one's faults only by hindsight. Couldn't Edwin, who now knew what it was to be obsessed by love for a woman, forgive her for her unconscious neglect?

But the young man sitting opposite her, the wooden table between them, the jailer at the door, seemed to have no emotion at all.

He only asked that the baggage that would be arriving from Germany be put in his room and left untouched.

"Don't let the servants unpack it," he said. "I'll do it myself when I come home."

In seven years? Beatrice's heart ached at the sight of the rigid figure.

"Edwin, *why?*" she cried. "Was it the money you needed? You had Grandmamma's legacy."

There was no answer.

"Was it that you really felt more loyalty to Germany than to your own country?"

Again no answer.

"This"—she wanted to say "adventuress"—"this baroness . . . you won't torture yourself over her, will you?"

She might have been speaking to a dummy.

"I believe we will be allowed to send you certain things in prison," she said, giving up the attempt to read his mind. "Books, for instance. What would you like? Some military histories, I expect."

Then he did speak in a strange abrupt voice.

"Grandfather's sword."

"Grandfather's sword!"

"No, I don't suppose that would be allowed. I might run myself through. Ha-ha. Don't worry, Mother. I'll survive. I'll even be lucky enough to escape the war that's coming. Now hadn't you better hurry back to Father? Or your customers?"

William said that the baggage from Germany must be opened. He couldn't allow what might be a potential bomb to remain locked up in his house for seven years.

The contents of three of the bags were harmless enough. They contained Edwin's personal effects, his good clothes, his beautifully polished riding boots and spurs, his pistols. The remaining bag was the odd disturbing one.

In it, carefully folded, was the uniform of a Uhlan cavalry officer, the blue tunic with the stiff red collar, the strange helmet that was a copy of the Polish czapka, the sword.

Where had Edwin managed to acquire this? What uneasy symbolism did it have for him?

"Our son!" William exclaimed incredulously.

Beatrice shivered and said, "Shut it up, William. Put it out of sight. I never want to look at it again."

She was remembering Edwin's sneering blue eyes, and thinking that he had been such a pretty little boy. She had been devoted to him until Mary Medway had come, and taken all her thoughts for far too long. . . .

Chapter 25

Edwin's admired Uhlan cavalry regiments went into action in August, 1914, along with other highly trained and well-equipped German regiments.

The Great War, long predicted by William, had begun.

Edwin, humiliatingly safe in Pentonville Prison, was going to miss it as he had predicted. William was too old for service. The only member of the family to be directly affected was Daisy. The war had isolated Daisy as efficiently as if she had gone to live at the North Pole. Letters from her entirely ceased. It seemed certain that Sergei would be called up and sent to the Eastern front. What would happen to Daisy and her small daughter? Would they have enough to eat, would they be protected supposing the victorious Germans overran the Eastern marshes and marched on Moscow and St. Petersburg, as they had already overrun Belgium and parts of France?

William, who deplored the possible capture of Paris by those "bloody Huns," nevertheless reserved most of his anxiety for the Russian cities and Daisy's welfare. He agonized over her silence and constantly wrote letters himself, hopefully posting them and praying that they would reach their destination.

He grew thinner and frailer and his hair was too liberally sprinkled with gray. If Beatrice could have looked at him with unprejudiced eyes, she would have seen a quiet, elderly man with a look of defeat, the merry twinkle in his eyes completely quenched. She saw his delicacy, that was true. She had always seen that. Indeed, when he was propped up in bed he had a disturbing resemblance to the old general, with a face too haggard, its bones too stripped of flesh. But his charm and his good looks remained indelibly printed in her mind. She thought that he was still the most handsome man in the world.

He had grown querulous, too, which was unlike him, with his usually unfailing courtesy. But what was there in life for a man with his only son in prison, his favorite daughter in exile, and his wife and remaining daughter as dedicated to the survival of a shop as to that of England and the British Empire?

Beatrice wanted to tell him that he still had her, she loved him as much as she ever had. But what was she now, a stoutish aging woman, with her hair pulled into a sensible knot at the back of her head, her manner brisk and competent? She wore her manner as she wore her plain gray shop dress. She was still afraid that too much tenderness would bore and suffocate her sensitive husband.

She was not grief-stricken about Daisy's silence. Daisy was one of those fortunate people who would always fall on her feet. Hadn't she done so from birth, with the undeserved advantage of a good home and a pampered upbringing? She had a much better instinct for survival than her frail and clinging mother had had. She would be all right, and better, as far as Beatrice was concerned, for being three thousand miles away.

Edwin, however, was a deep and humiliating pain. At first she had written to him frequently, and traveled once a month to visit him. But, with his handsome wooden face turned away from her, he had made it so clear that he was neither interested in her letters nor her visits, that she had finally given up the visits. She still wrote, however. She said that Overton House would always be his home. His room was kept for him. His grandfather's valuable collection of soldiers were now his, if he wished them to be. She would continue sending him books on history and famous campaigns. Contrary to what he thought, she had the deepest and most sympathetic interest in his future. She had only once been guilty of standing before the Overton vault and apologizing aloud to the old general for the blot her son had made on the family honor. It was surely her fault, and that of her forebears. It could not have been a hereditary trait of the Overtons.

With the war raging in France, this was a great opportunity for Bonnington's to renew its theme of patriotism. It was made clear to all the male staff of fighting age that they were expected to enlist. Beatrice didn't go about handing out white feathers, but the steely look in her eyes was almost as difficult to face as German guns. The young men obediently departed to recruiting offices, including James Brush who first proposed to Florence. Would she marry him now, before he left for France, or would she promise to wait for him?

Neither, said Florence unemotionally. She had no intention of marrying. She was fond of James, but second best was second best. Besides, she had a suspicion that his proposal was mainly concerned with making sure of his stake in Bonnington's.

Captain Fielding, her true love (or had he always been no more than a romantic dream?), had died in the retreat from Mons. He was awarded a posthumous Military Cross, and Florence put a black veil on the smart straw boater which she always wore to the shop. She intended to wear the veil until the end of the war. If James Brush and other young men from Bonnington's were also killed, the touch of mourning would serve a dual purpose. Also, the veil concealed the red-rimmed eyes with which she sometimes awoke. She only cried in secret.

From habit, Beatrice wanted to drape the shop in flags, and military emblems, and a great deal of mourning equipment, from widows' garb to funereal black plumes. This Florence resisted strenuously. On the contrary, everything must be gay. There must be color and life, dainty fabrics, scarves, ribbons, even silk stockings. There must be cheerful music in the Palm Court lounge, and the food, even if less plentiful and of poorer quality, must look attractive. Women must think of the shop as a refuge from gloom and sadness. There must never be the slightest sign of defeat.

"Who's showing defeat?" Beatrice grumbled.

"You are, Mother, if you hang out flags because we've just lost the battle of the Somme. It's too defensive. It's too dreary."

"Did we lose the Somme?" Beatrice asked uneasily.

"What do you think, with all those thousands killed? It could hardly be called a victory."

Florence tapped briskly about on her high heels. She had very thin elegant ankles which she now showed. She seemed to be enjoying the challenge of the war, in a masochistic way. She had the knack of turning events to advantage, just as Beatrice had once had. Now Beatrice's talent seemed to be static, or fading. It was simply that she was getting rather old, and she worried so much more. About William, about Edwin, even about Florence with her frighteningly competent and emotionless manner.

All the same Florence's costly Treasures department had to close, simply because foreign goods were now almost unavailable. Still, it could be revived after the war. All the countries of Europe could not have been plundered.

Florence turned her energies instead to training the women who had taken the place of the departed men. In this, as in other things, she proved adept. Her frosty eye was now looked on with more awe than Miss Beatrice's. Of course, Miss Beatrice, being elderly and a little too stout, and at times stiff with that annoying rheumatism, spent most of her time in the cash desk. She didn't walk the floors as she had once done. Perched on her stool inside the polished gilt cage (like a molting old thrush, she thought, with her pepper and salt hair, and her rounded bosom) none of the customers was aware of her stiff and halting walk.

Adam Cope knew about it, of course. But the war had done something odd to Adam. It had distressed him so much that all his long-repressed emotions had come embarrassingly to the surface. He frequently had tears in his eyes. As often as possible he took Beatrice's arm (he would never have presumed, once) and escorted her out of the shop to the waiting Daimler. He had developed a tremor in his limbs that made him stumble and drop things. It was time, Florence said crisply, that Adam be retired.

This was one more point of contention between Beatrice and Florence. When it came to these heated battles between mother and daughter (who would ever have thought Florence would grow to be so strong-willed and inflexible?) Beatrice always won, simply because of her position. *She* was Bonnington's. Florence undoubtedly would be, one day, but in the meantime, despite her bouts of rheumatism which made her so stiff and slow, Beatrice was absolutely in command. And would be so until her dying day.

In the same way Adam would stay. Loyalty must never be sacrificed to business. Looking into Florence's large pale eyes, Beatrice had doubts that her daughter ever listened

to these old-fashioned and profitless ideas. To Florence,
everything came down to simple economy. Adam Cope
was now quite uneconomic.

But he would stay, because Miss Beatrice said so.

However, as if he realized he was now an embarrassment
to his beloved old friend, he quietly dropped dead in the
basement where he had gone to check some stock. As if he
had consciously chosen a place where customers would not
be distressed.

Beatrice, again to Florence's disgust, closed the shop on
the day of Adam's funeral. It was the least she could do.
She shed some difficult tears in private. It was not easy to
cry nowadays. Her tears had dried up.

After that she felt very alone, with Miss Brown and
Adam gone and the younger generation pressing on her
heels, William, with the old hungry pain in his eyes (he
had used to look like that after Mary Medway's death),
and a growing obsession about all the letters from Daisy
which he was sure were piled up in some uncaring post
office, Edwin serving his long sentence, and Florence interested only in showing handsome profits in spite of the
war.

What would old General Overton have said about the
family that now inhabited his house? Would he have admitted he had made a mistake when he had thought that
the spunky little Bonnington girl was the person to provide
healthy new blood?

In the winter William was ill again, with his chronic
bronchitis. He sat up in bed, a plaid shawl around his thin
shoulders, and let the doctor tap his chest. They both
laughed hollowly at the suggestion that a winter in a milder
climate was to be recommended. Where, with the war
raging?

"Well, make the best of it," said the doctor. "You have a
comfortable home and a devoted wife. That's more than
can be said for most of my patients."

"Is he worrying about something?" he asked Beatrice
downstairs.

"Yes. Our daughter Daisy in Russia. He frets all the
time for news of her. Especially now there's a revolution
there. But everyone's fretting for someone nowadays. It
can't be helped, can it?"

"Well, don't sit up too much with him at nights, Mrs. Overton. I'll send a nurse, if necessary."

"Oh, no, doctor. I always nurse my husband myself." The doctor pshawed impatiently.

"Burning the candle at both ends. You're not young enough for that, don't you know? I hope your husband appreciates how lucky he is."

"I know he wouldn't care for a strange nurse," Beatrice said equably.

Neither he would. Because in the late hours of the night, when the room was shadowy in the light of the dying fire, he liked to hold her hand. And she knew he was perfectly aware that it was her hand and not that of some vanished ghost. There was just herself and him in the room. It was her deepest happiness.

At the end of that year a letter from Daisy arrived at last.

It had been written when she was ill, and it was full of a wild despair. If Beatrice had known its contents she would not have rushed excitedly upstairs, carrying it to William to give him pleasure, but would have quietly destroyed it and never told him of its arrival.

"Papa, Papa, you always made me happy, you took me on private treats, and bought me lovely clothes. Do you remember we went to Worth when I was only ten years old and you said this young lady must have a ball dress befitting her beauty? Oh, Papa, make me happy now. Send Sergei back to me. We have only had each other for three years and now they tell me he is dead. But this is a cruel country, full of witches like Baba Yaga, and the snow is so thick that even I know that none of the wounded could survive. Except that Sergei would live for my sake.

"Do you know that his eyes crinkled and shut tight when he laughed? It was comical and darling. And for a sober professor of languages he could do the most amazing jetés.

"There isn't much food and Anna cries with the cold. When I am better—I have been ill for several weeks—I will have to work. They need women for everything, factories, farms, hospitals. Sergei's mother will look after Anna. She says better a bit of hard work than the German guns, and I am as bad as the grand duchesses, with my uselessness and my tears. But I don't know how to be a tough Russian woman.

"Anna looks just like Sergei when she smiles. I can hardly bear it, and make her cry, just to stop her smiling.

"I think of Sergei's face with the snow falling on it. Pure and young. Young and pure. My dear, dear Sir Gay. . . ."

William was in a frenzy. It was no use Beatrice pointing out that many young women were in this tragic position, their husbands killed at the front. He insisted that no one's plight could be worse than Daisy's, alone with a small child in a foreign country. Why, she sounded almost deranged. Beatrice agreed about the derangement. It was the only excuse one could make for Daisy's behavior, writing such a letter when she knew how desperately it would worry her father, who was helpless to do anything.

It would have been difficult enough to pull strings at the Foreign Office, with Moscow shrouded in clouds of war, but with Edwin's shameful record still vividly remembered William was met with polite brush-offs or frosty silences. What was the life of one English girl in this maelstrom?

Anyway, women of Daisy's type, pretty and volatile, usually survived. Daisy would eventually find a protector, they said cynically.

So William could do nothing but sit at his desk and write repeatedly, with sympathy and advice, never knowing if the letters reached their destination.

No other communication arrived from Daisy, and the war ground its way with increasing misery into the third, then the fourth year.

All the same, in spite of her anger with Daisy for that self-indulgent melodrama, the thought of the girl and her baby was in Beatrice's mind too often for comfort. Austerity and hard work, even a little starvation, would do Daisy no harm. But a baby who was made to stop laughing because of her innocent likeness to her dead father—that was too painful to think about, and one could only hope such behavior had been a temporary aspect of Daisy's illness. Although it was not impossible that she had inherited some mental instability from her mother.

The war ended at last, but only six of the twenty young men who had left Bonnington's to enlist returned. One of them, James Brush, was without a left arm. The others were all suffering in varying degrees from shell shock and premature aging. They were reinstated in their jobs, including James Brush, although he had become petulant and unpredictable. He was a cross they must bear, said Beatrice firmly, while Florence congratulated herself that she had not married this thin, clever, vituperative man. She did not intend to be as patient with him as her mother was, even if he had fought for king and country.

Profits were down, and Beatrice decided that the little Crome watercolor she had wanted to buy William for Christmas had better wait another year. Although she hated denying him a pleasure. One never knew. . . . His health would be better if, now that the war was over, news of Daisy arrived. It surely must do so soon in spite of the Russian Revolution. Beatrice knew that he was haunted by the fear that, if Daisy had survived the war, she may not survive the revolution.

She did, of course. She was not only alive, but remarried, and a princess!

How she fell for these Russians! Her Georgian prince was a White Russian, of course, and, successfully escaping from war-torn Russia with his new wife and family, was now an émigré in Spain. Daisy wrote gaily that they were living on the proceeds of Vladimir's family jewels. There had been a great many, so they were not likely to starve. One magnificent ruby pendant he had promised never to sell, because it became Daisy so well. She wore it to parties in Madrid, and it was always a sensation. It was such *heaven* to be properly dressed and looked after again. Vladimir had literally saved her reason. And why hadn't Papa answered all those letters she had written when she was in such despair, frozen and starving, and trying to support Anna on the pittance she earned from teaching English to small Bolsheviks? That was how she had met Vladimir. He had brought his ten-year-old daughter (he was a widower) to her class. Unfortunately Olga and Anna didn't get on very well. Olga had exquisite patrician manners, but Anna had become very naughty and stubborn, and in addition had no looks to speak of. Vladimir called her a little brown sparrow.

It was a pity that Vladimir disliked England. They might come to Paris, but it was doubtful if Daisy could ever persuade him to cross the Channel.

Excitement brought spots of color to William's thin cheeks. He sat up in bed waving the letter and declaring that he must get ready to leave for Madrid immediately.

"Don't be mad!" Beatrice said. She seldom spoke sharply to William, but the contents of Daisy's letter had shocked and dismayed her. She should have been as delighted as William at the essential information, that Daisy had survived the war, and was apparently well and happy. But where was the deranged and grief-stricken girl who had written that moving letter about the death of Sergei?

"If you want to see her, she must come to you."

"But this new husband, this Prince Vladimir, refuses to come to England. Now I wonder how he got that stupid prejudice against this country."

"He must be a stupid man, and I wouldn't be taken in by his title. They say that anyone owning a bit of land and a few yaks, or whatever they have, in Georgia, can be a prince."

"Not with all that jewelry, surely. And don't be so cynical, Bea. It isn't like you. Our little Daisy is alive and has found a new life. Doesn't that make you happy?"

"She sounds so worldly."

"She's been through a great deal. She's also several years older, as we all are. She's a long way from that child bride in Paris with her bunch of daisies."

"That's clear enough. Wearing flashy ruby pendants. And I don't like her saying her child is so plain, when once she told us Anna looked so like Sergei."

"Well, he was an odd-looking fish if ever there was one. You can't think of those Mongolian looks in a little girl."

"We can't. But Daisy happened to love Sergei, and his appearance. Well, it's lucky she has an instinct for survival. Now lie down, my dear. It's time for your broth."

"Bea—where's your heart, for God's sake. A letter from our lost child, from the dead, almost—"

"She was never my child," Beatrice interrupted calmly. "You know very well that the doctor won't permit you to make a journey to Madrid. If you are to see Daisy, she must come here. Write and tell her so. And don't mince words. Tell her about your heart condition."

"That's nothing. A mere murmur."

"Enough to worry the doctor. And me."

"Today," William grumbled, "you sound just like Florence."

But he lay down, and allowed his pillows to be smoothed and his brow to be kissed. Later he would get up and put on his brocade dressing gown and come down to the library where he might do a little work. He was making an extensive catalog of his butterfly collection, which was now unique. It was to be left to the British Museum on his death. He enjoyed pulling the trays out of the cabinets and poring over the beautiful shimmering creatures, recollecting the circumstances of their capture. Sunny days on the Heath in the company of loved companions. Was Beatrice, for instance, forever associated with a rare swallowtail, and Daisy with a peacock? That seemed apt enough for Daisy now, peacocking about with her rich Byzantine jewelry. What was associated with Mary Medway? Nothing, nothing, nothing. . . .

Beatrice didn't know what William wrote to Daisy, but the answer which arrived several weeks later said airily that of course Daisy would adore to come to London and see darling Papa and Mamma and Florence and Edwin again—though why were Florence and Edwin not married, for goodness sake? Only at present Vladimir wouldn't agree to be parted from her. They were going to stay with friends in Portugal, on the Estoril, lovely gay people; she could never have enough gaiety after the terrible years of the war. Olga and Anna were being left behind at a convent in Madrid, where one hoped Anna was learning obedience. She would come in the autumn, perhaps. Although London might have too many painful memories of Sergei. She wanted to forget pain forever.

William grew very silent, after receiving this letter, and Florence commented that Daisy had grown hard. One had always suspected she would. After all, she had once been too insensitive to know what she was doing to Florence when she deliberately charmed Captain Fielding. So of course she now put her own comfort and well-being first. Presently she would grow tired of her new husband; she had probably only married him to escape from Russia. Then what?

Florence claimed to understand human nature. She had seen enough of it, and grown cynical in the process. No one was ever as kind and good and loving and generous as they hoped to be thought to be. Everyone, basically, was in pursuit of his own interests. Even Mamma, who claimed to be such an unselfish and loving wife. Wasn't hers a classic case of self-interest?

So one would see. Daisy wouldn't come to London unless for some ulterior motive.

She was proved right. Daisy didn't come to London. She and her Russian prince went to America instead, hoping, with their titles, to be a great social success in Manhattan.

In the end it was Anna, Daisy's and Sergei's daughter, who came to England, to London, to Overton House.

Chapter 26

The quivering child, thin as a chicken's wishbone, dressed in a straw boater, blazer and gym slip (the uniform of the last school from which she had run away), climbed into the old-fashioned Daimler and sat beside the little erect figure of her grandmother.

She had rebelled intensely about coming to London ("But there isn't anywhere you want to be, is there?" Mother had said in exasperation). Now she was here she hated it at once, that great smoky, crowded Victoria Station they had just left, and the gray streets along which they drove.

On meeting her, Grandmother had given her a hard stare, then had shaken hands briskly, and led her to the Daimler where she had tucked the fur-lined rug over Anna's skinny knees, and addressed herself to the chauffeur.

"Stop at Bonnington's, Bates. I have some business to attend to, and I'm sure Miss Anna will like to see the shop."

"Very good, madam."

"I always associated Victoria Station with meeting your grandfather," she said to Anna. "He was a great traveler. Well, then, so your mother has gone to America?"

Anna nodded, her mouth tightly closed, her eyes creased to prevent any inadvertent weak tears.

"Speak up, child, You've a tongue, I hope."

That old thing. Where's your tongue, Anna? Cat got it?

Just for a minute, when Grandmother had shaken hands instead of giving her a messy kiss, she had imagined she might now be treated as an adult. Or someone who wasn't half-idiot, at least. But it wasn't to be.

So she would have to do her mute act. She was very good at it. She had gone for a whole week without speaking

277

when she had been told of the plan to send her to her
grandparents in England. That was after she had run away
from her third boarding school and been found starving,
dirty and scared, crouched under one of the bridges over
the Seine. Who could she have told how desperately horrible that French school was? Not the kind gendarmes,
much less her mother or her stepfather. This stern-looking
old lady sitting beside her now? Impossible. She was alone,
as she had always been. A thin ugly little girl whom nobody liked.

"That," said Grandmother, pointing to a high brick wall
beyond which were large sprawling buildings, "is the back
of Buckingham Palace where King George and Queen
Mary live. We are coming now to Hyde Park Corner. We
will drive across Hyde Park to my shop in the Bayswater
Road. If you look to your left you will see Rotten Row
where ladies and gentlemen ride. On the other side is Park
Lane, and there are some of London's finest houses. A lot
of our customers live in them. Since my father died and I
took over Bonnington's, we've always dealt with the aristocracy. My daughter Florence says we should turn to the
masses now—isn't that an unpleasant word, like herds of
animals? After all, it was by pleasing the upper classes that
I obtained the royal warrant. You're not too young to know
what that is, I hope. I wonder if by any chance you'll have
a head for business."

The shrewd gray eyes surveyed her. "I, of course, was
far ahead of my time. A woman in business at the turn of
the century was regarded as something of a freak. By the
way, your grandfather and I won't stand for any nonsense
like your running away from school. You may make your
choice, a day school, a boarding school or a governess. But
whichever it is, we'll expect you to honor your part of the
agreement. Now, this is Marble Arch, and see, there above
the trees, that Union Jack is flying from Bonnington's. I
believe in patriotism. I suppose you're quite mixed up as to
which country you belong to. Well, you're half English, so
you can't do better than give your loyalty to England. Stop
at the front doors, Bates. We seem to have a very silent
passenger, but perhaps under the circumstances we must be
patient. Come along, my dear. You can talk to your Aunt
Florence while I just run through the day's figures. Then
we'll be off home."

"Well, you don't look like your mother, do you?" said the tall thin woman in the severe black dress. She didn't smile. She merely looked at Anna critically, as if she were something that might be sold in this large glittering shop. But not something that was worthy of display on the front of the counter. Anna's touchy senses registered that at once. It was a familiar reaction. All those horrid headmistresses had been exactly the same.

"I'm your Aunt Florence. Would you like a glass of milk or some cakes or something while you wait for Mamma? She's going through the department figures. She'll take at least an hour. You know the roof of this shop would fall in if Mamma didn't add up all the sixpences every day. Well—don't you speak English?"

Anna put on her most vacant expression, the one that Mother, in exasperation, said made her look an imbecile.

Aunt Florence sighed.

"Oh, my lord. I see trouble ahead." Her voice was sharp but not unkind, and at least she hadn't said, "Cat got your tongue?" She took Anna's hand and marched her off to the gilt staircase covered with a beautiful moss-green carpet. At the top of this were frondy palms and ferns in pots, and dozens of small tables spread with pale-pink tablecloths.

Unexpectedly, Aunt Florence said, "I used to be sick when I was nervous. I hope you're not the same." Indignation at such a suggestion produced a vigorous shake of Anna's head.

Aunt Florence gave a faint smile.

"At least you're not deaf as well as dumb. Sit down and don't look so miserable. You can't hate this as much as school, if you ran away three times. I warn you not to try running away here, because if you do we mightn't bother to look for you. All the same, I think you'll like Overton House. Our family is all so odd nowadays, it might even be where a funny little thing like you belongs. One thing is certain, your grandfather will spoil you, but don't let that fool you because it will only be because of your mother. He always loved her best of the three of us. Love is a queer thing. It can be very cruel, very unfair. I have no truck with it. So I'm just telling you, young Anna, no scandals while you're with us. It's bad for business."

"Well, how did you get on with your Aunt Florence?"

Grandmother asked when they were back in the Daimler.
"I hope she didn't scare you. She used to be such a shy
sensitive child, and now she's as sharp as a knife. But that's
put on, I suspect. She's had disappointments. Largely due
to your mother, so if she doesn't like you, that's the reason.
Your Uncle Edwin has had disappointments too. But one
should have the strength of mind not to let these things
affect one's character. I don't suppose anyone ever gets all
the love they need—or want. People are so greedy about
love."

Grandmother's eyes, turned briefly on Anna, suddenly
had such a look of sadness that Anna almost broke her
vow of silence. She licked her lips and screwed up her eyes,
and then to her chagrin Grandmother burst out laughing.

"What a queer little thing you are. Like a little foreign
cat. I wonder whatever your grandfather is going to make
of you."

He didn't make much of her, the thin old man in the
gorgeous red quilted silk dressing gown. He was an invalid,
Grandmother had explained, and she must be very quiet
with him. Quiet . . . when she hadn't yet opened her mouth!
You couldn't get quieter than that. And she certainly was
not going to begin to talk after seeing the look of shock
in the old man's face.

He took her hand politely and said, "How do you do,
Anna," in a courteous voice. Unlike Aunt Florence, it
seemed that he was acutely disappointed that she did not
resemble her mother.

"Tartar," he said. "She's exactly like her father, Bea. I
remember him clearly, in that little French church, standing beside our exquisite Daisy. Anna has the same outlandish looks."

"She can't help that," said Grandmother. "Wait until
she's been fed up, then we'll see an improvement. I've told
her she can make her choice about a boarding school, a
day school or a governess, but there's to be no running
away."

"School will be best," said Grandfather in a weary voice.
"We don't want the child about the house all day. She'll
be too lonely and she'll take up too much of your time."
Grandfather reached out a frail hand and Grandmother
took it, her soft plump cheeks going pink with pleasure.

Anna, diverted momentarily from her own intense self-pity, stared in wonder. These *old* people, could they be in love? That was funny, even funnier than Mother and nasty fat Vladimir.

"Oh, I don't think so, William. Miss Finch will look after her until we arrange her future."

"How long is she to stay?"

"Daisy didn't say. How long is your mother to be in America, Anna?" Grandmother looked into the shut face and sighed. "No, well, we must just see how things go along. Come and I'll show you your room, Anna. It was your mother's, and it's exactly as she left it."

"You ought to have seen this house before the war," Finch said. "Cook, three housemaids, lady's maid, two gardeners, coachman, knife boy, governess for Miss Daisy. It was properly run then. Now there's only Cook and Bridget and Bates and Hawkins and me."

"Why?" Anna asked. She had no rule of silence with servants, and this strange birdlike little woman was not someone of whom to be nervous.

"The war, of course. Where were you during the war?"

"In St. Petersburg. At home."

"What was home like if I might ask?"

"All right. Not like this." Anna looked around the pretty room with its frilled curtains and bedspread, the little pleated petticoat around the dressing table, the rose-patterned carpet, the dainty white furniture. It must have exactly suited Mother. You could see her sitting up in bed in her swansdown-trimmed negligee.

"I suppose not," said Finch thoughtfully. "The master always worried about Miss Daisy. Myself, I've never had a home at all. I've always lived in other people's, not eating much or taking up much room. Lucky I'm so small. I can perch on a twig of someone else's tree. I was with your great-grandmother until she died. Since then your grandmother has been very kind to me. She's a good woman, whatever you may think of her."

"She makes you do what she says," Anna muttered.

"That's the prerogative of grown-ups, Miss Anna. Is that all your luggage? Different from your mother. She had trunks galore when she traveled. Never mind, the mistress will see you get some nice clothes from the shop."

"I don't care for clothes."

"Oh, dear, what a pity. A certain amount of primping and preening is right for a young lady."

"Where's the bathroom?"

"Down the passage on the right. You might like to take a bath before dinner and then I'll do your hair up. Make you look pretty."

Pretty, pretty, pretty! Was that all women thought of? Anna wondered scornfully as she wandered down the passage and opened the first door she came to.

She had made a mistake. This was not the bathroom. It was a large gloomy room with the curtains drawn and only one shaded light burning. There was a vast table in the middle of the room, crowded with ranks of toy soldiers, on the opposite side of which sat a terrifying figure. A soldier, a *German* soldier, wearing a strange flat-topped helmet, and field-gray uniform. He had a monocle stuck in one eye, and a clipped fair mustache over tight lips. As Anna entered he started up, slapping a cane to his side as he came toward her.

She stood still for one petrified moment, then fled, shrieking, *"Nyet, nyet, nyet!"*

Downstairs, William and Beatrice lifted their heads to listen.

"That, I think, is Russian for no," said William.

"It's the first word I've heard her speak," Beatrice answered. "Whatever that may prognosticate."

"Wandering about strange houses is a bad habit," said Grandmother later, addressing herself to the stiff bolt-upright figure in the bed. "I did it myself once, and found it was usually to my disadvantage."

"I was only looking for the bathroom," Anna muttered.

"Exactly. That's always the excuse. Well, what are you doing in bed at six o'clock? You're not a baby. Get up and dress and come down to dinner.

Anna shook her head violently. She didn't speak again. How could she put into words her fear of that utterly terrifying figure of the German soldier? She had seen plenty of soldiers in her time, and actual fighting during the uprisings in St. Petersburg when the wounded and dead lay in the snow along the pavements. But nothing had been so strange and macabre as that silent figure rising slowly and coming toward her in the gloomy room.

Did Grandmother know about the German soldier living in her house?

"Now don't be a silly girl. You're not overtired, and with all that moving about Europe you can't be shy. There'll only be Grandfather and Aunt Florence and Uncle Edwin and myself. Family. Or don't you want to be part of our family?"

Anna pressed the edge of the sheet to her lips, and tried to say that she would never leave the safety of this room. Never.

Grandmother stared at her some more, then shrugged and sighed.

"Very well. Finch may bring you a tray upstairs for this once. Perhaps today has been a little much for you. But tomorrow we expect an improvement." She came and kissed Anna's damp forehead. "It was only Uncle Edwin, you know," she said. "He's not at all a person to be afraid of. Poor boy."

But she was afraid, perhaps not only of Uncle Edwin so curiously dressed as a German soldier, but of everything, the strange house and the strange people, the inevitable new school and the English girls she would have to meet. It was all too much. She would stay safely in this, her mother's old room. She wasn't afraid of Finch, and an even older woman, Hawkins, very bony and wrinkled. They were two old hens who cackled softly about her and didn't scold.

But nothing else and nobody else could be faced.

"Send for the doctor," said William impatiently. "If the child isn't physically ill, then it must be something mental."

"It's plain stubbornness," said Florence. "Like a mule, that one."

Edwin gave his small secret smile. He spoke almost as little as Anna did. But they were used to that. The prison doctor and then Doctor Lovegrove had said that he was suffering a personality change as the result of his long incarceration. He had withdrawn into himself, perhaps permanently. He was not unhappy. He found his fantasy world made no demands on him. He had always had a too highly strung nature. The servants didn't mind him in the house, and he made no trouble.

But Daisy's young minx was another matter, said William. She was just willful.

"No," said Beatrice quietly. "Let her be."

"You mean just let her stay in that room forever!" Florence exclaimed.

"Until she's ready to come out. I think perhaps we made a bad start with her. She's more disturbed than we knew. She's been neglected. Yes, William, I am criticizing Daisy. It's quite obvious that she's never been very maternal and with Sergei dying and leaving that child to remind her mother of her loss she hasn't been able to cope. That sort of thing needs a stronger character than Daisy ever had."

"Her character's fine, Bea," William said stiffly.

"No, it isn't, it used to be shallow and selfish, and it still is," said Florence. "All that girl wanted to do was to preen herself in front of men."

"Women who love men too deeply don't make good mothers," Beatrice said. "Speaking for myself—"

"You have been a splendid mother, Bea." William had his withdrawn look.

"I fancy Florence and Edwin may not entirely agree. However, let's see if I have more success with Anna."

"You won't if you leave her shut up in her room," Florence said. "She'll go cuckoo."

"She talks to Finch. I think she has a large inferiority complex, poor child. That second husband of Daisy's seems to be a very insensitive person, and he has this spoiled daughter, Olga, who is pretty."

"It's a pity about Anna's looks," William commented. He was surprised and resentful that Daisy's daughter should be so plain.

"She may improve. Does it matter so much?"

"Bea, this isn't like you, spoiling the little brat."

It was even just a little amusing that Daisy's daughter should be such a failure with William. Beatrice gave him her usual loving smile.

"No, that used to be your prerogative, didn't it? But apart from dragging her screaming out of her room what else can we do but give her time to settle down?"

"I just don't want her taking up too much of your time," William said.

A week later, on a sharp bright afternoon, a small figure crept from the house and came upon Edwin preparing his spring borders. Crocuses, narcissuses, daffodils. He loved the flaunting yellow of daffodils. He wouldn't have any help in the garden. The previous gardener had left at the beginning of the war. He had died, in mud that was bereft of all seeds and growth, on the Somme. He hadn't been replaced and when Edwin had come home the garden had been a jungle.

Every soldier needed physical exercise for fitness. Since he didn't care to go on route marches over the Heath he decided to work in the garden instead.

Now he loved it passionately. He wasn't going to have any skinny little girl (Daisy's girl, they said) interfering with his work.

However, she didn't interfere. She merely came creeping up close, as silent as the advance of a caterpillar, and stood watching. After a long time he said, "I'm your Uncle Edwin."

"I know."

"You yelled when you first saw me."

"I know."

"Fair enough. I was a Uhlan *Kapitän* and they command respect."

"You're different now."

"This is my working kit."

"I like it better."

"You'll like the other when you're used to it. Would you like me to teach you the Napoleonic Wars?"

"The retreat from Moscow?"

"You know that, do you? I suppose you would, being half Russian. Waterloo, too?"

"No."

"Good God! We'd better repair that omission."

"When?"

"This afternoon."

"In that . . . room?"

"I'll be the Duke of Wellington this afternoon. Scarlet tunic with gold braid. Very fine. You can be my trumpeter and sound the battle charge. I say, that will be jolly."

With the child coming out of her shell at last, although speech still had to be dragged from her, Beatrice set about finding a suitable school. William was adamant that he couldn't have her and a hockey-playing governess about the house all day. He had felt so differently about Daisy, but then he had been younger and in much better health.

With his habitual courtesy and kindness, he had tried to
make one or two advances to the child, but when she re-
jected his famous butterfly collection, saying coldly that
she preferred Uncle Edwin's guns, he gave up trying.

"How long do we have to put up with her?" he asked
plaintively.

"I suppose until her mother has a settled home for her.
We can't be inhuman, my dear. You'll hardly notice her,
once she's going to school."

"Let's hope so. She isn't one of us, Bea."

Once she herself, a solemn little outsider, had not been
one of the Overton family but she had become one. The
years took care of those things. Beatrice sighed, and wished
that Anna's complex problems didn't take the valuable
time she would have preferred spending with William. But
such an acutely vulnerable child needed time and understanding. That was one thing experience had taught her.

"It's only a day school, my dear. You can come home
every night, and do your homework in the old nursery."

"I don't want to go."

"I'm afraid you must, and that's all about it. One thing I
won't tolerate is an uneducated granddaughter."

She gave the cold little paw a firm unemotional clasp.

"Uncle Edwin can teach you at weekends. You must
learn something other than wars, you know."

The next letter from Daisy came from California. She
had left Vladimir. He was a beast. She had renounced all
claim to being a princess; she didn't want even a title from
a man who had proved to be so selfish, gluttonous and
cruel. Ugh! He hadn't even let her keep the ruby pendant;
he was going to use that to lure a new wife. But what did
she care, she had met the most attractive film producer.
He was promising to make her another Gloria Swanson or
Mary Pickford. (Which?" muttered Florence. "Make up
your mind.") As soon as her divorce was through and she
had married Randolph she would send for Anna. Although
if the child were happy, as she must be with dear Mamma
and Papa, it was a pity to disturb her. Poor brat, she had
had such a lot of being dragged about in her short life. It
was a plain miracle that she was going to school and staying there.

Daisy had even acquired a breathless American way of expressing herself. She was a chameleon, taking on the color of her surroundings. Perhaps she actually would make a successful movie actress.

"Dear Daisy. Still the complete opportunist," said Florence.

"She's always looking for another Sergei," William said, but less certainly now. Sadly, he was finding his faith in Daisy difficult to sustain.

"No, no, Papa, she was an opportunist long before she met Sergei. Unconsciously then, perhaps. And you can't tell me that tragedy changes people. It only brings out their latent characteristics."

"Goodness, Florence, what a lot of long words," Beatrice murmured.

But Florence was right. Daisy was completely self-centered, or how could she feel so little guilt about abandoning her child?

School was hell, Anna told herself cynically. However, partly because she was scared of Grandmother, and partly because she was afraid of what the alternative might be, she endured it.

She hadn't made any friends and she was always bottom of the class because her previous education had been almost non-existent, and because she was still limited in her understanding of the English language. Her spelling was something to marvel at, one of the mistresses told the whole class.

But that wasn't why she eventually ran away. It was primarily because at last she had somewhere to run to. Uncle Edwin had told her that if ever the enemy were too much for her, he would defend her. She could hide in his room, and no one would ever think of looking for her there.

She did this for two days, crouching behind the bamboo screen in the corner during the day, and sleeping on the hearthrug in front of the fire at night. Uncle Edwin smuggled food to her, wedges of bread and butter and apples and glasses of milk spiked with rum. Rum was for fighting men, he said. He also gave her a gun, a revolver with a wicked little snout that she cradled to her breast and pretended that it comforted her, since obviously that was what Uncle Edwin meant it to do. She was half dazed with the rum, anyway.

The police came and searched the whole house. When they knocked on Uncle Edwin's door he demanded, "Who goes there?" so loudly that the constable who appeared gave only a cursory search to the room.

"Chap in there's balmy," he said audibly, as he left. "Shouldn't think he even knows the time of day."

They left the house, having found no sign of Anna, and from then on concentrated on searching the Heath.

However, after two days, Anna was thoroughly bored with the game. Fiddling with the revolver, it suddenly exploded and made her shriek with terror. The shot hit the ceiling, and bits of plaster fell.

When Grandfather and the servants burst in (it was during the day when Grandmother and Florence were at the shop) Uncle Edwin was standing defensively behind his serried ranks of toy soldiers, his sword unsheathed.

"It wasn't me," he babbled. "It was her."

Scruffy, exhausted, her eyes swollen into slits, Anna was dragged out. Grandmother was sent for, and the court-martial began. (Uncle Edwin had warned her that the operation would probably end in a court-martial.)

"Edwin, if ever you give Anna a loaded gun again, we will have to send you away," Grandmother said in her steady voice.

"It isn't Edwin, Bea, it's the child who'll have to go," said Grandfather, whose voice did betray considerable agitation. "She's uncontrollable."

Anna, using her only effective weapon, that of silence, stood looking at them defiantly out of her aching eyes. She was suddenly realizing that she loved this house. Not the people but the house. Although Uncle Edwin was all right, and Finch was tolerable.

Uncle Edwin had left off his monocle and put on thick-lensed glasses that made him look boyish and quite unimpressive. He hung his head and mumbled that he had forgotten the revolver was loaded. It would never happen again.

"Just to be safe, I think you had better give me all your guns," Grandmother said. "Oh, you can keep the old flint-locks, if you like. But nothing modern. And you must never play military games with Anna again, do you hear?"

"It was only a siege," Uncle Edwin muttered.

"It was very dangerous. The police will have to be informed. Have they been informed, William?"

"Not yet. I was wondering if we couldn't tell them Anna had just come home of her own accord. Haven't we had enough scandals?"

Grandmother suddenly looked very tired.

"We have, but I'm afraid we can't do anything but tell the truth. Anna's headmistress will have to know exactly what happened if she's to take the child back."

Alarm proved greater than Anna's capacity for silence.

"I won't go back to that school!"

"But that's what has been the trouble in the past, hasn't it, Anna?" Grandmother said quite kindly. "You had never had to go back and face your disgrace. This time you will."

"She isn't our responsibility," said Grandfather peevishly. "We're too old for this kind of thing."

"I know, my dear," said Grandmother. "I know. However, here we all are. Anna, you had better go upstairs and take a bath and change your clothes. Then you'll be ready to talk to the police."

The next day, sitting beside Grandmother in the Daimler, Anna was driven back to school. Quite apart from her dread of going back, she hated her ostentatious arrival. She knew that Grandmother had done it on purpose, but whether to show up her guilt, or to make things easier for her, she didn't know.

She only knew that once more she hated everything, and Grandmother had gone over to the enemy.

Chapter 27

Beatrice found her feelings about Anna extremely confused.

Here, with this upsetting affair, had been a chance to completely rid herself of those two troublesome women who had haunted her life, Mary Medway and her daughter.

Yet she couldn't take the chance. She could even defy William over it. She could quarrel over defending Mary Medway's grandchild!

The whole thing was completely ironic, for now William had only her welfare at heart. He didn't like to see her tired and frowning and troubled. The rheumatism in her hips were troubling her, too, and he kept urging her to rest.

"Stay home more, Bea. I'd be glad of your company." He meant that. His eyes were full of affection. Here they were in their sixties, a true Darby and Joan.

Beatrice smiled faintly, finding the situation wryly humorous as well as heartwarming.

"Perhaps I will. I could have the department figures sent up on the days I stay home. But business hasn't been too good lately. Florence says there's a depression coming. I don't know how she knows."

"She always seems to know everything," said William.

Florence's flat-chested narrow-hipped figure absolutely fitted the fashionable twenties. She wore the low-waisted dresses and the fringed shawls with great panache. She had her hair bobbed and smoked cigarettes in a long ivory holder.

Beatrice told her that at her age she looked ridiculous. She merely gave her faint supercilious smile and said that as the head of a fashion department one had to be in the vanguard of fashion.

"Miss Brown never found that necessary. She believed in

being inconspicuous. It was her customers who had to shine."

"Mamma, when will you realize that those days are past? Business is done in a different way now."

"Is it?"

Florence met her mother's impassive gaze and sighed.

"Oh, I don't mean one adds up figures differently or replaces stock differently. It's the way things are presented to the public. This is the age of advertisement, of public relations, of making the right *image*."

Beatrice looked at Florence's short-skirted clinging silk dress. "If that's what you mean by the right image—I just call it ugly and immodest."

"Mamma, where are our customers going to be if you flout the Paris couture houses?"

"Very well, I'll turn my attention to other things. At least people still want damask tablecloths and silverware. Your father has a point, you know, in cherishing beautiful old things."

"That's a disease of old people."

"Yes. Perhaps even you will have it one day, my dear."

"Who knows? Only don't interfere with me now. James and I are planning a willow-green week."

"What is that supposed to mean?"

"It's a new color we're launching. We're inviting actors and actresses to a luncheon."

"In my day it would have been royalty," Beatrice remarked.

"Which shows again just how old-fashioned you are," Florence cried in exasperation. "Is Princess Mary likely to be so daring as to begin a new fashion? Could she even wear it to advantage? Of course she couldn't, but someone like Marie Tempest can."

"Why don't you send for Daisy?" Beatrice said sourly.

"Daisy! In her dreamworld! To think she can begin a film career when she's in her thirties!"

"You know, you started all that for Daisy when you insisted on having your Russian exhibition."

"Stick to the point, Mamma. We're talking of a business venture, and it had better be a success because our figures are down on last year. If we're not careful Bonnington's is going to be too old-fashioned for words. Be reasonable, Mamma. You fought that with your father."

"I suppose so. But all this streamlining. So ugly. Bonnington's has always meant luxury and spaciousness."

"And prices that no one nowadays will pay, or can afford to. James says that before nineteen thirty half the big shops in London will have failed."

"Is James a prophet?"

"He doesn't look into a crystal ball. He merely understands economic trends. If you know what I am talking about."

"I still understand the department figures, if that's what you mean."

Florence sighed. "It isn't. It's the stock market, the whole business economy of the country. World trends."

"A willow-green week is hardly going to remedy all that," Beatrice said tartly.

She decided to take a slow walk through her beloved shop, covering the ground floor, always the gayest, most colorful part, with its banked flowers at the entrance, its glittering displays of crystal, jewelry, lamps and lampshades, silks and brocades, then mounting the stairs to the pretty restaurant, and beyond that to the furniture and carpets, the acres of gleaming white linen and damask, the ice-blue chilly fur department with its expensive minks and sables, the gentlemen's wear run by the one-armed astute James Brush, the colorful pottery and porcelain, and then Florence's domain, ladies' fashions, guarded by slim-hipped dummies in those unattractive straight dresses with dipping hems, and closely fitting cloche hats coming down to their eyebrows.

Before she had completed her perambulations her hips were hurting her rather severely. She had to make her way back to her refuge, the gilt cage that still stood on its dais facing the front doors. Recently Florence had been campaigning to get rid of it, saying it was hopelessly old-fashioned. Anyway, it was infra dig for the owner of a large department store to be sitting up there like a madam in a house of doubtful repute.

Florence's similes were unfortunate. Beatrice replied coldly that no better way for receiving cash and keeping watch on the honesty of salesgirls had yet been invented, and while she lived this method would not be changed.

But many things, she feared, would be changed when she could no longer take charge.

That day had not yet come, although her painful hips were a wretched nuisance. Although in another way they were a blessing in disguise, for she could make it the excuse to stay home more frequently with William.

He had had another mild heart attack in the summer. It had sapped his strength, and he was now a complete invalid, never venturing farther from the house than onto the terrace. He spent a great deal of time over his butterfly slides, as if he were reliving his youth, reminding himself where this and that specimen had been captured.

"Bea," he would call. "Come and look at these incredible colors. Did you ever see such a marvelous creation as a butterfly? I know that child of Daisy's thinks this is a sissy occupation. Therefore people who make stained-glass windows or wonderful tapestries must also be sissy. She must learn not to discount beauty in life. Teach her that, will you?"

"You could do it yourself," Bea said.

"We don't seem to have any means of communication, unfortunately. I'm a selfish old man. I resent her because she isn't like her mother. Because she upsets this household."

"It's time for your rest, my love. Shut up those cabinets."

"I suppose I wasn't much of a man, by the standards of our time. I cared too much for beauty."

"Well, you didn't get beauty in me," Beatrice said in her dry voice.

"Don't denigrate yourself, Bea. I don't like you doing that."

"We've grown to fit each other, that's all."

"Whatever way you like to put it. But I really don't want exhausting awkward grandchildren around. I've too little time left to have it dissipated in this way."

"I know, dear. I've forbidden Anna to worry you."

Yet when the next crisis with Anna occurred she could not follow both William's and Florence's urgent advice and cable Daisy to come and take her troublesome child away. She found that it was as impossible to turn out the exasperating creature as it had been to turn away the barefoot beggars who had haunted Bonnington's doors in the past. She simply could not live with herself if she did so.

The little strange closed face would haunt her always, as Mary Medway's had done. She had the entirely unreasonable feeling that she owed this awkward unattractive changeling a debt.

It seemed that on her return to school after the running-away episode, Anna had found herself a heroine. She had actually defended herself with a real gun! This notoriety had made her the leader of a small clique who flatteringly expected her to invent other daring exploits. She was not lacking in imagination. The summer term, consequently, was full of illicit excitement, until the inevitable climax. One day her grandmother was sent for by the headmistress, and told that Anna must be removed.

Anna had an exasperating ability to seem to shrink to half her size when she was in trouble.

The little figure, thin and wizened, facing Beatrice in the morning room, was too vulnerable for comfort. Or was the little wretch a remarkable actress, with a devious insensitive heart?

One must not be taken in by her pathetic appearance.

"Anna, I hope you're not imagining that I won't send you back to school. I will. You have to learn to face the consequences of your mischief making. So you will start tomorrow at a new school I have found for you in Highgate. Bates will drive you there in the morning, and pick you up after school. I won't have you lurking about the streets at all. And I warn you that the rules in this school are very strict. If you break any of them the headmistress has my permission to punish you in any way she sees fit. She knows all about you, but the pupils don't. So you have another chance. I hope you will find yourself equal to living up to it. Well? Did you want to say something?"

"I thought you might send me back to my mother," Anna said in a strangled voice.

"Did you want to go?"

"Nyet, nyet, nyet!"

Real emotion always made Anna revert to Russian, to her babyhood, no doubt. Beatrice wouldn't allow herself to be moved. It just may have been another trick.

"Then for goodness sake, behave yourself. Try to please people. It's so much nicer being liked than disliked."

After that, although Anna remained prickly and unfriendly, there was no more major trouble. Which was fortunate, because William's health was now causing Beatrice grave concern. Another attack of bronchitis had left him with great difficulty in breathing. All the usual remedies failed. Watching his thin bluish face, and listening to his shallow struggling breaths, Beatrice realized that the time had come to write to Daisy begging her to return home to see her father.

She shrank from the upset this would cause, not only to her household, but probably to Anna. For William's sake it must be done.

However, Daisy answered:

"I am desolated to hear about Papa, but all my life I remember these crises and he always gets over them. And you must admit, Mamma, that you always did exaggerate his illnesses. You went about on tiptoe if he only had a bad cold.

"It would be dreadfully inconvenient for me to come to England just now. Randolph has just begun a new film and I have a part—a small one, but vitally important for my future. I know Papa will understand. Kiss him for me and wish him to be well soon.

"I would say my prayers for him, but I stopped believing in God when my darling Sergei was killed and I had that terrible time just trying to keep myself and Anna alive. Now I know that in this life you just have to grab things for yourself.

"Tell Anna that I will be sending her a parcel of pretty clothes soon. I am eternally grateful to you and Papa for having her. I am sure you are mending all her awkward ways. She's such a funny little duckling, and I have always been mean to her because she reminds me of what I have to forget. Children, poor little devils, are so much at the mercy of their parents' emotions."

Beatrice didn't show anyone this disturbing letter. It contained too much truth. It highlighted Daisy's self-absorption, but absolved no one from guilt.

One simply had to find a way of telling William that Daisy was not coming home at present. In the summer when he was better and could enjoy her visit, she would come.

If he lived until the summer. Each day that seemed less likely.

Beatrice deserted the shop, and stayed at his bedside day and night. When Florence brought her the department figures she waved them away. Which was just as well, said Florence, because they were poor figures. There was still a slump in trade. Perhaps it would pick up in the new year. On the other hand, it might not. Department stores were terribly expensive to run, and the rent for that valuable site in the Bayswater Road which Grandfather Bonnington had obtained so cheaply was shortly going to be astronomical.

Florence studied her new bob, which was cute, but rather showed up the lines around her eyes, and wondered if a beauty department on the top floor would pay. Girls were beginning to spend fortunes on their hair and faces. She must talk to James about it. No use talking to Mamma, either now or after Papa's death. It was Mamma's stubbornness about changes that was making Bonnington's go downhill. She would simply have to retire. That old-fashioned cash desk could be swept away and something diverting put in its place.

Papa was going to die, of course. His chest rattled with every breath, and they were spending a fortune on day and night nurses, even though Mamma never left his bedside, and resented extremely the presences of the nurses.

What a greedy woman she was. She had always wanted everything, Papa's entire love, the obedience of her children, the absolute control of her shop and the consequent authority which that gave to her. Yet had she ever been happy?

"Well, happiness was the most elusive of human conditions," Florence ruminated. It was partly because one was the victim of one's own nature. Look at her, and the way she had deliberately allowed her heart to wither after Desmond had jilted her. It had been a dramatic gesture, a strange masochistic pleasure which now she could not do without.

And look at Edwin, with his retreat from reality. Look at Daisy, pursuing the fleshpots. What a family! Mamma and Papa should have been warned. Why hadn't they bred butterflies?

All the same, what were they thinking now, in that darkened too-hot sickroom? Were they remembering their romantic happiness, long ago, before any troublesome children had arrived?

Florence brushed her short hair furiously, and set her lips in a thin line. It wasn't fair. What was she to remember when she lay dying? Her business triumphs?

In the early hours of a November morning Beatrice drew back the curtains because William had asked her to.

The moon, hazed by mist, was sinking. The sky was dark, the night utterly still. William was trying to say something, something about Italy, the country he had always loved best. Venice? The gondolas on the darkly gleaming canals? The sea lavender? The islands drowned in sunshine?

"The white peacocks," he said distinctly. "You told me about them."

As she sat with his hand growing cold in hers she remembered the white peacocks on Isola Bella, and Mary Medway, and Daisy's birth.

And knew, with a deep aching bitterness, who had been in William's last thoughts. Had he even thought it was Mary's hand he held?

The bedroom door opened softly. The light from the passage illumined Anna's tentative face.

"Grandmother!"

"Go away!" Beatrice whispered.

"Is Grandfather dead? I'm not afraid of dead people. I've seen them before."

"Go away!" said Beatrice harshly. "Leave us alone!"

Daisy had sent an enormous extravagant wreath of white hothouse roses and carnations. The Overton vault was opened again, and one more slender casket was being added to its hoard.

Beatrice steeled herself to watch. Anna and Edwin and Florence stood beside her. Edwin was suitably dressed, thank goodness, in a neat dark overcoat, but when he let it fall open Beatrice was horrified to see the Death or Glory badge of the 17th Lancers, the macabre skull and crossbones, incongruously pinned to the lapel of his jacket. Really, she thought, fury exploding in her head, why hadn't Florence, why hadn't someone, checked his dressing? Now everyone could see what a doomed family the Overtons were, Edwin mentally deranged, Florence, with her flat sexless figure, opting out of marriage, only that queer little foreign child to represent the future.

The old general must be hating her for failing him so badly.

Chapter 28

After Grandfather's death Anna thought that life became frightfully boring. Grandmother spent a great deal of time shut in the bedroom where Grandfather had died. She wasn't saying her prayers because she wasn't a praying person. She dealt in facts, said Aunt Florence, not illusions, whatever that meant. It was a mistake, said Aunt Florence also, to live so much for one person. "Remember that, young Anna, if ever anyone wants to marry you."

An unlikely prospect, her expression said. Anna made faces at herself in the mirror, deliberately exaggerating her slanting eyes, until she looked positively Chinese. When a parcel arrived from Mother in California containing a party dress with ruffles around the neck and hem, she exclaimed scornfully, "Where would I wear it, even if it suited me? Mother must have forgotten what I look like."

"It's very pretty, Miss Anna," said Finch. "You should be grateful."

"Is it?" said Anna, and when she was alone she got a pair of scissors and cut the dress to pieces, a fiendish satisfaction possessing her as she did so.

Uncle Edwin understood. He said, "That's the spirit. Defy the enemy." But everyone else was deeply shocked. She would have to be punished again.

Grandmother, looking at Anna with her sad eyes (she hadn't really seen Anna or anyone else since Grandfather had died), said that even if the dress was one that she personally would not have chosen, she could not condone destructiveness.

"Are you going to send me away?" Anna asked belligerently.

"Where to, I wonder? That's the problem I can't solve.

I don't turn children, even such a bad one as you, onto
the street. But in the meantime I must warn you that you'll
have to wear your old clothes for another season. I am
not spending money on expensive clothes, simply to have
them destroyed."

Yours wouldn't be such silly pink frilly ones, Anna
wanted to say, feeling a sudden impulse of friendship (not
for the first time) to Grandmother sitting like a stout old
queen in her upright chair. Hawkins had told Finch, and
Finch had told Anna, that Grandmother suffered a good
deal of pain from her bad hips, and this made her short of
temper. But she didn't want pity. The best thing was to
pretend one didn't notice her limp, or her difficulty in getting out of a chair.

So Anna, relieved that she had got off so lightly from
this last escapade, went on one of her silent enjoyable tours
of the house. Being sent away would have been the greatest
punishment anyone could devise because she loved this
house.

But no one must know that. It made her too vulnerable.

So, like the tax men who, after Grandfather's death, had
studied and listed every picture and piece of porcelain, she
quietly gloated over the yellow Worcester and apple-green
Derby; she took a Chelsea sauceboat, decorated with flower
sprays, caterpillars and butterflies, in the palms of her
hands, feeling its cool smooth shape with pleasure; she
admired the little fluted beakers and cream jugs made so
long ago and still perfect, the Worcester teapot and teacups
decorated with fruiting hops and trellises, the strange bird
paintings in lacquered frames, the eighteenth-century Irish
and English glass, decanters, wineglasses, candlesticks.

These things were the blood running through the veins
of the old house, keeping it alive. Grandmother felt the
same as she did. Nothing was to be sold. Grandfather's
famous butterfly collection (the best in England, people
said) had been bequeathed to the British Museum, but
apart from that everything had been left to Grandmother,
so the treasures remained intact. The death duties would
have to be found out of revenue from Bonnington's,
Grandmother said, to Aunt Florence's anger and dismay.
Was Grandfather, even in death, going on soaking the shop?
she demanded. After all, who was to inherit all these things

eventually? Edwin only wanted the military collection, and she only wanted money.

No one thought of making the suggestion that Anna, the strange foreign child, should inherit them. But no one had forbidden her to look at them, and this was much easier to do now that Grandfather was not there to catch her prowling about. He hadn't liked her to touch a thing.

Now he was gone, no one noticed her. She might have been invisible.

She didn't understand her destructive urges, or the wild malevolent glee that seized her when she was being particularly wicked.

She simply didn't know why, shortly after Grandfather's death, she stole the string of beads from the shop near the school where she had gone to buy an exercise book. This act was all the more inexplicable because she didn't like beads.

But there they were in her school satchel when the woman behind the counter came rushing after her, and seized her roughly as she was going out of the door.

"Them kids from that school!" the woman said angrily. "Bert! I'll hold this one while you call the police."

Uncle Edwin knew all about being in jail. He said it wasn't to be recommended. The food was terrible, worse than the troops had lived on during Wellington's Peninsular campaign. This time he couldn't promise to hide her, because look at the trouble that had caused the previous time. She would simply have to stand up and face the music.

From the time the policeman had brought her home, and talked to Grandmother, saying a charge had been made by the owner of the shop, and therefore the young lady would have to be taken before a magistrate in the juvenile courts, Anna had lived in a cloud of terror. She couldn't run away because Grandmother had ordered that she was never to be left alone. One of the servants must be with her all day and Finch must sleep in her room at night.

At first, when Grandmother had said, "Why did you do it, Anna?" she had taken refuge in her mute act. But even that hadn't been effective for long, for she had burst out, in spite of herself, "I don't know. I don't even like those horrid beads."

"Well, I'm glad of that. I hoped you had better taste."

"What—what will happen to me?" Anna asked urgently.

Grandmother sighed and put her hand over her eyes.

"Whatever the magistrate orders."

"J-jail?" Anna whispered.

"Children aren't put in jail in this country. Aunt Florence insists that your mother be sent for."

"H-has she been?"

"Not yet. And don't stutter, child. Try not to do so in front of the magistrate."

"Will—will you be there, Grandmother?"

"Yes. I'll be there."

"Then I'll try not to s-stutter, Grandmother."

It wasn't so terrible in the little drab courtroom, after all. The magistrate was old, with a pink-cheeked kindly face, and oddly enough Grandmother did most of the talking. She was dressed in her gray shop dress, and looked particularly severe, her little round chin jutting out stubbornly, her eyes tired and angry.

But she was allowed to sit by Anna, and halfway through her explanation of how Anna had come to live in England, and of her earlier unsettled childhood, she suddenly took Anna's hand in her gloved one, and held it hard. She didn't seem to know she had done so.

Then the magistrate leaned forward and asked Anna if she would like to go back to her mother in America.

"Oh, no!" Anna gasped.

"Why not?"

"She sends me silly clothes." That was all Anna could think of to say.

"Would she give you a stable and loving home?"

"What's that?"

"I can answer that question," Grandmother interrupted. "She would not."

"You understand your daughter, Mrs. Overton?"

"I do."

"Then are you prepared to be responsible for this child, and to see that she reports to the probation officer once a week for the next year?"

"What would the alternative be?"

"She could be sent to an approved home."

"Certainly not!"

"Then can you keep her out of trouble, Mrs. Overton?"

"If I knew why she got into trouble, perhaps I could keep her out of it."

"These offenders usually act from the rather pathetic desire to draw attention to themselves. So perhaps, beginning on that basis, you could achieve something, Mrs. Overton?"

"The impertinent old fool!" Grandmother said as they left the court. "Telling me how to bring up a child. I can tell you this, my girl, if you let me down, and I have to go back and eat humble pie in front of that petty god, I will certainly never forgive you."

Anna climbed into the Daimler and sat as close to Grandmother as she dared. She was cold, and trembling violently.

"I'll never steal beads again, Grandmother."

"I should hope not."

"I don't always know why I do bad things."

"Because you want me to notice you. That's what the old fool said. Well, I'll try to do so more often. This is a situation we must just make the best of."

"Why didn't you let me be sent away?" Anna dared to ask.

"Because I won't have anyone telling me what to do with William's grandchild. That's why. Not even your know-all Aunt Florence. I'm still in charge, and if I say you stay, you stay. Wrap the rug round your legs and stop looking so nipped and frozen, like an east wind. I suppose I must give more time to you now. We could make a start by going to the Russian ballet when it comes to London again. Your father used to like the ballet."

"Did he?"

"Didn't your mother tell you? That's where she met him. He wasn't a member of the ballet, but Daisy said he should have been. He was a great admirer of Anna Pavlova. You were named after her."

"Was I really?"

"Well, don't sound so surprised. Most people are named after somebody. She was a celebrity, but that doesn't mean you will take after her. Those skinny legs don't look so artistic, do they? Perhaps you'll be musical instead. Piano lessons might be a good thing."

"Why?"

"Because all Overton women learn to play the piano.

Your great-aunt Caroline used to sing very prettily. Family talents can be inherited. Why are you squinting like that?"

Anna hastily smoothed her ferocious scowl.

"I—I hadn't ever thought of being part of a family."

"Of course you're part of a family," Grandmother said irritably. "Did you think you came into the world belonging to nobody? You're an Overton and you'll behave like one. You won't bring shame on the family. We've had enough of that from your Uncle Edwin."

"Yes, Grandmother," said Anna, speaking meekly for perhaps the first time in her life.

Chapter 29

So she had committed herself. Anna was to stay. The house was to echo once more with simple piano exercises; there would have to be the tribal rites of birthday parties, theater treats, excursions here and there.

One was too old and tired and too frequently in pain. On the other hand, even such a withdrawn and troublesome child as Anna did something to take the edge off the unbearable quiet and loneliness since William's death. One had to stir oneself to think of something other than bereavement and grief; and of someone other than oneself.

"You had to stop brooding, madam," Hawkins said, with the brisk familiarity of forty years of service. Hawkins, Beatrice was almost certain, had always known the truth of Daisy's birth. She had shared Beatrice's cool disapproval of that pretty, vain and self-indulgent child. But Anna, discarded and deprived, was another matter. Decency insisted on kindness toward forlorn children.

"Anyway, she seems to have turned a new leaf, wouldn't you say, madam? I think it's the piano lessons. She has talent."

"Oh, yes. Those sort of children usually do have, if you can dig it out. Fortunately, she hasn't advanced yet to Chopin."

"Chopin, madam?"

That had been an unintentional remark.

But of course only she had been acutely aware of those wistful Chopin ballades on spring evenings. And still heard them. . . .

"A composer who must be played with skill."

It was a great triumph when they got rid of that interfering probation officer at last, after a year of good behavior on the part of Anna Overton. (That outlandish name Pavel had had to be dropped—William, one was sure, would have approved, even though he had never got over regarding Anna as an unwelcome guest.)

The highlight of the year had been the night at the Russian ballet when Anna, her bony shoulders hunched forward, had sat on the edge of her seat and literally had not stirred an eyelash until the curtain had come down on the last gorgeous scene.

She didn't speak all the way home. But, as they got out of the Daimler, she whirled into Beatrice's arms, nearly knocking her over and sending a shaft of acute pain through her hips.

"Grandmother, thank you, thank you!"

It was her first spontaneous action since her arrival at Overton House. It suggested, more than her misdirected and miserable acts of destruction, a warm and fiery spirit. Something might be made of her, after all. Something would be made of her, Beatrice told herself doggedly. She did not embark on projects which were not a success.

Except her marriage?

But surely her constant desolation since William's death meant success of a kind.

At least she was feeling physically stronger, and able to oppose with her customary vigor Florence's latest plans for Bonnington's.

The lease Papa had bought so many years ago, at a reasonable rent, was due to expire. Property in the Bayswater Road had increased twenty times in value. After all, sixty years ago this had been a muddy road at the end of a straggling Oxford Street, and not considered desirable for business purposes.

Now the picture was changed out of all recognition. New commercial buildings were springing up everywhere, and the site of Bonnington's, an extravagantly sprawling shop, was quite uneconomic unless drastic increases were made in turnover.

Florence, aided by her crony James Brush, had plenty of ideas about this. Complete modernization, she said. This was to be carried out in spite of the fact that a new lease would cost a price that made Beatrice wince, and also that the anticipated Depression, beginning dramatically in Wall

Street a little while ago, had now spread like a creeping plague to England and Europe.

In addition to these problems, Florence pointed out bitterly, Bonnington's had also had to bear the burden of Papa's death duties. It was completely disloyal of Mamma to refuse to sell any of the treasures of Overton House (the porcelain collection alone would fetch thousands) to cover this cost. Papa had always drained the business, and due to his wife's weakness and sentimentality, seemed determined to go on doing so, even in death.

"That was why he married me," Beatrice said calmly. "We made a bargain and I kept it faithfully. I shall go on keeping it."

Then didn't Mamma care about the business she had nursed and cherished for so long? Florence demanded. She had thoroughly enjoyed being called Queen Bea once. If she no longer cared about that, then it was time she abdicated. And certainly time that archaic cash system was got rid of, as it would be when modernization was begun. The mourning department would go, also; it was hopelessly Victorian. And that out-of-date tropical department, now that brides no longer set out for India and other parts of the British Empire with a dozen of everything in their trunks. Travelers in the future would not want huge trousseaux of clothes; they would travel lightly because a great many of them would go by air. And Mamma could forget her snobbishness about titled customers. Hadn't she discovered that they were the most dilatory of payers? One could send them the same bill for several years! The customer of the future was going to be the one with cash in her handbag, not the one who employed a maid to carry her handbag for her.

Florence was becoming a bully in her clever brittle way. Beatrice agreed that there was wisdom in many of her ideas, but as long as she was physically able to she would mount the steps into the cash desk, and sit there surveying her kingdom. She had always prided herself on the personal touch in business. Didn't Florence realize that there were many customers who still liked to see Miss Beatrice, even though she often had difficulty in remembering their names? Some of them had similar trouble with unreliable memories. Old Lady Elkins persistently asked for Miss Brown, saying no one else understood how to dress her. One very ancient colonel even occasionally inquired after the health of old Joshua Bonnington.

Which was what came from living in the past, Florence said impatiently. One must live in tomorrow in business.

"And how many tomorrows do you imagine you have?" Beatrice asked sourly.

"Enough. James and I can put Bonnington's back on its feet. But we *must* get rid of the old-fashioned atmosphere. And those death duties will have to be paid back. We need the cash. The Depression is far worse than you seem to realize. Don't you know that we could go bankrupt?"

Bonnington's bankrupt! Beatrice glared at Florence for daring to utter such a heresy. Florence stared back and said in her cruelly sensible voice, "You must face it, Mamma. No business with a dead hand on it survives."

Beatrice's lips quivered suddenly. She hoped Florence hadn't noticed that weakness.

"My hand is still very much alive, thank you." She was longing, with an unbearable sense of desolation, for William. Had life dwindled away to nothing but these sordid fights with Florence?

"Then use it to sign a mortgage on Overton House," Florence said crisply.

"Never!" she exclaimed. "That house is not to be touched, nor anything in it. It's Overton property."

"Mamma, who are you keeping it for? Edwin?"

The pain struck more deeply. Her poor flawed Edwin in that lovely house, letting it molder around him?

"You know these old houses cost far too much in upkeep nowadays," Florence went on. "We ought to sell it and get a smaller place. We'd need fewer servants. There wouldn't be all those rates and taxes. After all, let's be honest, you and I are shopkeepers, not ladies living at leisure in a stately home."

Beatrice had overcome her brief spasm of useless and weak emotion. She said thoughtfully, "You're right, of course, but you must be very imperceptive if you haven't realized that Overton House is much more to me than a business transaction. If it came to a choice between Bonnington's and Overton House, I would choose the house without any hesitation. And I'll never change my mind about that, so stop badgering me."

"You didn't used to be so unrealistic," Florence cried.

"Perhaps that's a pity."

"Mamma, I hate to say it—"

"Is this another unpalatable truth?"

"Your judgment could be getting unreliable."

"Is that a polite way of saying I am getting senile?" Beatrice said tranquilly. "No, not senile, dear. Just obsessive. As I always have been."

The Daimler broke down on the way into the West End. Bates opened the hood and peered into a vaguely smoking interior while Beatrice fidgeted on the back seat.

"What is it, Bates? I'm late."

"I'm not sure, Madam. She's old, that's the trouble. She's wearing out."

"Nonsense, Bates! A car of this excellence doesn't wear out."

"I don't want to say you're wrong, madam, but—"

"Oh, I know. Everything wears out. Me, too. Then if you're going to take hours over your meditations, you'd better go and find me a cab. I'll expect you at the front doors at the usual time this afternoon."

The Daimler was successfully mended, for Bates was waiting for her punctually at four o'clock, the car polished and shining and apparently running sweetly.

It was a different matter when it came to herself. When she fell ill with a nasty cold that developed into fever and pleurisy, young Doctor Lovegrove (old Doctor Lovegrove in his top hat and frock coat had given up his practice some years ago) gave her a severe lecture.

"Mrs. Bonnington, you're an old woman and the time has come to admit it."

"Nonsense!" she croaked in a hoarse breathless voice that took the authority out of her voice. She was used to intimidating people who were a nuisance, but this young man didn't look as if he would be intimidated. "I'll be as fit as I ever was when I get rid of this cold. It's only settled on my chest, the way it used to do with my husband. Goodness me, I've nursed him through enough fevers to know what this is."

"There's also the matter of your hips."

"Oh, yes, that. A bit of rheumatism. You might give me another kind of liniment. The ones I've tried have been useless. Downright swindles."

"I'll just take a look at them, if I may. Which one is the worst?"

Beatrice fretfully let Hawkins turn down the bedclothes. She submitted to the doctor's painful examination—one wretched leg had been almost immovable since she had had to lie in bed—and listened in secret dismay to his diagnosis.

"You're right about liniment, Mrs. Bonnington. It would be a complete waste of time and money. You have a form of arthritis unfortunately progressive. I can prescribe pain-killers."

"What else?" Beatrice demanded.

"Nothing, I'm afraid. The bone damage is fairly extensive already."

Beatrice struggled up.

"What are you trying to tell me? Come on, doctor, I'm no coward. I want the truth."

"I think you must know that already, Mrs. Bonnington. You will become less and less mobile."

"A wheelchair?"

"Not immediately. Although it would be a help after this illness while you're still weak. There are long passages in this house. Perhaps a room on the ground floor later. Then you would have easy access to the garden. I don't need to tell you that most people reaching old age face some sort of disabling illness, and they're not all as fortunately placed as you are."

"Don't lecture me!"

The doctor grinned. He was perhaps not as young as she had thought. And he, too, would face a disabling illness one day, if that were any comfort to her. So would Florence. So would Edwin. So would young Anna with her skinny flying legs. One remembered Papa stricken when he was much younger than she was. But fortunately his stroke had blurred the intensity of his resentment.

She remembered, too, how she and Adam Cope had persuaded him, not to come into the shop, or at least to keep out of sight of the customers. Illness cast a gloom. She had been so intense about the atmosphere she wanted, gaiety, light, color. People whose senses were pleasantly titillated or soothed opened their purses.

So she wasn't too senile, Florence would be glad to hear, to know that Miss Beatrice being wheeled in an invalid chair down the moss-green carpet would be a spectacle that was out of the question. If she couldn't walk, Bonnington's was over for her. The Daimler could be put in its garage and kept as a museum piece, and she, making her halting way on sticks about the house, could be another one. If anyone ever bothered to come and see her. She had never been a person to make intimate friends. William had always been enough for her.

And this sentence, she told herself as she lay in the gloom listening to the fluid crackling in her lungs, was nothing compared to losing William. Really, the world had come to an end, then. The desolation of his loss never left her. So why struggle now? Why not give in? Who was going to care for an old woman in a wheelchair? Who had ever cared, except one or two of the servants, Miss Brown, old Hawkins, dear faithful Adam?

In spite of her brave youthful hopes she had at last to be honest and admit that life had defeated her. The love she had wanted had remained elusive. William had given her friendship, that was true. And, in later years, a possessive devotion. But he had died speaking of the woman she had sent out of the house.

So where was love?

"Grandmother."

"Eh? Who's that?" Beatrice struggled out of restless dream-haunted sleep.

"It's me, Grandmother. Would you like me to read to you?"

"Didn't they tell me you couldn't read properly?"

"I can now, Grandmother. I've been studying hard."

"You need Miss Medway to teach you."

"Who's Miss Medway?"

"Just a . . . very good teacher. Florence and Edwin never did as well with anyone else. I don't believe they ever forgave me—"

"What for, Grandmother?"

"For getting rid of her, of course."

"Miss Anna! You mustn't disturb your grandmother."

Beatrice opened her eyes, and was irritated by Hawkins' anxious face. Too much loving devotion—one was smothered. Really, what did one want? The child at the foot of the bed with her tentative slant-eyed face? A stranger here. Much more Sergei than Daisy. Perhaps that was why one suddenly felt friendly.

"Go away, Hawkins. Anna is going to read to me. I must hear how she's getting on."

"Do you have a favorite book, Grandmother?"

"No, I don't, but it's kind of you to ask. Just read what you have in your hand."

"It's *David Copperfield*, Grandmother."

"Splendid. You get more English every day. Miss Brown would have approved. Her mother used to claim she saw Charles Dickens going in and out of his house in Doughty Street. Not such an elevating sight, I should have thought. I was brought up to watch royalty. That was in Queen Victoria's day."

"Queen Victoria!"

"It's not that long ago. Only thirty, forty years. She was a great personality, but a dreary, dull person to a child. I always preferred her daughters. Princess Louise and Princess Beatrice used to shop at Bonnington's. Princess Louise was very elegant, though a little eccentric. Now Florence thinks it's the *nouveaux riches* whom we want as our customers. I don't agree. Do you?"

"No, but perhaps we're old-fashioned, Grandmother."

"We!" Beatrice laughed until she had a paroxysm of coughing. Hawkins came hurrying, saying that madam must rest. "I'll send the child away, madam."

"You'll do nothing of the kind," Beatrice gasped. "She's made me laugh. When did I last laugh, Hawkins?"

"I—I really can't bring it to mind, madam."

"Well, you never succeeded in making me. So go away."

"Once," came Anna's composed voice, "when I was very small I can remember Mother taking me to see Tsarskoe Selo. That was where—"

"I know where it was. The czar and czarina lived there. Was it as fine a palace as Windsor?"

"I haven't been to Windsor, Grandmother. But it was pretty, and the trees were green. We could just see it from the gates. Mother said it was best in the snow, when you went by troika. It was like a fairy tale. But then she cried, and we never went again."

"Must see that you get to Windsor. When I'm better. By

the way, what do you say to having an ancient grandmother in an invalid chair? Will you be ashamed?"

"Ashamed!"

"Anyone could be. A child your age——"

"I might be skinny but I'm strong," said Anna. "I could
easily push your chair. I mean . . . if you'll let me."

Beatrice began to cough again, until her eyes streamed.
With mucus, she told herself irascibly. Not tears.

"Hawkins!" she choked.

"Yes, madam. Let me give you a spoonful of the syrup."

"Get that child out of here! I'm tired."

The ridiculously narrow back, the little pointed shoulders
hunched forward. A sparrow ruffled and hurt.

"Oh, for goodness sake! Anna! I'm not scolding you. You
can begin *David Copperfield* tomorrow. It's a long book, if
I remember, but we've plenty of time."

Chapter 30

Anna was calling from downstairs, "Grandmother! Bates is here with the car. Are you ready?"

Beatrice made herself be patient with Hawkins who was taking forever to do her hair. Anna could have done it in a quarter of the time, but one couldn't hurt the old woman's feelings. She was dressing Miss Beatrice for her last visit to Bonnington's. The familiar gray dress with the spotless white fichu, the fur cape over the upright shoulders, the gray hair neatly tucked beneath the little feathered toque. She must look the personage that she had always been, said Hawkins.

Privately Beatrice agreed. She particularly needed to look a personage, to get her through the ordeal ahead. To be wheeled through Bonnington's for the last time, even with Anna pushing her and assuring her that she rode her chair like a chariot, was an experience that had to be faced with dignity and equanimity.

"There's no need for you to do this, Mother," Florence insisted. "It's unnecessarily sentimental. You'll only have everyone in tears."

"And why shouldn't they be? There was a time when I *was* Bonnington's. I still may be, for all I know."

"Oh, I expect you are," Florence said grudgingly. "Only don't overdo the sob stuff since you could have saved Bonnington's if you had wanted to."

It had all happened as Florence, with her alarming intelligence, had predicted. The day of reckoning for Bonnington's had come. The depression, with its aftermath of unemployment, poverty and hunger, had been the final cause. Beatrice still insisted that in terms of human misery the times were not as bad as they had been in her youth. The

314

ragged crossing sweepers, the barefooted frozen children huddled together sleeping in packing cases behind the store, the pathetic little match sellers at the front doors, the sight of whom had been such a blight on one's complacency, had disappeared. Certainly there were dole queues and bread queues and hungry children and a great deal of despair and hardship, but the country would emerge from this crisis, and pull itself together again.

Unfortunately, it would happen too late to save Bonnington's unless Beatrice poured in money from the sale of Overton House and its contents. This, as she had already warned Florence, she would never do. A shop or a family tradition? There was never the slightest doubt in her mind.

Nevertheless, the painful argument continued for weeks and months. Beatrice had been bombarded with statistics, falling sales figures, rising salaries and maintenance costs, an exorbitant price for a new lease of the site on which Bonnington's stood, and estimates for the costs of Florence's dearly desired modernization.

To all this Beatrice remained unsympathetic, almost uninterested. She had accustomed herself to being an invalid. That feat had taken her remaining mental strength. Now all she wanted to do was to spend her last years at Overton House in peace.

Was that being too selfish? One knew that Florence had always considered her to be the most selfish, stubborn old woman in the world. But if she handed over the contents and goodwill of Bonnington's to Florence, surely she was doing all that could be expected of her.

Florence, when she finally saw that she was fighting a losing battle, decided, almost with relief, to open a small smart couture shop in Knightsbridge with James Brush as her partner. After all, they were no longer young. The smaller premises and smaller staff would suit them admirably, and there was no doubt that she had a flair for fashion.

"I," said Beatrice, also greatly relieved, "will be responsible for Edwin and Anna. The three of us will remain at Overton House. You can be free of us, Florence, as you've always wanted to be."

"Very well," Florence answered. But her voice was unexpectedly subdued, and just for a flash, the nervous uncertain child looked out of her pale middle-aged eyes. She went on more firmly, "But at least, Mother, if you insist on this fare-well, you could let Bates push your chair. Why Anna?"

"Because I prefer Anna. Isn't that sufficient reason?"

"Mother, you're beginning to spoil that child."

Beatrice smiled faintly.

"On the contrary, she's spoiling me. I must say I find the experience new, and pleasant."

"It's not that long since she was a delinquent. I'd say, watch her."

"That's exactly what I am enjoying doing."

"Oh, for goodness sake, Mother. Mellowing in old age is one thing, but overdoing it is another."

"I know, dear. I should have practiced it a bit more when you and Edwin were small. You see, I can still read your thoughts."

Florence colored slightly.

"The only thing we really held against you was sending Miss Medway away without any explanation. We loved her and she loved us. I don't believe either of us ever felt we were loved again."

The pain was still there, Beatrice thought, testing its sharpness in her heart. But she managed to answer tran-quilly, "You're perfectly right, Florence. That's why I'm being particularly careful with Anna."

The Daimler, polished to the brilliance of mirror glass, behaved impeccably. They drew up outside Bonnington's on the stroke of three o'clock, and Beatrice, avoiding looking at the CLOSING DOWN SALE notices splashed over the windows, allowed herself to be helped out and settled in her chair. Anna whispered, "Chin up, Grandmother!" and the chair was set in motion.

They had lined up in two rows to allow her to pass between them, the doormen in their dark-blue and gold uniforms, the head floorwalker, the heads of departments, the salesmen in their dark jackets and striped trousers, the saleswomen in their neat white-collared black dresses. She had intended to stand up in her familiar territory, the cash desk, but it proved to be too difficult to mount the steps. Damn, damn, damn, she was a prisoner in this humiliating chair!

Then she felt Anna's fingers gently pressing her shoulder, and she was able to lift her head and smile, and say the few words they expected of her, of thanks, of appreciation, of good wishes for their future, of time being the traitor.

Someone put a posy of rosebuds into her hands. Everything was suddenly blurred, and she was afraid she would faint. It was as if she saw life passing away in front of her eyes.

"Get me home," she whispered to Anna.

In the car, she said furiously, "I was a coward."

"No, you weren't, Grandmother. You were like a queen."

"Which one?" she asked suspiciously. "Old Victoria?"

"Of course, Grandmother. You wouldn't want to be any other one, would you?"

Royal or not, she was human, too, and subject to bodily weaknesses. She fell asleep as soon as she got home. When she awoke it seemed to be late afternoon, by the way the sun slanted across the garden. There was no sign of Hawkins, who must have gone away to leave her in peace, but faintly, from the music room, she could hear the piano playing.

Chopin? No, it was a slow, slightly sad melody she hadn't heard before.

She sat up and rang the bell for Hawkins.

"Take me downstairs."

"Certainly, madam. Don't you want Miss Anna? She's in the music room."

"No. I don't want to disturb her."

Rather than give up this beloved room with its memories and move downstairs, Beatrice had gone to the great expense of having a lift into which her wheelchair would fit installed. Again, Florence had thought the expenditure unwarranted, but Florence didn't understand sentiment. Or refused to. She wouldn't have known that William still came to this room and touched her hand, and sometimes kissed her.

Once she had destroyed the beautiful mirror room from petty jealousy. She would not make that mistake again.

The French windows of the music room were open onto the terrace, and at the end of the garden Edwin was working in his herbaceous border. His head was scarcely visible among the tall goldenrod and sunflowers. After a day spent in the garden in the summer, he was amiable and peaceful, smiling in the candlelight at the dinner table. He sometimes now discussed other things than armies and old battles. That was Anna. In her quiet persistent way, she drew him out.

Anna was sitting at the piano with her back to the door. She didn't hear Beatrice come in. She sang softly, in her clear melodious voice:

> *Parlez-moi d'amour,*
> *Redites-moi des choses tendres.*
> *Votre beau discours,*
> *Man coeur n'est pas las de l'entendre. . . .*
> *Pour vu que toujours vous répétiez ces mots suprêmes,*
> *Je vous aime. . . .*

The plaintive notes died away and as the girl sat quietly Beatrice observed her. The rich brown hair (William's), the pale triangular face with the slanted eyes, the exquisitely fine wrists and ankles. The little duckling was growing. She might even surprise her mother now, if that restless unhappy person, last heard of in Reno, were to see her.

She was not going to have the gentle beauty of her grandmother, or Daisy's brilliant prettiness. She was always going to be strange and foreign. But intriguing, arresting. One day, without a doubt, a young man with perception was going to fall deeply in love with her. She would be no failure, Anna. The soil of Overton House had luckily proved to be just right for her.

Beatrice sniffed sharply, and said in her gruff voice, "Sing that song again, but in English. I was never any good at French."

"I didn't know you were there, Grandmother."

Anna began to sing softly the English words:

> Speak to me of love
> And say what I'm longing to hear,
> Tender words of love.
> Repeat them again, I implore you. . . .
> Speak to me of love
> And whisper these words to me, dear,
> I adore you. . . .

"Grandmother!"

"Yes?"

"You're not crying, are you?"

"No. Yes. That's not a suitable song for this house."

"Whyever not?" Anna's arched brows, another subtle

beauty there, like her slender wrists and ankles, had risen in perplexity.

"Because there has never been enough love here. It's been entirely my fault. Poor Edwin, Florence—I never loved them enough. Nor Daisy, but that was for another reason. As for William—"

"Now, look here, Grandmother! You can't say you and Grandfather didn't love each other. Why, you only had to see the way he looked at you as you went out of a room."

Beatrice held her breath. "Really?"

"Really, Grandmother. Goodness, you of all people don't need to be assured of love. I remember being astonished when I first came here that two people so old could still feel like that. Now I know better."

"You know nothing. Nothing."

"Grandmother, please! You've had a sad day today."

"Yes, I have. I've suddenly decided you know, that I'm going to leave you Overton House. If you will promise to always give Uncle Edwin a home."

"But of course! Oh, Grandmother, have I any right?"

"Of course you have a right. More than anybody. You'll keep Grandfather's treasures, of course, the pictures and the furniture and the family portraits."

"And the yellow ground Worcester and the apple-green Derby," Anna breathed.

Beatrice turned the sudden trembling of her lips into a smile.

"And if you see an old man dusting his porcelain or taking out his slides of butterflies, or a stout old shopkeeper out of her element, you will know they are friendly ghosts." Some compulsion made her add, "There may be another one."

"Yes?"

"Never mind. Just remember that you can't fight ghosts. It's taken me long enough to learn that. Now put that sentimental song away and show me how you're really getting on with your music. Play me some Chopin."

ROMANCE From Fawcett Books